HARVEST of RUBIES

HARVEST of RUBIES

TESSA AFSHAR

Tessa Afshar (signature)

MOODY PUBLISHERS
CHICAGO

Scripture references are from Psalm 46:1–2; Job 3:25; Psalm 18:1–3; selections from Psalm 25; Psalm 25:7; Psalm 31:8–9; Hosea 2:14–15a. *Achor* in the Hosea citation in chapter 26 means "trouble."

Some Scripture quotations are taken from the *Holy Bible, New International Version*®, NIV®. Copyright © 1973, 1978, 1984, 2011 by Biblica, Inc.™ Used by permission of Zondervan. All rights reserved worldwide. www.zondervan.com

Some Scripture quotations are taken from the *Holy Bible, New Living Translation,* copyright © 1996, 2004. Used by permission of Tyndale House Publishers, Inc., Wheaton, Illinois 60189, U.S.A. All rights reserved.

Published in association with the Books & Such Literary Agency, 52 Mission Circle, Suite 122, PMB 170, Santa Rosa, CA 95409-5370, www.booksandsuch.biz.

Moody Publishers editor: Pam Pugh
Interior Design: Ragont Design
Cover Design: Brand Navigation, LLC
Cover Images: iStock, Dreamstime, and Shutterstock

Library of Congress Cataloging-in-Publication Data

Afshar, Tessa.
   Harvest of rubies / Tessa Afshar.
      p. cm.
   ISBN 978-0-8024-0558-6
   1. Scribes—Fiction. I. Title.
PS3601.F47H37 2012
813'.6—dc23

                                    2011045869

We hope you enjoy this book from River North Fiction by Moody Publishers. Our goal is to provide high-quality, thought-provoking books and products that connect truth to your real needs and challenges. For more information on other books and products written and produced from a biblical perspective, go to www.moodypublishers.com or write to:

River North Fiction
Imprint of Moody Publishers
820 N. LaSalle Boulevard
Chicago, IL 60610

3 5 7 9 10 8 6 4 2

Printed in the United States of America

For my mother and father:
Thank you for teaching me to laugh and to love.

587–586 BC	Judah is captured by Babylon, and the Temple is destroyed.
559–530 BC	Cyrus the Great establishes the largest empire the world has ever known and founds the Achaemenid dynasty. In 538 Cyrus sets Israel free from its Babylonian captivity as foretold by Isaiah (44:24–45:5). He donates money from his own treasury toward the rebuilding of the Temple in Jerusalem.
530–522 BC	Cambyses, Cyrus's eldest son, conquers Egypt. His reign is briefly followed by his younger brother, Bardia, who dies shortly thereafter under strange circumstances.
521–486 BC	Darius the Great expands the Persian Empire so that at its height it encompasses approximately eight million miles of territory. Next to Cyrus, he is the most admired Achaemenid king. He is probably not the king referred to in the book of Daniel 6:1–28, since Daniel would be quite old at this time.
486–465 BC	Xerxes takes over his father's great dynasty. He is best known for his notorious attack on Greece and for choosing a simple Jewish girl named Esther as his queen. The date of this event is not known. For details, see the book of Esther.
465–424 BC	Artaxerxes is known as a benevolent king who replaces several harsh laws with more humane rulings. He sends his cupbearer, Nehemiah, back to Jerusalem in 445 in order to rebuild its ruined walls.
334 BC	Alexander the Great conquers Persia.
Approx. 33 AD	Jesus of Nazareth is crucified.

CHARACTERS in order of appearance or mention

Sarah—senior scribe to the queen

Simeon—Sarah's father

Leah—Sarah's aunt

Nehemiah—relative of Sarah and Simeon; cupbearer to the king

Artaxerxes—king of Persia

Damaspia—queen of Persia, wife of Artaxerxes

Amestris—the queen mother

Frada—steward to Damaspia

Nebo—scribe to Amestris

Parisatis (Pari)—handmaiden to Sarah

Gaspar—scribe under Frada

Alogune—concubine to Artaxerxes and mother of his son Sogdianus

Lord Darius—Sarah's husband

Lord Vivan—Darius's father

Teispes—steward of Darius's household

Shushan—cook in Darius's household

Teispes—steward of Darius's estate

Bardia—the gardener

Mandana—an *arassara*

Gobry/Gobryas—Bardia's grandson

Aspasia—a courtesan

Arash—Damaspia's nephew

Vidarna—Darius's new steward

Chapter One

The Eighth Year of
King Artaxerxes' Reign*
Persia

O n my twelfth birthday, my father discovered that I
could read.

He came home long before the supper hour that night, an
occurrence so rare that in my shock I forgot to greet him.
Instead, I sat stupefied, clutching a forbidden clay tablet.

"What are you doing?" he asked, his gaze arrested by the
sight of the tablet clasped to my chest.

My father, a royal scribe in the Persian court, treated his
writing tools as if they were the holy objects from the Ark of
the Covenant. Before I had learned to walk or speak, I had
learned never to go near his scrolls and tablets for fear I might
damage them.

* 457 BC

"You know better than to touch this," he said, when I didn't respond right away.

I swallowed the ball of gathering dread in my throat, knowing myself caught. Truth seemed my only option. "I was reading," I said, as I replaced the tablet on the floor with extravagant care.

He studied me from beneath lowered brows. "Even if you could read—which you cannot—you should not be anywhere near my scribal supplies. It is very wrong of you to lie, Sarah."

"I am not lying, Father."

He heaved a sigh. Spreading his hand in mock invitation toward the tablet, he said, "Demonstrate."

The tablet was in Persian, one of the most complicated languages of the world. I could have chosen to teach myself Aramaic, a simpler language for a beginner and more appropriate for a Jew. But most Aramaic documents were recorded on parchment, and I had decided that there would be fewer chances of accidentally damaging clay or stone tablets than fragile parchment scrolls.

Licking my lips, I concentrated on the complex alphabet before me. The symbols looked like a series of delicate nails standing upright or lying sideways, an occasional incomplete triangle thrown in for confusion. With halting accuracy I began to read the first line from left to right. Then the second and the third.

My father sank to the carpet next to me, his movements slow. He was silent for a long moment. Then he asked, "Who taught you to read Persian?"

"Nobody. I learned by myself. I've been studying for five months."

He seemed speechless. Then, with jerky movements, he fetched three small clay cylinders and placed them before me.

"What's this word? And this? Can you make out this sentence?"

We must have sat there for hours as he tested my knowledge, corrected my pronunciation, and demonstrated grammatical rules. He forgot about my months-long transgression of secretly handling his scribal supplies. He forgot to remonstrate with me for having taught myself to read without his permission.

But then he also forgot to ask me *why* I had wanted to learn. Although I was surprised by his lack of anger at my behavior, his lack of interest was all too familiar. In the years since my mother's death when I was seven, my father had rarely spoken to me of anything save mundane household matters, and even that was rare. My desires, my motives, my hopes, held no appeal to him.

Late that night, after so many hours of his company, when I crawled onto my thin cotton-filled mattress, my mouth spread in a wide smile. I had finally found a way to hold my father's attention. He had spent more time with me on this one night than he was wont to do in a fortnight. Months of hard work had won me the desire of my heart; he had found something in me worth his while.

After we lost my mother, Aunt Leah, my mother's only sister, began coming once a week to our home to help us with the housework. She tried to show me how to sew and clean and cook. Our conversations around these topics tended toward frustration—for her—and pain for me.

"Weren't you paying attention when I showed you how to pluck the chicken?"

"No, Aunt Leah. I beg your pardon."

"You can't use a broom like that, Sarah. You only move the

dust from one spot to another. That's not called cleaning. That's a migration of dirt."

"Yes, Aunt Leah. I beg your pardon."

"This pot won't clean itself just by you staring at it and sighing."

Silence seemed the best response at times like this. I could not offend my only aunt by telling her the truth: that I would rather hit my head with the pot and make myself lose consciousness than have to face the frustrating boredom of scrubbing its black bottom.

My one consolation was that our house was small—four rooms and a hallway with a tiny garden the size of a large carpet in the back, so there wasn't much to clean. The few rugs we had were woven rather than knotted, and I just beat them against the stone hedge outside. Our furniture, modest to start with, had served my family a good twenty years; even my impatient treatment of the pieces could not ruin them more than they already had been.

Aunt Leah came to visit the day after my twelfth birthday and discovered me practicing the Persian alphabet on a fresh clay tablet. The tablet fit comfortably in the palm of my hand; I held one blunt end with my thumb and used a stylus to carve new words on its wet surface. Since my father had uncovered my secret and seemed to sanction it, I felt no reason to keep it hidden any longer.

Aunt Leah slapped a hand against the crown of her head. "Are you writing now?"

"I am," I said with pride, stretching my cramping legs on the crude carpet.

"It's a scandal. What will your father say?"

"He is teaching me."

"It's a scandal," she repeated. She made me put the tablet

and stylus away and help her with the laundry until my father arrived.

Although I was dismissed from the room so that they might hold a private discussion, I could hear snatches of their conversation through the drawn curtain that separated the rectangular room into two parts. My heart beat an uncomfortable rhythm as I considered the possibility that Aunt Leah might convince my father to stop teaching me. I waited with fuming resentment, barely able to keep myself from marching in and demanding that she stop interfering with the first good thing that had happened to me in years.

"The child just wants to learn to read and write, Leah. There's no shame in that. She even shows a glimmer of talent." I was surprised to hear my father defend me; I couldn't remember his ever doing so before. The simple words soothed my rising anger.

"The child is a girl."

"Literate women are not unknown. The queen reads as well as any scribe, they say."

"Sarah is not a royal Persian woman. She's a simple Jewish maiden."

I could not make out my father's answer. Aunt Leah's response came heated and fast, though. "No good will come of this, Simeon. You mark my words. Your stubborn refusal to listen to reason will cause that child nothing but harm."

She stormed out of the house, not taking the time to put her shoes on right. As soon as she left, I gathered my practice tablet and borrowed tools and walked into my father's room. He sat on the floor, his head bent, a hand covering his eyes.

With care I laid my bundle in front of him. "Would you like to see what I did today, Father? It's not much; Aunt Leah interrupted my practice."

This was new for me, this bold approach to my father. I had known for years that I was a bother to him. He found my conversation trying; my presence aggravated him. But my literary endeavor had given me a new confidence. I knew my father loved his work. *I* might be a nuisance, but the work wasn't. I thought he would bear with me as long as we had a clay tablet between us.

He lifted his head and focused on me for a long moment. One corner of his mouth lifted. I let out my breath when he made no protest. "Let's see what you have accomplished, then."

Aunt Leah came back with mighty reinforcements the following week. I had met my cousin Nehemiah years before during the time of my mother's sickness. But in recent times I only heard the stories of his great accomplishments at court. He had risen to the position of cupbearer to the king.

In Persia, rank was measured by proximity to the person of the king. Only those of consequence were given positions that placed them in constant contact with royalty. Nehemiah tasted the king's wine as a human shield against poison. But he also acted as one of his advisors, for it was common for the king to ask the opinion of those closest to him. Even I, a child of twelve, knew that Artaxerxes held him in high regard. This was enough to make him a frightening visitor. However, the fact that he came with his pomp and circumstance in the wake of my aunt petrified me. Had she persuaded him to intervene against my desire to become literate? If so, he was too great a man to be denied.

"Bring Lord Nehemiah some refreshments, Sarah," my aunt ordered as I stood gaping at them in the hallway.

"No, no, I need nothing. Let the child join us, Leah. It's been an age since I saw her. You have grown up into quite a young lady."

He was a tall man with startling dark red hair and flawless manners. Even his fingernails were trimmed and neat, so different from my father's stained, rough hands. I made an awkward bow, unused to palace protocol. "Welcome, my lord. This way, please," I said, my voice faint with anxiety. "I shall fetch my father for you," I added and slipped out, glad to escape his august presence.

My father rushed out of his cramped chamber. "You honor us," he said, addressing Nehemiah and sparing Aunt Leah a short nod. He motioned everyone to sit on our skinny cushions, which had been arranged along the floor.

"It's been too long, Simeon, since I came to your home. You know how the palace drains one's time. But that is no good excuse; forgive my long absence. I am glad to see you."

"And I you, my lord. Though I fear that my sister-in-law has bothered you needlessly with the small matters of my household."

"As a matter of fact, Leah did mention something about an urgent matter concerning Sarah."

I rolled my eyes. My father only said, "Indeed?"

My aunt bristled, sitting up straighter and raising her voice. "A Jewish maiden has no business reading and writing Persian. She needs to learn womanly graces, not stuff her head with knowledge that will be of no benefit to her."

I grew hot at her words. "How can it be of no benefit if I can help Father with his work? Or keep the household accounts and relieve him of one more duty?"

"Keep your tongue, Sarah," my father ordered, his voice sounding tired.

"Let us hear from the child. This concerns her most, it seems to me." The sharp brown gaze of my cousin landed on me, making me squirm. "Tell me, Sarah, do you want to learn?"

"Oh yes, my lord. More than anything. And I am very good at it. Ask my father. I taught myself how to read Persian."

"You see?" Aunt Leah struck her hand palm-up into the air for emphasis. "She has already forgotten the value of humility."

"It's only the truth," I said, my voice trailing.

Nehemiah covered his mouth with his elegant hand for a moment. The faint lines around his eyes deepened. I wondered if he might be smiling beneath the cover of his fingers, but when he lowered his hand, his expression was serious. "If the Lord has gifted the child, then perhaps it's because He has a plan for her life that requires such skills. And who are we to stand in the way of the Lord?"

"The *Lord*?" My aunt's voice sounded like a broken shepherd's pipe.

Nehemiah ignored the interjection. "Leah, do you remember Queen Esther?"

Every Jew in Persia knew about Esther. Only one generation ago the entire Jewish population of Persia would have been wiped out if not for her courage and ingenuity. We celebrated Purim in honor of her victory.

"Of course I remember Queen Esther."

"She had the gift of extraordinary beauty. Yet what struck one most about her was her sweetness. I met her once when I was a boy, you know. An unforgettable woman." Nehemiah's face became inscrutable for a moment and I wondered if his memories had become more real than our company. When he spoke again, his voice seemed softer.

"Her intelligence and grace made her queen of the greatest empire the world has known. But it was God who placed her on that throne. The Lord who knew the danger to His people, groomed her for that very position."

"I don't understand," my aunt interjected, looking as though she had been sucking on sour cherries. "What has Esther to do with this situation?"

"My point is that we must be ready to follow the Lord wherever He leads us. Esther came into royal position not knowing that one day her gifts and influence would be needed for God's great plan of salvation for His people. We must walk through the small doors that the Lord opens for us, in case they lead to a greater path. I say again: who are we to stand in the way of the Lord's plans for Sarah? If her gifts prove a useful tool in His hand, then we must build them up, not crush them."

I brightened as it sank into my brain that Nehemiah was championing me. I tried to wipe the smile from my face, knowing my aunt would take exception to my smug victory. Inside I felt like jumping up and dancing. Outwardly I schooled my features to reflect a modicum of the humility I had lacked earlier.

"Lord Nehemiah, you want a Jewish girl to learn to be a scribe?" Aunt Leah finally burst out.

"I want a Jewish girl to fulfill her destiny. I don't know what that is. But I want her to be prepared for whatever God may send her way."

At that pronouncement we all fell silent. I felt the weight of his words with a new insight. Nehemiah's interpretation of my childish desires was concerned much more with the will of God than the will of Sarah. This was too disturbing a concept to grasp; with the ease of youth, I buried it somewhere in the recesses of my heart. It was more pleasant to focus on the fact that I was about to receive my dearest dream.

"So then, Sarah, you must promise to study hard and hone your talent," Nehemiah said to me.

He might as well be making a child promise to eat rich honey cakes. Unable to stop the grin from spreading across my face, I said, "I promise, my lord."

My father began to teach me in earnest after that. By the time I was sixteen, in addition to Persian I knew how to read and write Akkadian, another complicated language practiced only by royal scribes for the keeping of important administrative records.

Ironically, the most popular tongue in the Persian Empire was not Persian—a language too complex for the common folk of foreign nations to learn. Aramaic, simpler to understand and record, and already practiced by the many peoples displaced through the Assyrian and Babylonian wars for the past two hundred years, grew more popular than other tongues in the Eastern empire. So I became proficient in Aramaic also.

I learned how to write on tablets of clay using a sharp reed to carve into their wet, unfired surface. Father would also bring me parchment made of calf or sheepskin, alkalined and stretched on a wooden frame to render its surface smooth for easy writing. Sometimes, he would even give me a large roll of papyrus, which was the most fragile of the writing materials, susceptible to both moisture and heat.

Becoming a proficient keeper of records in an empire that relied on its administrative skill to prosper made me a valuable commodity to my father. I developed the ability to speak and interpret several languages in a kingdom that faced multitudes of linguistic barriers, and daily needed to overcome them in order to function. I also learned to practice the art of accounts keeping. I could now help my father increase his commissions.

Aunt Leah visited less and less often once I began to apply myself to learning. I suspect she never fully reconciled herself to Cousin Nehemiah's pronouncement. Yet it was more than that. As I gained free access to the scribe's world, I grew less tolerant of hers. I spent fewer hours in her company. My intense work schedule gave me a reasonable excuse to escape her attempts at drawing me into her woman's world. My father hired a servant to help with housekeeping once a week, and I did my best to care for our daily needs.

Once my aunt would have fought me and brought me under some form of discipline. But I think the combination of my father, Nehemiah, and me was too much for her.

I doubt my cousin had intended that I should grow into womanhood with no feminine influences. Yet that is what I managed to accomplish by my stubborn refusal to give my aunt room in my life. By the time I was twenty, I was more scribe than woman. My aunt, tired out by my constant rejections, finally gave up.

Cousin Nehemiah would visit us on occasion to check on my progress. Once he brought his own parchment and asked me to read. I unrolled the fragile papyrus on my father's small desk to find a beautifully crafted Hebrew text.

"I cannot read this, my lord."

"You do not read Hebrew?" He raised one eyebrow. "The language of your own people?"

I shrugged. "It's of little use in court documents."

He pressed his lips. "Perhaps you remember the words. I will read a few lines for you:

God is our refuge and strength,
A very present help in trouble."

I remembered them well, though it was a painful recollection I would as soon forget. I wondered what had provoked him to bring this particular psalm to me. Shying away from the emotions that were tethered to the words, I merely said, "I remember."

"I once heard you recite the whole psalm when you were a little girl. Did you know that?"

"No, my lord."

He lowered his head. "It was when your mother was sick. She had been my favorite cousin growing up and I was sorely grieved at her illness. I visited your home often in those days, praying for a miracle.

"Once, toward the end, I walked into her room. You were alone with her. She held your little hand. Neither of you had noticed me come in, and I remained silent, hoping not to disturb you. That's when I heard you recite this psalm to her. You did it from beginning to end without flaw. You could not have been more than eight."

"I was seven."

He nodded. "Her eyes were closed. She was emaciated by then, and yet somehow still lovely. In those moments, there seemed to be such holiness about her. An utter lack of fear. I thought, *God has truly become her refuge and her strength.* Even that vile sickness could not rob her of her tranquility."

I cleared my throat and stared at the floor. How nice for him to have happy recollections of my mother's illness. I could not share them.

"Do you still remember the words to the entire psalm?"

"Yes, my lord."

20

"You believed them then. Do you believe them now? Do you believe that God is your very present help in trouble?"

I looked up. "No, my lord."

He had the kind of face that reflected his emotions. Disappointment settled on his features like a light veil. "I suspected as much. It's hard to see those we love suffer without questioning God."

"I haven't become an idolater," I said in quick defense of my feelings. "I believe in the Lord. It's only that these lavish promises have lost their meaning for me. Perhaps we are meant to help ourselves by our own efforts. Perhaps God is too busy to bother with our daily needs."

"I have never come across that principle in the Torah."

"That may be. But I have come across it in life."

He left shortly after this conversation. I wondered if my forthright admission had cost me his favor. But he came again for other visits, acting as though we had never spoken of my mother's favorite psalm. And he made certain that I learned how to read and write Hebrew after that.

My scribal work occupied my days to such a degree that I had little opportunity to enjoy the typical pleasures of young women. I never whiled away the hours in the company of girls my own age. I had no interest in what I considered to be their superficial pastimes. Few invitations came to my father and me, and our social life shrank to a few obligatory annual feasts.

My world grew narrow and inward as a result. Father never noticed the lack, but perhaps Nehemiah did, for with one swift stroke he chose to expand the boundaries of my life.

Nehemiah's visits, though infrequent, were common enough that his appearance at our door late one evening gave me no cause for alarm.

It was suppertime and I offered him barley soup and fresh bread. He examined the watery concoction I had prepared and declined.

"So how is Sarah progressing?" he asked my father.

Taking a slurping mouthful from his bowl, my father hesitated. "She is a dismal cook, but her skills as a scribe now surpass mine. What she lacks in experience, she makes up for in knowledge."

Nehemiah smiled. "That should satisfy."

"Satisfy whom?" I asked quickly, pleased at the thought of being satisfactory to anyone.

"The queen."

My father straightened with an abrupt motion. "What have you done?" he asked, his voice faint.

Nehemiah leaned back. The flowing sleeve of his silk robe moved like a billowing wave in the lamplight. "I have acted in Sarah's best interest."

"Acted, *how?*"

I was taken aback by my father's hostility. The realization began to sink into my consciousness that my cousin had taken some momentous step that concerned me. "My lord?"

"Sarah, you shall be the queen's senior scribe."

Chapter Two

The Sixteenth Year of King Artaxerxes' Reign* Persepolis

Earlier this week the queen dismissed her senior scribe," Nehemiah said. "He had proven incompetent one too many times." My cousin leaned back against a cushion. "She has since sifted through every eunuch available from Susa to Persepolis, but none has met with her approval." He stopped speaking in order to brush an invisible fleck from his shoulder.

"Here is where you come in, Sarah. It so happens that the queen has lately been reading the account of a female scribe in ancient Mesopotamia. Last evening, while she partook of supper with the king, she bemoaned the lack of such a woman in Persia.

* 449 BC

"I was present during this conversation, and was given the opportunity to tell Her Majesty that I knew just such a woman. I mentioned *you* to her, Sarah—your ability, your training, your passion. I said you were the very woman she sought." Nehemiah gave a bland smile, as though his pronouncement had not just turned my life on its head.

"You told her *I* was such a woman? What did she say?"

"That she wishes you to be her scribe, for a trial period at first. And if you please her, which I have no doubt you shall, then the work is yours."

"She would have to live at the palace for such a post!" My father's protest sounded loud in the quiet room.

"That she would, Simeon."

"You want to take my daughter out of my home?"

"What would you prefer? That she should remain in this house and spend her days in isolation? Without a single friend-ship, without companionship?"

"And who in the palace is going to offer her all that—the queen? Have you given a thought to her future? Who would ever want to marry her: a royal eunuch?"

I would have laughed at my father's biting humor if the tension between the two men hadn't reduced me to a jumble of nerves. I sank into my cushion and bit my nails.

"Royal servants are not in lifelong bondage. She's more likely to meet a prospective husband at the palace than she would here. There are plenty of Jews in the service of the royal family. She could marry whomever she chooses," Nehemiah countered.

All this talk of marriage and husbands seemed to drive the conversation away from the topic that was of most inter-est to me. "I thought you said something about my being a scribe, my lord."

"A *senior* scribe. You would never have to cook again, or wash your own laundry, or dust and sweep. The queen's servants take care of her staff's general needs. And you could still see your father frequently since he works at the palace too."

I could not digest the immensity of Nehemiah's words. I felt like I had swallowed one of the king's dancers and she was busy turning summersaults in my belly. The thought of moving away from the only home I knew was overwhelming; the thought of reporting to the queen of Persia even more so. "I cannot do it," I said. "It is too much."

My father heaved a sigh that seemed to come up from his toes.

"Sarah, you can." Nehemiah slashed his silk-clad arm through the air for emphasis. "I have worked with eunuchs and scribes over half my life and have seen none more gifted than you. The Lord has prepared you for this day."

Nehemiah's words of praise settled over my heart like a pleasant balm. Did he really think me that talented? Then I remembered the plethora of other deficiencies I'd have to contend with. "I haven't the faintest glimmer of palace protocol. No doubt I shall offend the queen before I even open my mouth, and after *that*, my doom is sure."

"Members of the queen's retinue will give you whatever training you need. You will not be the first outsider to move into the palace who needs a bit of polish."

Among Nehemiah's talents was an extraordinary ability for persuasion. Half of me thought the whole idea ludicrous. I could not imagine myself adjusting to such an inconceivable change. The other half began to catch the spark of my cousin's enthusiasm. To live in the palace—to be surrounded by beauty and culture and new wonders. To occupy such a high position— one rarely enjoyed by a woman, no less. To have my abilities acknowledged in such a public fashion. These realities presented an irresistible pull, while fear pushed back with equal force. I sat frozen, caught between the two forces within myself.

As if sensing my weakness, Nehemiah pressed his advantage. "Think of it Sarah: you shall have more tablets and scrolls than even you can count. Your own scribes will report to you and do your bidding. The queen will rely on you to administer her vast holdings. Many will depend on you; your life shall serve a purpose you could not have conceived."

"I . . . I don't know what to say."

"This is a unique opportunity, Sarah—a once in a lifetime moment. Ponder this: what are the chances that the queen should read an obscure account about a female scribe? What are the chances that she should want such a scribe and express her desire in my presence? What are the chances that I should happen to know such a woman—to have intimate knowledge of her fidelity, her ability, and her wisdom—qualities most esteemed at the court? What are the chances of such a configuration of far-fetched circumstances?

"None! There is no *chance* at work here, my dear. This is a door that the Lord holds open for you. Walk through it. He who has called shall also equip. Everything you lack shall be provided."

I hesitated. I could not proceed blindly for the sake of faith; I was not like Nehemiah. I needed human assurance. Human reasoning.

"Tell me what holds you back," he said.

He already knew the answer, I reckoned. He merely wanted to hear me say it. "Fear," I admitted, and then decided to open my heart to him. "Fear that I'll fail. Fear that I will not fit into the palace and make myself and my father and you into a laughingstock."

26

"You may fail; I cannot deny it. But if you go through life making every decision based on what is safest, you will look back one day and discover that you have missed out on the best. Do you think you can reject the offer of the queen and return to your quiet existence without regrets? No, Sarah. Allowing fear to run your life will only rob you of your future."

I drew my knees up against my chest. "How long do I have to decide?"

"Until tomorrow."

"Tomorrow?"

"Queen Damaspia is sending a servant to fetch you and your things in the afternoon."

I turned to my father. "What do you think, Father?"

He shook his head. "You must choose. I know not."

In the end, in spite of Nehemiah's advice, it was fear that determined my decision, not the Lord's will. I was more afraid of turning down the queen's offer and regretting it the rest of my life than I was of my own deficiencies. One fear beat the other in its urgings.

A eunuch from the household of the queen showed up the afternoon of the following day to transport me and my meager belongings to the queen's apartments in Persepolis.

"Good-bye, Father," I said, while the eunuch waited outside. If I had expected an emotional display, I would have been disappointed. But as my father had not held me in a tender embrace even once since the death of my mother, I was prepared for his awkward distance.

He pulled on his beard. "Well, I'll see you at the palace, no doubt."

"How shall I contact you?"

"You can send me a message through one of the servants."

And that was the end of my life at home. I would have wept as I walked out, except that I was too occupied with thoughts of Persepolis to dwell on what I was leaving behind.

The eunuch had strapped my wooden chest to the back of a cart. I climbed up next to him and covered my hair with a long scarf, hoping not to arrive at the palace looking dusty as well as provincial.

Persepolis was famed as the most exquisite structure built by human hands that the world had ever seen. The palace, surrounded by walls as thick as the height of an ancient oak, was nestled on a terraced landscape so that it was visible from a great distance. Like everyone else living in the area, I had seen glimpses of it most of my life. I had even peeked within the entrance through the massive gates, which gaped open during the day. But to drive past the guards and *into* the wide avenue that led to the grounds of the palace itself was a heady experience.

My father traveled this path every day and had grown accustomed to the stunning sculptures and reliefs carved on every surface, the tall columns that seemed to hold up the heavens.

For me, however, each sight was new and awe inspiring. We had entered through the Gate of Xerxes, an imposing portico made of carved limestone. On either side stood two giant statues of winged bulls. I almost fell backwards into the cart trying to see to the top of them. The marble that covered the winding driveway was more luxurious than the floor *inside* my childhood home. On either side of us majestic cypress trees lined the road. The heady scent of thousands of white and purple hyacinth blossoms made my head spin.

The Gate of Xerxes was the entrance closest to the main royal stables. The eunuch left the cart and donkey in one of the larger stalls housing royal carriages and carts, and we continued our journey on foot.

As we left the marble courtyards and wide limestone staircases rising to stupefying heights, wall friezes gave way to silver, ivory, and ebony carvings; gold, lapis lazuli, and carnelian details covered many surfaces, as if to blind visitors by the overwhelming display of riches at every step. It seemed impossible that human hands could have wrought such luxury—such immensity.

Another wonder that struck me that first day was the lack of foul odors. The whole atmosphere of the palace seemed saturated with perfumes. I learned later that palace engineers had installed covered drainpipes underground to carry sewage away from its grounds.

To any observer that may have caught a glimpse of me, I would have seemed a callow outsider. I doubt I closed my mouth for the length of time it took us to walk from the stables to the women's quarters.

My guide delivered me to a cramped, windowless room and informed me that I would be sharing my quarters with three other women, also servants of Queen Damaspia, who were currently occupied with their work.

I sank on the carpeted floor and looked about me. Even this small place, out of the way and created for servants, held more luxury than my childhood home. The walls were painted a faint blue and two plain columns stood at each side of the door. Shiny green tiles covered the floor where the carpet ended. Rolled against a wall rested four sets of mattresses and bedding; someone had clearly prepared for my coming.

I was wondering what I was supposed to do next when a

woman with curled hair, dressed in crisp linen garments, appeared at my door.

"I am the queen's senior handmaiden. She has assigned me to welcome you."

Was I supposed to bow to her? Should I introduce myself? Was she considered my social equal or was I expected to address her as a superior? I felt the weight of my own ignorance crushing me.

My visitor frowned as she examined me from head to foot. Flustered, I scratched the side of my face nervously, hot under such an unflinching evaluation.

"That won't do." She knocked my fingers away from my face. "When you come before the queen, there will be no scratching, no fidgeting, no picking, no coughing, no speaking unless you are spoken to. And don't even think about blowing your nose. Do I make myself clear, scribe?"

That was only the beginning of my training. For eight days I was deluged with more information than my father had poured into me in eight years. And this merely prepared me for my first interview with the queen.

Damaspia, the only lawful wife of King Artaxerxes, was not what I expected. When later I grew more familiar with royal practices, I'd learn to appreciate how understated her court was. She expected few honors, though she was due every form of them.

Not many people were present in her chamber when I was ushered in for my first meeting. I had been bathed so thoroughly I doubt even the angels could smell cleaner. But no amount of soap could hide the coarse fabric of my garment or the rough edges of my manners. If she noticed, she made no mention.

Damaspia was the most beautiful creature I had ever set

eyes on. Even clad in a simple long linen garment with no jewelry, she took one's breath away. Although she was past the first flush of youth, her skin remained taut and her fashionably tall figure retained its willowy charm. Everything about her was narrow; her waist; her nose; her fingers—everything except her lips and eyes, which were both wider than most people's. Her hair, unlike mine, curled naturally and had been rolled and tucked under with gold combs so that it looked far shorter than it was. The cerulean blue gaze rested on me and she gestured for me to approach.

"So you are my new scribe," she said, when I straightened from my imperfectly executed bow.

"If Your Majesty pleases."

"I will tell you what I please. Be honest. Be loyal. Be competent. Do the work I give and do it well, and we shall have no problems, you and I."

"Yes, Your Majesty."

She flicked a hand. "Well, go and do it, then."

That was the end of my introduction to the queen, though my full training in royal formalities went on for months.

The only time in the palace when I did not feel like I was blundering were the hours I spent in my cramped office, which I shared with two eunuchs, scribes who reported to me. The first day or two they had little to say to me and spent entirely too much time staring at me, the way they would have an exotic animal in a cage. I suppose they had never had to work with a woman before. In time, as they saw that I knew my craft and they could rely on me to provide adequate guidance, they forgot that I was a woman, and treated me as an equal. With them, I need not worry about palace etiquette or social niceties. Our work was our code of conduct. I would squirrel myself in that closet of a chamber as long as I dared, until the queen's sharp-tongued senior handmaiden found me and dragged me out for more lessons on royal propriety.

There were other things I needed to learn. The king's household traveled with predictable regularity to different nerve centers of the empire: Susa, Ecbatana, Passargadae, even Babylonia. I came to see more of the world's wonders than I had ever thought possible. Suddenly I wasn't a sheltered daughter, hardly leaving home from month to month. I had to learn to be mobile. I had to adjust to traveling and learn to become ambulatory without losing any of my efficiency.

Late at night I would crawl into my chamber, often finding my roommates already asleep. The few times I saw them long enough to converse, I was so impressed by their sense of superiority and their disapproval of my simple appearance that my late hours began to offer more of a relief than an inconvenience.

In spite of its aggravations, I grew accustomed to palace life. Nehemiah's opinion of me was borne out; I had been made for this work. It came easily to me.

The Persians used few slaves; the majority of their labor force came in the form of paid servants. Each servant's wages was paid in rations—grain, wine, livestock. Among the vast array of my responsibilities was the need to keep track of every single payment made to each of the queen's hundreds of workers. I ensured that everyone received fair and timely payment, and that none of the queen's possessions found its way into someone else's pockets. As a linguist, an accountant, an administrator, a librarian, and a keeper of records in triplicate, my job had many facets. And I proved adept at every aspect of them. Before one month was done, the queen offered me the position on a permanent basis.

I was twenty. And I was the Queen of Persia's Senior Scribe.

Once a week, I would meet with the queen herself. Shrewd and well educated, she knew every detail of her far-flung enterprise. The night before every meeting I suffered from stomach pains and nausea. I would not sleep the whole night through no matter how well prepared I was. This anxiety only grew worse with the years, although she was not stingy with her praise.

Once, after a long and complicated meeting, she gave me an exquisite fan in appreciation. "You have been doing well, scribe," she said. "You have sharp eyes and a keen understanding."

That night, I sat up filled with fear. I worried that I would lose her good opinion. I thought that eventually she would come to realize that I was not as satisfactory as she had thought. It was as if the more praise she lavished on me, the less confident I grew.

Every accolade became a new high standard I had to maintain. I knew that I could not retain such a standard no matter how hard I strove.

On the one hand, my success was my lifeline. After a childhood of disappointing my father, I had grown into an adulthood that at long last reaped approval. I swallowed that approval with greed; but I found I never grew quite full enough. So on the other hand, my achievements drove me to anxiety. I always feared that I would fail in the end.

Beneath my apparent success, my father's daughter brooded with fear. She knew better than anyone that if I failed at my work, I had nothing else to offer.

The months melted into years while I remained occupied with my vocation. After three years of service to the queen, the

court became my whole life. I was certain—that like my father
—I was meant to be a scribe until I grew old. I was certain that
I would serve the queen for years to come. I was certain. But I
was wrong.

Chapter Three

The Nineteenth Year of
King Artaxerxes' Reign*
Persepolis

I never thought a day would come when almost being devoured by a lion would be the least of my problems.

I had snuck out of the gilded walls of the palace, the normal bustle of the queen's quarters having become too much for my benumbed mind, and taken refuge on my favorite hill. Even after three years of working for the queen, I had precious few occasions for solitude. I was an oddity in the court, a woman doing a job normally given to eunuchs. To prove to the queen that I was worthy of this unusual privilege, I spent every waking moment at work and allowed myself few opportunities for leisure.

Though I paid the price for the demands of my post with

* 446 BC

a willing heart, there were moments when I grew desperate for rest. On such days I would slip out for a solitary walk on what I had come to think of as *my* hill.

Far from being a majestic spot, the hill looked like something God had heaved up as an afterthought—low, squat, and neglected—unworthy of attention in a place as glorious as Persepolis. Perhaps God had molded me from the same dust, for I too was short and round, unimpressive and overlooked.

It was a hot day for that time of year; we were only fifteen days past the Persian New Year, which was celebrated on the first day of spring. Yellow and white narcissus grew in bunches around me, waving in the lazy breeze. Under the warmth of the sun, the tensions of the week began to drain out of me. I had brought a large roll of flat wheat bread, liberally spread with creamy butter and sweet grape jelly, one of my favorite repasts. Munching slowly on my meal, I leaned back against an elbow, considering the merits of a short nap.

The sound of pounding hooves made me snap my half-closed eyes open. The horse, a pure black, thundered across the terrain, heedless of rocks and debris. I could not see the rider's face, though he was near enough for me to make out the aristocratic linen tunic, the bejeweled belt, the soldier's bearing.

I shot up with an abrupt lack of grace, realizing that he was on a collision path with me. He saw me and slowed his horse, but continued to trot until he was almost on top of me.

Having lived for years in the palaces of the king of Persia had taught me to recognize rank. I bowed and stood again to study him with silent curiosity.

His dark hair, though long and waved in the fashion of the court, was not bewigged or over-coiffed. Eyes the color of the lush forests of Ecbatana stared at me through a ring of thick lashes. I had never seen a man with such disconcerting beauty.

"I take it you haven't seen a lion?" he asked.

For a moment I was struck dumb. Speaking to young, handsome noblemen was not a common occurrence in my world. But being faced with one who began his conversation with such an unusual—one might even say ridiculous—question, was downright confounding. Wild animals were routinely imported for royal hunts, but they were kept in well-maintained hunting grounds and were not allowed to roam the countryside, terrorizing the natives.

"Have you lost one, my lord?" I asked, trying not to smirk.

One dark eyebrow arched a fraction. "In a manner of speaking."

"They generally don't come here," I said, and refrained from adding that he should try the royal hunting grounds as most sane men would.

"The hunt started in the royal enclosure," he said, as though reading my thoughts. "Then the beast seemed to vanish into air. Everyone else is still in the park looking for him. But I followed his tracks here."

I looked about me casually, not worried that I might come across an actual lion. "I've seen no sign of him."

He dismounted and began to examine the ground with minute attention. Straightening, he shook the dust off his hands. "Well, he was here, and not too long ago."

Not wanting to sound skeptical of his hunting prowess, I held my peace. We stood in silence surveying the landscape, I in one direction and he in another.

Suddenly he hissed, "Don't move!"

I froze at the urgency in his tone. My mouth grew dry as with perfect incomprehension I saw him reach for his bow and arrow. What was happening? Was he planning to shoot me? Persian men were legendary for the accuracy of their marksmanship. He could have skewered me with ease from ten times this distance; this close, he was not likely to miss if he wished me dead.

"Don't move," he said again, his voice a gentle whisper.

A soft rustle low to the ground behind me caused me to hold my breath. For the first time I began to believe that a lion had truly managed to get itself loose from the well-guarded hunting grounds, which did not make my situation any more secure. Instead of being murdered by a sharpshooting courtier, I was about to become the noonday meal of a ferocious animal.

Too close behind me I heard a roar so fierce, I almost toppled over with terror. How I managed to hold still, I shall never know, but it saved my life. Within a moment the whoosh of an arrow passed within a finger's breadth of my cheek and then I heard another roar followed by a crash. The first arrow had barely been loosed when the rider had a second notched into his bow.

Frozen to the spot, I stayed unmoving, even when he lowered his weapon, indicating that the danger was past.

"I found my lion." In my frazzled state I managed to notice that his voice remained cool as he spoke, as if he had pet a kitten rather than confronted a menacing feline.

"How fortuitous for me," I said through dry lips.

"Don't you want to see him?"

For a moment I could not find my voice; fighting nausea, I staggered to the ground. Could he not tell that I was too busy having an attack of the heart to admire his skill?

He hunkered down and studied me. This close I saw that the symmetry of his face was even more stunning than I first had thought, magnified by the unusual contrast between his bright green eyes and olive skin. In those unusual eyes I was surprised to find kindness.

"I thought you very brave. You hardly flinched."

"That's because I didn't believe there was a lion behind me," I blurted.

He laughed, revealing a white smile marred only by the overlap of one crooked tooth. The sight of that blemish brought me relief somehow. It made him more human.

"You thought I had been in the sun too long."

"I thought you had a gourd for a brain and the skills of a sparrow in tracking game." Almost being killed had clearly affected my sanity. Even in the best of times I had a tendency to speak with unwise forthrightness, but this was ridiculous. I covered my mouth with my hand.

He stood with a slow flexing of athletic limbs. I noticed to my relief that his smile did not fade. "You are very forward for a servant."

I forced myself to my feet. "I beg your pardon, my lord."

It was unwise to offend the nobility, and I had managed to do it with stupendous success. Hoping to cover my rudeness by some empty flattery, I put on my best fawning expression and said, "You are an extraordinary hunter." Even to myself I sounded insincere.

His smile disappeared. It was like seeing a mask settle over his face. His cold expression confused me. He had been welcoming and kind when I had been offensive. But in the face of my compliments, he acted with icy disgust, as though I had soiled his shining shoes.

Perceiving the change and concerned that I had indeed antagonized him, I turned around to find more fodder for my desperate praise. The sight of the massive carcass not five steps behind me brought the gears of my mind to a crashing halt. My vacuous comments turned into sincerity. "You saved my life," I said with a catch in my throat. "It would have killed me if not for you."

"How kind of you to notice." His voice dripped with sarcasm.

I tried again. "I am grateful for your marvelous skills, my lord."

He flicked a hand as though swatting at a fly. "This flattery will avail you nothing, and it only bores me."

"But I am sincere!"

"Of course. Now that we have established your pure motives perhaps you would be so kind as to offer me your assistance?"

I finally understood that while he had not cared about my earlier rudeness, he found my flattery distasteful. I hadn't offended him by comparing him to a sparrow; he was annoyed that I had called him a great hunter in order to coax his favor. That one brief indiscretion had lost me his respect.

I had started my words with flattery; he was right to suspect me of it. However, I could not have been more sincere once I saw how close to death I had come.

He was a stranger to me; even his name remained a mystery. Why should I care for his opinion of me? Yet care, I did.

It was clear that he had no patience for my explanations. Swallowing my pride, I asked, "How may I help, my lord?"

"Send me two guards from the palace. I cannot carry this beast down by myself."

I bowed, one hand on my heart. "As you command. And, my lord? I do thank you for saving my life. It may not seem like much to you, but it is all I have."

He turned his back to examine his prey. "You will not last long in Persepolis with that mouth," he predicted with cool detachment, and I knew myself dismissed. For a moment longer I tarried there, staring at that broad back. Something in me—some strange unknown longing—stirred at the sight. Illogically, my heart constricted at the knowledge that this would be the last time I would ever see him.

I walked back into a storm. Barely had my feet touched the marble floors of the queen's apartments when one of her hand-maidens grasped me about the arm.

"Where have you been? The queen has asked for you a dozen times."

I frowned, irritated by the handmaiden's inquisition. "I had an engagement with a lion."

"*What?*"

"Never mind. Where is Her Majesty?"

Queen Damaspia was not in the habit of calling me unexpectedly. On most days, my life worked on a schedule as exact as the rising of the sun. Once a week, I met with the queen to help manage her vast personal holdings. Outside of these pre-established appointments, she showed no interest in me. I accomplished most of my work in the confines of my airless office or amongst the records of the queen's library—far from the glamour of the court.

As I walked to Her Majesty's inner sanctum, I grew increasingly uneasy about this urgent summons. Had I made an error? A grave mistake that had displeased her? Was this the disapproval I had been dreading? If so, I would have preferred the mouth of that wild lion. My head began to pound.

I found Damaspia pacing about her bedchamber. The flowing hem of her garments, made of endless lengths of lavender silk, dragged on the floor behind her like the tail feathers of an exotic bird. Before I had a chance to bow with sufficient humility, she dismissed her attendants. I studied her from beneath lowered lashes, trying to guess her mood.

"Read," she commanded, pointing me to a clay tablet. With considerable relief I saw that it had not been prepared by me. Not my mistake, at any rate.

I looked at the seal and found that it belonged to the queen mother.

Amestris.

More alarming stories about that lady haunted the palace walls than any other member of the royalty. Her intrigues and political machinations excited more rumor than all the governors of the empire put together.

Whether the queen believed the worst of the rumors, or entertained her own reasons, my lady could not forbear the sight of her fierce mother-in-law.

I began to examine the tablet with care, trying to put behind me the terror of the morning, which had robbed me of my equilibrium. The record spelled out an official complaint against a man named Frada, a steward in charge of considerable royal holdings. I did not need to read further to know the exact extent of his duties; I was already familiar with them.

Frada worked for Damaspia. He was one of her favored servants. And according to this tablet, he was being accused of stealing from Amestris. The queen mother was requesting his life in punishment for this crime.

To accuse Damaspia's trusted man amounted to accusing the queen herself. This was no less than a declaration of war, a public battle between the two most powerful women in the empire: the king's wife and the king's mother. Frada was merely a pawn, poor fellow. I had worked with him on many occasions and knew him to be a scrupulous and honest man. Whatever Amestris sought to accomplish by this suit, it held no truth in it.

I studied the details of the accusation again. It spoke volumes of Damaspia's ironclad control that she did not interrupt me in her agitation, but allowed me to read undisturbed as she paced her enormous chamber with rapid steps.

The queen owned a sizable village a day's ride from Persepolis, over which Frada had charge. A rich and fertile land, it produced more fruit and grain than any of her other villages. It had only one drawback; the land shared a border with a large walnut grove owned by Amestris. During the last harvest, Amestris's document charged, Frada had stolen *her* walnuts and had counted them toward Damaspia's share.

"Well?" the queen snapped, when she saw me straighten from my study.

I chose my words with care. "There seems to be some confusion."

"Confusion! This is an evil-hearted attempt to destroy a good man for the sake of harming me."

The queen's conclusion was the most obvious one, I had to concede. There was no love lost between the two women. If Amestris wished to embarrass her daughter-in-law, this might not be a bad plan. Yet in the language of the document I noted a genuine sense of outrage. The words sounded more emotional than legal in places, as though dictated by the wronged party rather than a disinterested scribe.

Furthermore, the document was written in Persian, the prestigious language of the court. If the legal document had been meant for the average man, it would have been prepared in Aramaic. For a royal brief such as this, tradition would require the use of Akkadian, the complicated language of old Assyria, still held in high esteem amongst the educated. But Akkadian was known predominantly by scribes, not by aristocratic women. Once again the personal nature of the document struck me; this was not a detached legal construct. Affront leaked out of every accusing word.

I had another reason for hesitating. The queen mother's chief scribe, Nebo, happened to be a friend of mine. In our own fashion, palace employees at times forged unique bonds of camaraderie. Nebo and I did not share the intimate secrets of our hearts, but we stood together as scribes sometimes strove to do, and exchanged what information we could without violating confidences. Nebo had told me that his mistress, though proud, was a fair woman. In over fifteen years of service, he had never known her to punish anyone without provocation. The picture he had painted was not of a woman who would cause harm through petty fabrications.

"Your Majesty," I began, and hesitated. Without my bidding, the lion hunter's last words echoed in my mind: *You will not last long in Persepolis with that mouth.*

"I have not known you to mince words before, scribe. Speak before you give me a sour stomach." Damaspia clasped her hands behind her back, causing her thick gold bracelets to jingle like bells.

I bowed. "Give me a week to look into this charge, Your Majesty. I see no benefit in your rushing into open enmity with the queen mother."

The queen raised a shapely eyebrow. "When I invited you to speak, I meant as a scribe. You forget your place. Your job is to tell me if this document is binding. Should I wish for political advice, I would appeal to greater minds than that of a mere girl who can read and write."

"I beg your pardon." It seemed my day for apologies. "The document is wholly legal, though . . ."

"What?" she snapped with impatience.

"The language is odd in places. For one thing, it is written

44

in Persian. It does not sound like the work of a scribe, but of one who is personally outraged."

"I would not be surprised if she dictated the whole of this malevolent document with her own wrinkled lips," the queen said with a dismissive wave of her hand.

"Another irregularity is the date of the crime. The robbery happened during the last harvest, which would have been months ago. Why has the queen decided to complain of it now?"

"She is capricious and unreasonable. Who knows what is in the mind of that woman?"

I decided that I had said as much as I could and that the matter was out of my hands. The queen clearly had no interest in my opinion.

Damaspia dismissed me with a regal nod of her head, and with one final bow I retreated. I was at the door when she barked, "Wait."

How could I have known that reluctant order would change my life?

"Explain your reservations."

Like a fool, I did.

"You are saying you do not believe this to be a plot hatched by Amestris? You think she truly believes this drivel about Frada?"

"Quite so, Your Majesty."

"How could this be when you know as well as I do that Frada would never steal a single shriveled walnut from that woman or anyone else? It is either Frada or Amestris. For my part, I know whom I believe."

"I, too, believe Frada is innocent." I shifted my weight from one leg to the other. The tension of the long formal audience with the queen was beginning to wear on me. My arm itched and I had to force myself not to answer its irritating demand.

Persian court protocol was fierce. "I cannot explain this mystery. I merely suspect that all is not as it seems."

"What do you suggest? That I sacrifice Frada based on your unlikely suspicion of Amestris's innocence?"

"Of course not, Your Majesty. But give me a week—or better, two—to try and solve this puzzle."

"I give you three days."

My heart sank. I could not get an audience with someone as lowly as an assistant apothecary in that time, let alone investigate such a complicated matter with the delicacy it required. I knew better than to argue, however. Resignedly, I bowed before retreating.

Chapter Four

Damaspia sent the queen mother's clay tablet containing the details of the suit to the office I shared with my two assistants. The young servant bowed before handing me the covered document. "Her Majesty sends me with her compliments. I am to serve you for the next three days, mistress."

Taken aback, I took the tablet from her hand. The queen was not in the habit of sharing her servants. Nor was I in the habit of having them. "Er, thank you," I said. What was I to do with her? In her flowing yellow robe she seemed more suited to applying the latest beauty treatments to elegant women than to serving a harried, sweat-stained scribe. "What is your name?"

"Parisatis, mistress. Everyone calls me Pari."

She was about my age, and pretty; her long limbs and slim neck made her appear like a new fawn when she moved. "Well, Pari, you are most welcome," I said, trying to put her at ease.

After some moments of awkward silence I thought of a useful task for her. Scratching off a short note on parchment,

I gave it to her and instructed her to go to my father's quarters in the bowels of Persepolis. Her eyes lit up; the royal palace held many wonders for a servant often restricted to the women's apartments. I shook my head and turned to study Amestris's clay tablet once more.

Had I made an enormous error in judgment? Would three days fly by with no breakthroughs as the queen mother spun her web to inflict irreparable damage upon my lady? Had I placed her and myself in a hopelessly precarious position?

I made my way to the exotic formal gardens for which the Persians were so famous. Their presence here in Persepolis was a minor miracle, for the climate of this part of the empire remained dry most of the year. Before the great king Darius's engineers had dug qanats—a system of delicate shafts and tunnels that tapped into underground rivers—this land had been an arid desert. The qanats forced the earth to give up her secret waters without drying them, and transformed the land into a paradise of beauty.

I was blind to that exotic allure as I weaved my way through a marble avenue shaded by sycamore trees that had been planted with such exact spacing, it had required the skills of a scribe to work out the angles. I gripped the clay tablet with trembling hands. The sight of the familiar stone bench beneath the black mulberry tree calmed me a little, and I sank onto its smooth surface to await my father.

He had served as royal scribe for thirty years. In that time he had heard of more schemes and conspiracies than I had hair in my unplucked eyebrows. Perhaps he could help me solve this puzzle.

Now that we had our work to bind us together, we spent more time in each other's company than we had when we lived in the same house. We were colleagues. In this we found common ground. Through my vocation, I had finally managed to earn my father's esteem, if not his tender attachment.

I saw him walking toward me in the distance and rose to greet him. I was my father's daughter in more ways than one; his black straight hair, his dark eyes, his short stature had all been repeated in me, looking even less prepossessing in a woman than in a man. I suspected that he had never fully forgiven me for that—for looking like him rather than my mother, who was, according to everyone who had known her, a woman of no small beauty. When she died, she took most of my father's heart with her.

"Since when have you had a servant assigned to you?" he asked after greeting me.

"Since today. And the honor will last a mere three days."

He frowned as he sat. "A temporary servant and an urgent summons to your father in the middle of the workday. Sounds important."

I described my dilemma to him.

"Why have you become involved in this?" He pushed an agitated hand through his hair. "This is folly. You should never have said anything to the queen."

"I couldn't very well bear false testimony."

"It is not false testimony to hold your tongue. You know nothing of the matter."

"I know all is not as it seems." Taking the cover from the tablet I urged him to read it. "See for yourself if I am right."

My father took the tablet reluctantly and held it close to his nose; the years had not been kind to his eyes. I wondered what I would do if he told me that I had arrived at an erroneous conclusion. The skin of my chest began to itch with annoying intensity; it was a reaction to acute anxiety that I had developed in recent years. I sat on the tips of my fingers, squashing the urge to scratch myself, and waited on my father's pronouncement.

At last, he raised his head.

"Am I right?"

He shrugged. "Unlike you, I am not a mind reader. But yes, the language is unusual. Personal."

I sighed with relief. "If the queen mother was indignant when she dictated it, it means that she believed this crime happened. She believed Frada stole from her."

"So there really is a thief. All you have to do is find him. In three days."

The itch on my chest spread to my arms. "It's worse than that."

"How could it be worse?"

"There are two possibilities. First, that a third party stole the walnuts and Amestris jumped to the conclusion that it must be Frada. This is a matter of simple theft though the wrong man is accused of the crime."

My father, I could see from his intense gaze, had become interested in spite of his annoyance. "And the second possibility?" he asked.

"Not a simple robbery, but an intentional plot to rile Amestris against Damaspia. This is the more likely scenario. Why does the document accuse Frada of stealing the walnuts to count them toward *the queen's* share? Why not say that he took the crop to enrich his own coffers? Surely a thief would take the crop and run, without leaving a trail to Frada or Damaspia. But someone interested in stirring trouble would make certain to implicate Frada as well as my lady."

My father leaned back. "This is a bad business, Sarah. You have landed yourself in a hornet's nest. Do you know anyone in the queen mother's household?"

"Her chief scribe."

"You had best send for him, then."

Nebo was a Babylonian by birth and a mountain by girth. Next to him, I was a willowy wisp. That he agreed to meet me with such alacrity was a sign of his courage, for if we were implicated by the current circumstances, we would both be severely punished.

I explained to him my suspicions. "Can you tell me what you know?" I asked. "It is to both our ladies' advantage if we resolve this disastrous misunderstanding."

He hesitated, thinking through my story no doubt, trying to find trickery behind my words.

"It is as you say," he conceded finally. "Amestris has been robbed, and she is convinced that this Frada is the culprit. More importantly, she believes he did it by the order of the queen. I have rarely seen her so angry. Your lady should have a care for her health."

I heard a sudden noise behind me in the oleander bushes and held my breath. Night had fallen and I hoped no one could see us. But sound carried. Had we been overheard? A small rabbit ran out from beneath the thick foliage. Relief made me light-headed for a moment. How had I managed to go from a seden-tary scribe to one who jumped at the sight of rabbits?

I tried to gather my thoughts again. "Why is the queen mother so convinced the culprit is Frada? What proof has she?"

"The thief left behind an expensive robe. It was recognized

by the people of the village as belonging to your lady's man."

"One man could not rob half an orchard!"

"No, he had help. But he must have been there himself, and in his hurry left behind this garment."

"Why is the queen mother convinced that Frada was stealing on behalf of Damaspia?"

Nebo looked about him and dropped his voice even lower so that I had to move my face almost against his mouth to hear. "A few days ago an assistant scribe working for Frada sought an audience with Amestris. He had with him a parchment that clearly proved Frada's perfidy. What's more, it had the seal of your lady, indicating that not only did she know about his actions, but she herself instigated them."

"May I see this parchment?"

"Impossible."

"The name of the scribe? That at least, you can give me."

Nebo groaned. "You endanger us both."

"I swore loyalty to my queen and you to yours. Is that not worth some danger?"

"You are a young fool. And I am an old one. His name is Gaspar."

I bowed as if to an aristocrat; I wanted him to realize how grateful I felt for his help. "Talking of danger, why did Gaspar take the risk of dismissal by exposing his superior?"

"He said he could not live with his conscience, knowing the queen mother was being cheated."

"How noble."

"Indeed."

"Why did he take so long to come to Amestris? After all, the theft happened months ago."

Nebo scratched his bald head. "I suppose his noble conscience needed time to be convinced. He must be afraid to go back to his employer, though, for Gaspar has not returned to his post, but lingers somewhere in the city. Before you ask, I don't know where."

"That makes no sense. Frada is not the kind of man one fears. Why give up a well-paying job before anyone has threatened to dismiss him?"

I took my leave of Nebo more troubled than when I had first arrived. This mystery grew increasingly complicated with every step. I knew my lady had put her seal to no such document. I needed to speak to Frada, but it would take more precious hours to summon him than I had. I decided that I would have to content myself by sending a message. In the meantime, there was this conscience-stricken fellow, Gaspar, to find.

The dinner hour had long passed when I found one of the queen's couriers and entrusted him with a letter for Frada, impressing on him the urgency of the situation. The speed of Persian couriers was legendary. The Achaemenid kings seemed to know of every important occurrence throughout their far-flung kingdom almost the moment it happened. Their secret was in part the dazzling speed of their messengers. But even that legendary swiftness might not be enough to give me my answers in time.

It had been a grueling day, but I was too fretful to think of sleep. My grumbling stomach reminded me that I had not eaten since breakfast. I made my way to the servants' kitchens in the women's quarter, knowing there would be little to choose from this time of night. I managed to scavenge a large piece of Lavash bread and a generous slice of sheep cheese. In the herb garden I spied some mint in the dark and rolled it into my bread with the cheese. I sat near a clump of tarragon and chewed thoughtfully. Water trickled soothingly somewhere near. The scent of mint and tarragon filled the air. All appeared to be well with the world. My mind knew better.

I wondered what would happen if I could not find the answers to this riddle in time. I knew my father feared the worst —feared that by involving myself in a political intrigue I had endangered my life. This, I realized, was not my fear. Damaspia was not a violent woman, nor was she in the habit of killing servants who disappointed. She did demote them with rapid decisiveness, however. Or, like my predecessor, got rid of those who ceased to please her. The idea of such public shame made me break into a cold sweat. The thought of failing to win her approval—failing to accomplish what was required of me—was enough to reduce me to a shaking mass of nerves. I could not bear the weight of failure.

With a sigh, I retired to my narrow, windowless chamber. My three roommates were already asleep when I came in, an unhappy but regular circumstance, as I still needed to unroll my bedding and would probably raise their ire with the noise I was bound to make. To my surprise, I found my bed already made. At the foot slept my temporary servant, Pari. I blessed her under my breath as I crawled under the fresh sheets. From somewhere, she had acquired essence of orange blossoms and had scented my bedding. I decided that I could grow accustomed to having a servant of my own, and before long, fell into a deep and dreamless sleep.

I woke up to a headache and Pari's unsmiling face. "You're in trouble, mistress," she said.

She made it sound as though this was a personal reflection on her. Alarmed, I said, "What?"

"The cook says you took food without permission last night."

I sighed with relief. "Is that all?"

Yawning, I reached for my tunic at the foot of my bed where I left it every night, and found it missing. I looked about me, puzzled.

"You need a fresh one, mistress," Pari said in her soft voice. "This one needs to be washed."

"It's fine."

From behind her, she pulled out the disputed garment. "I will show you: these are sweat stains, you see? Here is a dried-up crust of food from two days ago; I recognize the sauce from the dinner in the servant's dining hall. And here, I think, is plain dirt, from sitting on the ground." She sounded shocked at the idea.

"Oh. I hadn't noticed."

Pari was too polite to scold me. "Where do you keep your clean ones?"

I showed her the chest that contained all of my worldly goods. She rummaged for a few moments and handed me a long white cotton tunic. I felt too embarrassed to tell my borrowed servant that the dress was tight and forced myself into it like a stuffed grape leaf. Pari sighed when she saw the results and went off to wash my clothes.

I found a scarf and wrapped it around my shoulders for modesty and retired to my office. Setting the Persian tablet before me, I sat and stared at it again, trying to pry out more clues. If only I could convince Damaspia to give me a little more time. If only I could find this man Gaspar and force him into confessing the truth. If only Frada could unlock the key to the source of the parchment bearing the queen's seal. My life hung in the balance of too many *if onlys*.

One of two assistant scribes who reported to me sat studying a parchment on his cramped desk opposite me. Letting the parchment roll, he turned to me. "I cannot work out this payment for the queen's records."

The queen's records! Of course! Meticulous records were kept of every transaction made to or from members of the royal household throughout the years. In those records, one could sometimes find precious details about the servant who was being recompensed.

"You are a genius," I cried as I flew to find my way to the hall of records, leaving my assistant shaking his astounded jowls in my wake.

It took me three hours to locate the documents pertaining to Gaspar. Most of them referred to him as a resident of the village where he worked. My persistence finally paid off, however, when one of the earlier records gave me enough details to locate his parents.

Conveniently, they lived not far from the palace walls. Although technically Persepolis was a sprawling collection of palaces, gardens, and pavilions as well as the administrative nerve center of the Persian Empire, it was also surrounded by a city and several villages, which had sprung up to accommodate the thousands who worked in conjunction with the palace. The name of *Persepolis* invoked all these things: capital; palace; hunting grounds; city; the most magnificent structure the world had ever known.

I decided to take Pari with me, hoping that the presence of a servant would give me a more official appearance. Excited at the prospect of visiting the town, Pari forgot that I was a cook-displeasing, filth-encrusted, lowly scribe, and looked at me with adoring eyes. Only her threat of giving me a bath and treating my hair with perfumed olive oil and the angels knew what else when we returned home darkened our pleasant stroll. That and the prospect of the upcoming interview.

Gaspar's parents lived in a rundown dwelling located on a narrow lane. Flies gathered around a dirty puddle next to the front entrance; we disturbed their feasting as we took our places near the mud wall and they began to try to land on us with dogged persistence.

I was waving my arms about in an attempt to discourage them when the curtain was swished open by an old woman with leathery skin. Her eyes widened as she saw Pari and me. I lowered my arms with haste and tried to look dignified.

"I am Sarah, Senior Scribe to Queen Damaspia. I am here on official business."

She took a step back and placed her hand on her chest. "What do you want?"

I stepped forward. "May we come in?"

She looked around for a minute and stepped aside, allowing Pari and me to enter. After the brightness of the day, it was too dark to see well inside. I waited to be invited to sit as was polite. The invitation never came.

"I am looking for Gaspar," I said without preamble. "I have some questions I need to ask him."

She shrugged. "I don't know where he is."

I felt sure she lied. "It would be to his benefit to speak to me," I pressed.

She shrugged a thin shoulder again. My eyes had finally adjusted to the dim light inside and I looked around me. The dirt floor was bare, the mud walls unpainted. The flies outside had many cousins, most of which seemed to live here. Against one wall, I spied a tunic woven in rich wool, with purple and green embroidery at the edge. Not a garment belonging to a poor household.

"Who does that belong to?" I pointed.

The old woman blanched. "My husband."

"Very fine."

"Our son sent it to him to keep him warm in his old age."

"Tell your son, should you happen to see him, to look for me at the palace. He is in trouble, you must know. I will try to render him what service I can and spare him the worst."

She glared at me with defiance. I suddenly felt sorry for this woman who was trying so hard to protect the child of her womb. Hanging my head, I thanked her for her hospitality before getting out, Pari behind me.

"You didn't believe her, did you, mistress?"

"No." I was squirming inside my mind. What good would come from this crazy chase? Someone was bound to be hurt. Damaspia, Amestris, Frada, Gaspar, that sad old woman whose crime was to love a dishonest son. Me.

We made it to the palace in time to have dinner with the rest of the servants. Afterward, Pari made her threat good and forced me into a bath. Although I was clean, I was no closer to the answers I sought.

Chapter Five

The next morning marked the final day allotted to me by the queen. I rose up with sore legs, realizing that I had walked more in two days than I normally managed in two weeks. My routine responsibilities, neglected for too long, had piled up, awaiting my attention. Distracted, I found myself making slow progress, half my mind on what Frada's letter might illuminate.

The courier arrived long after evening had fallen. Still covered with the dust of the road, he handed me a leather cylinder. I knew he had neither slept nor enjoyed a respite since starting his journey many hours ago. Expressing my thanks I dismissed him to his rest, knowing I would have none that night.

Inside the leather cover I found a roll of parchment. First, I examined the seal to ensure it was intact. Breaking it, I sat down in my deserted office to work through Frada's response.

He told me how shocked he was at the allegations raised

against him and assured me of his innocence. Regarding his cloak, he said that it had been stolen several months ago, and included the testimony of one of the king's men as to the veracity of this claim.

He had heard about the theft at the queen mother's orchard the previous autumn, but knew nothing about it. At the time it had occurred, he had increased the watch over Queen Damaspia's lands in case other robberies should be attempted. He had thought no more of it after that.

He wrote that two weeks before, Gaspar had left his employ abruptly, without giving prior notice. In the short time he had had to respond to my missive, Frada had searched for clues of Gaspar's activities before his departure, but had found little worth remark. These few details he described in the hope that they would be of help to me.

Several weeks ago, a young servant boy had been asked by a royal courier to fetch Gaspar. Before leaving the scribe in the company of the messenger, the boy heard the courier announce that he had come from Alogune of Babylon.

I leaned away from my desk. *Alogune!* She was one of Artaxerxes' concubines, I knew, and the mother of his son Sogdianus. What had she to do with the queen's servant? Why would she send him a message?

I returned to Frada's letter. He explained that the young boy had thought the courier's visit irregular; village officials were not in the habit of receiving missives from royal households other than the queen's, and then the letters always came directly to Frada, not to the assistant scribes. Afraid to bear tales against his betters, the boy had maintained his silence, however, until Frada had begun questioning everyone. Unfortunately, he could provide no other details regarding this odd occurrence, such as the reason for the messenger's visit. He only knew the name of the one who had commissioned the message.

One final oddity: a missing parchment regarding the purchase of a piece of land, originally sent by the queen and bearing her seal. Frada had discovered its disappearance by accident some days ago when he had needed to refer to it.

I could recall the exact document to which he referred. Damaspia had been in a hurry the day she commissioned it and less patient than usual. She did not wish to wait for us to fill the parchment with other instructions and send it the following day, but urged us to send it immediately to protect the land purchase. This made it an uncommonly short missive, with a wide margin of unused parchment. She had been turned around at the time I placed the document under her hand for her seal. Distractedly, she brought the seal down low on the parchment; with perfect clarity I now remembered the blank space between her seal and the Aramaic text.

I offered God cursory thanks for the exacting Persian procedure of making every document in triplicate form, and the fact that somewhere in the queen's own records we could find a replica of the original letter that had gone missing. At least we had a minor piece of real evidence.

With painstaking precision, I read the letter twice more, slowly working through the different pieces of the puzzle. Alogune was at the root of everything; Gaspar was an insignificant tool in her hands. With cold calculation, she had set Amestris against Damaspia, and worse, planned to ruin the queen's reputation. Did she hope to supplant the queen? To turn the king's affections against the wife he loved so well by making her out to be a common thief and liar? Did she plot to place her own son, Sogdianus, in line to the throne instead of Damaspia's son? Was that the instigation for all this evil: the dissatisfied ambitions of a woman who already had so much?

I sighed, rolled up the parchment, and began to prepare an oral report for my audience with the queen on the morrow. My only companions for the night were a large platter of meat and chickpea patties, and my own troubled thoughts.

Early the next morning I found Pari had washed and pressed my best robe. I would not submit to her desire to curl my hair, but I conceded to let her gather it into a neat knot at the base of my neck. I knew I failed her high standards and felt guilty for letting her down.

Anxiety made me ravenous that morning, but I dared not eat much under Pari's worried scrutiny lest I spill anything on my clean garments. After a long wait, the queen called me to her chamber. She was dressed in full royal attire, her green and purple garments richly embroidered with dark purple thread. Upon her brow she wore a fluted gold crown that must have weighed as much as the head of a man. Jewels the size of goose eggs sparkled upon her chest and arms and fingers. She must have just returned from a formal reception with the king, I realized.

"Have you found any validity to your wild suspicions, scribe?" she asked without preamble.

"Yes, Your Majesty."

She eyed me with her wide blue stare and dismissed her attendants once again. I told her everything I had discovered. When I described the letter bearing her seal, and explained Gaspar's likely use of it, Damaspia sprang from her gilded chair.

"That slanderous dog! He falsified my letter?"

"Yes, Your Majesty. Although I have not seen it, I suspect

he added a few instructions of his own at the end of the parchment, instructions that implicated both you and Frada. This would have been the source of the delay between the robbery, which occurred last autumn, and the queen mother's lawsuit. After arranging for the theft, Gaspar had to wait to lay his hands on a letter that would suit his purpose. He then showed that letter with the forged addition to Queen Amestris as proof of your guilt. I don't believe he would have dared move forward with the scheme without the evidence of your royal seal. That is why Queen Amestris did not lodge a complaint until three days ago."

Damaspia paced with restless steps about her chamber. I watched her silently, giving her time to absorb the enormity of the plot that had been woven around her. "You have done me a good turn, Sarah," she said with sudden good humor, coming to a stop.

Caught off guard, my jaw fell open. In three years, she had never called me anything but *scribe*. I was not even aware that she knew my name. Snapping my mouth shut, I bowed.

"I see Pari has even managed to keep you clean. Well, you can hang on to her a little longer, and take your clean self to Queen Amestris and explain the truth to her."

"My lady?" I squeaked.

"Someone has to speak to her. She still assumes I am the villain who robbed her."

"But . . . Your Majesty, surely . . . If perhaps you were to—"

She began to laugh, her shoulders shaking with mirth. "You will have need of more eloquence than that when you speak to Amestris or . . . " she made a garroting gesture against her long neck.

I stared at her wide-eyed.

She laughed harder. "You should see your face. Be at your

ease. She will not dare touch you. Not right away in any case."

I collected my tattered dignity about me as best I could. "But Your Majesty, would it not prove more effective if you were to speak to the queen mother?"

"I have not spoken to that woman in ten years and I don't intend to start now."

"Consider, Your Majesty, I am a mere"—I almost said *girl who can read and write*, but feared she might not appreciate my sarcasm and emended my words to "mere scribe. The queen mother will not even deign to see me."

"*Senior* scribe. And she will see you because she knows I will have sent you. Her curiosity will get the better of her pride. I cannot risk sending another. You know the details of the matter, and will have the best chance of convincing her. Our trouble is that we have very little hard proof, and she is not an easy woman to sway. You must tread carefully with her, Sarah.

"In the meantime, I will send for Frada and the boy who witnessed the arrival of Alogune's courier. Their lives are in grave danger. Alogune would have counted on the queen mother and me falling into her trap and blaming one another over this theft. Which we would have, were it not for your sharp eyes. But now that we have unearthed the connection to her, she will need to cover her tracks.

"If Alogune has spies other than Gaspar planted in my household, she will know that her only safety is in destroying the witnesses that can point to her involvement."

Appalled, I lifted a hand to my mouth. Would my letter to Frada bring about the servant boy's death?

"Fear not; Frada is an old campaigner. He will have thought of the danger and hidden the child somewhere in safety. Still, I will rest better when I have them under my guard here in Persepolis.

"I will also send in search of this Gaspar. You did well to find his hiding place. His testimony would have cleared Frada, but I doubt I shall recover much more than a body now."

Alogune could not let him survive, I realized. He held too many of her secrets. It dawned on me that my naïve desire to pursue the truth had placed the innocent and guilty alike in the path of danger. I prayed that I had not acted out of arrogance; that I had not violated the will of God in pursuing so single-minded a path. I should have prayed *before* undertaking this assignment, I thought, with a bitter taste in my mouth.

In her most famous act of revenge, Amestris had put to death the wife of Masistes, her husband's brother, after first cutting off her nose, ears, lips, and tongue. Some whispered that this was an action motivated by jealousy, for the woman's daughter was said to have become King Xerxes' lover. I doubted that the queen mother had committed the murder out of romantic jealousy. Given that Masistes and his sons rose up against the king in a revolt but a short while after, I thought it most likely that Amestris had caught wind of the plot before everyone else and punished the instigator without waiting around for lawful proof. Which did not help ease my personal anxieties.

The queen mother was the most powerful woman in the empire—more powerful even than Damaspia. And unlike my lady, she would not hesitate to condemn me to death if she believed me guilty of treason. I had little solid evidence, as Damaspia had pointed out. My words alone were my emissary. If I proved unconvincing and Amestris came to the conclusion that I lied in order to help her son's wife, she might vent her anger on me while her daughter-in-law remained out of reach.

The king's mother deigned to receive me, but not until first making me wait in a stuffy antechamber for four hours. She had been Xerxes' third queen. The first, the lovely Vashti, had been banished forever from the presence of the king for refusing to come to him when he sent for her during a public feast. The second, Esther, a Jewess like me, had never borne him any children and lost her place as queen because of it, though the king was said to have treated her with kindness all the days of her life.

Perhaps not having been Xerxes' first choice rankled too much, for Amestris allowed no one to dismiss her grand station. She was the daughter of Otanes, one of Persia's seven most prominent leaders, and woe to anyone who forgot her lineage or her position. I did not intend to make that mistake.

When finally permitted into her presence, I approached her with my hand before my mouth in the tradition of formal royal audiences, lest the odor of my breath offend her. I walked the length of her long audience room with my back bent low, as though she were the king himself instead of his mother. Even the king only required such honors on tribute days, when delegates and courtiers from different parts of the empire brought before him the symbolic gifts of their fealty to the empire.

The queen mother did not object to my excessive obeisance, however. She let me stay bowed a good long time until I grew quite familiar with the colorful pattern of the tiles on her floor. Each tile was made of a precious stone; nothing but the most exquisite materials the world had to offer would do for Amestris. Finally I rose when she gave me a signal, being careful to keep my hands to my sides.

In spite of her wrinkled face, it was plain to see that she had once been a handsome woman. She shifted on her gold throne and studied me through cold eyes, then nodded at the handmaiden who stood by her side.

The handmaiden barked, "Proceed."

I took a deep gulping breath and prayed I would remember my speech. "Your Majesty, Queen Damaspia has sent me with her compliments. She asks me to inform you of the recent developments regarding Your Majesty's case against Frada." In my best courtly Persian, I presented everything I knew of the case. The only detail I did not divulge was what Nebo had told me about the letter Amestris had received from Gaspar. Nebo would fall under suspicion if I were to reveal my knowledge of that document.

The old lady pinned me with her faded eyes. "You are accusing the lady Alogune of a serious charge."

"I lay no charge before the lady, *duksis*," I said carefully, using the Elamite title for *princess*, a term I knew she preferred. "Perhaps there is no link between this courier's visit to Gaspar and the theft of Your Majesty's orchard. I am merely describing the facts as I know them, so that Your Majesty might arrive at your own decision."

She gave a snort. "You want to lead me by the nose to a decision, you mean." She turned to the handmaiden at her side and whispered something I could not hear before turning to me again. "What you don't know, scribe, is that I have your own lady's seal to prove her perfidy. Talk your way out of that if you will."

"My lady's seal?" I asked with false innocence of which I would have to repent later, and gaped at her like I was hearing about it for the first time.

She turned her face away as though bored. "You shall see." Then ignoring me, she turned to whisper to one of her attendants.

Not being dismissed, I stood before her ramrod straight, desperate for a seat.

A few minutes later Nebo came puffing through the door, bearing a parchment. He blanched when he saw me. I looked away as though he were a stranger to me, a gesture that must have reassured him. Amestris pointed a bony finger toward me and Nebo handed me the document. I did not have to make a show of studying it; I needed to find any telltale discrepancies of script between the first part and the second.

Gaspar clearly had a talent for forgery. Even knowing exactly what I held in my hand, it took me many moments of careful examination before I found what I looked for in the simple Aramaic script. Lifting my head I waited on the pleasure of the queen mother to speak, which she granted at her own leisurely pace.

"We have a copy of this letter in the queen's record room, *duksis,*" I said. "I shall have it fetched that you may see the original wording. It was much shorter than this, ending at this portion dealing with the purchase of land. But by accident the queen placed her seal lower down on the parchment I now hold in my hand. This later section, which convicts Frada and my queen, is in fact a fraudulent addition. The forgery is very good, I grant you, and hard to detect. It is no fault of your own scribes, *duksis,* that they did not perceive it. I myself have only discovered the irregularities because I wrote the original in my own hand."

"Send for this original now," Amestris demanded. I realized that she did not want me to have time to forge a document of my own. I nodded for Pari to come forward and gave her instructions to take to my assistant. She looked fearful enough to faint as she glanced at the old queen from the corner of her eyes.

As Pari began to withdraw, the queen mother turned her

attention back to me. "Show my scribe here these discrepancies of which you speak."

I began to point Nebo to the difference in the strokes of the ink when Amestris barked, "Louder!"

In her old-fashioned court, she considered it beneath her dignity to become directly involved in such plebian matters, yet she was also unwilling to give up the least bit of control. I thought how differently she directed her household from the queen and was grateful to work for the younger woman. Pitching my voice louder, I began my explanations once more, pointing to each letter, with Nebo following carefully. When I finished, Amestris nodded once and Nebo went to her side for a whispering conversation that I could not hear.

Pari appeared at the door, and at my signal made her way to me with rapid steps.

Glancing at the record to ensure it was the correct one, I handed it to Nebo. He studied it before engaging in another long whispering conversation with the queen mother. Finally Nebo stepped aside, and the queen mother's attendant shouted, "You may leave."

I may leave? But what was the verdict? I looked at Amestris in confusion, but could read nothing in her impassive face. Nebo gave me a reassuring smile, and having to be content with that, I took my official leave. I wondered what I could report to the queen. *Nebo smiled, so all is well?*

Damaspia demanded for every detail of my audience with Amestris. Far from being disappointed, she laughed like a child and clapped her hands. "What I wouldn't have given to see her face. She hates to be proven wrong."

"It was not very entertaining, Your Majesty. Her face never changed expression; she certainly showed no sign of remorse for falsely accusing Frada."

The queen laughed. "She is like the Sphinx—old and expressionless. We can leave everything in her hands now."

I frowned. "Your Majesty, I doubt she will take any action. Why, she dismissed me without even telling me if she believed me."

"Oh she believes you, my little scribe, or you would have heard the sharp end of her tongue."

"I don't think her tongue has any other end."

Damaspia's eyes twinkled with merriment. I was proving to be quite entertaining apparently. I found it a heady experience, being in the confidence of the queen of Persia, basking in her approval.

Suddenly I remembered that all danger was not yet passed. "What of the lady Alogune?" I feared greater mischief from a woman who had gone to such extremities already.

Damaspia waved a hand. "The queen mother will take matters into her own hands. Amestris will not allow such maneuvering to go unpunished. You don't tamper with the queen mother without suffering for it."

"What do you think she will do?" I asked in fascination.

"She'll go to the king, and Alogune will find herself packed up and back in the bosom of the mother who birthed her in Babylon. And here is the beauty: I shall not have to approach the king and complain of one of his dear concubines. His mother shall do me the service. To help herself, Amestris must help me." The queen twirled with grace in the middle of her room. "How glorious an outcome! Not only have we foiled an injurious plot, but we have forced the queen mother to do our dirty work for us."

She laughed and tapped me on the cheek affectionately. "I am very pleased with you, scribe."

Now that my special assignment was over, I sent Pari back to the queen's apartments. I missed the girl's unobtrusive ministrations. She had proven to be a congenial and useful companion.

Three days later, the queen's men recovered Gaspar's body. The queen told me it was inevitable; he had riled too many powerful people, and if someone had not done it in the dark of an alley, the king's justice would have punished him as severely in the light of the day for daring to commit fraud upon a royal person. Rather than chastise Gaspar's parents for hiding him, however, Damaspia gave them a little money and packed them off to a village she owned near Susa. She wanted to ensure their continued safety.

I thought it typical of her to show clemency to an old couple who would have caused her harm in their desperation. She often said that the greatest king of the Achaemenid line, Cyrus, won nations by his mercy as much as by his sword. He had set my people, the Jews, free from their captivity in Babylon, so I held him in great esteem myself. He was the only Gentile to whom our prophets referred as the *anointed one*. I honored the queen's efforts to follow in his footsteps.

We had not even started packing for our annual summer journey north when the lady Alogune was officially exiled to Babylon in public disgrace. Artaxerxes, who had lived through the murder of his own father and older brother in a palace coup, had no patience for plots. I breathed easier after that, knowing Frada and the young servant boy under his care were safe now from threat of harm. I thought life had returned to normal, and busied myself with the tedious work of preparing for our summer move to the cool mountains of Media.

Chapter Six

The queen ruined my life with kindness.   .

The Achaemenids regarded special acts of faithful service worthy of reward. For generations, they had grown accustomed to bestowing tangible favor on those who provided them with notable aid. Usually these gifts came in the form of a luxurious offering—necklaces and bracelets fitted with precious stones, handwoven garments, silver and gold chalices, rations of fine wine and grain. If Damaspia had given me any of these in appreciation for discovering and foiling Alogune's plot, I would have wallowed in grateful excitement for months. If she had even given me a decorated saddle for a horse I did not own and could not ride—another common royal gift—I would have soared on wings of joy.

But no. The queen chose to bestow on me the highest honor imparted from royal hand: she gave me a husband. A Persian aristocrat.

A week before our departure for Ecbatana, Damaspia sent

for me. Puzzled at this irregularity, I tried to forget that the last time she had summoned me like this, I had become embroiled in a web of perilous intrigue. Ignoring the knot in my stomach, I forced my reluctant feet to walk faster, and found myself ushered into her presence.

She smiled widely when she saw me. She was in good humor, I thought, a little reassured. It seemed that every member of her court had gathered about her; her handmaidens and eunuchs and lesser servants turned in unison to gaze at me. I began to feel myself perspiring under the scrutiny of so many people. I was not accustomed to such attention.

Disconcerted as the stares continued, I approached the queen with misgiving.

"You are very good at uncovering secrets, scribe. But I have kept a few from you for some days now," Damaspia said.

I made some inane comment about her wisdom and began to feel a prickling of worry. It was clear that everyone in the room knew of this secret and was amused by it at my expense.

"Some nights ago as I supped with the king my husband, he told me of the predicament of one of his cousins, the lord Vivan. This predicament, I wish to share with you, Sarah, for it concerns you now. Before I do, however, I must tell you Vivan's story.

"Many summers ago, when Lord Vivan was still a young man, he fell in love with the daughter of his steward, a beautiful girl named Rachel."

My eyes widened at that name, which was not Persian, but Jewish. The queen acknowledged my recognition with a faint nod and continued. "She was one of your people—a Jew. Lord Vivan's love for Rachel was so consuming that he refused to take her as concubine, which befit her station, but married her instead and elevated her above his other wives. Her son, whom they named Darius after the great king, became his heir.

"Of course Lord Darius was not raised as a Jew, but a Persian. When he was seventeen, to the sorrow of father and son, Rachel died.

"Since then, Darius has proven himself an honorable son in every regard save one: he has refused to take a wife, though well past marriageable age. This has been a sorrow to his father, whose greatest desire is to behold the children of his son. Vivan holds this one shortcoming against Darius, for in every other regard he is a man of honor and the epitome of what a Persian nobleman ought to be."

I did not understand why the queen would wish to parade this young man's admirable qualities before me. I bobbed my head up and down like a fool and waited the queen's good pleasure to explain.

"Some weeks ago, goaded by his father's great unhappiness, Darius finally confessed to his father the reason behind his stubborn desire to remain unwed. It happens that before her death, Rachel made her only son promise that his first wife would be a Jewish girl. He knew that his father wished him to marry into Persian nobility. Caught between his youthful promise to his mother and his father's certain disappointment and wrath, Darius kept quiet, hoping that in time a solution would present itself.

"By this time Lord Vivan was so relieved that his son was willing to marry at all that he cared little where the girl came from. His remaining dilemma was in finding the right Jewish girl for his son."

An uncomfortable prickling sensation made me squirm where I stood. Why had the queen expressly called me to her chamber to share family gossip?

Damaspia went on. "As I said, the king told me this story as we supped two nights ago. His cupbearer, Nehemiah, was in attendance as usual. He is your cousin, I believe, is he not, Sarah?"

"Yes, Your Majesty, on my mother's side."

"A good man." Damaspia waved a bejeweled hand, to emphasize her words. "The king admires his wisdom. So I asked him, when the king had finished regaling me with his tale, if Nehemiah could recommend a worthy wife for Prince Vivan's son. Before he could answer, however, I said that I myself had a name to suggest.

"The king and his cupbearer turned to me as though I had suddenly learned to speak the language of the Greeks. 'Who do you have in mind, my love?' the king asked me. Do you know whose name I gave, Sarah?"

"No my lady," I said, beginning to feel sick.

"Yours, you simpleton!"

"*Mine?*" I croaked.

Everyone around the room laughed. The sound came as though from far away. I felt the room sway and feared that I might faint. Perhaps I would wake up and find that this whole scene was a nightmare—that I had fallen asleep while overseeing the packing of records. I would wake up drooling over a pot of ink and have a good laugh over the absurdities that my mind could conceive.

"Yours," the queen repeated remorselessly, unmindful of the effect her words had on me. "I told the king you were the one who had discovered Alogune's perfidy, and that it was you who had approached the queen mother with the truth. Then I asked Nehemiah what he thought of you and your family.

"He said he held you in the highest regard; though you were poor, you were trustworthy and loyal. Well, I could have said as much myself. I told the king that I owed you a reward for protecting my good name. Marriage to a Persian aristocrat—the king's own cousin, no less—seemed as good a prize as anyone could have. And Lord Vivan would have his heart's desire, which was marriage for his son. It was a perfect solution for everyone. The king and his cupbearer agreed with me heartily and the next evening we invited Lord Vivan and told him the good news."

I kept waiting for the ending of the story, the part where the queen would tell me that someone came to his senses and stopped this disastrous chain of events. The world operated according to rules and regulations. Insignificant Jewish scribes simply did not marry Persian aristocrats. It was rare enough for Persian aristocracy to marry outside their own ranks. But when they did, they did not choose women who brought no political advantage, no wealth, and no beauty. Someone must have thought of this at some point and recognized the impossibility of such a scheme. I would be all right, I kept assuring myself. There would be no marriage to some spoilt courtier who would stifle the life out of me with his lofty expectations. This was a jest.

"There is one difficulty," the queen began, and I breathed out in relief. Here it was: the voice of reason. "Lord Vivan must leave for Ionia before we depart to Ecbatana. He will be gone a full year on an assignment from the king. And he does not wish to wait that long to see his heir married. He wants to celebrate his son's wedding before his departure at the end of the week."

My jaw dropped open. I put a hand against my neckline and pulled it down to give myself some air. "End of *this* week?"

"I am afraid it shall be a hurried affair, a one-night feast instead of the appropriate seven-day celebration. In his gen-

76

erosity, the king has offered the use of the new Throne Hall in Persepolis; he hopes the magnificence will make up for the shortness of the celebrations. Lord Vivan shall have to foot the bill of course; the king is not *that* generous." Everyone laughed. I began to believe that this wedding was something real in the queen's mind. That she counted on it taking place at some point in the future.

"But, surely, Your Majesty, I am too insignificant for such a lofty lord from the Passargadae tribe to marry. It would not be fitting," I said, desperate to remind her of reason, and to escape this unbearable fate. The Passargadaes were the greatest family in Persia. Even the Achaemenid kings descended from them.

"Nonsense. It is fitting if I say it is. You need not worry about anything, Sarah. I myself have given you some furnishings and a few robes so that you shall not go to your husband's house empty-handed. There is no reason for you to be ashamed when a queen stands behind you. The contracts were signed by your father and Lord Vivan this morning. Everything is taken care of."

At the mention of contracts I collapsed on the floor; my legs could no longer support me. I heard the twittering of laughter around me, and did not care. Then I felt a gentle arm go around me and a cup was placed against my lips. I tasted wine. I saw that the queen herself held me.

"Come, come, it has been too much for you, poor child. You had best go and rest now."

I thought if I left her presence, I might not be able to secure another audience until it was too late. "I beg your pardon, Your Majesty," I mumbled, and forced myself to my feet. "I am well." I grasped wildly about, hoping for inspiration. "But my lady, who shall be your chief scribe if I marry? There will be no time to replace me. I cannot bear to think of the shambles your records shall fall into without proper care."

Damaspia took a half step away. "You have uncovered the one weakness of my plan, I admit. It is most inconvenient to myself, this marriage of yours. You were the best scribe I ever had. Such is my regard for you, however, that I have willingly made the sacrifice."

"You need not—"

"Enough!"

I knew that tone. The regal voice that declared the end of discussion.

I remembered that I had not thanked her yet, and that I could not afford such a breach in protocol. In a choked voice I said, "I am very grateful for your undeserved generosity, my queen." Then bowing, I left.

My father, I told myself, would find a way out of this. I collapsed on the familiar bench in the king's garden, utterly blind to the beauty that surrounded me, and tried hard to hold on to my sanity as I waited for my father's arrival. Scant hours ago, it seemed, my life was just as I wanted it; I had my work, I had the respect of my queen; I had the satisfaction of knowing I chose my own path.

Damaspia had told me that my marriage would inconvenience her, yet never had she thought of my inconvenience. Everyone in her chamber had looked at me as though I had been handed the keys to happiness, as though I ought to kiss the hem of the queen's robes with utter thankfulness.

But I knew about aristocratic marriages amongst the Persians; I saw my queen, cherished by her royal husband, yet having to share him with many women. He called Damaspia *beloved* and yet sired children by others. I would not have the luxury of love. I was nothing but the appeasement of a promise to a dead woman. How many women would I have to share my home with? How many women would bully and despise me?

In the palace, I shared my humble room with others; but that little spot was mine; no one begrudged me its use. I earned it with my service.

The work of my hand brought me respect as well as wages. I knew I had earned the admiration of the queen and as a result, her household. In spite of my relative obscurity, I was worthy of esteem by those who knew of me in the palace. In the house of the cousin of the king I would be nobody. Worse. I would be a disappointment. These thoughts filled me with such panic I began to tremble and could not stop.

I saw my father walking slowly toward me from a distance and ran to him.

"What is this thing you have done?" he asked without greeting. He sounded tired.

"It was the queen's doing. I only found out about it this morning. Father, how do we stop this madness?"

"It cannot be stopped, Sarah. I sealed the contracts myself."

"Why?" I cried. "Why did you not refuse?"

"Refuse the king's own cousin? Are you mad? He came armed with the king and queen's blessings."

I turned away from him to rest my head against the trunk of a sycamore tree. "Why me?" I moaned. "No doubt there are many sweet-tempered, beautiful Jewish girls who would love to become wife to a Passargadae. I will find one myself and deliver her to the door of Lord Vivan before the week is out. *Why me?*"

79

"Sarah, it is done."

"It is not!" I screamed. "I will find a way. I will go to Cousin Nehemiah."

"He was there when I signed the contract," my father said softly. "There to help, not to hinder."

His resignation made me furious. "You have no care for me," I said, my face cold. "You never have. This marriage will kill me." I was pleased to see the sheen of tears in his eyes. Something hardened in my heart as I walked away from my father. In those moments, it was as if all the years of desperate love and unfulfilled yearning I had carried for him twisted into bitter anger. I knew now that I was truly alone in the world.

I was working in my cramped office, trying to put Damaspia's records in perfect order before the court's departure to Ecbatana, when three of Damaspia's handmaidens traipsed in. My chest began to itch ferociously at the sight of them.

I spied Pari standing in the middle. "What is the meaning of this?" I asked, half rising.

A middle-aged woman, clearly acting as the head of the small army said, "The queen's chief handmaiden sends us with her compliments. We are to help you prepare for your wedding."

I gulped as I surveyed their baskets overflowing with oils and what seemed like torture instruments to me. The thought of spending my remaining hours of freedom in their company made the itch on my chest spread to my belly.

"How thoughtful." I threw a surreptitious glance at the eunuchs who acted as my assistant scribes. "But there must be some mistake. I already have been assigned help."

"Oh. Pardon our intrusion. Her Majesty's apartments have been in upheaval the past day. The queen mother has announced that she will be visiting her daughter-in-law this week. We have all been very busy making preparations. No doubt the chief handmaiden forgot that she had already sent you help."

I gave a fake smile, though I could not help reddening with guilt. It was only a little lie, I told myself. After all, I *had* been given help. Was it my fault that their support was of a scribal nature? Besides, I would not be surprised if my eunuchs knew more than I about Persian beauty treatments.

To my relief, the queen's servants left my room without further discussion. At the door, however, Pari turned around. "Who did she send to assist you?"

"I can't recall."

She crossed her arms. "How unlike you, mistress."

I narrowed my eyes and hissed, "It's none of your affair."

She raised her perfectly plucked eyebrows. "If I don't do my job, mistress, who do you think will be in trouble for it?" I had nothing to say and she turned as if to leave. At the door she hesitated. "Have a few hours then. Mind you, I will return."

It took me two days to secure an audience with the king's cupbearer. Since my wedding day was four days hence, the delay of this crucial meeting—my last hope for reprieve—proved hard to bear. On my way to Nehemiah, Pari stopped me for the fifth time in two days.

"Mistress! I must prepare you for the wedding. There is so much to do: your hair, nails, skin—"

"Later," I said and pushed her away.

"But there is no time. You cannot go to your marriage bed thus! Your bridegroom—"

"Can sit on his spear for all I care." I threw Pari a fierce look, and walked off, leaving her openmouthed.

Behind his back I may have called him *Cousin* Nehemiah, but he was too important an official to treat with casual intimacy. I greeted him with a bow; it took every bit of my strength to wait to be addressed by him before opening my mouth. With apprehension, I studied him for signs of his humor. As always, he was impeccable; his dark red hair had been neatly arranged into waves and covered at the crown by a pristine felt cap. His rich robe fell to the floor in colorful splendor; not a wrinkle could be found anywhere in that garment. I doubted the fabric would dare.

He gazed at me through cool eyes, and I remembered with discomfort that in contrast to his fastidious appearance, I was even more of a rumpled mess than usual, having in my great agitation neglected the finer points of personal grooming for some days.

"The bride," he said finally, after studying me for a long time, his voice drenched in disapproval.

"I don't want to be," I wailed.

He sat on a stool and stretched leather-shod feet before him. "How tragic."

I gaped at him, thrown by his lack of sympathy. "Will you not help me?"

"How? The queen has chosen you; the contracts have been sealed; the date is set; the king has planned an elaborate feast. It is the will of the Lord, Sarah. As our countryman Mordecai told *his* cousin Esther but one generation ago, *Who knows but that you have come to royal position for such a time as this?*"

"The will of the Lord? It is *your* will! You could have told the queen the truth when she suggested my name; you could have said that I was unsuitable to be the wife of a Persian nobleman."

"That is not the truth or I would have said it."

I crossed my arms in exasperation. "Would you please just look at me? There is nothing in me to please a spoilt young man interested only in beautiful girls and hunting."

The barest hint of a smile touched Nehemiah's lips. "I don't know which you insult worse: yourself or your bridegroom. Either way, you underestimate both. You are a quick-witted, discerning, warmhearted woman. I have always thought you very pretty, Sarah, though you take as much care of yourself as a mangy dog."

I did not find being compared to a dog offensive; to my mind, it was the closest thing to the truth he had said thus far. Again, I tried to make him see reason. "My one talent is as a scribe. My husband will not care how many languages I speak, but at the palace they do. Here, I am worth something."

"You are not worth something because of how many languages you speak," he said, beginning to sound exasperated.

My eyes filled with tears I could not control. His implacability hit me with the weight of one of Persepolis's giant columns. "Please, please, Cousin. I beg you! Stop this marriage."

At the sight of my tears Nehemiah's face softened. He came to stand near me. "Child, trust God. He would not have placed you in this position without a reason."

I shook my head. "I trust your ability to make mistakes more than God's ability to make His plans succeed!" I blurted, and without permission ran out of his chamber, knowing with certainty now that he would do nothing to stop the wedding.

I made my way to my favorite hill, and collapsing on its soft dirt, I cried myself to sleep. It was morning when I awoke. With shock I realized that the following evening, I would be a married woman.

Chapter Seven

I went back to my office and spent several hours making certain that I left the affairs of the queen in good order for the scribe who would replace me. Lost in my work, I could pretend that there was no bridegroom and no new home waiting for me at the end of the morrow. I had just finished when Pari came in, her arms piled high with things so that I could barely see her face.

To my astonishment, she dropped everything at my feet. Her face was white and tear-stained. "Mistress, I must prepare you for your wedding. I know you have no other help, and there is much to be done. I am not leaving until I finish." She burst into tears.

The sight of her misery smote my conscience. Had my refusal to mind her these past days landed her in trouble with her superiors? "I am sorry, Pari. You can do what you please with me. Did someone scold you on my account?"

She jerked her head toward the ceiling, the Persian gesture for no.

"What then?"

"My father is very ill, mistress. I received word earlier; my mother says he is dying."

"I am so sorry! Does he live in the city of Persepolis?"

"Aye."

"Then you must go to him. Why do you linger here? Go, go!"

"It's impossible! We must hasten to ready you."

"I'll do it myself, Pari. How hard can it be? Long before the queen sent you to me, I learned how to bathe."

"Mistress, the queen has sent hair and skin treatments and cosmetics. Also, depilatories to remove," she waved a hand toward my face, "excess hair. She even sent her own robe, which I'll have to adjust to fit you. I do not think you can manage alone."

Neither did I. I knew I could get rid of the dirt on my skin, but I would probably not be able to tell the difference between the depilatory and the hair-conditioning cream, which could prove problematic.

"I don't have to use all of it."

"Most assuredly you do. Her Majesty sent express word that you were to use everything she sent." Pari wiped her tears, but fresh ones replaced them.

"Then I shall use everything. Go home. I will not tell anyone. Go home and bid your father good-bye."

Eventually, I was able to convince Pari to leave. I took the bundle the queen had sent to my room. Being early afternoon, the women with whom I shared my quarters were busy at their posts and would not return until supper. Sifting through the pile, I tried to decipher the purpose of the creams and oils in each jar and amphora. The world of women remained a mystery to me. Ironically, though I lived among them, I occupied a narrow world of scholarly administration. Sums I understood. Cosmetics made as much sense as Egyptian burial rites.

I grasped the robe the queen had given me. Pale blue silk had been shaped into a simple bodice and full skirt, with wide, pleated sleeves that hung low, almost to the ground. Damaspia was narrower and longer than I. However, because the robe was open fully in the front, designed to be crisscrossed over the chest and held closed with a belt, I managed to put it on. No doubt Damaspia would have worn it over a tight silk under tunic, which would have peeked modestly under the blue robe. She had not sent me such an undergarment, knowing I could not fit into her form-fitting clothing. So I had to make do with one of my own homespun tunics.

In the pile I found a polished silver mirror and gazed at my reflection. The dress gaped in the front, showing far too much of my stained tunic underneath. At my feet the excess fabric pooled unflatteringly.

I sighed. To this at least I could attend. It was the one feminine accomplishment that Aunt Leah had managed to drum into my head. I fetched my sewing kit and sat down to hem my wedding dress. It took me hours; there was so much fabric in the gathered skirt that no matter how much I sewed, I still had more left. I was exhausted by the time I took the last stitch with my ivory needle, for while my fingers had remained busy, my mind continued to grapple with overwhelming thoughts.

What kind of man would my husband be? He was named after the second greatest Achaemenid king. Was that an indication of his pride, his sense of self-importance? Would he be cruel? As the wife of the king's cousin, I would not be allowed to work, of course. But would he allow me freedom to read and write? Would I find him repulsive? Overbearing? Tyrannical? And my greater fears: Would he be disappointed with me? Would he disapprove of me?

Anxious questions swirled around my mind with brutal intensity until I thought I should go mad with the weight of them. I had had no time to adjust to my fate. Fighting against this marriage had taken my whole focus for the first few days, and now less than a full day's cycle remained for me to grow accustomed to the finality of the change in my life.

I flung the exquisite blue garment at the foot of my bedding and began to sift through the jars sent by the queen. The women who shared my room came in and seeing my pile of goods, began to sigh over each article with enthusiasm. Why couldn't it be one of them getting married, I thought. They would be happy now. They would be celebrating their good fortune rather than bemoaning their cruel fate.

Their incessant cheer grew annoying and I crawled into my bed to put an end to their unwanted comments. My bed! I realized this was the last night I would sleep in its comfortable narrow confines. I had truly lost everything.

When I awoke, it was late morning and I was alone. I picked up the silver mirror sent by the queen and stared at my slightly blurred reflection. My hair needed a good washing and my eyes were red and bloated from my disturbed night. My lips, perhaps my best feature, normally soft and full, had grown dry and chapped. Just above them, a dark fuzzy shadow reminded me that I was supposed to remove all excess hair from my body. Persian women attacked facial and body hair like it was an enemy of the empire. I had never seen the point; it only grew back again. Besides, I had no idea how to manage it.

I pulled a jar of cold wax and the strips of cloth that went with it out of my pile. Thanks to the enthusiasm of my companions the night before, I could now identify most of the objects Damaspia had sent me, though I still had no clear understanding of how to use them.

I decided to try some wax on my leg. A sticky goop reminiscent of honey sat on my skin in an uncooperative lump. I spread it about a little and stuck a strip of linen fabric on top. Then I pulled hard. I yelped with surprise at the stinging pain. How did women do this with such regularity?

I hadn't done it properly, obviously, for my leg had only yielded some of its stubborn hair while others clung tenaciously to their roots. A couple of more attempts and I gave up with disgust. I had become a sticky mess and not lost much hair for my painful trouble. Frustrated, I set the wax aside. Darius Passargadae would have to deal with a hairy bride, God help him. I had no sympathy for his hardship.

Without enthusiasm, I grabbed a few jars of cream and skin treatment and went off to arrange for a bath and stayed in the water until it grew cold. I had never been covered with the scent of so many different perfumes. My hair smelled of jasmine, my skin like roses and fresh lime, and my breath reeked with the strong odor of mint. I felt like a giant bowl of fruit and flowers. I hoped my bridegroom would appreciate all this finery; I was giving myself a headache.

The queen expected me to curl my hair, no doubt, and I wrapped my wet hair into strips of cloth. It occurred to me that I should have done this the previous evening for my hair, which was thick and straight, would never be dry by late afternoon.

I remembered that the dress still needed to be loosened on top, but when I examined the fabric I saw that the seams had no room. I would have to wear it as it was, with the front gaping in a wide crisscross of fabric that showed a large expanse of my homespun, cotton under tunic. There was no time to do laundry and I only had two garments left that could serve. One was old and faded and looked even more decrepit peeping beneath the exquisitely woven blue silk. The other was respectable enough, and I put it on to ensure that it provided the right fit under my wedding dress. I decided that it would have to do.

The grumbling of my stomach reminded me that I had not eaten anything since the previous morning and with some relief I abandoned my preparations to go in search of food. Fifteen thousand people, including the king's soldiers, were fed daily in Persepolis. It was said that a thousand animals were killed each day to feed the appetite of so many. Yet there was hardly any food to be found in the deserted servants' kitchen. After scrounging, I found a large batch of thick herb soup with soft wheat noodles, which someone had uncharacteristically left to one side. Pouring some in a bowl, I managed to sneak back to my room without being seen.

The first spoonful almost made my eyes cross; enough garlic had been put into that soup to make a herd of wild horses faint. No wonder they had abandoned it in the kitchen. I decided that I was too hungry to care. To my horror, I landed a full spoon of the soup on my good tunic, which I still wore. In spite of my best efforts I could not get the stain out, for the soup had been seasoned with turmeric and its stubborn yellow tint clung to the fabric right in the middle of my chest.

Now I had two choices to wear under my wedding dress: an old faded tunic frayed at the edges or one stained with soup. I chose the old one. With shock I realized that I had very little time before I would be fetched for the wedding feast.

Frantically, I pulled the rags out of my hair; as I had feared, it was still too wet to hold anything like a wave. I grabbed the curled hairpiece Damaspia had provided and stuck the comb into my head. Wigs were all the rage in the empire; each one cost so much that owners were required to pay a special tax to the government for the privilege of having one. In spite of its value, this one did not sit right on my head. Wavy false hair mixed in with my own wet straight tresses, looking oddly out of place.

The appropriate application of cosmetics hardly seemed relevant in the greater scheme of my troubles. I went through the motions for the sake of the queen's command, but my heart was filled with defiance.

I covered my face with white powder. A filigreed silver amphora held freshly made kohl, which I applied to my brown eyes with an unsteady hand. There was a red pot for my cheeks and another for my lips; these I applied with faint hope that I put the right one on the appropriate feature.

When I had finished using every single luxurious item sent by Damaspia, I examined myself in the mirror and gasped.

I looked hideous.

I had used too much white powder, and against my strong, never plucked eyebrows, which joined in the middle of my forehead, the feigned whiteness of color overlaying my skin made me look more like a corpse than a living woman.

The way I had applied kohl to my eyes made me look like a loser after a serious fight. With some discomfort, I began to realize why Persian women removed excess hair, for my downy mustache sat atop my unnaturally red lips like an insect over a ripe berry. The image in the mirror squeezed every last drop of bravado and defiance out of me.

Before I could wipe my face, one of Damaspia's ladies in waiting rushed into my room.

"Where have you been? Everyone has already assembled—!

Oh great, holy fires, what have you done to yourself?"

"I—I was about to clean my face and start again."

"There is no time!" she wailed.

"Won't you please help me?" I begged, taking a step toward her, finally panicking at the thought of the disgrace that surely awaited me.

She lifted a hand to her mouth and nose. "What have you been doing, chewing on raw garlic all morning? Your breath reeks!"

I slapped a hand in front of my mouth. "What do I do?"

"There is no time," she said again. "You already run the risk of offending the queen, not to mention Lord Vivan and his son by tarrying so long. Quickly, put on your robe and let us go."

Later I would think of that moment—of my decision to obey her—with great regret. Obedience to palace protocol had been drummed into my head for three years, so I fell in with her command too easily. For her part, she must have been thinking of the fulfillment of her duty, which was simply the punctual delivery of the bride to the wedding feast. Taking the paint off my face would have consumed a good bit of time; we would have arrived late. Yet looking back, I am certain that my tardiness would have been less offensive to the queen and to Lord Vivan than my current appearance. I suspect, however, that the handmaiden was panicked over the thought of not performing the duty assigned to her. Not that her decision saved her from recriminations later. I would not be surprised if Damaspia took her to task for delivering me to the feast looking as I did. We both miscalculated.

We walked through the long corridors of the women's quarters and made our way toward the Gate Tower, leading into the Processional Way. The wedding feast was to be held in the Throne Hall, a majestic structure recently completed by

Artaxerxes, which stood at the end of the Processional Way. But the wedding ceremony itself was to be more private, located in a smaller assembly room to the east of the Throne Hall.

Caught in a dream-like trance, I hardly noticed the splendor that passed before my eyes as I ran. The queen's handmaiden pulled me behind her, forcing me to keep up with her hurried steps, the clicking of our heels echoing on the stone floors. And then with an awkward turn we arrived.

Persian weddings required the bridegroom and close family and friends to arrive first. The bride entered the room when everyone had already gathered, and she sat next to her betrothed at the head of the room where a pavilion was set up under a delicate overhang of fabric. Before them was laid a number of exquisitely decorated items, each bearing a symbolic significance: a large loaf of flat bread, cut in half; wheat and barley painted and decorated into patterns on a silver tray; honey and sweets; mirror and candelabra.

I was to enter the room and process under everyone's watchful eye and take my seat next to my bridegroom now. Though I had known all this, I was unprepared for the force of everyone's gaze as they turned to study me when the queen's handmaiden shoved me into the room and disappeared.

I heard the twitters before I was able to concentrate enough to see faces. The scene that greeted me made me lose my power to move: strangers covering laughter behind raised hands; Damaspia looking outraged; Nehemiah's mouth open with utter shock; my father, head bowed, hands trembling. And then I saw him—my bridegroom. Instantly, I recognized the vivid green eyes, the molded face, the broad shoulders. Darius Passargadae was none other than my lion hunter.

For a fraction of a moment I saw a myriad of expressions flash over his face. Perplexity. Shock. Embarrassment. Betrayal.

Wrath. Then suddenly it was as if he pulled a veil over his features. His face became inscrutable, a stony mask that gave nothing away. I noticed several young men, his friends presumably, trying to hold in snickers, and failing.

The last of my defiance vanished as I realized how I had demeaned him in my foolishness. An avalanche of shame and regret covered me with such force, I almost cried out. I turned to leave, to run away from this devastating disgrace, to free Darius Passargadae from the humiliation I had brought upon him.

An iron hand closed about my wrist. To my amazement I found that it was the king himself who held me in his grip. With the added height of his *kidaris*, the gold-fluted crown of royalty on his head, he towered over me like a giant.

He smiled at me with mild amusement and bent close to whisper in my ear so that only I could hear, "I don't know what you are about, girl. But you must finish what you started. You will shame him more if you run now."

I managed to jerk my head into a nod.

He did not release his hold on my hand but held it—a rare sign of astounding royal favor—and led me to the wedding pavilion himself. That right hand, famously longer than the left through a tragic defect of birth, remained near me like a protective shield until I stood before my bridegroom. Then Artaxerxes placed my hands into Darius's and helped me sit on my stool.

No one laughed now. The king lifted an eyebrow toward my hands, lying limp and cold in Darius's rigid hold, and nodded at Darius. Belatedly, my betrothed remembered to lift my hands to his lips for a kiss that touched the air above my skin, stopping short of touching my flesh. No one perceived his icy rebuff save me and perhaps the king; to the casual observer

94

the required customary welcome kiss had been performed.

At the king's signal, the ceremony began. Does any bride remember the details of her wedding? I know not. I only know that for me that night is covered as by fog. I remember the moment we fed one another of the bread, signifying our union, remember his mouth opening for the morsel, which I placed there with trembling fingers; I remember him swallowing without chewing, as though he tried to get rid of bitter poison best taken untasted. Then the magi's blessing and the bowl of honey was lifted before us, and again I saw to my astonishment that it was the king's hand that held it.

My husband dipped his little finger into the bowl and I followed suit, imitating him in a mindless haze. And there was the taste of honey on my lips—a symbol of the sweetness of our lives together. I made the mistake of looking into his eyes for a fleeting moment and almost choked as the impassive curtain lifted, replaced by a flash of loathing so hot, I thought my heart would melt.

"Now you," the king hissed in my ear, reminding me that I must reciprocate my husband's actions by feeding him honey with my fingers. Anxious lest he should scorn me before the guests, my fingers shook as I lifted them to his mouth. But he hid himself behind his stony expression once more and licked the honey so quickly that I barely felt his touch. The king expelled a long breath as this last part of the ceremony concluded.

Apparently we were to have an unusual wedding in every way, for Artaxerxes, a committed follower of the Persian deity Ahura Mazda, called upon Nehemiah to speak the blessing of the Lord over us. In a peripheral corner of my mind I was aware that by this public acknowledgment, the king had placed his seal of approval upon my husband's choice of a Jewish bride, and by extension, upon me. Nehemiah came forward and blessed us first in Hebrew and then in Persian. My eyes pricked with unwanted tears as he began with Solomon's tender words: *I am my beloved's and he is mine.*

I felt utterly bereft in that moment; bereft of my father's protection, of my queen's esteem, of Nehemiah's friendship, of my dearest dreams. I thought, not without considerable irony, that perhaps the only other person in that room who understood even a fraction of my internal turmoil was my husband.

Darius and I rose up to stand side by side, careful not to touch, awaiting the customary congratulations that tarried awkwardly. Again the king took matters into his hands and embraced my husband with open warmth. From the corner of my eye I saw a man barreling toward me. There was no mistaking his identity for his features bore a remarkable resemblance to my husband's. His eyes, though, were a powdery blue instead of green, and his skin had the fair coloring of his forbearers. I took an unconscious step to the side as I registered the outrage boiling to the surface of Lord Vivan's countenance. Unlike his son, he either had no talent or no desire to hide it.

My hasty step brought me too close to the person of the king, and suddenly the golden-tipped spear of one of the Immortals, Artaxerxes' personal bodyguard, was shoved in my face. The golden apple at the end of that distinguished spear almost slammed into my nose. I was sorry it did not; I thought a bloody nose might give me a good excuse to sneak out of the coming interview with my father-in-law.

Artaxerxes noticed the guard's gesture and waved him aside. Before Lord Vivan could reach me, the king took hold of my hand once more. This time he bent down to kiss me on both cheeks.

This rare gesture of favor, of welcome, of personal conde-scension was so astonishing that the gasps of the guests filled the room. His lips were cool and dry and his meticulously curled beard tickled my face.

"You've been a most entertaining bride," he said so that I alone could hear him.

There was no room for proper obeisance; he stood too close. Bowing my head, I croaked, "I beg your pardon, Your Majesty. It was unintentional."

"Nonetheless, you shall pay for it. I can only aid you so far. There are too many people in this room who would like a piece of your hide at the moment, not the least of whom is my dear queen."

Chapter Eight

Under the thick layer of powder covering my face, I blanched. Artaxerxes gave me a bear-up-you-must-be-courageous smile, then turned and gestured to his cousin, Lord Vivan.

"Meet your new daughter, Vivan," he said aloud, his voice stern with warning. Lord Vivan understood the underlying message of the king's words, as did everyone else in that banqueting room. He expected this evening to proceed with the full honor due a noble wedding.

Artaxerxes stepped aside to give Lord Vivan room to draw near. Trying to make up for the disrespect implied in my appearance, I bowed low before my father-in-law. His voice was cold as he said, "Welcome to your new home, daughter."

I bit my lip and mumbled, "Thank you, my lord." What could I have said in the space of those short moments that might have explained my strange appearance? Had I consented to Damaspia's arrangements and permitted Pari's ministrations days before, I would still have been a disappointment to father and son, for I knew myself to fall vastly short of their expectations of beauty. But my stubborn resistance and bold-faced lie had turned mediocrity into repulsiveness. I hoped Lord Vivan could detect the regret on my face. If he did, he showed no sign of it.

Artaxerxes hovered near us in conspicuous splendor until the last greeter had passed. His presence forced every tongue to be civil and every malicious smirk to be wiped clean. I had heard tales of his kindness before; tonight I had tasted of it. I would never forget it.

My bridegroom and I were ushered into the Throne Hall, a magnificent square structure decorated with a hundred fluted columns made of black marble, and opening to eight carved doorways that made the hall seem even bigger. The north portico was flanked by two massive gilded bulls. Beneath our feet priceless handwoven carpets sparkled with the shimmer of gold and silver thread, and above us the ceilings stretched so high that twenty tall men standing atop each other's shoulders would still not touch the cedar rafters. Hundreds of lamps lit up the room like twinkling starlight. The effulgence was lost on me, however, as I wallowed in my own private well of misery.

Darius and I were seated next to each other once more. He grabbed a silver goblet of wine and stared into its fiery depths before taking a long swallow.

"Why?" he said in a voice at once soft and dangerous. "Why did you pester the queen into arranging our marriage and then demean me publicly?"

I whipped my face toward him in astonishment. "Pester the queen to arrange our marriage? I did no such thing!" I cried, too outraged by the lie to remember that I *had* wronged him, though without intention.

99

"The whole palace is abuzz with how you manipulated Damaspia into arranging this union."

"And everyone knows that palace rumors are utterly reliable."

He took another deep gulp of his wine. "Not always, no." His green-eyed glance in my direction was brief and sufficiently insulting to make me blush. "But why else would Damaspia want me to marry *you*?"

The smell of our sumptuous wedding feast surrounded us: roast ostrich and deer, smoked quail, lamb cooked with quince, duck marinated in pomegranate paste, herbed meatballs seasoned with garlic and onions, cinnamon and saffron and cumin, fresh breads still hot from the ovens. Servants ate a different diet from aristocratic guests and royal residents of Persepolis; I had never seen such a feast. I wrapped my arms about my middle and thought I might be sick.

"You'd have to ask her yourself."

"What would be the use?" He signaled a servant to refill his cup. "You've had your way," he said when the servant had left. "But mark my words. You will have no joy of it."

Beneath the well-modulated tones I heard an implacable threat. At that moment I would far rather have faced his hungry lion. "Please, Darius—"

"Do not presume to be familiar with me, woman; you may call me *my lord*, for that is all I shall ever be to you." He finished his wine with a quick tip of his head and grabbed the whole flagon from the hand of a passing servant.

Darius spent the next hour with his wine and several merry friends, while I, neglected, sweltered in Damaspia's blue silk dress. My lonely terror proved a poor companion on the eve of my wedding.

I noticed the king reclining on his private couch near the queen, eating his food abstractedly. It was an open secret that he had no sense of taste. Every day of his life the richest man in the world was offered the most delectable food available to mankind and tasted nothing. Tonight, I could commiserate.

He must have sensed the weight of my attention for he turned my way and lifted his bejeweled cup in a salute. Damaspia followed his movement and turned away quickly when she realized that it was I Artaxerxes had acknowledged.

My cousin Nehemiah came over at that moment, bearing a gift for Darius. He waited until Darius turned his attention on him before placing a papyrus roll before him.

"I knew your mother, my lord," Nehemiah said.

Darius's bored countenance turned hostile. "And?"

"She loved the psalms of King David. I thought you might appreciate having a collection of some of them for your library. Your wife also used to have a particular liking for them in her childhood."

"My *wife's* likings are not of the least interest to me, cup-bearer. And neither are you, being her cousin, and party to this insult of a marriage. My father *trusted* your word!"

"Not everything is as it seems," Nehemiah said in measured tones, though bright color suffused his cheeks. "You may find one day that what seemed like an insult is in fact a blessing."

"And you may find one day that you are too clever for your own good." Darius picked up the priceless roll and crumpled it between his fists before throwing it back down.

Nehemiah tightened his mouth and took a step closer. "Those words used to comfort your mother in her times of trial and loneliness. She used them to draw near to the Lord and find His strength and direction. Treat them with respect!"

Darius lurched forward, his fist smashing down on the table before him. Suddenly the king stood before us, the queen on his arm.

I heaved a sigh of relief and forced myself to my feet to bow. Darius and Nehemiah followed suit, their hostilities veiled for the sake of the royal audience. At Artaxerxes' gesture, Nehemiah retreated.

"The queen and I take our leave now. I have arranged a room for you here in Persepolis this evening; it is too late to navigate the dark roads to your palace, cousin."

"You are both ever thoughtful, your majesties," Darius said, his words syrupy with sarcasm.

Horrified, I held my breath. Damaspia flushed and threw me a look as sharp as a dagger, but the king merely gave a bland smile. "Don't forget it."

"I am not likely to."

"Come. We will accompany you to your chamber. It will save having to bear the raucous company of others should you leave later. I don't suppose you would wish for that kind of fanfare?"

Darius pulled a hand through his hair. "No, I don't wish for that kind of fanfare."

I grabbed Nehemiah's crumbled roll, the scribe in me unable to bear such a waste, and followed the king and queen and my husband out of the Throne Hall. For a short moment I felt relief flood over me at the thought of leaving the scrutiny of so many condemning eyes, until I remembered that I was walking away from my wedding toward my wedding night.

Alone in our well-lit chamber, Darius homed in on the flagon of wine and delicate glass goblets left out for us. I sat at the edge of a hand-embroidered couch, but then found that I could not remain still and began to pace instead. In the oppressive quiet of the room I came to the realization that I needed to speak to my husband. I needed him to understand that I had had no part in this marriage, and more importantly, that I had not meant to humiliate him by my appearance. Resolved at last toward some action, I stuffed my shyness into a corner of my mind and sat near him on his couch.

He had already made impressive inroads into the wine. Though he held the fragile glass with a steady hand, something about the careful manner he maneuvered it warned me that he was not precisely clearheaded. I sighed and leaned close, trying to make sure I had his attention. "My lord, allow me to explain—"

An odd look came over his face. With some haste he placed a palm, callused from wielding swords and arrows, against my lips. He wrinkled his nose and scooted back from me. Belatedly I remembered the overpowering stench of garlic on my breath, and the fastidiousness of Persian aristocracy toward unpleasant smells.

"Please don't speak. And if you can help it, don't breathe," he commanded, withdrawing his hand.

I put my head in my lap, mortified. "I ask your pardon," I mumbled into my hand, hoping to cover the worst of my offensive breath. Trying to put some distance between us, I rose, thinking it safer to speak to him from the other side of the room. To my shock, he grabbed me around the arm and pulled me back down.

"Let's get this over with," he said, and I realized from the grim angle of his jaw that he wasn't speaking about conversation. Before I could react, he put a hand on my leg and pulled so that I was sprawled before him on the couch. He bent over me, his brows knotted in a grim frown as he studied me through unfocused eyes. To my relief he jumped up, but I realized that he was merely leaving to douse the lamps. The room drowned in darkness.

I had used the time to swivel back off the couch, but he grasped a handful of my dress and pulled me back. He put his hand into my hair to get a better grip on my wriggling form; Damaspia's wig, which I had attached too loosely to my straight hair, came away in his grasp.

"What—?" He jumped back, staring at the offensive headpiece. "I can't do this!" he cried. "It is impossible; I can't do this." He got up and struggled in the dark to light a lamp. In its faint light, he found his way to the elaborate bed at the end of the chamber. After setting the lamp down with exaggerated care, he threw himself across the feather-filled coverlet with a heavy thud. Within moments the sound of his soft snores filled the room.

Relief flooded my body. For the first time in many hours I found myself alone with my thoughts. Tomorrow Darius would be clearheaded enough to listen to reason. Tomorrow I would explain how I had meant him no disrespect.

The relief was short-lived, however. Even I could not believe that so much mistrust and hatred could be banished with a few simple explanations. The very sight of me was detestable to him.

His words rang in my mind: *I can't do this! It is impossible.* My worst fears about being undesirable had proven true. It was not the poorly applied cosmetics or the ragged tunic or the scent of garlic he rejected. It was Sarah herself. It was the whole of me that he found unlovely. Helplessly, I began to weep until my nose ran and I had to use one of the royal napkins to mop my face. My world had unraveled. And now I would have to bear a lifetime of belonging to a man who loathed me. The thought made me cry harder. The sound must have disturbed Darius's sleep, for he stopped snoring for a moment and mumbled, "Shush. It will be all right." Then he turned over and began to snore again. Those sleepy words, I knew, were not for me, but for some more fortunate figment of his dreams.

No, it will not be all right, I thought with fierce conviction.

Finally, when my tears had run their course, I found a pitcher of water and scrubbed my face until it was free of the hated cosmetics. Unlike Darius, I did not have the benefit of too much wine to help me into unconsciousness and I stopped in the middle of the king's sumptuous chamber, wondering what to do to keep from losing my mind.

Abandoned on a table I spied Nehemiah's wedding gift and picked it up. The papyrus was rolled over wooden cylinders, decorated with ivory carvings in the shape of lotus flowers on both ends. Darius's rough handling had damaged the papyrus, but with the right tools, I would be able to repair it.

For long years the children of Israel had memorized the sacred words of our prophets and leaders. But in recent times, Jewish scribes had begun to record our law and Holy Scriptures. Copies such as the one Nehemiah had given to Darius were rare and priceless.

Nehemiah's words echoed in my mind, evoking a flood of guilt as he no doubt had intended that they should: *Your wife also* used to *have a particular liking for them in her childhood.* Once, I had recited the words in this scroll with childish wonder and awe. I had believed in their promises. I had cherished their wisdom about God and humanity. But my mother's death changed everything.

I had few memories left of my mother. One memory lingered vividly, however. When she grew sick, she often asked me to recite the psalms. It was on one such occasion that Nehemiah had seen us.

God is our refuge and strength,
An ever-present help in trouble.
Therefore we will not fear, though the
earth give way and the mountains fall into the heart
of the sea.

In my childish fervor, I had recited the words of the psalm as a prayer, and told myself that I could trust God's promise to be an *ever-present* help in trouble. That I could accept such a promise on face value. So I asked His help for my ailing mother. I asked for it with a child's confidence and hope.

My mother died. Hollering in pain. I could no longer remember the color of her eyes, or the shape of her cheeks, or the touch of her loving hands. But I remembered those screams.

I did not understand why God would allow one of the sweetest creatures who ever lived on His earth to go through such agony. Initially, I had shielded my questions. I had held on to my faith. With grim determination I had prayed for my father's love. With David I whispered: *Delight yourself in the Lord and He will give you the desires of your heart.* Only, He hadn't.

At that point I stopped reciting the Scriptures and relying on the Lord. I still kept the outward form of the Law when possible, living amongst Gentiles as I was, but my heart no longer made room for God. I learned it was far better to rely on myself. I became the guardian of my own safety, the builder of my own dreams. It seemed to me that my strength, my cleverness, my abilities proved far more reliable than God's ever-present help.

Except that they hadn't, of course. That's why I was in this chamber, with a resentful stranger for a husband and a bitter future that promised no joy. I had reaped what I had sown with my own hands. This was the reward of my strength and my talent.

Now I had no help: not from myself, nor from God. Despair overwhelmed me, and I sat clenched in its brutal claw hour after hour that night, so that I came to a place almost past hope and past endurance.

Just after dawn the queen sent her handmaiden for me. Darius still slept when I left. I had known this interview would come, though I was surprised at the hour of it; Damaspia was not in the habit of being awake at the rising of the sun. She met with me alone, still wearing her garments from the previous evening, and I realized that she had not been to bed yet. I noticed her loose hair, her smudged eyes and bruised lips, and amended my conclusion; she had not been to *her* bed.

I prostrated myself and said with my face lying half against the cold marble and half on the edge of the silky carpet, "Forgive me, *duksis.*"

She turned her back to me. "*Why?* Why would you embarrass me like that? Why would you go to such lengths to make yourself and me and your new husband appear ridiculous before the whole court? I thought of you as a loyal *friend.* How could you betray my trust in you?"

Her words made me want to give in to another storm of weeping. I swallowed the tears, knowing she would have no patience for them. "I never meant to harm anyone, least of all you, my queen. My great fault was my ignorance; I would never willingly betray you."

"Your ignorance! What did you lack that I did not give you? Did I not provide you with more riches than you deserve in order to overcome that ignorance? Did I not send you my own servants to help prepare you for your wedding? It never occurred to me that you would be so stupid as to turn them away. If it had not been for Amestris's impending visit, I would have discovered your deceit and put a quick end to it. But that woman turned my household inside out by the threat of her mere presence.

"Still, my servants shall have to face my wrath for their disobedience. They should have seen through your excuses and insisted on doing their job."

Her reference to the serving women, especially Pari, caused my whole body to tense. It was the one reason I had wanted to come to Damaspia. I knew she would not heed my excuses about my own conduct. These women, however, were innocents caught in the net of my foolishness. I had to try to help them.

"Your Majesty, it was not their fault. I lied to them. I said I already had help. Pari was not deceived and returned four days in a row to try and help me. I sent her away every day, thinking myself too busy. And that final day I insisted to her that I could prepare myself, and in my arrogance, I truly believed that I could. She had no choice but to obey me."

"So, you admit to lying. Not to mention that in the meantime, you were busy trying to throw my gift back in my face."

Guilt kept me silent and Damaspia bobbed her head up and down. "Busy wriggling out of the marriage I had chosen for you. Yes, I knew about that. And I am half convinced that last night was not a matter of naïve ignorance so much as one final ploy on your part to escape this union. Perhaps you hoped that your bridegroom would put a stop to the marriage once he saw you?"

I gasped and lifted my head from the floor. "No, Your Majesty! What would such a ploy have gained me but your wrath? I would have devised a better plan, if that had been my intention."

The corners of Damaspia's mouth quivered. "That's the first time anyone has told me they could concoct a better plot against me than I can think of." She folded her long limbs into her gilded chair. "Oh, stand up. You look ridiculous down there."

I scrambled to my feet. "Thank you, *duksis*."

"So you are really *that* incompetent?"

"I'm afraid so, Your Majesty."

"Artaxerxes thought so. When I railed against you, he championed your innocence; for some reason he took a liking to you. He also bet me a gold coin that Darius would not consummate the marriage. Did he win?"

To have the most humiliating experience of my life the subject of a royal bet seemed a fitting conclusion to the last twenty-four hours. "The king won."

With a sluggish movement of long limbs she twisted on her chair to make herself more comfortable; it occurred to me that she must be exhausted. Her voice was as strong as ever as she addressed me, however. "No more than you deserve. You would have scared a child last night. For such a brilliant woman you certainly can be a dolt." Meticulously groomed fingernails drummed on the armrest. "Well, let's see if we can undo the damage you have wrought."

"It's beyond repair," I blurted.

"As we have already established you are extraordinarily incompetent in such matters I believe we shall disregard your opinion."

"Yes, Majesty." She was wrong, of course. But I couldn't tell her that. I was already in more than enough trouble.

"Now, regarding Pari. If she suspected you of lying, she should have reported it to the chief handmaiden. Obviously, she failed to do so, or I would have heard about it."

I gasped, horrified that in my attempt to prove Pari's innocence, I had caused more trouble for her. "But . . ."

Damaspia waved a silencing hand. "Since she sees fit to obey you over me, she can leave my employ and enter yours. You shall have to pay for her, of course. You still haven't collected the full wages you have saved over the past three years. From that sum you shall pay for Pari's training, for her clothing and food during her entire stay at the palace, for a year's upcoming salary, and for damages to me, given the inconvenience you cause by taking one of my servants from my household. This does not leave you with much, I believe."

"Your Majesty is most generous," I said, unable to make my face match my grateful words.

She laughed. "I am doing you a favor, sending your own servant with you into a household where you may not find a friend for some time."

I saw the wisdom of her actions, though they cost me too dear, and said with more genuine feeling this time, "My thanks."

"You shall spend the rest of today preparing as a bride. I myself spent a year getting ready for my marriage to the king, so one day will hardly suffice. It is a start, however."

I tried to hide my dread, though not well enough. Damaspia rolled her beautiful eyes. "Don't be such an infant, Sarah."

"I shall do my best."

"I leave for Ecbatana tomorrow with the rest of the court. Shall you and Darius be joining us?"

"I don't know, Your Majesty."

"I see. I don't suppose Darius would have been in a mood to wax eloquent about his future plans last night."

"Not exactly." Her question only reiterated how little control I had over my future . . . and how little knowledge of it.

The queen frowned and bit her lip. "Do come and visit me if he brings you. I should like to know how you progress."

Chapter Nine

*E*vening had long since fallen when I wound my way back to the chamber the king had assigned to Darius and me. Pari walked in my wake, her small bundle of worldly goods clutched against her chest. The poor girl had just lost her father, and now thanks to me, a position she had loved. Yet she had not murmured one word of complaint since I had fetched her an hour before. She turned her long, slim neck my way and startled me with a pale smile. She might be unhappy, she seemed to say, but she didn't hold me responsible. In the whole palace, she must have been the one person who didn't hold me accountable for some grave failing. I cannot express how dear that made her to me.

My skin smarted everywhere; I had been waxed, plucked, rubbed, sanded, and oiled for the better part of the day. Instead of looking rosy and soft, I was now covered in red welts from my face to my toes. My skin, unused to such rigors, had responded by breaking out into unattractive, angry-looking bumps.

At the door of the chamber a sleepy servant came to attention as I approached. "My lady! Lord Darius said you are to join him at home when the queen dismissed you. I am to take you there directly. Your belongings have already been sent ahead."

Relief flooded me at the thought of two more hours without having to face my husband. While in the women's quarters, something of Damaspia's strength and the familiarity of my surroundings had buoyed my spirit. That thin veneer of hope vanished the closer his plush cart drew me to his palace.

We had been riding for an hour when Darius's man informed me that we had entered the boundary of his lands. In the dark, I could make out the vague outline of farms. It was common for the aristocracy to lease land to farmers and give them seed and supplies in exchange for a portion of the harvest, so I was not surprised by the cultivated land. What did surprise me was how much of it there was. We rode a full hour before approaching Darius's personal estate and gardens. My husband was wealthier than I had imagined. I found the thought depressing. How could I fit into such a world as a mistress rather than a servant? I had even less in common with Darius than I had assumed.

In the dark, my new home seemed menacingly large. Marble walls and fluted limestone columns shone an eerie white in the moonlight. My husband's palace was every bit as overbearing as he was himself. The steward, a tall thin-lipped man with a lantern for a jaw, met me at the door. His eyes, cold and dark, held no welcome for me. He told me that Lord Darius awaited me in the great hall and showed me there in person. His manner, though impeccable, left no doubt that he held no welcome for me. I sent Pari to find my room and prepare it for my arrival as best she could.

Bereft of excuses for delaying the upcoming interview, I

allowed the steward to show me to the hall. The light of many lamps blazed in the large room so that I was momentarily blinded when I walked in.

Before my eyes had adjusted, Darius towered over me. A corner of my mind registered his immaculate appearance— knee-length coat of rich handwoven wool with tight long sleeves, held closed by a belt of golden roundels, skin-hugging buff colored trousers, not a hair out of place. I still wore my ridiculous wedding outfit.

"What happened to your face? Did the queen beat you?" he asked, his voice puzzled.

"No, my lord."

"Oh." He sounded disappointed.

I wasn't about to tell him that this is how I looked *after* a beauty treatment. So I said instead, "She sent a servant with me."

He crossed his arms. "And I'm supposed to pay for her, is that it?"

"I paid for her out of my own wages. Her first year's salary has also been recompensed."

"I see." The corners of his eyes creased as though he were holding back a smile. "Damaspia didn't beat you; she merely bankrupted you."

I shrugged. "She spared me the worst when I explained the circumstances."

"There's Queen Damaspia for you. She believes any drivel if it pulls her heartstrings."

"Are we speaking about the same queen? The one who reduces grown men to tears with one glance? That queen?"

Instead of answering, Darius's brows knit into a frown. He pointed a finger in my direction and cried, "I recognize you now! Last night it kept niggling in the back of my mind, this sense that I had seen you before. You seemed so familiar, and yet under so much paint I couldn't see what you really looked like. But now it comes to me. You are the girl from the hill—the girl with the lion."

"I'm the one whose life you saved, yes."

"Ha! And you claim that you did not manipulate your way into this marriage? You saw me that day, and hatched this plan! Do you know, I thought you sweet and honest and brave when I first saw you. How wrong can a man be? You showed your true nature even then with your insincere flattery. I've dealt with your kind all my life. Brazen creatures who use their cunning to make their way in the world."

He struck his forehead with the end of his fisted hand. "By all that is holy, *this* is to be my wife? It's beyond bearing." He seemed past words for a few moments. Swallowing hard, he addressed me again, his voice rough. "There are thousands like you in the palaces of every great king, men and women who scheme their way into higher stations. You seem to be better at it than most, I concede, for it is no small matter to claw your way into the king's family. Congratulations, woman. Your skills are impressive even to me; I have faced vipers less venomous and calculating than you."

"What? No! I did not scheme to marry you. I didn't even know your name. The first time I knew that Darius Passargadae was the same as the man who saved my life was on our wedding day."

"I cannot stomach your lies."

I threw my hands up in the air with vexation. "I am not lying! I never wanted to marry you or anybody else. I liked my life as it was. I liked being the queen's chief scribe. You are mistaken in your assumptions about me, my lord."

"What I don't understand," he went on as though I had

spoken in a language he could not comprehend, "is why you embarrassed me and my father with such perversity last night. What was the point of it? You had already slithered your way into the position of a lady. Why diminish your prize in front of the court? Why did you shame me so?"

He had pelted me with so many false accusations that an avalanche of resentment buried the feelings of regret I had felt about my behavior at the wedding. "It was unintentional," I said, pronouncing the words with slow deliberation through clenched teeth. "I had never worn cosmetics before last night. I did not know how to apply them correctly."

"Come now. You expect me to believe that Damaspia did not offer you guidance or help? She did not send you her own servants to minister to your needs?"

Shame smote me at this reminder of my most foolish moment; I lowered my gaze to my feet, too much of a coward to answer him.

"I knew it. She did send you help. How did you manage to evade their assistance? They would not have left you without fulfilling the queen's command."

I looked up for a moment feeling sick.

"You lied?" he guessed.

The skin of my chest began to burn. "Yes, my lord."

"You told a bold-faced lie? Of course you did. This, at least, is a fragment of truth. You sent the servants away because no one working for Damaspia would have allowed you to come into your wedding banquet looking like a demon from the outer darkness."

"At first, I sent them away because I did not wish to face my upcoming marriage. I wanted to pretend it wasn't happening, I suppose, and thought I could get out of this union, somehow. That last day when I knew there was no hope, I found out that Pari's father was dying and sent her home to say good-bye to him. I would have asked for help from another if I had known what would happen."

"That is a most convenient story."

"I assure you, my lord, I have never known such inconvenience."

Darius turned and walked away from me. I had a momentary insight into why he was so set against believing me. He had spent his life with the knowledge that he was a prize. Most women would swoon at the opportunity of becoming the wife of a rich, devastatingly handsome courtier with connections to the king. The idea that I had no interest in marriage to him was so foreign to his world that it sounded like a lie. I considered explaining the circumstances that led to our betrothal, hoping that if he knew why Damaspia had chosen to reward me with a royal marriage, he would grow convinced of my story. But I had given my pledge never to betray the queen's confidences. I could not bring myself to share her secret with this man whom I hardly knew.

His steps, rapid and aimless, took him around the room several times before he returned to me. "I cannot abide liars. I do not think I can abide you. Your very presence is like a poisoned dagger pressing against my flesh."

"I am very sorry," I said, wrapping my arms around my middle.

He held up a hand motioning me to silence. "This is what we shall do. You will remain here for now. I will spend the summer in Ecbatana with the rest of the court. When I return, I shall decide your fate. But madam, if I were you, I would grow accustomed to loneliness, for though you have married into nobility, there is nothing noble in your character. And I will see to it that you live accordingly."

Before I could attempt to defend myself again, my husband turned his back and left me in the vast emptiness of his opulent reception hall. I could already feel the walls closing in on me. If he had buried me alive in an Egyptian tomb, I would not have felt more abandoned.

"My lady, you can't stay in bed all day again. It is past noon. You must rise."

Through a haze of sleep I heard Pari's admonitions and waved her away. "Leave me alone."

"This will not do, my lady. You shall make yourself sick."

I growled at her. "You are the servant; I am the mistress. You are supposed to do what I tell you."

"And I will. As soon as you rise."

Giving up on the precious dregs of unconsciousness, I sat up and tried to focus bleary eyes. "What for? There is nothing to do."

"For one thing, you could use a bath. After that, we shall think of something."

I ran a hand through my uncombed hair. How long had it been since I had been out of bed? How long since my life had served any purpose? Weeks had slipped by since Darius had deserted me, leaving me to rot in his empty palace. Days and nights blended together until I lost count of the calendar.

By the end of the first week, my hands had begun to shake. I could not control them. When the second week of my marriage concluded, I stopped speaking; when I tried to talk, my words sounded jumbled and stupid. I only ate and slept. Sometimes, it seemed that I ate mountains of food, long past hunger had been satisfied. I ate out of boredom. Out of anger. Out of fear. And I slept to forget. To forget that my life was a ruin and I had no escape.

"You are an annoying girl," I said, angry with Pari for interrupting my one refuge.

"I beg your pardon, my lady."

It occurred to me that this sudden show of stubborn disobedience had cost my sweet-natured servant a lot of courage. In many ways, I held her life in my hands. If I should discharge her, she would have no recourse. Without a reference from me, her chances of finding gainful employment would be non-existent. Her brave objections began to melt the edges of my resistance. For her sake, I pushed myself out of bed.

"Fetch me a bath then," I said more gently.

When I was finished bathing and dressing, I asked for my lunch. I was sitting on a sturdy footstool combing my wet hair, when Pari brought me half a bowl of thin broth and a plate of peeled pomegranates.

"What is this?"

"Your noonday meal, my lady."

"Is the cook sick or something?"

She turned her face away. "No."

"Then where's the rest of my food?"

Pari tangled her fingers in front of her and twirled them this way and that. "It's not good for you."

"What do you mean it's not good for me?" My head was beginning to throb and I started to long for the comfort of my bed.

"My lady, your clothes barely fit you anymore. What shall you do, parade around here naked? We do not have access to my lord's storehouses. That pigeon-headed steward, Teispes, will not let me anywhere near them."

Something in the tone of her complaint caught my attention

so that I let go of my focus on the parsimonious lunch as well as on the fact that my servant had just implied I had grown fat beyond recognition. "Has the steward been mistreating you?"

She shrugged. "He is a rude and impertinent man."

"He's probably following his master's orders."

"Oh no, my lady. I do not believe it. The lord Darius is well known for his good manners and kindness."

I made a disgusted sound. Pari's staunch defense of my husband's character grated on me. What did she know about him beside palace gossip? She ought to spend a few hours alone with him before singing his praises.

"He may be angry with you, but he would never allow a servant of his to disrespect his wife," Pari said with dignified insistence.

I grew still. Darius was a true Persian nobleman, this much I conceded. Even at the height of his anger would such a man tell his servants to treat his wife with impertinence? "You are a wise one," I said with only marginal sarcasm and took the bowl of broth from her.

It dawned on me that by hiding in my rooms and giving in to despair I had allowed the servants of the household to lose what little respect they might have for me. And I had treated Pari even worse, for she had borne the brunt of dealing with them. My cavernous plunge into self-pity had caused an innocent young woman daily pangs of humiliation and hardship. With sudden though inconvenient clarity I realized that I could not continue to hide from my fate, for I was now responsible for someone else's well-being in addition to my own.

I drained the dregs of my broth in a hurried gulp and said, "Let us go and face this monster, Teispes."

"Yes, my lady. Right away, my lady."

Pari jumped up and with an unmistakable spring in her

movements pulled the heavy carved door of my chamber open. For the first time in many days I stepped beyond its threshold. And promptly, stumbled over a hairy bump, nearly landing on my head. Steadying myself against a wall, I turned to find what had caused my near collision and found myself staring into the liquid brown eyes of a powerful fawn-colored mastiff.

"What is that?" I cried.

"This is Caspian, my lord's hunting dog."

"Charming. And what is he doing, camped outside my chamber? No, don't tell me. You've been feeding him my food, haven't you?"

"I get so lonely, my lady."

I closed my eyes and shook my head. "Why did his master not take the beast with him? What's wrong with it?"

"Nothing! He is wonderful. His lordship took his falcon with him to Ecbatana this time. Caspian and the falcon are not the best of friends, and Lord Darius takes turns bringing one or the other on his trips."

I studied the dog's massive frame, its stocky shoulders, its long thighs and shanks. He returned my gaze with apparent intelligence, his black broad muzzle held in a dignified pose that seemed to look down on me. I frowned. "This is a dog trained for war and the hunt. Why is he not in the kennel being cared for by the groundskeeper?"

Pari dropped her voice. "There is no groundskeeper. Teispes has discharged him, as well as a host of other servants, claiming there is no need for them with my lord away so often. There is only a handful of servants left. Some are his spies and a more useless bunch of workers you have yet to see. There are a couple of old retainers that he has not dared discharge, and Teispes runs them ragged. You should see this place. It's a disgrace."

I was beginning to like this steward less and less. As Pari and I traipsed through the house in search of him, the mastiff following us like a conscientious guard, I began to understand Pari's outrage. Although the house was magnificent in size and structure, dust covered every surface. Agate and lapis lazuli floors had not seen a broom for a month at least. In one room I actually found mouse droppings on the wool carpets.

There was one unexpected benefit to our fruitless search: it forced me to grow acquainted with my prison. With so few people about, I had a freedom not afforded to most aristocratic women, and was able to examine every unlocked room of my husband's sprawling home at my own leisure. Cedar pillars, carved cornices, embroidered hangings, gold and silver tables, and latticed windows made this palace a jewel of beauty. Though much smaller than Persepolis, it contained an element of charm that was lacking in the king's own palace.

In the corner directly opposite my chamber we discovered a lush set of apartments facing east, filled with light pouring through the windows. As soon as we stepped in, I knew it belonged to Darius. For one thing, no speck of dirt besmirched any surface. Someone had kept these rooms pristine. I imagined even Teispes dared not abandon Darius's own rooms to filth. For another, the apartment was exquisitely decorated with riches from around the world: textiles from Egypt, carved ebony furniture from India, gold from Sardis, urns from Ionia, tapestries from Babylonia. These rooms reflected my husband's vast travels.

The distinct stamp of his personality present in every corner of the room made me uncomfortable and I withdrew quickly. I knew he would feel that I was violating his privacy by being there.

But having entered in, I could not banish his image from my

restless mind. Without my volition I recalled his words to me my first night there. *Do you know, I thought you sweet and honest and brave when I first saw you.* I had focused so much on his belligerent accusations that I had forgotten the only kind words he had said to me during that encounter. For a short while, when he had originally met me, he had liked me. He had thought I possessed admirable qualities. He had thought me *sweet*.

What might my life be like if my husband had continued to think of me in such terms—to think of me as honest and brave?

I could bear this thought even less than the bitter accusations he had hurled at me. There was too much loss in it. The sum of my stupidity and his misdirected suspicions had robbed me too well. To escape the dark sorrow of my conclusions, I picked up the pace of our tour through the rest of my husband's home, making Pari and the dog hurry behind me in their effort to keep up.

To my relief, I found a measure of order in the kitchens. A woman with bony shoulders and wide hips rose as we walked in. She was smooth-skinned and could not have been more than thirty-five, though her long face made her appear older.

"Don't you bring that dog into my kitchen," she said in a raspy voice, raising her wooden spoon and pointing it at Caspian for emphasis.

"Ah, cook, this is my lady Sarah," Pari interjected.

The woman gave me a measured look and with shock I realized that she had a stone marble for one eye. I did my best not to stare. She bowed her head with a motion so quick it would have been lost on me if I had not been watching her with such close attention.

"Right then. Don't you bring that dog into my kitchen, *my lady.*"

I nodded to Pari and she led Caspian out. "As the kitchen seems to be one of the few clean places in this palace, I can see why you wouldn't want a dog in it." An awkward silence was the only reward I received for my attempt at conciliation. I tried again. "I wanted to thank you for the delicious meals you have provided for me."

"I do my best with what I'm given."

I was taken aback by her biting tone. At first I bristled, thinking her hostility directed at me. Then it occurred to me that in the span of the past several weeks I had not eaten meat above once a week. Often the food consisted of vegetables and grains. The cook managed to make it palatable, even delicious. But for a lord's house, the fare was too modest.

"You do not receive a sufficient allotment of what you need? Like meat and fowl and rare spices, as befits Lord Darius's table?"

"I made no complaint."

"I'm aware of that. I am also aware that you do a marvelous job with what little you are given. The fault is not yours."

The rigid shoulders began to droop. "Lord Darius deserves better. He owns more sheep and cattle than a man could count, and yet fresh meat has not passed the threshold of this kitchen once this week."

"Are you the only cook working here? Do you have no help?" The idea seemed ludicrous. At Persepolis there were two hundred and seventy-seven cooks plus an additional thirteen cooks who specialized in dairy dishes, twenty-nine kitchen helpers, and seventeen beverage preparers. Granted, this was no Persepolis, but it was still a nobleman's palace. The lack of a multitude of cooks was an outrage.

"The steward has assigned one of his servants to part-time kitchen duty. I prefer to work without his help. Our numbers are so diminished that I can manage alone. It's more difficult when Lord Darius and his full retinue are here."

I remembered Pari telling me that Teispes's hired servants acted as his spies and could not blame the cook for preferring to work alone. "I understand. I'll see what I can do. Do you know where I can find the steward?"

"He left this morning. Said he wouldn't be back until evening."

I nodded and turned to take my leave.

"My lady," she called, and handed me a bone. "For the dog. It's been cooked clean. But he's still bound to enjoy gnawing on it."

I smiled. In spite of her awkward sharpness, a kind heart beat inside that scrawny chest. "May I ask your name?"

"Shushan."

"That's an unusual name." Shushan was the Persian pronunciation for the citadel of Susa.

"Born there, that's why. My parents served in Lord Vivan's household from the time he was a young man. They were traveling with him from the north when my mother went into early labor. They made it to Susa just in time for me to be born there."

"They must have a soft spot for Susa then."

"The humorous part is that Lord Vivan came up with the name. My father said that he was covered in sweat at the thought of a woman giving birth on the side of the road. He was so relieved when we made it to Susa and the safety of his palace before I made an appearance that he rewarded my mother with a gold coin. You can understand; he was no more than twenty-five at the time. It's on account of him that I'm still alive," she said.

Fascinated, I asked, "He saved your life?"

She pointed to her false eye. "Accident. It happened the last year of King Xerxes' rule, when I was still a child. I was play-ing swords with one of the servant boys and his stick slipped and jabbed my eye.

"Instead of sending me to the town physician, Lord Vivan gathered me in his own arms and galloped to the palace, demanding the services of a royal physician. No one dared refuse the cousin of the king. An Egyptian physician tended me. He said I would have died if not for Lord Vivan's quick response. My lord even paid for a false eye," she said, pointing to the painted marble that occupied her eye socket.

"How did you become a cook?" I asked. Usually, men occu-pied that post; certainly no women became the kind of chief cooks that Shushan seemed to be in this household. Having occupied a masculine post myself made me wonder about Shushan's story.

"It took months for me to recover from my wound. One summer day, they brought my bed outside into the garden to cheer me. I lay in bed and watched a servant girl washing clothes in the sun. I felt so wistful at the sight, thinking I would never be of any use with only one eye. Lord Vivan happened to observe me; he would sometimes come and visit me during my time of convalescence.

" 'Shushan, I make you a promise,' he said. 'When you are better, you can do whatever you wish in my service.' He was as good as his word. I always wanted to work in the kitchens. When he found out, he apprenticed me to his best cook."

I thought about these stories. My father-in-law, who scorched me with his frowns on my wedding, had seized up with worry over the possibility of a servant woman birthing a child outdoors. He had cared for a wounded peasant child with the same fierce protectiveness he would have shown a child of his own. He had opened the doors of high employment to a woman who would have been scorned by another person of rank.

"How came you to work for Lord Darius?"

She beamed. "My lord always favored my cooking. It didn't matter to him that I was a woman, and blind and bony besides. He made me promise that I would become his chief cook as soon as he set up his own household. His father grumbled that Lord Darius had stolen his best cook, but it was all in fun. He would have given my lord the moon, if he had but asked.

"We used to have such magnificent feasts in the old days whenever Lord Darius was in residence. And then, at the end of the feast, he would sometimes call me to him and introduce me to his great guests. He said he was proud of me."

I could see that Shushan doted on my husband, and was baffled by this picture of him, which showed him as a generous and loving master. I did not like to think of him in those terms; it was more comfortable believing him to be harsh and unreasonable.

Hearing the dog barking outside, I grew concerned that he might, in his enthusiasm, burst back into the kitchen and annoy Shushan. Waving the bone, I said, "My thanks, Shushan," and was startled to catch her in the act of smiling.

I realized that I had made my first sally toward friendship in my husband's home. Suddenly the thought of abandoning my bed was not so overwhelming.

Chapter Ten

Get this creature off me," I cried, huffing around the mastiff's long tongue, which was trying to plant wet kisses on my face. Avoiding another enthusiastic lick, I pushed him away. He weighed as much as a large man. "I don't have any treats for you."

Pari laughed. "He isn't looking for food. He wants attention."

It was clear that Caspian was used to human companionship and affection. Most Persians were hunting mad and spent prodigious time in the company of their animals. Next to their children and families and the empire, they loved their horses best. Many extended that love to their hunting dogs as well. From Caspian's peremptory expectation of affection, I concluded the mastiff enjoyed Darius's particular attachment. I was amazed that Teispes had dared to mistreat him.

"Let's take him for a walk in the garden." As soon as I mentioned the word *garden*, Caspian began to whine and bounded forward, then rushed back to lick my hand, then leapt ahead again.

"It figures. The dog understands Persian better than his master," I grumbled.

It was a glorious day. Blue skies stretched over us like a ceiling carved out of turquoise. I breathed the fresh air and felt my soul coming back to life.

Darius's formal gardens had been designed in the traditional style, cut into four enormous parks by means of two long intersecting avenues. A long man-made stream ran along the center of one of the avenues. We chose a side lane that led us through a fruit orchard. Pink and white blossoms perfumed the air. Pari reached for a cluster of them and wove them into my hair.

I was no gardener, but I could see that in spite of its beauty, the orchard showed signs of inattention. Piles of leftover leaves from the previous autumn still remained decrepit and wrinkled at the base of tree trunks. Weeds grew with abandon. And yet the orchard must have once been well maintained, for the trees appeared strong and healthy. Again I was puzzled by the state of this palace, at once so rich and strangely neglected.

Caspian bounded toward me and began to bark. I found a smooth stick on the ground and threw it for him to fetch. As he approached it, I began running behind him, crying, "Race!" and before I knew it, Pari, the dog, and I were running like carefree children through the trees, the sound of barks, hollers, and laughter mingling with one another. The blossoms flew out of my hair and landed on the ground; I squashed them under my feet as I ran past, unable to avoid them. Their scent rose up more pungent for being crushed, sweetening the air.

It didn't take me long to grow winded, and I collapsed against a peach tree, out of breath.

"I think you lost that race, my lady," a man's voice said behind me, making me jump and hit my head against a branch.

Grabbing the crown of my head with a rueful hand, I turned in the direction of the voice. "Who are you?"

Under a shock of white hair, the man's craggy face split into two, courtesy of a wide smile, showing off his five remaining teeth. "My name is Bardia, my lady. I'm the head gardener."

I was too polite to tell him that he seemed ancient for a job that required so much physical exertion. No wonder the orchard appeared neglected. "Did Teispes hire you?" I asked, thinking it just like the parsimonious steward to employ an aged man for less pay.

"Teispes hire *me*? I should say not. My family has worked for his lordship's family three generations now. I have tilled Passargadae land since I remember. Teispes has barely been around three years."

"I beg your pardon."

"That's all right, my lady. You didn't know any better."

I tried not to smile. Such show of magnanimity from servant to mistress was unusual, not to mention inappropriate. It was clear that his long years with the family had taught him to take certain liberties with an earnest and unself-conscious temerity.

"Do you have many men helping you manage the land?"

The white head bent. "I used to."

"Let me guess. The steward has dismissed most of your workers."

"You don't think I would allow the orchard to fall into this condition if I had sufficient help, do you, my lady?"

"Why don't you ask for Lord Darius's help?"

That wide, gap-toothed smile flashed out, accompanied by the wave of a veiny hand. "No need. No need. The young lord has too many responsibilities to be bothered with my concerns. Every year sent to a new province, a new war, a new trouble to deal with. This is the longest he's been at home since he was a lad. And shall I embitter his time at home with my grumblings?"

I took a step toward him. "I can see that you're a good man and a devoted retainer, Bardia. But don't you think that Lord Darius would prefer to bear the inconvenience of dealing with this problem rather than allow his estate to fall into ruin?"

He pulled on a wrinkled earlobe. "I'll take care of the place myself, as long as I can. When I've lost my strength, I'll burden the young lord. No sense harassing him now."

I wondered what kind of man could inspire such devotion. The Darius I knew was ruthless and cynical. I would be happy to add to his burdens. Clearly, Bardia saw him with different eyes. Perhaps he still perceived him through the prism of his memories as a young boy, amiable and dependent, needy of his protection.

He should see his master slay a lion without batting an eyelash. Or skewer my future at the end of his sharp tongue. I bore no illusions about that man. He could manage every inconvenience thrown his way. Besides, after marrying me, dealing with a bad steward would hardly ruffle his hair.

I did not delude myself, however, into thinking that I could convince the gardener to tell his young master the truth. It was obvious that his commitment to shielding Darius from every form of aggravation was his primary concern.

If I managed to bear some influence upon this stingy steward, perhaps I could force him to hire some help for the old man. I might be able to improve his hard life a little.

"As you wish," I said and turned to leave.

"It's good to have a lady in residence here again. There hasn't been one since my lord Vivan passed the estate to his son. This place could use a mistress like you."

He would not say that if he knew the circumstances of my marriage or the reason his master had gone to Ecbatana with the rest of the court, abandoning me here. "I'm not much of a lady," I said with a brittle smile.

"Of course you are. Don't take to heart his lordship leaving like that. Young men are proud. He will come to his senses; you'll see."

I coughed, choking on my saliva. How much did he know about my relationship with his master? Servants were notorious for their knowledge of household gossip. And yet he had said nothing that hinted of criticism. He seemed actually glad to have me here.

"Thank you," I said.

"Come and visit me tomorrow if you wish, my lady. I'll be in the orchard again."

Here was another lonely soul trapped in my husband's gilded cage, I thought. Perhaps that was why he seemed so accepting of me—a woman who had betrayed his beloved master. Perhaps I was better than nothing. Clearly he was parched for company.

A head gardener would normally have an army of helpers for companionship. He could even expect regular visits from his master, for the Persians were mad over their gardens. The king was known to tend his garden with his own royal hands whenever his schedule allowed. More than one Achaemenid king had raised a talented gardener to the position of governor, for if a man could transform a piece of barren land into a blooming orchard, what could he not do with a province?

In the old days Bardia would have been considered an elevated and worthy retainer. He would have enjoyed his master's devotion. Now he was ancient and abandoned. Unwanted, like me. I resolved to visit him on the morrow.

The next morning I sent Pari in search of the steward once more. We had waited past midnight the previous evening, but he had not arrived. She returned with the news that the steward had left earlier in the morning.

"Earlier? It's barely sunup! Where has he gone this time?"

"Nobody knows. He isn't in the habit of explaining himself."

"Well, he is about to change his habits." I pulled my robe over my head. I had to hold my breath to pull it down over my belly. "A small breakfast for me," I mumbled.

Pari threw me an I-told-you-so glance, which I ignored. Caspian bumped his wet nose against my arm. "Stop that, you mangy monster. I can't believe the howling outside my chamber last night."

"I can't believe you let him in," Pari said with a giggle.

"As long as he doesn't get onto my bed. Do you hear me, dog?"

Caspian whimpered. "Perhaps we should stop by the kitchens to get Caspian something to eat."

Before we made our way to the kitchens, however, I had one more stop to make. I wanted to examine Teispes's accounts. Did Darius keep him on the strength of the money he saved the household? If so, I had to find other ways of economy so that my husband would not resent the additional expense of the changes I wished to make. We found the records room as locked and sealed as my husband's treasury, however. Teispes was really beginning to irritate me.

Caspian could be obligingly obedient when he chose, and at my bidding, he waited outside the kitchen door without fuss.

Shushan stood as we came in. "Good morning," I said. "Do you perchance have any leftovers for the dog? He is behaving like a gentleman at the moment, but some food might help keep his temper biddable."

"Yes, my lady. In fact I've been saving him a few things." Caspian was in ecstasy over his meal. I wondered what he had eaten before Pari took an interest in him. Surely Teispes would not be so foolish as to neglect his master's favorite hunting dog.

"May I have a little yogurt and honey?" I said when I returned to the kitchen. I had decided that I would tame my unhealthy appetite and stop consuming food as a pastime. Pari refused to join me, as it was not proper for a servant to eat before her mistress. In the end I convinced her to eat in one corner of the kitchen while I ate in the other. I could not have her walking about the estate suffering pangs of hunger.

"We are going to visit Bardia in the orchard again today," I informed Shushan over the expanse of room that separated us. She was a little scandalized to see me eat in the kitchen, I think, and I wanted to try and put her at ease. "Since we cannot find the steward, I thought we would converse with the gardener to see what he lacks."

"Oh my lady, if you are going there, perhaps your handmaiden would be willing to take the old man some food that I have set aside for him. He forgets to eat, sometimes. Before the new steward arrived, Bardia's men came daily and picked up his rations for him. Now he has little help and is so concerned over his trees and flowers that he doesn't give his stomach a thought."

"We would be happy to help."

We could not find Bardia in the orchards, however. I asked Pari if she knew where the old man lived and she led me to a small cottage built at the edge of a diminutive pond. We knocked and found no answer.

"We should leave the food inside, out of the heat of the sun," I said. Feeling awkward at my intrusion, I walked in, intending to leave the bundle and go. What I saw froze me in place. The room stank of mold and was covered in dust. Walls, needing repair, had been left to crumble in spots and a large damp stain on the floor indicated the source of the moisture. There was only one chair, and when I examined it, I found it to be broken. His bedding, rolled neatly against the wall, had absorbed the smell of mold and needed a good washing.

I fumed over Darius's lack of care for his faithful retainer. The old man deserved better.

"This place needs a cleaning," Pari said, pulling up the hem of her skirt to keep it from touching the floor.

"It needs a great deal more than that. That poor man spends his whole time in the gardens of his master; he has no time left to care for his own home."

I left the food on the lopsided chair and walked out. Back in the palace I bid Pari to gather together what cleaning supplies she could and we headed back to the cottage.

"My lady, you can't scrub the floor! Why don't you just go outside and let me do the work?"

"I want to finish before he returns; it will shame him to find us here, picking up after him. Even with the two of us we shan't make much dent in this disaster of a cottage in one afternoon. This needs workmen, not cleaning women."

"But my lady—!"

"Stop making speeches and join me. I can't bear for that man to come home to such a mess one more time."

We returned to the palace again to fetch clean sheets and a sturdier blanket, which I took off my own bed. I also brought a footstool made of mahogany and ivory—one of the gifts of the queen for my wedding. After several hours of labor, the cottage was cleaner, but we had not been able to rid it of the damp, which was seeping through the foundations.

We would have to find a more permanent solution to Bardia's living conditions. Either the building would have to receive appropriate repairs or he would have to move to the palace. I had little hope of convincing him of the latter and resolved to find Teispes and force him to attend the situation.

In one of life's inexplicable coincidences, on our final trek back to the palace we ran straight into Teispes. His jaw grew even longer as he gaped at me.

"Just the man I wanted to see," I said, taking advantage of his surprise. "Bardia's living conditions are deplorable. His cottage is overrun by damp and mold and must be repaired."

"Bardia?"

"The head gardener, though head of whom, it's hard to tell; he seems to be working the gardens and orchards almost single-handedly. He needs more help."

"My lady need not concern herself regarding the running of the estate. That is my job."

I bit the side of my mouth in an attempt to control my temper. "It is a job that comes with much responsibility. I am happy to assist you where I can."

"No need for you to become involved."

I noted the dropped title, the hardening of the tone, the crossed arms; it seemed wise to change tact. "I would like to go into the records chamber and examine the accounts."

The steward took a long step back. "That chamber is locked."

"So I found. You have the key, I presume?"

He did not answer, but gazed at me without flinching.

I took that as a *yes*. "Good. In that case, let us proceed."

"I could not possibly open that door without his lord-ship's permission."

"Don't be ridiculous. I am his lordship's wife. I demand that you show me the accounts."

He had the temerity to smirk at me. "Then perhaps you should write your husband and ask for his permission."

If my hair were not so dark, it would have turned red with the rest of me. Shame lashed me like a physical force. I had never felt so belittled. It was clear that Teispes knew of the state of matters between my husband and me. And he believed himself safe from any form of reprisal no matter how he treated me. It occurred to me that I was utterly vulnerable to this man's power. In Darius's absence, he controlled everything. I could not even send a missive without his approval.

Anger replaced shame. He had abused his position by mis-treating so many. What I did not know was if his master stood in agreement with his methods or if he was guilty only of trusting the wrong man. In either case, I resolved not to give in to Teispes's intimidating manner. There were people who needed me now; I could not afford the luxury of fear.

Chapter Eleven

woke up to the sound of low giggles. Pari stood at the end of my bed, a hand covering her laughter without success.

"You let him on your bed," she said, pointing at the hairy creature lounging at my feet.

I yawned. "He insisted. Anyway, as long as he stays on top of my bed and doesn't try to get in it."

"That's what you said about him getting *on* your bed."

"He cries. What am I to do, ignore him?" I bent down to pet the massive fawn-colored back. He turned his black tinged face to lick my hand. "Phew! He reeks."

"He's a hunting dog. He spends his time chasing animals in the woods."

"He used to be a hunting dog. He sleeps on my bed now, so perhaps we should bathe him."

"I will make a fair exchange with you, my lady. I'll bathe Caspian if you submit to a few beauty treatments."

That girl should have worked for the king as a royal merchant; her haggling skills were mind numbing. Within moments, she had me agreeing to her terms with benign good nature, as if I myself had come up with the idea.

Satisfied now that she had her way, Pari sat on the edge of my bed next to the dog and petted him with absentminded tenderness. "What are we to do with that awful Teispes? Perhaps the Lord will help you deal with him."

Her odd non sequitur caught me off guard. "The *Lord*?" I leaned against an overstuffed pillow, astounded that she knew that name. "What do you know about the Lord?"

"When I was a little girl, a Jewish washerwoman lived in our neighborhood. She loved children and had none of her own. Sometimes, she would allow me to accompany her when my mother did not need me. She told me some of the stories of your people. My favorite was of the shepherd boy David who slew a giant with a slingshot."

"Goliath," I murmured.

"That's the one. Perhaps you are David and Teispes, Goliath. He certainly has the jaw for it."

I laughed. "I don't think pelting him with stones will solve our problems."

"No, but Teispes's power is great, like Goliath. You are small in comparison to him. You don't have riches or connections or the ear of your husband. The odds are not on our side, just as they weren't on Israel's. Yet sometimes the odds aren't what matter."

I was quite impressed by Pari's sagacity. Nehemiah would like my servant, I decided.

A knock on our door reduced us to silence. I could not remember anyone seeking entry to my chamber since my coming to this palace weeks ago. Caspian raised his head, wrinkled his forehead, and then replaced his snout back on the blanket without a single objection. So much for his protective hunting skills.

Pari rose, straightened her skirt, opened the door. Bardia waited outside, his hat twirling in crooked fingers.

I pulled on a robe and rushed outside. "What's wrong?"

"Nothing, my lady. I came to give you this." He bent down and retrieved a bowl filled with delicate jasmine. I buried my nose in the scented heap of flowers and breathed deep. You can almost forget your troubles when your nose is buried in a bowl of freshly picked jasmine.

"My mother used to pick jasmine for me in the mornings. She would put them on my pillow while I was still asleep, so that I would rise to the scent of them." I picked a tiny blossom and twirled it. "It's been long years since anyone brought me jasmine."

"I brought them to thank you."

"Thank me? Whatever for?" I had hoped that he would not guess I was behind the change in his habitation.

"You cleaned my home. I'm sorry I allowed it to fall apart like that." He would not look up as he spoke.

"I don't hold you responsible for this, Bardia. As it is, you work more hours than two of the king's servants together."

The white head remained bowed. "It's that arrogant steward, Teispes," I continued, trying to coax him out of feeling disgraced. "I cannot understand what he gains by running the estate in such deplorable manner. If only I could examine his accounts, I might find some answers. But that crafty fox keeps them under lock and key."

"Aye, and keeps the key on a chain around his neck night and day. I even saw him wearing it in the bathhouse once." Bardia pulled on his white beard.

I heaved a sigh. "How can we convince him to give up his precious key?"

"I know this: he would be easier to convince on the third day of the week."

Pari chortled. "How can one day of the week be different from another with regard to a man's temper?"

"Well, for one thing, he sleeps sounder on Mondays."

Teispes took every Monday off, leaving before sunrise and arriving in the middle of the night somewhat the worse for wear. No one knew where he spent his time, but it was clear from the lingering odor as well as his less than steady gait that wherever he had been was well-stocked with wine. So we picked Monday as the ideal day to *borrow* Teispes's keys.

Bardia insisted that he should attend to the actual retrieval of the key, as it would be inappropriate for a woman to enter a man's chambers. I told my accomplices that either I would deal with Teispes myself or else the whole plan was cancelled. I figured that if I were caught, the steward could not have me thrown into the streets no matter how Darius felt about me. Servants would be more vulnerable to his power.

When midnight came, Bardia, Pari, and I waited for the steward's return in a dark corridor near his chamber. I lingered in our hiding place a good hour after he returned to ensure the steward was sleeping soundly. I had no lamp for fear that I might wake him as I entered his room. Having waited in darkness for over an hour my eyes had adjusted and I could see enough by the light of the moon to make out the form sprawled across the mattress on the floor.

A cracked tile flipped noisily under my bare feet as I stepped into the room. I stopped dead as Teispes turned on his side with a restless motion. What was I doing here? I had placed myself in a compromising position by being in a man's room unaccompanied. Somehow, while planning this hare-brained idea, such details had not seemed as important as they did at this particular moment.

If I were caught in the chamber of a strange man, I could be banished into some backwater part of Persia with an unpro-nounceable name and a winter that was longer than the river Nile. And that was if Darius were feeling generous. As if that weren't bad enough, I had turned thief in my husband's home. This venture marked a slippery slide in my character, I was sure; I had never stolen anything before that moment.

I considered turning around and walking away from this madness. Then I recalled the deplorable conditions of Bardia's home and the cook's empty cabinets and the lack of help for all of them, and forced my feet forward.

Too soon I stood over the steward. His face was turned away from me. One arm was flung across the bed, the other folded under his head. I knelt down and bent over him as qui-etly as I could. He reeked of sour wine. This close, I could see the glint of the chain around his neck. There would be no way, as long as he stayed in this posture, to remove the object from around his neck without waking him.

I could sit and wait, hoping that he would shift position. Or I could do something about it. Doing something seemed the lesser of two evils; at least it would end my torture more quickly. I lifted the hem of my skirt and held a small piece of the linen in my hand. Whispering a quick prayer in my mind, I tickled the end of Teispes's nose with the fabric. His nose twitched like a rabbit's and he raised a hand to swat my intrusion away. I man-aged to dodge his sleepy reach and tickled him again.

Teispes groaned and turned on his back. I froze, afraid to move a single muscle. He settled down and started to snore. His movement had made the chain accessible. With painfully slow movements I grasped the key to prevent it from jingling and drew chain and key up in one motion. Soon the key was over his head, but the back of the chain still rested against his neck, which was pressed into the pillow. To remove it, I would have to pull hard alongside his neck and head. He would not sleep through that intrusion.

I squeezed my eyes shut and stood so for a moment to bolster up my courage. Then I blew in his ear. He lifted his hand with unexpected vigor to swat me away. I barely managed to remove myself from the path of his backhanded slap. Just as I thought I would have to resort to more drastic and dangerous measures, he turned his head away from me on the pillow, releasing the imprisoned chain.

With more speed than I knew I possessed, I grabbed that chain and key and tiptoed my way out.

Our hope was to keep Teispes in the dark about the loss of his key. I would have a better chance of opposing him if I could catch him by surprise. This gave me a handful of hours to examine the records and find clues to his behavior. I ran to the chamber that held the family's records and left Pari behind to keep an eye on Teispes's room, while Bardia stood guard in the darkness outside the records room, where I settled to spend the rest of the night.

I compared the records pertaining to different aspects of Darius's estates from one year before Teispes arrived with the three years following his stewardship. There were too many details belonging to a variety of properties to allow me more than a cursory examination. I would need at least a month for a thorough job. But I had enough training under my belt to pick up a few curious irregularities in the short hours I had. Just when my search was growing interesting, Pari and Bardia skidded into the records chamber.

"He's coming! He's coming!" they hissed in union.

I jumped to my feet, panicked for a moment. Then I grabbed two thick rolls of parchment, and placed the rest carefully on their shelves.

"Hurry mistress!" Pari hissed. "He's coming this way."

My heart pounded so hard in my chest, I could feel the blood roaring in my ears. "Get out! Get out right away," I ordered. My accomplices rushed out and I followed suit, lingering long enough to lock the door.

From the opposite direction I saw Caspian bounding toward me. I had no idea how that dog had managed to loose himself from my room, where I had barricaded him hours ago for fear that he might give us away with an untimely noise. Seeing him now, I formed the germ of an idea. I had not time to think it through, for I could now hear Teispes's heavy footsteps around the corner.

I bent down and offered the chain to the hound. "Take this to Teispes," I said. "Teispes. Understand?"

He gazed at me with intelligent brown eyes and for a moment I was convinced that the dog spoke Persian as fluently as I. He took the chain obediently in his mouth, letting one long end dangle down his jaw with the key, and ran in the direction of Teispes's footsteps while I ran in the opposite direction.

I stopped short of my own chamber and held my breath. In the darkness I heard the steward's outraged voice. "You filthy beast. Where did you get that? You monster. Give it back to me."

I heard the dog's low growl and feared for the fate of Teispes's fingers. For a moment I thought that I should go and rescue him. Then I heard Caspian's whimper and knew the steward had hurt him in some way. I saw red. Shoving the hard-won rolls of parchment into Pari's hands I hissed, "Hide these," and pointing to Bardia I said, "You help her."

I followed the noise of Caspian's barks and Teispes's curses across the dark corridors of the palace until I came in sight of them. Feigning a huge yawn and sleepy manners as though I had just abandoned my bed, I came to a sudden halt.

"What on earth are you doing, you lout? How dare you hit his lordship's favorite dog?"

Arrested mid kick, Teispes's mouth fell open. "I . . . I . . . He is a thief! He stole my chain and keys."

"Don't be ridiculous! He's just a dog. If you will leave your things around, he will play with them."

"This chain never leaves my neck. The dog stole it from me, I tell you."

"You've lost your mind, steward. Take your chain and give me the dog. Your master shall hear of this behavior. You can count on that."

Without another word, Teispes disentangled his chain from Caspian's toothy grip. The dog gave up his prize with innocent obedience while I stood near. Then he trotted over to me and we walked away.

Ensconced in my room and safe at last, I bent to pet Caspian. "Brave boy. Why did you let him beat you? You could have snapped his hand off." It dawned on me that although Caspian had been trained to fight in battles, he must have also been carefully tutored to honor those he considered his masters. Extraordinary beast. I lay my head against him. "My valiant friend."

"Won't he find out that you stole those rolls?" Pari asked me, her voice worried.

"Chances are good that he will not. He is a steward, not a scribe, so most of his work concerns current accounts, and I took two older ledgers. Unless he goes searching for them for some reason, we should be safe."

We had congregated in the herb garden where Bardia was busy working. Pari and I had joined him, pulling out persistent weeds and helping to plant some late seedlings. As with most things, Bardia was running behind with the planting of his herbs. His part-time assistant was busy in the almond grove, which left him with us for help.

He made no objection to our assistance, for this was considered a noble pastime, suitable for people of high or low rank. Pari made me wear linen gloves to protect my hands, however, and insisted on bringing a parasol to shield me from the sun. I always felt like a fraud when she treated me like the lady I was not. I may be married to a nobleman according to official documents, but in truth I remained the daughter of a scribe and a servant at heart. It did not help knowing that my husband and I were in perfect agreement on this one subject. For the sake of peace, I bore Pari's shows of courtesy with leashed unease.

"My lady, I want to show you something," Bardia said and beckoned me to go to him. He was standing near a willow tree with sweeping branches, its narrow leaves already unfurled and twinkling their green reflection into the irrigation canal that flowed past. It was a breathtaking sight. I had a soft spot for the willow, a fairly recent transplant to this part of the empire. An adventurous traveler had brought it along the Silk Road to Persepolis, where it gained wild favor and quickly spread across the rest of Persia.

"She is lovely," I said. "When did you plant her?"

"I did not. My Lord Darius did when he was no more than a lad."

"Did his father command him to do it?" I asked, thinking it unlikely that Darius would have the patience for agricultural pastimes.

"Oh no, my lady. His lordship sought me out himself. He was home on a rare leave from the palace. The magi had just completed an agricultural training for the lads his age at court. With so few hours at his disposal, he elected to spend a good deal of his time planting this tree."

It was hard for me to imagine my husband as a young lad at his studies. Sons of aristocrats were sent to the palace at the age of seven to receive a rigorous and comprehensive education. Through their years of training, they learned the arts of war and leadership. They were given breathing lessons to make their voices audible on a noisy battlefield. A Greek scribe had once told me that Persian warriors were known to have the loudest voices in the world. I had never heard my husband shout; he didn't have to. His quiet tones were sufficient to reduce me to a state of near panic.

The magi also taught the older pupils ethics and right living, and trained them to hold truth more sacred than every other virtue. Their goal was to raise honorable leaders who practiced the principles of truthful living. I had not realized that the magi included gardening in their training.

"Did you choose the tree for him, Bardia?"

"No, no. He chose his own tree."

"That's odd. I wouldn't have thought a willow as typical of his taste. Perhaps a walnut tree. Or even a cherry—something strong with a useful harvest." The willow bore no edible fruit and offered little practical use other than cool shade on hot days.

"He loved the willow—loves it still—not because of its usefulness, but because of what it is. It touches the soul, that's all."

I shrugged, not comprehending. In fact, I could not see why Bardia was so bent on sharing the story of this tree with me. I would rather plant my own herbs than hear stories of my husband's prowess in the garden.

If Bardia sensed my impatience, he ignored it and continued with his tale. "His lordship came and sought me out. *I haven't had a chance to talk with you for months, Bardia,* he said. *You can supervise me, but you are not to touch anything. I'll do the work. Just keep me company.*

"He chose this spot himself, and as he worked, told me stories about life in the palace. Wouldn't let me dig one shovelful of earth for him. He was a young man to be proud of—strong, humble, caring. He was everything a lord should be."

I ground my teeth. "Why do you tell me this?"

"Because you don't know your husband. You see the state of this palace and you blame him. You think he takes ill care of his people."

"I never said so."

"You didn't have to. It's plain to see on your face. You have no respect for him. Begging your pardon if I speak out of turn, my lady, but you commit a grave mistake in what you think of him."

My jaw would have landed at the base of the willow tree had it not been attached to my head. "*I* commit a grave mistake in what I think of *him*? Here is irony."

Bardia pulled on his beard. "Did you really appear at your wedding looking like a creature of darkness?"

Was there anyone in the entire Persian Empire who did not know the full extent of my disgrace? I felt like Job, for what I feared had come upon me; what I dreaded had happened to me. I had turned myself into the laughingstock of courtiers and servants alike.

"It's true."

"So you cannot blame my master for being mistaken in you."

I sank to the ground and leaned against the tree my husband had planted. "Given what you know, how is it that you never held me in contempt, Bardia? Why do you not resent me for mistreating your beloved master?"

"I'm privy to a few things that Lord Darius cannot know. He was away attending school at Persepolis at the time and will not remember, but years ago my lord and lady had a great friendship with the king's cupbearer."

"*Nehemiah?*"

"The same. He'd often have supper with Lord Vivan and Lady Rachel. Sometimes they would stroll in the gardens. Whenever I was present, Lord Nehemiah engaged me in conversation, and treated me with cordial respect.

"I am a good judge of plants and trees. I can tell you with one glance what is hardy and what sickly. And I am a good judge of men too, and I judged this man to be wise and trustworthy. Every word that passed his lips was truth, though sometimes he was fiery with expressing it." Bardia flashed a gummy smile. *Fiery* was a good word for my cousin, I thought.

"In time, Lord Vivan was transferred to a different region, and then my lady died. The king's cupbearer's visits grew rare, though I think the spirit of the friendship remained strong through the years.

"Knowing that both Nehemiah and the queen had approved of you, I concluded that there was more to the story of your wedding than met the eye. Nehemiah is not a man to put his kin forward solely for the sake of advancing his connections. If he thought highly of you, then he must have had just cause."

So Lord Vivan had known Nehemiah and trusted him. Now I saw why he had rushed into drawing the marriage contract. He had not only the Queen of Persia's recommendation, but also the confidence of an old friend. He had anticipated no problems and had expected the best for his son.

I recalled with clarity Darius's livid accusation flung at my cousin: *My father trusted your word.* He had placed his life in the hands of friend and monarch and they had both failed him. A man who had resisted marriage against every conceivable pressure and reasonable expectation had finally given in, relying on the word of one who had been friend to his mother. No wonder he had been so angry with Nehemiah. *And with me.*

I stretched my legs and dangled my feet into the canal. The water was bone-chillingly cold. It soothed my fire-hot thoughts. "Why is it that you were able to forestall your suspicions when my own husband concluded the worst and denied me the benefit of explaining myself?"

Bardia began to strip the tree of broken limbs. In spite of his age, there was a confident agility about his movements. His forearms, wiry with muscle, flexed and relaxed as he ministered to the needs of the tree. "If I may be so bold to point out, you're not *my* wife, my lady. Much as I love my master, I can still think straight regardless of the circumstances, which he, caught in the center of them, undoubtedly cannot."

"You have an answer for everything, old man. I am going back to my stolen records. They don't pester me with such convoluted arguments." On the way back to my room I stopped by a flower border to pick a bouquet of pale yellow lilies. Bardia had inspired a passion for flowers in me. The sight of their crisp, beautiful petals cheered my heart as I headed away from one difficult situation and into another.

Chapter Twelve

The problem was that my precious stolen records were turning out to be as tricky as Bardia's revelations. I tinkered with them for days, growing more puzzled at each turn, for Teispes was not saving any money by stint of his parsimonious actions.

To add to my vexation, it seemed I would hardly sit down to work when some interruption or other drained my time. Caspian broke my train of thought with his barking and nipping until I gave in and took him outdoors for extensive walks. Bardia kept me busy in his gardens, forcing me to enjoy the fresh air, he said. Mostly, I reckoned, I was cheap labor and human company. Pari dragged me away from my records by subjecting me to some ridiculous treatment designed to improve my looks and revive my mood. Even Shushan joined in by insisting that I eat long formal meals at table as befit such a great lady. My portions remained small in spite of the fact that it took the cook and Pari an hour to serve them.

In the old days, I would have spent unbroken hours drowned in figures and translations, my only human company those who participated in my work. My world had taken a turn, however, so that companionship became its new center. Hard as I tried to force my existence back into the old mold, I could not. Living creatures vied for my attention. While I found their interruptions frustrating, even depleting, I could also see that spending time with them met a deep yearning in my soul. And with an unexpected twist I discovered that I could not deal with Teispes without them. Their aid proved essential to the fulfillment of the arduous task before me.

"The oddest thing about these records," I told Bardia, Pari, and Shushan eleven days after I started my search, "is that there is no change in the amount of money being spent on Lord Darius's estates since Teispes's coming. Same incomes. Same expenditure. He's not saving any money by his drastic . . . *industry*, shall we say?"

We were in the herb garden working. "Industry?" Shushan lifted her head and made a rude noise with her tongue that startled several birds into flight. "I give that for his industry." Everyone laughed.

"He is a clever man, that one. But not so clever that he can outwit me." I stopped for a torturous pause. My audience straightened from their various tasks.

"Well, what is it?" Pari burst. "Have you solved this puzzle?"

"Not solved it, exactly. No. What I have discovered is that the money he saves by impoverishing this estate is being poured into another of Lord Darius's properties. A textile factory that his lordship owns in Ecbatana. It is run by an *arassara*."

"Isn't that some kind of female overseer?" Shushan asked, squinting her good eye.

"Precisely. The royal family uses them often. The *arassara* supervise a variety of factories, particularly those that require child labor. These women are skilled in management and earn good wages, sometimes as much as a man, though they remain unmarried. When I worked for Queen Damaspia, I supervised the payment of allotments to several such *arassara*. So I'm familiar with the range of their rations."

"And this one is getting paid more than she should, is that it?" Pari asked.

"A lot more. The first year Teispes arrived here, the records show that Mandana, that's the name of Lord Darius's *arassara*, gave birth to twin sons. As you know, mothers of newborns receive larger rations according to Persian law. They receive even greater rations when they give birth to boys. Imagine the tidy raise when it's twin boys. Here things become interesting. Mandana's raise in rations and wages were ten times above that which would normally have been given to a woman in her position."

"Wait! I thought you said she was single," Pari interjected.

"Never met an *arassara* who wasn't."

"You can forget thinking those children belong to Lord Darius, right now," Bardia said, shoving his earth-crusted finger on one of my favorite theories. "If my lord had twin sons, never mind by whom, he would acknowledge them publicly rather than sweep them under the carpet, and supporting them on the sly. This is not a family to deny its children."

His objection rang true. The aristocracy was not too fastidious about where its sons came from as long as it produced them. Nothing pointed to a man's virility, outside of his achievements in combat, more than the number of his sons.

Having sired twin boys was a cause for public pride, not something to be hidden in a dark corner.

"Teispes, then?" Shushan said.

"It's not impossible," I said. "Mandana's rations have gone up with each year so that according to the records she now receives the equivalent of twenty honored *arassara*. It's unnatural."

"That worm of a steward has been beggaring this estate in order to support his paramour?" Shushan burst out.

"Support in style," Pari said. "She must be as rich as a satrap by now."

I straightened a crooked sleeve. "Suppositions and conjecture. We cannot prove any of it. And though it sounds reasonable, there could be ten other explanations. Lord Darius might be behind this arrangement." I held my hand up as a peace offering before Bardia could object. "Not because he has sired the twins, but for reasons unknown to us."

"My master wouldn't allow this estate to fall into ruin on purpose. It was his mother's favorite and he bears a tender regard for it."

"Then why would he allow this? Why would he not stop it for three years?"

"He doesn't know. Those of us who have been around since his childhood did not wish to burden him with our complaints. The newer servants would have been afraid to approach him. Besides, Teispes always hires temporary servants during his visits. He makes sure that the areas most often visited by Lord Darius are in good order."

"Bardia, it's in the records. Can he not read?"

"My lord can read and write. He can even speak three languages. But keeping up with accounts is not one of his strengths. You said that the income and expense of his estates have not changed since Teispes came. I doubt if his lordship

154

would have examined more than that. You are a scribe and it took you days to find the source of the problem. He would not have seen it."

Aggravated because his reasonable argument poked holes into my own theories, I raked my hand through my hair, a movement impeded by the combs Pari had stuck there. I was hampered at every side: by Darius's absence, by Teispes's dishonest secrecy, by my inability to travel, by my lack of access to royal messengers. Now even my hair was tied up. I sent Pari a grumpy glance.

"We need more information. If only I could get my hands on a royal courier." Every answer we needed resided in Ecbatana. And we were stuck here. A courier, however, would be able to go where we could not.

Royal messengers had special permission to travel on public roads. Though Persia had some of the most intricate road systems of the world, they were vigilantly guarded. Travelers needed special visas, something I no longer had access to without my former employer's power or my husband's influence. Teispes was the one who acted in my husband's stead. He had Darius's seal. If I wanted to travel, or even send a messenger, I would need Teispes's permission, which would not be forthcoming any time soon.

"You need to send a message?" Bardia asked, his face brightening. "I can help with that."

The next morning started with some excitement. Pari, the dog, and I were clattering down the stone steps leading to the garden when one of the stones became inexplicably loose. I had my whole weight on it when it went flying under me, twisting my right ankle in the process. My balance gone, I went over, headfirst. Caspian somehow managed to place himself where I landed, breaking the worst of my fall.

"Are you all right?" Pari and I shouted at the same time, she addressing me, and I addressing the dog. The dog had miraculously escaped injury, but my ankle ached with a persistent throb that prevented me from attempting to move for some time.

Bardia must have heard our cries of alarm, for he hurried over to us after a few minutes, a young man I had never seen before trailing in his wake.

"My lady! What happened?"

"She fell down the stairs and bruised her ankle," Pari said.

Bardia bent to examine the injured limb. "Doesn't look broken. Shall I send for a physician?"

"No. I merely need a few moments to catch my breath."

Pari shook her head. "One of the stones came loose. This place is falling apart from lack of proper care. It's dangerous."

The young man moved to examine the stone. He crouched next to it for several moments before straightening. "Odd," he said.

"I should introduce this young lout," Bardia said. "This is my grandson, Gobry. When he was a boy, he helped me here, but now, he is a royal messenger."

Several things fell into place at the same time, making me forget the discomfort in my ankle. First, Bardia's grandson was a courier, the very person I needed in order to further my investigations.

Second, Gobry was short for Gobryas, a name familiar to me in my study of Darius's records. To my puzzlement, I had discovered that for a number of years, the majority of Bardia's income had been directed to one Gorbyas, presumably the same young man who stood before me. And now I knew why.

By theory at least, every man in Persia was free to receive the education afforded a lord's son. In practice, however, financial matters made this an impractical dream. Most families needed their young men in the workforce as early as possible in order to augment their income. There was the further complication of cost; educating a young man required additional funds—food, drink, horse and saddle, feed, stable fees, armor, weapons—all this cost money. It was an expensive undertaking. No wonder Bardia had so little. He had poured most of his wages into the education of his grandson for years. Now Gobry could ride like a nobleman and be entrusted with the speedy delivery of the secrets of an empire.

The third thought that came into sharp focus was the realization that Gobry had pronounced my upturned stone *odd*. "Pleased to meet you, Gobry. What is odd about the stone?"

"My lady," he said, making a credible though brief obeisance to me. "That stone was not loosened by accident." He picked up the flat slab and showed me its underside. "See here, this dent? This comes from repeated beating by a blunt instrument. Someone beat this stone out of place."

"I see," I said.

"Do you mean someone broke it on purpose to cause a fall?" Pari asked, her cheeks bright red, whether from anger or self-consciousness at addressing a comely young man, I could not tell.

"This is my handmaiden, Pari," I said.

Gobry turned grave eyes upon my blushing servant. "It would seem a reasonable assumption."

I bent to play with the ribbon on my shoe. "Teispes may have discovered his missing parchments, I fear. This could be his warning to us to stay out of his business."

157

"The steward?" Gobry said. "I will knock his head off. It's enough that he has mistreated my grandfather, but when he starts plotting to harm the lady of the house—"

I cleared my throat. "We cannot prove it. Not this, not any of it. But you could help us find the truth, Gobryas. Then we could present our case to Lord Darius and leave him to decide the matter."

He laid his hand flat upon his chest. "I live to serve, my lady."

Quickly, I explained the tangle of our situation to Gobry. "What I need is someone who can go to Ecbatana and unearth this mystery." I couldn't send a royal messenger on a personal errand for myself, of course. I hadn't the authority. "Is it possible that you might be given a mission in Ecbatana soon? That way, while there, you could perhaps do a bit of extra reconnaissance for Lord Darius's household?"

"Easy to arrange. With most of the court at Ecbatana, messages are sent there almost daily. What is it that you would like me to do, once I am in the city, my lady?"

I needed no reminding that the court resided in Ecbatana; but for my marriage, I too would be there now.

"We have to find out if Mandana is truly involved with Teispes," I said. "Does anyone in town know who the father of the twins may be? Bring me back whatever news you can, even if it is only town gossip.

"And meet with Mandana face-to-face. Take the measure of her. Sometimes direct questions are the best way to find information."

Royal messengers were trained to be discreet as well as fast. While spying was somewhat outside the purview of Gobry's usual work, I felt certain that he could manage it. But I had also seen that our resident fox had sharp teeth. "Be careful,

Gobry," I said. "This might be more dangerous than we bargained for."

He flashed a smile. "My lady, that would only improve my journey."

"Nonetheless, you must promise that if you sense any threat, you will seek out Lord Darius in the palace and tell him everything we have told you."

I managed to rope the young man into helping me back to my chambers though I had no real need for his assistance. He held me by one arm and Pari by the other as I limped my way forward. I had my reasons for this devious dependency.

I was certain that the steward had watched us from the moment we had left the house. He could not have heard our conversation, but no doubt he had positioned himself where he could see the result of his mischief. He must have been disappointed that I hadn't landed on my head. Now, I wished him to believe me more hurt than I actually was. The more helpless he thought me, the safer he would feel. Criminals, like wild animals, preferred safety; they proved less dangerous while they felt secure.

I had another reason for drawing Gobry away from his grandfather. I didn't want Bardia around while I gave his grandson my final missive. In my chamber, I unearthed my modest bag of gold and silver coins, payment from the queen for my years of service. It had been her idea to pay me in royal coins rather than in rations as was common, for she said it would be wiser to have financial resources that required no dependence on others. Three years' worth of rations needed storage space, connections for a fair exchange, letters, meetings, all of which would have required a steward. Damaspia could have had no notion of Teispes's dishonesty, yet her instinctive cautiousness had proven indispensable.

I hadn't many coins left after having discharged my debts to the queen. I gave a few to the young man.

"Gobry, use this during your search if you need to. Try to save what you can. When you return, I want you to buy the necessary materials to fix your grandfather's cottage if Lord Darius should refuse to do it. The damp is seeping in and I worry for him once autumn arrives. Do you think you can manage?"

He bent low at the waist. "My lady is most kind."

"One last favor. I don't want your grandfather to know where the money came from. He is a proud man."

Waiting on Gobry's return proved hard for me. I had squeezed as many secrets out of Teispes's scrolls as they had to give. My ankle was too sore to allow for extensive activity. I felt useless.

"Are you going to mope the day away again?" Pari asked as she gathered my sheets for laundering.

"Leave me be."

"Why don't you talk about it? It will make you feel better."

I groaned. "Go away."

"I don't think so."

I gave a humorless laugh. My servant was unhappy with my choices and disregarded my commands on a regular basis. My husband's dog was dissatisfied with my performance as a mistress since I had become lame and sedentary. My gardener disapproved of my attitude toward my husband. My cook didn't think my manners grand enough. The Lord was surely disappointed by the fact that I had barely spared a passing thought for Him. I pleased nobody including myself. "What a life," I mumbled under my breath. I hadn't thought Pari could hear me, but she had sharp ears, that girl.

"What's wrong with it?"

"There's no point to it. I accomplish nothing. I help no one. I am a great big waste."

"Help no one? Are you serious? What have you done but help since you got out of your bed?"

"What have I actually achieved? Nothing. Just riled up that crooked steward."

"My lady, you've cared for us, which is the most important thing anyone can do for another. You showed interest in what we needed. You made us feel worthwhile by taking notice. Even if nothing comes of your efforts, we've still been cheered by your concern."

I shook my head and waved her words away. She ignored me, which was an irritating habit she had formed of late.

"Do you remember the willow tree that Bardia showed you? Remember what he said about it: that the master didn't love it because of its usefulness, but because of what it was. *It touches the soul, that's all,* he said."

"What of it?"

"You're like that tree, my lady. It's not what you produce or achieve that makes you lovely. It's who you are. Your kindness, your caring. The way you consider everyone's well-being, even a dog's. The way you make us laugh. The way you get on your knees and clean the home of a servant. The way you face a bully like Teispes without letting fear stop you.

"The sharp mind that teases mysteries out of parchment is only a small part of you. In this house, I have seen so much more of what you are. And my lady, I tell you, you are our willow. We all rest in your shade."

She turned around with an abrupt move and began to

shake the sheets with furious motion. To my amazement, I saw that she was crying. I rose from my couch and approached her, not knowing what to do or say. She noticed me lingering near and dropped the sheets. Without warning I found myself enveloped in a fierce hug. This was so far out of the realm of my experience that at first I did not know what to do. Then I raised a wooden arm and patted her on the shoulder once or twice.

She laughed and stepped back. "You'll have to learn to hug better than that, my lady."

I laughed too, freed in some inexplicable way from my dark thoughts. In the background of my mind was planted the inconceivable idea that my very presence—not what I could do or how I might serve—but my mere being might be a joy to another.

Chapter Thirteen

That night I dreamt that I still worked for the queen. She burst into my office and screamed, "You aren't satisfactory. Leave at once." I had no time to explain or beg. Palace guards stripped me of my clothes and I stood before everyone naked and mortified. Then I was turned out of the palace.

I burst into consciousness with a racing heart, covered in perspiration. I buried my face in the pillow. O God, when would this wound be healed?

Two days later my ankle had improved enough to take a long walk in search of Bardia. He was in the vineyards, a hilly stretch of land situated just outside the estate gardens, beyond the eastern gate. It took us an hour to find him; Caspian chased every rabbit and bird on the way. He terrorized them so thoroughly that I doubt they dared return to that part of the land for a week.

Bardia threw us a cheery wave as soon as he caught sight of us.

"What are you doing?" I cried as I saw the mountain of branches at his feet. He had cut back the vine until there was nothing but a few skinny scraps of bark and puny leaves left. The unpruned plants seemed healthy and robust in comparison.

"Pruning." I found neither the economy of his speech nor the remarkable calm with which he continued cutting reassuring.

Half of me thought that a man grown on the land knew his job better than a scrivener of letters like me. The other half thought plain common sense could see that the head gardener was going too far. He was ruining the vine. The common sense half of my brain won.

"Bardia, stop!" I demanded. "You'll kill it."

The busy fingers went still. "Kill it, my lady?"

"There's barely anything left rooted in the ground."

He gave a wheezing chuckle. "That's what pruning means."

"It means that you destroy the vine?" I tried to gentle my voice, but it still came out with an edge.

Sighing, the old man laid his short knife on the ground. "The vine doesn't have enough nourishment to feed all these branches. In two springs, the plant may be bigger, but most of its clusters of grapes won't even ripen. And the ones that do will be scraggly and of poor quality."

I pointed to the ground. "Perhaps if you fed them better, they could handle the growth. The soil looks quite bad here." I don't know why I was so harsh. I knew Bardia hadn't enough assistance. How was he supposed to feed this grapevine? He had done what he could.

Bardia didn't seem offended by my outburst. With calm he

said, "Yes, it's very poor soil. But this is what the vine needs, my lady."

"The vine needs bad soil?" I raised my eyebrows. "You just said that it doesn't have enough nourishment."

He seemed to consider his answer for a few silent moments and I thought I had finally caused him to see reason. Instead he beckoned me to stand beside him. We were near the top of a slope and he pointed below us. "What do you see, my lady?"

I shielded my eyes against the sun. "A vineyard," I said with a shrug.

"Not any vineyard, but one of the best in Persia. The king himself asks for the wine from this land each year. My lord owns many vineyards, but none produces wine that compares with this one. Its crop is small, but excellent.

"Could it bear more fruit if we fed the land richly? Possibly. But then it wouldn't taste the same." He bent down and picked a handful of rocky soil to show me. "This is the secret of the vine. This poor soil, and this sun and this slope."

"I don't understand," I said, beginning to remember that he had exquisite skill and years of experience. With a wince I realized that I had been making a fool of myself trying to correct a man with more knowledge in his back tooth than I had in my whole being.

He gave me a gentle smile, as if he could sense my dawning discomfort and had no interest in gloating. "Let me share with you the riddle of the vine, mistress.

"The vine needs to *suffer*. Going down into this earth— fighting to survive among the stones, among the lime rock— this is what gives it its aroma. Its taste. Its unique character. These grapes will create a wine few other vineyards can compare with not because their life was easy, but because they had to struggle to survive."

165

I grew still. "The vine *needs* to suffer?"

"To be at its best, it needs to suffer, yes. And fight."

"I'm sorry for it, then. No creature should have to bear pain."

"Pain is part of this life. No one can escape suffering. Not the vine, nor we humans, as you well know, my lady. But what if we are like the vine and that affliction only makes us better?"

Bardia was right in one thing; harsh struggle was the order of life. The world I lived in was no Eden; I did not need faith to teach me that. The evidence of my eyes was more than enough. This world by its very nature was full of the bitter brew of sorrow. Had I not drunk of that cup since my childhood? Had I not lost a beloved mother? Had I not known the detachment of a father who could not love me? Had I not, even when I found a calling that fed my soul, spent nights and days in the grip of fear lest I should fail? Had I not lost the very thing I held on to so tightly? Had I not found myself in a barren marriage? Had I not become trapped in the grip of a treacherous man who sought even now to destroy me?

I bent to grab a branch Bardia had recently cut and discarded. It was still green and fresh looking, but in the hot sun, cut off from its stem, it would shrivel and die in a matter of hours. I studied the jaunty, wide leaves and said, "It's bad enough that these poor plants have to battle the very ground they're rooted in. Do you have to add to the vine's pain by cutting off its branches, Bardia?"

Bardia picked up his short knife again and examined it with silent intensity. In the sun, the blade glinted like a shaft of starlight. "Consider my lady, I'm the gardener and I know what the vine needs in order to thrive. You only see the stripping, but I cut the vine in order to restore it. I take away from it to enrich it. You hold in your hand a withering branch and

that's all you see now, but I know that [...]
more abundant life."

Without his knowing it, Bardia's v[...]
in my heart. As a Jew I believed in o[...]
heaven and earth. One Creator with[...]
God, in a metaphor that Bardia cou[...]
sometimes referred to Himself as a ga[...]
vineyard.

Two things stole my breath as Bardia taught me the riddle
of the vine. First, that suffering improved the character of the
vine's fruit. Perfect ease and comfort would only ruin it. If my
life were anything akin to the vine, then these calamities I bore
need not ruin me. They could very well be my redemption.

Second, come the right season, Bardia, the expert gardener,
Bardia, the tender caretaker, Bardia, the one on whom these
plants depended in order to survive, slashed and hacked into
the vine. He added to its suffering. He stripped it until, from
my vantage point at least, there was hardly any life left. Yet the
vine needed this implacable care. Bardia had claimed that he
cut the vine in order to restore it; he took away from it to
enrich it.

I knew that he was selective in what he called the vine's
suffering. He would not allow pests to brutalize the plants,
for example, or let weeds anywhere near them. Though he
was shorthanded, I had seen no sign of a weevil or beetle near
the crop. He knew what to destroy, what to improve, what to
protect.

If Israel was God's vineyard, was I one of His little vines?
Was He the Bardia of my soul? Did He shield me from what
would destroy me? Was He stripping me now on purpose only
to give me a more abundant life? Would I, one day, bear fruit
worthy of a king's table?

ought brought tears to my eyes. I would not let
ll. I gripped the dying branch Bardia had cut until my
rs grew numb. This was the life I wanted, and God had
ken it from me. I did not want more abundant fruit. I just
wanted what I'd had before.

While we waited for Gobry's return, I formed a plan. We needed to find out as much about Teispes as we could. His habits, his connections, and his pastimes could give us clues to the mystery of the mismanagement of the estate. Which led us to Mondays. Where did Teispes go for so many hours? And who did he spend his time with?

The only way to find out was to follow him. I could not take everyone; he would be bound to notice such a crowd. Nor did I dare go alone in case something went wrong and I needed to send for help. In the end I took Bardia with me and convinced Pari and Shushan to stay behind. They could seek assistance in case we failed to return.

I did not sleep on Sunday night. I whiled the hours away questioning the validity of my precarious plan. Teispes was not a man to play games with. I knew him to be dangerous. My scheme placed Bardia's life in as much danger as my own. And for what? The capture of a dishonest steward? If my husband did not care about the state of his property, why should I?

But it was not about the property or the money. This concerned the well-being of . . . of my friends. With dawning realization I acknowledged that it had been some time since I had thought of these people as my servants. I saw them as my friends. They had offered me a kind of friendship that I had never known. They had sought my company and called it joy.

They had heard my fears and comforted me. They had known me at my worst and abided with me. I had to do what I could to relieve them of their growing distress.

While the horizon was still cloaked in darkness, I dressed myself with Pari's help and met Bardia outside the steward's room. We did not have long to wait. He came out looking well rested. There was a spring in his long stride as he headed for the stables. I groaned inwardly, resenting his cheerful expression; resenting his refreshing slumber; and most of all, resenting his choice to ride to his destination.

I had thought of this eventuality, of course. It was the most likely possibility given the palace's distance from town. I just didn't like it. I couldn't ride a horse to save my life, and donkeys made me queasy. We chose a donkey. At least we didn't have to worry about travel documents; we were considered a suburb of Persepolis.

Bardia and I shared a docile beast as we followed Teispes at a safe distance. Bardia, accustomed to riding the brute, sat in front and dealt with its ornery nature, while I sat behind him, clutching the gardener's skinny middle, praying that I would not fall off.

By the time Teispes entered the heart of Persepolis, the sun was rising in the east, looking as magnificent as a royal crown. Its showy glory made no impression on me. I had one desire: for the steward to arrive at his mysterious assignation so that I could get off that swaying beast. I received my wish soon enough. On a street lined with shops, he brought his mount to a stop and handed the reins to a waiting lad.

Bardia and I stopped a long way off for fear that he would notice us. Teispes seemed unaware of our presence, however, and bounded up a set of wooden stairs to the top floor of a commercial building. I stood back and examined the street. Many of the lower buildings were occupied by modest shops—cobblers, potters, taverns. The top floors in contrast seemed residential. Though it was not a luxurious neighborhood, it was not a cheap one either. The buildings appeared in good repair, the street wide and clean, with miniature flowerpots boasting cheerful colors in front of many of the stores.

"Wait here," I told Bardia; he stuck to me like glue, following my every step. I rolled my eyes. "Fine. Keep quiet then, and don't interrupt no matter what I say."

One floor below the apartment where Teispes had headed, a portly merchant began opening his diminutive shop.

Cosmetics. Fabulous. The only cosmetic I knew anything about was kohl; I had once seen the queen's maids making a batch of the black powder used for darkening the eyes. With painstaking patience, they had burned almonds and pistatues one at a time. The soot had been gathered on the bottom of a clay bowl, and scraped off to use as kohl.

"Do you have any kohl? Made from almonds, mind, and fresh," I said, trying to sound like I knew what I was talking about.

"I have twenty-three varieties, mistress. Which would you like?"

I nearly choked on my saliva. *Twenty-three varieties?* How many blighted ways were there of burning an almond to cinders? I pointed haphazardly to a silver amphora. It was small enough not to cost a fortune. He named a price that almost made me choke again.

After a few more tries and severe haggling I became the owner of kohl I did not need. However, my merchant was in an expansive mood, which is what I did need.

"I'm looking to rent a place in town. A friend told me that apartment above your shop might be available."

"That one there?" The merchant straightened his rounded hat. "That's well occupied. You've been misinformed."

"Are you sure? My friend seemed certain that it was becoming vacant."

"Never. That set of rooms is occupied by Aspasia. She does pretty well for herself. She might be a courtesan, but she only has the one customer, and he takes good care of her, he does. In fact you just missed him; he's up there right now."

Bardia started clearing his throat. I jammed my elbow in his side and he quieted down. "A *hetaira*, is she? Do you know if she needs any help? I could always use a partner."

Bardia began to cough violently. I slapped him across the back.

"Is he all right?" the merchant asked.

"Oh yes. Just getting on in years, you know. So hard to find good help these days," I said. "About this Aspasia."

"That's right. You wanted to know if she was in the market for a partner. I doubt it. Doesn't need to, with this long-jawed fellow who visits her at least once a week on Mondays come rain or shine, and more, when he gets the chance. He pays for everything—her rent, her clothes, her food. What need would the likes of her have for a partner?"

His gaze was bold as he examined me from the top of my head to the tip of my toes. "Now, if you're looking for a protector, I might be interested in a classy girl like you. What's your rate then?"

This was the first time in my life I had been propositioned, although I suppose I had unwittingly set myself up for it. I couldn't make up my mind whether to be flattered or disgusted. It seemed impossible that a man should actually be interested enough in me to be willing to pay for my attentions.

Before I could respond, Bardia stepped forward. "You'll

have to talk to me about that, and I'm busy today." Then he grabbed my hand and pulled me behind him until we reached our tethered donkey, shoved me onto its back, and joined me before I could wave good-bye to my new admirer. He rode home so fast, my teeth were nearly jostled out of my head.

As he strode out of the stables, he was muttering under his breath; I could not hear him well, but I caught something about his fate if Lord Darius ever found us out. I followed behind feeling subdued. Then I noticed that his shoulders were shaking. And he wasn't coughing either.

"You're back early!" Pari cried as soon as she spied us walking toward the kitchen.

"Not early enough," Bardia said. "She almost got herself contracted as a courtesan to a shopkeeper."

"*What?*"

"I was trying to get information out of him. And it worked."

"What did you find out?" Shushan asked.

"We'll tell you if you feed us," I said. Minutes before, green from riding that swaying mule, the thought of food would have been the end of me. Now, standing on solid ground and free from the stress of spying, my stomach reminded me I hadn't eaten anything since noon yesterday.

Forgetting the differences between our ranks, we sat together around a simple meal of sheep cheese, hot flat bread, and cooked lentils with onions as Bardia and I shared our adventures with our comrades.

Pari whistled. "Quite the ladies' man, that shifty steward. One woman in Ecbatana, another in Persepolis. Where does he get the time?"

"There's something fishy here," I said around a mouthful of lentils.

"We know *that*," Shushan said.

"No. I mean something doesn't line up. All the money he saves from the running of this estate is being poured into the factory in Ecbatana. Assuming that's how he is supporting Mandana and his twins, what is he using to support Aspasia? The full-time upkeep of a courtesan isn't cheap. He can't do that on a steward's salary."

"He must be mismanaging another of Lord Darius's estates."

"I don't believe so." I had considered Shushan's suggestion myself and had spent time amongst the records to ferret out similar violations elsewhere. "He is only in charge of a handful of properties. From what I could see, only two of them showed considerable irregularities. This one, and the one in Ecbatana."

"So he's the sole supporter of a courtesan he cannot afford and the father of twins he never sees," Pari said.

"Precisely. Fishy, as I said. We need Gobry's report, and then perhaps we'll be able to put this puzzle together."

"In the meantime, my lady, I hope your days as a *hetaira* are over. I don't think your lord husband would approve. And I dread to think what your father-in-law would say." Bardia tried to look stern. The sight of his five teeth peeking through his widening mouth ruined the effect.

I lifted up my hands as if in question. "I don't see why they should object; I'm a *classy* girl."

Three people groaned in perfect harmony. "Fine," I said. "I am retiring. But I want you to remember it was an illustrious career while it lasted."

Chapter Fourteen

obry arrived five nights later. He showed up at his grandfather's doorstep without warning; he had had no chance to send us word of his coming. As it was, he must have pulled some strings to be able to complete his mission for us.

Royal couriers usually traveled in stages. At the end of each stage, the messenger handed his missive to a fresh courier waiting at an appointed royal staging house. This process sped up the delivery of messages throughout the far-flung kingdom of Persia. In every kind of weather, in sunlight or darkness, royal couriers delivered their dispatches with undreamed of efficiency. But rarely did a messenger carry a missive to its appointed end by himself if the ride was longer than one day, which the ride to Ecbatana certainly was. Somehow Gobry had managed to get himself sent all the way to Ecbatana and back, which meant he had persuaded someone of authority to shift the rules. It was not unheard of, though it required both ingenuity and good standing in the ranks. That he had completed this mission spoke highly of his abilities.

"My lady, I cannot linger. I have yet to report at Persepolis." It was clear that Gobry had ridden directly to see us. His face was grey with fatigue and the dust of the road.

"Of course," I said. "Tell us what you can."

"For a start, there are no twins."

"No twins?" I squeaked.

"Not even one child, male or female. It's a fabrication. Mandana has never borne children. Also, I asked around, and there are no rumors of Mandana ever being involved with a man."

"Did you meet with her face-to-face?"

"I did. She claims that she has never received a raise in pay in the past three years. Her lifestyle is simple and seems to bear out that claim. I interviewed a few of her workers. Everyone thinks highly of her. She is honorable and fair according to her employees. There's never been even a breath of scandal attached to her conduct."

"I don't understand," Pari said. "Where does the money go if not to her?"

"Teispes has a middleman in Ecbatana," I guessed.

"That he does, my lady. His brother, to be exact."

"What does that mean?" Pari asked.

I leaned against the back of my chair. "Rather than sending wages directly to Mandana, Teispes sends them to an agent. This agent then pays the *arassara*. But he pays a fraction of the wages he has received.

"Meanwhile, in the records here, Teispes claims the larger payment and has the receipt from his agent to prove it. There is no one to dispute the difference. The *arassara* has no reason to object to the amount of her payment; she only knows she is being paid as usual.

"The whole story about the twins is a fabrication to make the increased allotments for Ecbatana acceptable in case someone wants to ask cursory questions, which I doubt Lord Darius ever has. As Bardia pointed out before, he, like most landowning aristocracy, is not interested in the details of his accounts. If they seem to make sense on the surface, he is satisfied and leaves the rest to his steward."

"So Teispes and his brother are splitting the extra money between them?" Shushan asked.

"Precisely. It's not a sophisticated scheme. We can easily prove their guilt now that we have uncovered the details. Mandana will have her receipts for the lower amounts from the agent."

"Wait. Doesn't this only implicate the agent? Perhaps Teispes is as much in the dark as Mandana."

I gave Pari an approving nod. "Good point. However, as we have established, unlike Mandana, Teispes has been living above his means for a long time. He must be smitten with his courtesan if he refuses to share her with other men. How far would he go to keep her?

"Another detail that points to Teispes's involvement is that Mandana's current wages are ridiculous. Any steward would investigate such an enormous irregularity.

"You add to this his secretiveness, and the fact that his agent is not a stranger, but his own brother, and well, the pile of evidence against him grows as high as the tower of Babel.

"Of course Lord Darius will have to make his own investigation and get the local judge involved. But it's time to make his lordship aware of what's been going on behind his back.

"Gobry, you have lingered long enough with us. I am most grateful for your excellent work. I could not have found a more capable man in the queen's own employ." Bardia blew out his chest as if I had been singing *his* praises.

"Make your report at the palace," I went on. "However, come and see us again when you can. In the meantime I will draft a letter to Lord Darius, outlining the case against his steward. If you could help get this missive to Ecbatana, I would be most grateful, Gobry, as his lordship also will be, no doubt. Any courier would do; you need not ask for any special favors that would send you all the way up there again. We simply need a missive delivered to Lord Darius."

The letter to my husband proved complicated. I decided to draft it as an official document rather than a personal letter. Nonetheless, I had a problem. He was likely to suspect me of trickery, deceit, and thievery by the time he had read the first line. The very fact that I accused his steward would probably turn the man into a hero in Darius's mind.

I composed fifty different versions of that scroll in my head and discarded every one. At one point I considered making Bardia write it, except that Bardia was not literate.

Four days had already gone by and I still had no letter. To clear my head, I went for a solitary walk along the main avenue of the garden. Out of nowhere, Teispes appeared before me.

"I want my scrolls back."

"Pardon?"

He took a step toward me, standing too close. I did not want to show how intimidated I was by him and stood my ground.

"The scrolls you stole from me. I want them back." His breath reeked of onions.

"They belong to my husband, not you. If he asks for them,

I'll give them back." I pulled my scarf closer about my shoulders.

"Do not meddle with my business, woman. You will be sorry if you do."

"Do you dare threaten me?"

He picked at the black substance lodged under one nail. "I will dare more than that. Keep in mind that you are alone here. Who has come to visit you since his lordship deposited you at my doorstep? Who has sent you a letter to ask after your well-being? You are nobody and no one cares what becomes of you, least of all Lord Darius."

I swallowed hard. I had agonized for hours over the fact that not just Darius, but everyone in my life seemed to have abandoned me. My father, Nehemiah, my aunt, my old coworkers, the queen—none had seen fit to inquire after my well-being these past four months. I could be dead for all they knew.

Teispes could poke my hurt until he turned purple, I decided. I would not give in to his dirty tactics. "In spite of what you think, I have prominent friends." I was astounded to find that my voice was steady. I forced my lips into a smile. "It is you who will be sorry if you meddle with me."

He locked his teeth. "Give me my records back."

"I'll think about it," I said and whirled around to walk back to the palace. I did not feel safe until I was within my chamber with Caspian and Pari at my side.

I needed those records to show Lord Darius when he finally came to investigate my claim. He was not going to take me at my word.

My one advantage was that Teispes had no idea of the extent of knowledge I had against him. I certainly would not want to face him once he found out that there were five of us who had enough evidence to land his head at the end of a very tall pike.

After my encounter with Teispes in the garden I went nowhere without company. I knew Teispes had not exhausted his threats. Caspian, with his usual uncanny sense of timing, developed an intense aversion to the steward, which meant that the very sight of the man sent him into feral snarls and threatening barks. The dog and I grew inseparable.

We took the precaution of stashing the two scrolls in the kitchen. It seemed the safest place. Shushan came up with the idea. She had a faulty bread oven that hadn't seen the sight of a fire in a year. We wrapped the scrolls in leather bindings and stuffed them in the back of the oven, covering them with wood chips and old ash. I doubt even Caspian could have unearthed them.

Our precaution proved wise. One day when we returned to my chamber after a visit with Bardia, we found the place in complete disarray. Teispes hadn't even bothered to cover up his search. It took us hours to straighten up the place.

On top of my bed lay the crumbled parchment of the Psalms that Nehemiah had given to Darius on our wedding day. In his rude explorations, Teispes had further damaged the scroll. I unrolled it with delicate care and found to my relief that it could be repaired. Without thinking, I began to read.

I love you, O Lord, my strength.
The Lord is my rock, my fortress and my deliverer;
my God is my rock, in whom I take refuge.
He is my shield and the horn of my salvation,
my stronghold.
I call to the Lord, who is worthy of praise,
and I am saved from my enemies.

To my surprise I found a strange comfort in those verses. I felt as though the man who had penned these words could understand the condition of my own heart. He would know my fears, my sense of insufficiency, my continuous battle not to lose heart.

He had been pursued by a powerful king, intent on killing him. He had lost everything through that incessant pursuit—home, wife, friends, comfort. And yet somehow, through every soul-crushing trial, through every mistake of his own making, he had battled against despair and won. In the end, he had found peace in the Lord. And the Lord had brought him through what seemed impossible odds.

"What's that?" Pari asked.

"Do you remember the boy David who fought Goliath the giant? He grew up to be a wise and powerful king. But before that, he was a musician, a soldier, a mercenary, a madman, and a poet. This is one of his poems."

"That's a man who held many jobs."

"He made the best of what he was given. Perhaps it was God's way of training him for the future. Perhaps David needed to learn humility before he could be trusted with great power."

"Did the Lord rescue him from his enemies in the end?"

"He did."

"Then we should ask Him to rescue us. I will be honest, mistress; sometimes I think Teispes is too strong for us."

I knew how she felt. I thought it ironic that a Persian would have to remind a Jew to go to the Lord for help. It was just like God to use Pari to humble me. So I did as she asked, and taught her how the children of Israel pray. It had been a long time since I had turned my face toward God. I found afterward that I was surrounded by an unexpected peace. I picked up Nehemiah's parchment and placed it lovingly in my chest.

The next day, Bardia reported that his cottage had met with the same fate. While I could bear the intrusion into my own domain, the thought that Teispes had infringed upon my dear friend and reduced his cottage to a shambles outraged me. I had a mind to set the dog loose on that thieving, carousing miscreant. Later I was sorry that my scruples had held me back.

I had now lived in my husband's palace for four months; over three months had passed since I had risen from my bed of darkness and chosen to live.

Shushan insisted on a formal meal at least once every other day, to keep me in practice of my station, she said. One evening, I was lounging at a priceless gilded table carved by Ionian slaves. I was even more gilded than the table, thanks to Pari. She had insisted on doing my hair in an elaborate concoction of curls. I was overdressed, garbed in one of Damaspia's royal garments. Deep blue silk had been fashioned to sit tight around the waist and flow into a full skirt made of tiny pleats that looked like waves every time I moved. Cleverly, Pari had used the extra fabric she had cut from the bottom to create a modest panel for the top.

Out of nowhere, Shushan exclaimed, "You look so lovely, my lady. Lord Darius will fall over his feet when he sees you."

I was swallowing a ripe fig when Shushan made her comment. I spat it out. I was that shocked.

No one had ever called me lovely before. That was my mother. I—well, I was just good with languages and sums.

"Don't be silly," I said. "I'm not lovely."

Pari made a small noise in her throat. "Are you blind? Of

course you're lovely. You always were; you just didn't know how to take care of yourself."

I was beginning to grow annoyed. "Nonsense."

I was aware that I had changed a little under Pari's constant attentions. For one thing, I had lost weight. My conscious decision to eat healthier meals coupled with the daily exercise that my new routine entailed had caused me to shed the excess weight I had gained since girlhood by my sedentary life. I would never be a Damaspia; I would never gain her narrow bones and long sinews. I was short and I was round. But now that roundness was shapely and feminine. It was acceptable, I supposed. But no one in their right mind would consider me lovely, and I did not wish to build up empty hopes in my own heart.

I retired to my room, ignoring the women's startled looks as I left. What I needed to focus on was Darius's blasted letter. I could not afford to put it off any longer. Gobry was bound to find an available courier for us soon, and I had to be ready.

Settling myself next to Caspian, I pulled out a sheet of clean parchment and began my missive.

To Lord Darius Passargadae, Friend to the King of Kings, Captain of the—

Caspian's growls interrupted my train of thought a short moment before there was a knock on the door. Pari would neither have caused the growl nor bothered with the knock. I pulled the door open to find Teispes on the other side of it.

"My lady," he said, and bowed low.

This was new. "Yes?"

"I've come to apologize."

I tried to school my features into something like nonchalance. Or at least not to give away the fact that I was about to swallow my tongue. "Indeed?"

182

"I have behaved abominably. Even though it was his lordship himself who bade me most forcefully to treat you—I pray you'll forgive me for plain speaking—to treat you with contempt, I feel ashamed of my own conduct. I ought never to have addressed you in such a manner, no matter what my lord may have commanded. I blame the pressures of this job. I manage so many properties and with my lord always absent, the responsibility falls on my shoulders alone. I would never have mistreated you if I had not been stretched with so many concerns."

"I see." Which I did not. I trusted the steward about as much as I would a spider spinning a web for a wounded fly. I supposed he wished to soften me up in order to undermine my guard. So I forced my lips into a smile and said, "Under the circumstances, shall we start afresh?"

He bowed. "My lady is too gracious. That is indeed what I hoped for." He bent down and picked up a tray. "A peace offering," he said.

He had brought me mulled wine and dates. What captured my attention, however, was the sight of a vellum parchment resting at the side of the tray. I picked up the parchment, worried about its proximity to the wine. It was a Babylonian copy of the Epic of Gilgamesh.

"I found it in my lord's library. I thought you might enjoy it."

Since my husband's personal library was kept in the same room as his records, I had not had the opportunity to get my hands on any reading material since I had arrived. Giving a scroll to a starved lover of stories was bribery at its most elevated. I almost succumbed. "Thank you," I said. I put the vellum on a couch, took the tray from him, and closed the door in his face before I gave in to temptation.

An hour later, I was lost in the story of Gilgamesh when

Caspian went rigid beside me. He leapt up and ran to the door and began barking and whining, scratching the door with such force, I thought he might gouge the door.

Then I heard it too, the sound of men speaking in the distance. Caspian was going wild at the door. I worried that if I let him out, he might try to take a bite out of whomever was visiting. I tried to soothe him with comforting words, but he would not be quieted. Finally, I grabbed a hold of his collar and opened the door with caution, hoping to learn the identity of the visitors.

Caspian leapt with such wild strength that I lost my hold on him. He stood on his hind legs, and placed his paws on the shoulders of the man standing just outside my door. The man was trapped under Caspian's ecstatic reception, his hand still raised, clearly arrested in the act of knocking. The dog began to lick his face with delight.

I took an involuntary step back, transfixed by the sight. My missive would remain unwritten, it seemed. My husband was home.

Chapter Fifteen

I had a few moments to wrap my mind around Darius's unexpected arrival while Caspian kept him occupied with his delirious welcome. He had shaved his face in the manner of the Egyptians. I had seen a few other young Persian men follow this fashion in the summertime when the heat must have made a beard uncomfortable. Clean-shaven, his face was even more stunning than before, and yet the absence of a beard made him appear strangely vulnerable. For the first time I noticed that when he laughed there were grooves on his cheeks, and that his whole face softened when he was happy.

I also saw that he was weary. Shadows marred his eyes and he seemed pale. Tired or no, he clearly enjoyed Caspian's playful presence.

"What are you doing here, you mangy monster?" he said with the edge of a laugh coloring his voice. "Get down. *Sit.*" To my surprise, Caspian obeyed immediately. He had never responded to my commands with anything more than superior disdain.

Part of me would have preferred a toothache to the upcoming conversation. Another part of me, however, grew limp with relief. I knew in my bones that Darius would take care of the problems with Teispes. I knew that I would no longer have to bear the burden of responsibility.

Of course I still had to make him listen to me, which was simpler said than done.

With Caspian well heeled and quiet, Darius now turned his attention to me. Frowning, he said, "Pardon, I was looking for my . . ." He stopped speaking for a moment and stared. "Is it *you?*" he blurted.

This, I had not expected. Had I changed so much from the girl on the hill? I bowed. "It is I, my lord."

"Well. You seem to have many faces." His smile was not pleasant. "How fitting."

I chose to ignore his barb. No doubt many more of a similar vein would follow in its wake. If I chased after every bitter accusation in order to defend myself, I would never resolve the issue of the crooked steward.

"My lord, your arrival at this time is most fortuitous."

Darius leaned a shoulder against the wall and crossed his arms. "Is that so?"

"Yes, indeed." I cleared my throat. "The fact is I have some bad news."

"My arrival is fortuitous because you have bad news? How like you to find sharing bad news a fortunate thing. Tell me, wife, what is it you have up your silk-covered sleeves this time?"

I turned away from him in a half circle of exasperation. "My lord, I did you an ill turn, and I am heartily sorry for it," I said, turning back, willing him to believe me. "One day, I hope you will see that I did so unintentionally. But in the meantime I am in a position to do you some good."

"By all means, do your good deed. Play your little game. You will not find me as easy a target as Damaspia."

Again, I ignored his sarcasm. "May I ask you something? Did you warn Teispes of your coming?" I thought of the steward's peace offering a scant hour before and wondered if that was because he had received warning of Darius's arrival and was trying to hedge his bets.

Darius lowered his brows. "Teispes? No. We left Ecbatana too suddenly to send word ahead. Why?"

"Because now you will see for yourself how he runs the estate when you are not here."

"I see. It's about Teispes then, this bad news of yours? Perchance you think you would do a better job running my estate for me?"

"My lord, I know you have ridden hard and must be bone weary. But would you mind coming with me to visit Bardia in his cottage right away?"

He straightened up and I realized that he had merely been baiting me until now. Everything about him turned hard and wary. He was still encased in summer riding clothes, tan linen trousers, and a form-fitting knee-length linen tunic split on both sides for ease of movement. There was nothing of the aristocrat about him; he stood before me a warrior through and through. And the dagger of his anger was pointed at my heart.

"If you have harmed one hair on that old man's head—if you have tried to manipulate him to get your own way—I promise you Sarah, I will make your life a misery."

Far from growing annoyed by his threat, I cheered up to find him so protective of Bardia. I could at least respect that.

"I would never harm him in any way," I promised. "Come and see for yourself."

The sun had set long ago and I knew we would find the head gardener in his cottage. Darius bade his mastiff to stay in my rooms as we departed. We walked the path together in silence. I had to admire Darius's patience. I would have pelted him with questions by now.

Before we arrived at the cottage, Bardia pulled the door open and rushed out to greet us. "My lord! My good lord!" he cried and grasped Darius in his ropy arms as if he were hugging a little boy instead of a man twice his own size. With amazement I saw my husband settle into that embrace without self-consciousness or hesitation.

"How are you, old man?"

"As well as can be expected. Why did you not tell us you were coming? Your timing is incredible, master. We were about to send for you."

"May we come in, Bardia?" I said.

He looked down. "My cottage is—"

"The perfect place to start."

Bardia nodded and led us in. Darius followed with unhesitating steps until he stood inside and his eyes adjusted to the lamplight. "What's happened here?" he exploded as he looked about him at the peeling walls and the damp ground. "Why are you living like this?"

"The damp has been seeping from the pond," I said.

"Why have I not been told about this? Does Teispes know?"

"Yes, my lord. I told him myself, but he refuses to do anything about it."

"Is this true?" he asked Bardia.

"Yes, lord."

"Wretched man! I'll deal with him." Darius marched out

and it was all Bardia and I could do to keep up with him.

"My lord," I panted. "There is more, much more that you should know first."

"*More?*" He came to a halt and I almost plowed into him.

"Perhaps if we went to my chambers first, I could tell you. Bardia can join us if you prefer. He knows as much as I."

Darius nodded and headed down the path with his single-minded gait again. When we arrived at my door I was out of breath. As soon as we walked in, Caspian sat up guiltily. The goblet of wine the steward had brought me was overturned on the floor, its contents spilt over the tiles; the dog had obviously been having a good lick.

"Caspian!" I cried, pulling him away from what remained of the wine. "You should be ashamed of yourself. Look at this mess."

"Why is he in here anyway?" Darius asked.

"He sleeps here."

"Here? You've turned my best hunter into a lap dog?"

My chest began to itch. "He was half starved when we found him. What was I to do? Turn him away hungry? Besides, he's the one who has decided he is master of my chamber. I had barely let him in before he made himself at home. He tolerates my presence out of magnanimity; otherwise, I'm sure he thinks these are *his* rooms."

"Where is the games keeper? Why was my dog left unattended? Where are the other dogs?" Ire flowed out of every pore as he stood in the middle of my chamber, making it shrink with the force of his presence. "What's going on here?"

"Will you not have a seat, my lord?" I suggested, hoping to calm him.

"I don't feel like sitting."

"Well, Bardia and I can't sit unless you do, and it's going to

189

be a long night if you make us all stand as we answer your questions. It's a complicated story."

He gaped at me as if I were one of Persepolis's mythical stone creatures come to life. I realized that as usual I had spoken my mind without thinking, and that the onslaught of such a rejoinder must be a new experience for a young Passargadae lord.

"I beg your pardon. I didn't mean to be so blunt."

He shook his head and looked at me again through narrowed eyes. Without another word he sat on a stool. I perched myself on the edge of a couch and Bardia folded his legs and made himself comfortable on the floor.

"Bardia, tell his lordship how many men work under you now."

"Two. One is part-time, and the other is a bumbling fool who knows as much about plants as I do about stars, which is to say nothing."

Darius leaned forward. "You mean twenty."

The gardener shook his head. "I mean two."

"That's impossible. How can you keep up with the land and the vineyard with two men? Where are the rest?"

"Teispes let them go, master. He's been dismissing the staff steadily for almost three years now. We have few of the servants you or your father hired anymore. He didn't dare cast Shushan and me out, and kept on a few others, but he got rid of most of the rest. The small staff he has hired is useless and lazy. They're just his spies. The rest of us, he runs ragged."

Darius sprang up. Out of respect so did Bardia and I. "Great holy fires, will you two sit down?" We did as he commanded.

"Bardia, why have you not told me this before? Have you been trying to keep up with the gardens alone? You must be beyond exhausted. This is not the old age you deserve."

"I didn't wish to add to your burdens, my lord."

Darius slapped his forehead with the palm of his hand. "My burdens? It's not a burden to look after you properly. This is my fault. I ought to have looked to your welfare better than I have. I ought to have made sure that the steward was proficient at his work."

I warmed to him in that moment. He perceived his failure before anyone had to point it out to him, and he took on the responsibility of it without excuse. The simmering anger and blame I had nursed toward him for his careless management of the estate drained out of me. In that one moment I saw him for the man he was; I saw his heart and it was not selfish and undependable as I had assumed. He was the man Bardia claimed him to be.

I swallowed a ball of sorrow, for to have a self-serving man think ill of me didn't hurt nearly so much as knowing that a truly good man found me wanting. "My lord," I said, forcing myself to speak. "I fear this is not merely a matter of incompetence. Teispes has been robbing you for three years."

Darius went still. "That is a serious charge. Do you have proof?"

"We do, my lord." Bardia nodded. "The mistress, her servant Pari, Shushan, and I, and even Caspian here have banded together to find you proof for over three months. My grandson Gobry joined us in the end, and helped us to find the evidence we needed to bring matters before you. That's why I'm so glad you have arrived. We have finally managed to solve this mystery ourselves and were about to send for you."

"I see." Darius sat down slowly. "You had better present this evidence, then."

Bardia slipped out to fetch the parchments we had hidden in the kitchen. His absence left an awkward silence. I knelt beside Caspian and scratched his back. He gave me an appreciative lick, then ambled over to his master and sat at his feet. Darius gave a satisfied smile.

"He's a good dog," I said to show that I held no grudge.

"More loyal than some people." His voice had an edge of bitterness. I couldn't tell if he was referring to me or to his steward. Both probably.

I remembered that he had just completed a grueling journey and was about to be showered by a lot of unpleasant information. "May I have some refreshments fetched for you?"

He pointed to a water pitcher and bowl. "Is that fresh?"

"Yes, my lord." I brought them over to him along with a pristine Egyptian towel. He waved my help away and poured the water himself before washing his face and hands. The way he sank his wet fingers through his hair, I could tell he wished for nothing more than a hot bath and a good meal and the comfort of his bed.

"We could speak tomorrow, if you wish," I offered, feeling guilty for dumping my unpleasant news on him without giving him a chance to draw breath. "Perhaps you should rest after your long journey."

"You expect me to rest after what I have seen and heard? I'll not move until I get to the bottom of this mess."

Bardia returned just then bearing the leather-wrapped parchments. To my relief, he was followed by Pari who bore a large tray of food. Shushan hadn't had time to prepare an elaborate feast, but she had sent a warm dish of pureed eggplants and onions sautéed in olive oil, turmeric, and dried mint, along with fresh bread and strained yogurt. In her usual efficient manner, Pari set the tray up on a table near Darius. I expected him to wave her away with impatience and begin grilling Bardia and me. But the aroma of Shushan's cooking proved too tempting and he dipped his bread into the eggplant and dropped the morsel into his mouth before Pari had a chance to hand him a napkin.

A deep sigh escaped his lips and he closed his eyes as he chewed. "No one cooks like Shushan, not even the royal cooks at Susa or Persepolis."

I was glad to see him eat. For one thing, I was still feeling guilty for depriving him of any form of respite with my ill-timed revelations. For another, I knew he would be in a better mood with the taste of Shushan's food on his tongue.

As if sensing my thoughts, he opened his eyes and gestured with his hand. "Please. Proceed."

With painstaking detail, I laid before him the tale of our investigations. I explained how I had grown suspicious of Teispes, and how he refused to allow me into the records room. I tried to gloss over the way we took Teispes's key by merely saying that we stole it from him.

"Wait a moment," Darius said, halting my rapid narrative. "How did you do that? As I recall, he never removes the thing from around his neck. Or is that not true?"

"Oh, it's true," Bardia said.

I squirmed uncomfortably on the couch. I now had to tell my husband how I sneaked into the chamber of a man alone, and how I laid hands on him as he slept in his bed. Darius listened to my tale of indiscretion and theft with a sardonic gleam in his eye.

"My wife, it turns out, has greater talent than I was led to believe. Remind me to take you on our next military campaign. You can sneak into the enemy general's tent at night and get me whatever information I need. And if perchance he should wake before you are finished, tell him he can keep you with my compliments."

To my shock, Bardia, usually so respectful, shushed him.

"He does not mean it, mistress. When he knows the full story, he will ask your pardon, I am sure."

"He will not, *I* am sure," Darius said, grabbing another piece of bread loaded with yogurt and eggplant.

Before we lost the thread of our conversation altogether, I picked up where I had left off and told of Caspian's part in the plot. Darius roared with laughter, a sound I had never heard. I could grow accustomed to it, I decided.

"Clever beast. He saved the lot of you."

"He did," I admitted, "though he paid a price for it, poor fellow." I described how I had found Teispes beating him. Darius turned pale. I could see it took all his control to keep from jumping up there and then to fetch Teispes and give him a taste of his own medicine.

I gazed at the dog who had saved me with such courage that night; he seemed strangely subdued and sleepy given that his beloved master was nearby after such a long absence. I reached over to pat his head. Darius must have had the same thought, for our hands connected in a brief caress over Caspian's bristly fur. I pulled my arm back quickly and hid it in the folds of my skirt. I didn't dare look up at Darius; I didn't want to see his sarcastic expression. I wondered if he assumed I had purposely reached out my hand for an excuse to touch him.

He refrained from making one of his cutting remarks. "What happened after?" was all he said, and even that sounded bored.

So I told him about my discovery of the discrepancies in the accounts and showed him the ledgers that had caught my notice. I had to kneel close by his stool to explain the figures. The flowing pleats of my sleeve brushed his thigh every time I pointed out something on the parchment. Without warning, he grabbed the silk and moved it off his lap and stood up so abruptly that I lost my balance. With a thud I ended up sitting on my rump.

He rolled the parchment and threw it on a table. "Fine. I can see there is unusual activity. It does not prove he is a thief, however, though he certainly needs to explain himself. Do you have more?"

"We do."

Before I could divulge the secrets of Teispes's pastime on Mondays, Bardia told him about the loose flagstone on the garden steps.

"You think he intentionally tried to hurt my wife? That's beyond belief, Bardia. The man would have to be mad."

"Or very brazen. My grandson is the one who discovered the stone. He told us it was pulled out by someone on purpose."

Darius sank back on the stool. "Gobry would know. He's had ample training. I can scarcely believe this. But why?"

"He must have discovered the missing parchments," I said. "He was warning us to leave him be." I had moved back to the couch, a safe distance away from my husband. "Anyway, Gobry agreed to do a bit of spying for us in Ecbatana. We had assumed that Mandana's twins belonged to Teispes. But it turned out we were wrong."

I described Gobry's findings and Bardia filled in the details of our spying trip into Persepolis. Thankfully, he omitted to tell my husband about my short career as a courtesan.

Darius was silent for a long time. I could see that he was trying to digest the ramifications of our revelations. The profound betrayal. The cost of it to people he loved. The damage of it to his estate. And the fact that his own carelessness had allowed Teispes's duplicity to go on for three interminable years.

At his feet, Caspian tried to rise, then fell. He did this several times. At first I thought he was drunk from the wine, until I noticed his unnaturally fast breathing. He seemed to have trouble drawing air into his lungs. All of us rushed to his side.

"What's the matter, boy? What's wrong with you?" I cried.

Suddenly the hound began to quake in great jerking motions, his massive body shuddering with uncontrollable movement.

"He's having a seizure," Darius said. "Has this happened before?"

"Never! What should we do? Can you not help him?" I began to tremble, looking at the poor creature's suffering.

Darius shook his head. After a few moments, the shaking seemed to stop. A large glob of spittle came out of his mouth. He shook twice more before losing consciousness. Darius went rigid. He bent his head and sniffed the dog's mouth. "Bitter almonds," he said and turned to look at Bardia. Something passed between them in that look, something I didn't like.

"What does it mean?" I asked, horror sinking me to the ground.

"Tell me, Sarah, what has he eaten today?"

"He ate what I ate at dinner."

"What *you* ate?" Again I saw that indefinable secret pass between the two men. They turned to gaze at me. Darius's green eyes were intense and unflinching. "Did he eat anything else?"

I remembered the spilled wine. "He drank of the wine Teispes brought me earlier, remember? And the dates too."

Darius rushed over to the almost empty goblet and began to sniff it. "Bitter almonds," he said again, cryptically.

I put Caspian's head on my lap and began to stroke his now inert body. "But what does it mean? Why is he so sick?"

196

Darius crouched in front of me. "Sarah." I was too miserable to pay him any mind. He tangled his hand in my hair and forced my head up until I focused on him. "Did you drink of the wine, Sarah?"

"Why?"

"Because it was poisoned."

Chapter Sixteen

"**P**oisoned?" I remembered Teispes knocking on my door, and delivering the tray with a pleasant smile. "Of course. It was Teispes." I felt completely paralyzed as I beheld Caspian's unconscious form, his belly rising and falling with fast, shallow breaths.

"Did you drink any of it?" Darius asked again, and now I understood the intensity of his manner.

"No. No, I didn't."

Darius let out a breath and let me go. "Does he always deliver your food personally?"

"No. This was the first time. He said he wanted to ask my pardon, and that he was sorry he had followed your orders to treat me with contempt."

"I gave no such order."

I shrugged. "He said he came to make peace. His mistake was that he brought me a copy of the Epic of Gilgamesh from your library. I became too engrossed in the story to touch the food or the wine. I would have drunk it soon enough, but then you came. And Caspian got to it first."

Darius became a whirl of motion. "Bardia," he said, his voice calm, but commanding, "do you have a purge we can give him? It's probably too late already, but we should try."

"I don't know how it would work on a dog, master. It might just send him over the edge."

"It's a chance we must take. He'll die anyway, if we do nothing."

I couldn't hold back a cry at that news. I laid my head against Caspian's and wept. Bardia said quietly, "I'll fetch the herbs right away."

Darius rushed to the door. One of his men stood at attention outside my chamber. I overheard enough of his command to know that he had sent the man to arrest Teispes.

When he returned, he knelt by Caspian. Gently, he began to rub the dog on its chest. "Do you think he is suffering?" I asked.

"Not anymore. He is in a deep sleep."

I nodded. I had begun shivering and I couldn't stop. Darius's hands on my shoulders made me jump. I realized that he was wrapping me in my cloak. He must have risen with the silence of a cat, for I never noticed his movements. He came back to crouch before me.

"You've grown to love him?"

I nodded. He had been my champion through danger and my companion through many lonely hours.

Darius pulled the cloak closer about me and settled the fabric around me until I was covered from neck to feet. "Thank you," I whispered. He rose to fetch a blanket with which he covered Caspian.

"He is the brightest dog I ever had," he said. "And the most faithful."

I realized that although he wasn't weeping, he too was mourning; he merely held his grief deep inside. "I'm so sorry," I said. "Perhaps if I had managed this affair in a different way, he wouldn't have been hurt."

"This is not your fault. It is that man's doing and he shall pay for it. What manner of evil would unleash such murderous behavior? What will become of Persia if our men turn into cheats and murderers? And to think I gave him the run of my household."

There was a knock on the door. In days past I would have just bid them enter, but the palace was now milling with Darius's men and I could not very well ask one of them into my apartments. Without comment, Darius rose to open the door. "It is your maid. She wishes permission to enter."

Of course with Darius in my room, Pari couldn't barge in unannounced as was her wont. "Oh, please tell her to come in. She loves the dog too."

Pari entered; wordlessly we clasped each other in a comforting embrace. More commotion at my door drew our notice. It was Darius's man, reporting that Teispes was missing.

"They searched everywhere," Pari whispered in my ear. "There's no sign of him, and one of the horses is missing too. He must have left in a hurry."

Darius came to give the same report. "I must go and find him. The sooner we leave, the better our chance of apprehending him."

"I think I know where he has gone. His courtesan's lodgings in Persepolis would be my guess. He will think himself safe there, not realizing that we followed him and know about it."

"It's a good starting point," Darius conceded. "Even if he hasn't gone there directly, he is bound to try and get in touch with his *hetaira*. I will post a few men at the house. We'll catch that rat sooner or later."

I gave him the directions. "Will you go yourself?" I asked, trying to keep my voice from wobbling.

"Of course."

"My lord, I . . . I don't know what to do for the dog. When Bardia comes with the purge I mean." From what Darius had said earlier, there was not much any of us could do. But at least he had some training in the healing arts from his years of study at the palace. If any of us could help Caspian, it was he.

He chewed on his lip. I knew the struggle before him: the need to capture a man who had wronged him grossly, to bring him to justice and end the trail of his destruction, or to remain and do what he could for a beloved animal.

My heart melted with relief when he said, "I will stay." I was too distraught to know my own feelings then, but I believe that was the moment I began to fall in love with Darius Passargadae, the man who despised me for my public betrayal.

He was accustomed to command on the field of battle. He knew how to organize and mobilize under pressure. By the time Bardia arrived with his bag of herbs, Darius's men were on their way in three separate detachments—one bound for the house of Teispes's *hetaira*, another searching for general clues, and the last back to Ecbatana to arrest Teispes's brother and gather evidence from Mandana.

I had no interest in Teispes anymore. My whole attention was focused on the creature that lay dying before me. Bardia and Lord Darius made up an infusion of herbs, discussing between them the advantages of mixing one over another, and poured it down Caspian's throat. How the poor dog retched! He hardly had any strength and I worried that the struggle to empty his stomach would be enough to kill him. Several times he choked and Bardia and Darius had to manually help open his throat. I was astounded by my husband's patience and gentleness. Was this the same man who had sat next to me at our wedding, fuming with cold bitterness?

Finally, there was no more in the dog's stomach to purge. We could only wait.

"It's a good sign that Caspian has survived this far, mistress," Bardia assured me. "He is strong."

I sat with Caspian's head on my lap hour after hour, counting his breaths, praying he would survive. I must have fallen asleep some time during the night, for I awoke with a start. My head was on Darius's shoulder, and I was leaning heavily against his side. I turned to him hoping to find him asleep and unaware of my transgression, but found him watching me.

"Pardon." I scooted away, putting a bit of distance between us. He said nothing, but continued to watch me as if I were a puzzle he could not make out.

"How is he?" I asked. My throat felt parched and scratchy.

"The same."

Bardia had gone to sleep in a corner of the room, wrapped in one of Pari's blankets. Pari too was asleep at the foot of my bed, where Caspian usually lounged. I looked longingly at a flagon of pomegranate juice that sat on a desk nearby, but I did not want to disturb the dog's rest by moving his head. To my astonishment Darius rose and poured some into a silver goblet and brought it over to me.

"I . . . thank you." We sat in silence for a while. Having witnessed his kindness, I felt emboldened to ask, "What brought you home? I thought you were in Ecbatana for the summer."

He sighed. "The queen."

He said no more, which was cruel. He must have known that I was writhing with curiosity. I could not resist prodding, "The queen?"

"Yes. You know, King Artaxerxes' wife. I believe you are

somewhat acquainted with her."

"I believe I am. So *that* queen sent you home? Why? Were you naughty?" That would teach him to try and torment me.

He smiled into his goblet before taking a deep swallow. But he said nothing to satisfy my curiosity, the wretch. Not a man to be goaded into giving information, I concluded.

"Bardia said you cleaned his cottage for him. With your own hand, he said."

The swift change of topic caught me off guard. I shrugged. "He wasn't supposed to know. Pari did much of the work."

"I thank you for that."

I looked at him through the veil of my lashes. "I didn't do it for you. I did it for him. He has become very dear to me."

"You were right; you have done me a good turn, and I am grateful for it. But it doesn't undo the past, Sarah. It doesn't make what you did disappear."

Sometime in the night my hair had come undone from its elaborate arrangement and now it fell about my back in loose curls. I bent my head until a curtain of hair hid my face. I didn't want him to see how much his words hurt.

Darius leaned back. "Let me tell you how I came to hire Teispes. His uncle held the post of my steward before him. When his uncle passed away, Teispes was very helpful to me in the chaos following the loss of a trusted steward. I hired him on the strength of these circumstances: his connection to my last steward, who was as honest a man as the world has to offer, and his own good service to me when he had little to gain by it.

"Even bad men can have trustworthy connections. Even evil men are capable of doing good upon occasion."

"You mean you can't trust me merely because you have seen a better side of my nature. For all you know my current

203

actions are as much of an anomaly as Teispes's behavior after his uncle died."

"I'm not soon going to forget becoming the butt of every courtier's joke because of what you did. Nor can I respect a woman who would so publicly humiliate another for the sake of her own ends. How can I place confidence in you when you will not even admit what those ends are, but hide behind feeble excuses?"

I stroked Caspian's head. "What if you're wrong? What if you are being cynical rather than perceptive?"

"Sometimes the two are the same. The best a man can do is weigh the evidence before him and make the wisest judgment he is capable of. This I have done with you."

"Is it not better to commit the error of thinking others better than they are rather than mistakenly consider them worse?"

"You ask me that on *this* day, with the damage of Teispes round about us, because I thought better of him than I should have?"

What could I say? He considered my explanations *feeble excuses*. I clenched my teeth. Just as well, I thought. He probably wouldn't enjoy being married to a former courtesan with a shopkeeper for a potential customer. I drank the rest of my tart juice and shifted my legs, which had begun to fall asleep.

"The queen sent me to fetch you," he said without preamble.

"What?"

"I came home because Damaspia sent me to fetch you to Ecbatana. She wants you there for the feast of the equinox."

"I see." So Damaspia had *commanded* him to personally escort me to Ecbatana. She, after all, had not forgotten me. The thought of her kindness brought no comfort. That very kindness had landed me in this plight to begin with.

A dark mood descended on me as recent events sank deeper into my consciousness. I had escaped my own demise by the merest wisp of circumstance. Now I held in my arms a beloved animal whose impending death cast its pall on all our hearts. Once again, my husband had rejected me, though with more benevolence this time. The fact that my adversary was finally about to be caught didn't assuage the larger miseries of my life. With longing, I thought of the peace I had felt when I had prayed with Pari. I felt none now.

Why Lord? I cried out in the privacy of my thoughts. *Why have You allowed so much hurt in my life? Why did You take my mother? Why would You not turn my father's heart toward me? Why did You take away the work of my hands? Why did You marry me to a man who will never care for me? Why did You allow this poor creature to be poisoned? Why?*

God, it seemed, had no answers for me. I railed against Him to no avail. I pummeled Him with my demands for an explanation, an excuse, a justification. He only gave me His silence.

I thought of King David and the many disappointments he had suffered. He too had put God to the question. *Eli, Eli, lamah azavtani? My God, My God,* why *have You forsaken me?* I hurled David's question at God, hoping that He would honor His beloved king where He had chosen to ignore me.

And then I went still.

I remembered that in the Hebrew Scriptures you sometimes asked a question not because you expected a literal answer, but because a question was another way to express your feelings. King David had asked God *why*, but he had never intended to take Him to task with that question. He was not asking the Lord to explain Himself. He was merely pouring his heart out to God. He was telling his Lord that he felt abandoned.

I became mindful of how differently I had addressed the Lord. I had asked my whys of Him for years, expecting an explanation that would satisfy *me*. I had put Him on trial for what I perceived to be His insufficiency—His failure—and refused to surrender my heart to Him unless He would answer me. Unless He would give me a satisfactory explanation of His ways. How different was my heart from David's.

It occurred to me that the Lord must have cherished David's simple *lamah*. That was the cry of a child, who not understanding, still clung to his father. My *why*, on the other hand, was an indictment. It was a finger pointing at God. It held no trust.

In those moments of inward examination, with three other people and a sick dog in the same room with me, I felt myself completely alone before God. And I saw the state of my soul for the first time. I saw how arrogant I had been to judge Him. To reject Him.

I was faced in that moment with a decision. Surrounded with reminders of the disappointments of my life—a husband who was only here because of a queen's command, a dog who lay dying in my lap, a house that was little more than a gilded prison—surrounded by these very sorrows, would I turn to God as a trusting child instead of a demanding judge? Would I lay down my accusations and exchange them for the intimacy of a weeping infant's arms who clung about her Father's neck? A child, who, not understanding why her Father took away her favorite prize, still turned to Him for comfort?

Would I exchange my *why* for David's *why*?

It occurred to me that even if God wished to give me an accounting of Himself, His explanation would make as much sense to me as Bardia's elucidation of pruning would make to the vine. I simply could not comprehend a God who was so far above me.

But, like David, I could have His comfort. I could have His love. I could have His peace. I could have all this without understanding.

This was the choice before me then: an unreasoning surrender that paved the way to love, or a stubborn distance from God until He justified Himself to me. Until He chose to run the world my way.

I was so tired of battling God. It had availed me nothing but bitterness. He had allowed me to wander far, to have my own way, to follow my own will. To taste the sour fruit of running my own life. I had had enough. I wanted David's heart. I had started that night with sharp accusations against my Lord; I ended it with the desire to love Him. I chose to give my life back to God on His terms, not mine.

Since King David had led me to this new path, it was in his words that I prayed silently:

O Lord, I give my life to you.
I trust in you, my God!

Show me the right path, O Lord;
point out the road for me to follow.
Lead me by your truth and teach me,
for you are the God who saves me.

Do not remember the rebellious sins of my youth.
Remember me in the light of your unfailing love,
For you are merciful, O Lord.

How can I describe what happened to me after offering this simple, earnest prayer to God? I had prayed hundreds, perhaps thousands of prayers before this. I had even meant some of them. There was something different this time, however. Perhaps it was the offering of my whole life. Perhaps it was allowing God to be Lord on *His* terms. I know not. I only know that some of the walls I had built against my Lord since childhood began to crumble.

As I finished praying, I remembered with sudden clarity the first time I had visited the king's palace in Ecbatana. For days we had been traveling, until one afternoon we made the final ascent through the mountains along the Khorasan Highway. Without warning we came in sight of a mammoth wall, circular, tall, and gold. The Medes who had built the wall originally had attached thin shields of gold plate to the stone beneath, so that as the sun shone on it, we were blinded.

When we rode through the gates, we came upon a second wall, this one silver, equally massive and overwhelming. On and on we went, circuit after circuit of wall, each taller than the next, each in a different color: red, blue, crimson, black, white. As we went, I was mostly aware of walls, for only the merest glimpse of the palace or the city peeked from behind the seven gleaming concentric circles of colored stone. I knew a magnificent palace was there because others had taken shelter within and had borne testimony of its existence. But the evidence of my senses pointed me to high walls, not the palace beyond.

Until this moment, my life with God had been like the ascent into Ecbatana. I had only seen the walls. I had never entered close enough to take comfort within. I was near, but I was on the outside. Some of these walls had been of my own making: my rebellion; my resistance; my arrogance; my need for control. Some had been built around me by the misfortunes of life: my loneliness; my orphaned heart; my fear of rejection. I had kept God at bay, and cheated myself of the warmth of His mercy.

That night, as I prayed, it was as if some of the walls I had raised up between God and me came down, and I drew near.

An inexplicable peace filled my soul. I held a precious dog in my arms as he struggled for breath. But I was devoid of all bitterness. I had nothing left of what I thought I treasured. But a burgeoning hope strengthened me. I had begun to care for a man who could never regard me with equal tenderness. But I felt that it was well with me.

"What's wrong?" Darius whispered close to my ear. "Are you feeling unwell?"

I realized that tears ran unchecked down my face. I couldn't even feel self-conscious about it. With a smile I said, "I've never felt better."

He reached over and laid a hand against my forehead. His palm was dry and rough. "You're not feverish," he said.

I laughed. "I was only praying. It's all right. I'm not losing my mind."

"You sound like my mother."

He couldn't have paid me a better compliment and I flushed with pleasure. His expression changed, became shuttered and withdrawn. I realized that he had spoken the words without thinking, and that he did not wish to invite me into a conversation about his private life.

I took the hint and leaned over to check on Caspian. "He seems the same."

"We should try to get some water into him," he said. He held his hand out to me as he stood.

"I don't want to move him," I said.

"You have sat in the same position for hours. Your muscles will cramp if you don't move a little. Come. He won't feel your absence. His sleep is too deep."

As softly as I could, I shifted Caspian's head off my lap before reaching out my hand to Darius. He pulled me up with a strong heave. He was right; my legs were unsteady beneath me, and I tumbled against his chest. Long fingers wrapped about my waist, holding me steady. For a moment I rested there, against his hard rock embrace. Then I forced myself to step back. The air around me became thick and awkward.

I tried to act as if I weren't horribly self-conscious, and said the first thing that came into my head. "I have a confession to make."

"I'm listening."

Chapter Seventeen

"I took your wedding gift. Remember the collection of psalms from Nehemiah? You abandoned it at the wedding. I didn't think you wanted it, but I should have asked."

"*That* is your confession? You can keep it. I care not."

"My thanks. It means more than I can say."

He shook his head and fetched water and Caspian's bowl. Together we crouched near the dog's sleeping form. His heart still beat far too fast from the effects of the poison, and I worried that it might burst itself from working too hard. Darius had me hold Caspian's head while he poured a thin stream of water into the slack mouth. The dog began to choke and Darius stopped his efforts. It was clear that Caspian could not ingest anything anymore.

Darius sat back on his heels and observed Caspian in silence. Without turning to me he said, "Go to bed."

"I'll keep vigil with you."

"You will not. Perhaps you don't realize that we must still

leave for Ecbatana. I'll linger as long as we can. But we must leave soon. It will be a fast and hard journey if we are to make Damaspia's feast as she demands. You'll need your strength. I won't have you falling sick on me. I'll probably be blamed for it."

I wavered, knowing I should obey him, but wanting to remain with the dog. "What if he should die while I'm asleep?"

"I promise to wake you if there is any change."

I hesitated too long. He pointed a tapered finger. "Bed." He didn't say it, but I knew from the tone of his voice that if I didn't move fast, he would deposit me there himself. My bed was located in a modest nook, which could be curtained off from the rest of the room. I took off my cloak as I dashed toward it, squirming under the covers while trying not to dislodge Pari in the process. The curtains that separated me from the rest of the chamber were too sheer to make changing an option, so I gathered Damaspia's lavish silks and spread them about me as best I could to prevent them from wrinkling.

"Don't forget to wake me."

"I made a promise, woman. Now, be still."

I didn't believe that I would be able to sleep, but no sooner had I closed my eyes than I drifted off. The sound of someone knocking on the door brought me bolt upright. It was Shushan. She had made us breakfast and brought it over herself.

Pari stirred as I rose out of bed. Stifling a yawn she said, "How is Caspian?"

"I'm about to check on him." The sound of my husband's voice made me uncomfortably aware of my bed-tousled hair and my rumpled appearance.

"Good morning," I said as I knelt by Caspian and found him unaltered from the night before. The same unnaturally deep sleep, the same fast heartbeat, the same panting breaths. But he clung to life, so I clung to hope.

It couldn't have been long past dawn; I hadn't slept for more than a couple of hours then. Bardia was awake too, folding his blanket into neat squares.

Darius turned toward his cook. "Shushan has brought a feast fit for an Egyptian pharaoh. We had better eat."

"I already fed his lordship's men. They threatened mutiny if I didn't. This is their leftover." Shushan was sporting an eye patch, which made her look more like a highwayman than an aristocrat's treasured cook. I knew her eye must be irritated, or she would never have resorted to the patch.

I whispered so that only she could hear, "Is the eye causing you much discomfort?"

"It's bearable."

I couldn't help smile at the sight of my friends about me. The extraordinary circumstances had blurred the normal rules of propriety even more than usual. It wasn't every day that I slept with *two* men in my room. After washing my hands and face and allowing Pari to brush my hair, I joined Darius at the breakfast table.

As unobtrusively as I could, I thanked God under my breath. It was a ritual I had performed countless times. Today, however, the words seemed full of significance. I blessed God with my whole being, for truly every good thing I had came from Him. And I *had* many blessings for which to be grateful.

When I lifted my face, once again I found myself the object of Darius's watchful gaze. I remembered that he had been raised as a Persian prince, taught to honor the Persian god Ahura Mazda and to live by the principles of justice. Yet he was also half Jewish, influenced by a beloved mother who had been devoted to the Lord. My simple acts of worship were bound to call forth memories. I wondered if he felt any con-

213

flict in his soul, caught between two worlds as he was. Did he have any hunger to know more about the Lord? And if he did, how could he satisfy such hunger when the pursuit of it would mean the disappointment of a dear father?

I decided that such questions were not my concern. Darius would not thank me for entertaining them. For now, while we were thrown so close together, I'd have to bear the brunt of his curious scrutiny. But that marked the end of my involvement. I lectured myself to keep my own counsel, to hold my tongue, to be discreet. I lectured myself, not sure that I could abide by my own wise advice.

"Any news of Teispes?" I asked, setting my disturbing thoughts aside.

Darius bit into a perfectly baked piece of warm bread filled with sweet cream and quince preserve. "Not yet." He seemed exhausted to me. I recalled that before staying up the whole night to deal with an unpleasant and stressful situation, he had spent a full day in the saddle.

"My lord, you ought to retire to your apartments. Bathe, rest, change from your travel clothes. We will send for you if there is news. As you pointed out to me, you still face the journey back to Ecbatana."

He raked long fingers through his hair. "It would be good to wash off this dust." One long leg stretched before him. "There's as yet so much to organize. I need to replace the servants Teispes discharged and get rid of the useless ones he hired."

"I can help you with that, my lord," Bardia volunteered. "I know how to reach many of our old people. If they are available, they will come back, I'm certain. Tell me the terms and I will see to it that the work is done. Shushan can help me with the indoor staff."

Shushan nodded. "Easy enough. Just leave us a couple of your men, lord, so that we can send them with messages."

Darius grinned. "With you two about, maybe I won't even need a new steward." He heaved a sigh as he rose. "Nonetheless, I shall have to find one."

I could have given him three suitable names without even thinking hard. I held my peace, imagining that I'd be the last person he would trust with the welfare of his estate.

"Until we find the right man, I shall leave my personal scribe here with you. He will need your help with the practical side of running a household, but at least he can straighten the accounts and see to the rations for the new servants." To my surprise, he turned to me. "In the meantime, if I need the services of a scribe, I imagine you can help me?"

"Yes, my lord. Of course."

"This must be a distressing state of affairs for you. You married yourself to an aristocrat only to find yourself back in a scribe's chair. Fear not. I will free you from the responsibility soon after we arrive at Ecbatana. The king is bound to have dependable contacts."

"Nothing about working as a scribe distresses me. I shall be glad to help."

He raised an eyebrow in that maddening way he had, which seemed to question the world and all that was in it, not to mention everything that came out of my mouth. "Call me with updates. I'll take your advice and go to my own rooms."

Bardia and Shushan left to see to the hiring of new staff. Pari remained and helped me tend Caspian. We tried to give him more water without success, and settled for a rubdown instead. I doubt if our attentions made any difference to him, but it made us feel better.

My long night and short hours of sleep were catching up with me, and I gave myself over to Pari's care as she bathed me and dressed my hair again. My chamber was growing hot and I wished nothing more than to wrap myself in my oldest, most comfortable robe, but Pari admonished that with Lord Darius in residence, I needed to look the part of the lady. So I covered myself in exquisite Egyptian linen and went to take up my vigil by Caspian. It seemed ridiculous to don such finery at the bedside of a sick dog.

Pari left to help Shushan in the kitchen; Shushan, I knew would be happy for the help now that she had a larger household to feed. Alone for the first time in two days, I found my room too quiet. My thoughts wandered and I remembered Darius's request that I help him with his personal scribal needs while his man remained at the palace. A sudden shaft of excitement pierced my soul. This, I could do. This, I could do *well*. Perhaps seeing my ability, he would come to hold me in higher regard. He would learn to ascribe value to me. If I worked hard and exceeded his expectations, he might see my worth. I thought perhaps the Lord had opened this door for me. Tenaciously, I held on to that hope.

I checked on Caspian again and found that his breathing had slowed. I laid my hand against his chest. His heart continued to beat erratically, but it seemed fainter to me. He was still in the hold of a deep sleep. I tried to shake him awake; he remained unresponsive. I thought I had best send for Bardia to see if we needed to inform Darius of the change. He had posted a man outside my door and I dispatched him to fetch the head gardener.

Bardia came with a bowl of plucked jasmines "to cheer you, mistress," he said. Since hearing how much I loved their scent, he often brought me fresh blossoms in the mornings. He agreed with my summation of the dog's condition and went to inform Darius. I didn't expect him to come since the change was minor and the dog still unconscious. But within the hour he was back in my chamber.

He too had changed into fresh clothes. He had not slept, I could tell from the circles under his eyes, but his wet hair indicated that he had at least had a chance to bathe. He sat with Caspian for a few quiet moments, stroking his back.

"Could he stay like this?" I asked.

"Not for long."

"Then what?"

"He'll fade. His body has been under tremendous strain, and he has not been able to eat."

"But he could awake."

"It's possible."

"You don't think it likely, though, do you?"

"I won't give you false hope, if that's what you want."

"No, I want the truth."

"The truth is it's a miracle he has survived this long."

He left shortly after that to see to the arrangements for the estate. I lay down near Caspian. "Be a good dog and live," I said. "I don't want to lose you." Then I fell asleep.

Darius found me there when he came back to check on Caspian. "Why don't you go to bed? He won't get better because you lie on the floor."

I sat up. "I'm sorry, I didn't mean to fall asleep. I was supposed to keep watch."

"It isn't a situation where your staying vigilant can make a difference."

"My lord, what if he lingers like this for days?"

"I don't believe he shall." His voice was grim.

He thinks Caspian will die soon, I thought. I buried my face in my hand, trying not to cry. After a few moments of silence I said, "I don't think we'll make it to Damaspia's feast, even if Caspian were to . . . to recover by this evening." I was thinking of my previous travels to Ecbatana, which had taken weeks. I journeyed there with the queen's other servants in carts that bore her furnishings and clothes.

Darius lowered his brow. "If you take the royal road to Ecbatana, the journey lasts twenty days. But we would take the more direct routes, and arrive in ten."

"The more direct routes? The ones that cross mountains over narrow, skirting precipices?"

"They are difficult in places, I grant you. On horseback, they are manageable enough."

I shot up in dismay. "I cannot ride!"

Darius gave me a look of perfect incomprehension. "What do you mean you cannot ride?" He had grown up with Persian ladies who had been in the saddle from childhood and rode as well as some men. He had hunted and traveled with them. The idea that there might be a woman who had never sat astride a horse had not occurred to him, I was sure.

The Persian Empire was only six kings deep. The great Cyrus, the first Achaemenid ruler of an empire covering the vast majority of the known world, had started life as the king of an insignificant nation whose women were as fierce as its men. It wasn't so long ago that Persian women wore leather trousers and went to battle if their men were losing. Persian nobility might be civilized and covered in silks and perfume, but they still remembered the strength of their women. I even knew some princesses who were proficient at the use of the bow and lance. So the idea of a woman who could not ride landed like a foreign object in Darius's world.

Ashamed of my ignorance, I said, "I mean I don't know how to ride."

Darius lowered himself on the carpet next to me. "Well, then, you have two options. You can either ride with me and my men—an extremely uncomfortable prospect if you have never ridden before—and please the queen by your obedience, or you can travel in a cart and face her wrath for your lateness. The choice is up to you, as you will be the one paying the price in either case."

The speed and reach of Persian cavalry was unequaled. I thought of trying to keep up with that and lost my color. "Perhaps it won't come to that. Caspian might save the day by waking up after the feast."

My hopes were dashed not long after as Caspian's heartbeat became noticeably slower. He labored for every breath. Darius became still and watchful. Although Caspian remained unconscious, I thought he must be suffering, for his breath rattled with a horrible sound in his great chest. Darius bent over him and gave him a gentle stroke. "Hush boy. I'm here."

I couldn't keep the tears at bay; I knew Caspian was dying. In spite of Darius's warnings, I had held on to a thread of hope. "Thank you for everything," I said in his ear, my voice reflecting my broken heart.

It was almost a relief when he stopped breathing. I don't think I could have borne to watch him suffer much longer. I raised anguished eyes to Darius, knowing that he understood this awful loss. The sheen of tears blurred the green irises. For a moment we looked at each other with a pitiful understanding. Then I rose up and ran to my bed and burrowed under the covers and gave vent to a storm of uncontrollable weeping.

This was to be the first test of my young faith. Once again, the worst had happened. I had desperately wanted God to give me a miracle. I had longed to have Caspian back in my life. Instead, I had lost him forever.

Would I turn against God because He had allowed my faithful companion to die at the hands of a vicious criminal? Would I reject Him, call Him uncaring or weak? Or would I turn to Him for comfort?

"Help me!" I cried. "Help me cling to You." He had not answered my prayers to spare Caspian's life, but this prayer He answered with astounding speed. I was suddenly filled with peace, with comfort. I felt held in the grip of a presence so real, it almost seemed like physical touch.

I thought suddenly of the intricate series of coincidences that had caused my life to be spared. The queen sending my husband home after months of absence. His journey bringing him to my side moments before I would have tasted of that poisoned wine. Caspian knocking down the cup and drinking it—strangely out-of-character behavior for a dog that had never tried to consume my drink before. Had he not died in my place, I would most certainly have drunk that poison. It would have been my heart that stopped beating on this day.

I began to realize that my life had been spared not through a coincidence, but through a convoluted series of occurrences that seemed to point to God's provision. My Caspian had not died in vain. He had laid his life down for me. Instead of focusing on his death, I focused on this miracle. God had used Caspian to spare my life. Far from being indifferent to me, He had proven His care for me.

This thought made me miss Caspian all the more, but it also comforted me. His death was not a waste. He had purchased my life and health with it.

"Sarah." It was Darius's voice. I felt my bed dip under his weight as he sat next to me. "Will you come out from under there?"

I lowered the covers and sat up. I looked a mess I knew, with my hair standing on end and my eyes red and my skin splotchy. What came as a surprise to me was that Darius too seemed unlike himself. The perfect planes of his face had lost their usual sparkle, had turned sallow with dark, deep circles under his swollen eyes. I wished so badly to throw myself in his arms, to give and receive comfort, but the habits of a lifetime would not easily be broken, and I held myself back, stiff and miserable.

"My lord?"

"Bardia and I wish to bury Caspian in the garden. Bardia thought under my willow. Would you like to join us?"

I didn't trust my voice and just nodded. He rose to give me room to get out from under the covers. I straightened my skirts and slid out. Caspian was lying under a soft sheet of Egyptian cotton. Darius hefted his body into his arms. Though massive in life, he seemed diminished and vulnerable in death.

Shushan and Pari joined us by the willow and we watched as Darius and one of his men dug a deep trench near the willow tree. Softly, he picked up Caspian's body, held him close one last time, and laid him in the cold earth. Before they filled his grave completely, Bardia planted a number of bulbs over where his body lay. Next spring, this spot of death and sorrow would be transformed into a colorful garden of life.

Darius lingered over the fresh grave a few moments. "Not even Cyrus the Great could boast of a dog like you."

"You saved my life," I said. It seemed the perfect epithet for such a faithful creature.

A few hours later Pari and Shushan served a late lunch in my rooms. Shushan handed Darius a sealed letter before laying out our table. I noticed that he smiled grimly when he read the message inside.

I had no appetite for the duck cooked with walnuts and pomegranate paste, and the three different kinds of oven-hot bread. Darius had obviously managed to fill the kitchen's empty cupboards in short order. But I would just as soon have avoided the sight of food.

Darius seemed no more hungry than I. Into the silence he said, "We leave for Ecbatana tomorrow."

"Tomorrow?" I gasped. "What of Teispes? Don't you want to find him first?"

"I already have. The missive that I received earlier informs me that he was captured. He went into hiding overnight, but as you surmised, he surfaced late this morning at his courtesan's door. My men there picked him up and are bringing him back. With Caspian gone and Teispes in hand, we must leave for Ecbatana at first light." He stretched his arm behind my chair and turned in my direction. "Which means you must decide whether you will join me and my men in the morning or come later with your handmaiden."

Clearly he expected me to make a decision right away; my mind was in a confused jumble, however. The grief over Caspian's death seemed to have dulled my reasoning process. I lowered my eyes in a futile effort to shut Darius's body, leaning so close, out of my mind and tried to think through the choices before me.

I considered the hardship of riding with Darius and his men—unrelieved hours in an unfamiliar saddle, not to mention nights spent in a tent instead of the comforts of a posting station. On the other hand, I'd have to face Damaspia's disappointment if I chose the relative ease of a carriage. She had exerted her influence to intercede for me when she had sent Darius to fetch me. It was no small thing for the queen to interfere with a high aristocrat's personal life by issuing a direct command. In return for such thoughtfulness, she would have every right to expect my timely arrival. She was sure to perceive my lateness as an affront. Damaspia would not credit my inexperience as a rider a suitable excuse for lateness. One couldn't tell the queen of Persia that riding a long distance to see her was too inconvenient.

It occurred to me with sudden certainty that the Lord would give me the strength to do the right thing.

"I had better come with you, my lord, if you can put up with me, though I fear I will slow you down with my inexperience."

Chapter Eighteen

"Tell him you don't have riding clothes," Pari whispered in my ear.

I threw her an annoyed look. "Tell him!" she whispered louder.

I acknowledged to myself that I could not undertake such a journey without the proper gear. But the idea of turning to Darius in my need made my stomach churn. I did not wish to ask anything of him. He had resented me when I cost him nothing; now if I started asking for favors, he would no doubt be even more annoyed.

Well, there was no help for it. "My lord. I ask pardon, but I own no clothes that would be suitable for riding."

"So take them from the storehouse. Your servant can surely make adjustments where needed."

"Uh, we don't have access to the storehouses, my lord."

"What do you mean you don't . . . Ah. Teispes?"

I nodded.

He strode to the door. "Come with me." He motioned to me. "And you," he added to Pari. He marched us to the storehouses and used his own key to let us in.

"Take everything you need." He lingered with us for a few moments, rummaging through shelves. "Here are some clothes that would serve." He handed them to Pari. I turned to leave, but he signaled me to remain and continued searching.

"Here they are." He pulled several packages from a row of shelves at the far end of the room. "It's too dark here to see. Come into my chamber and I will show you."

Since the storehouses were closer to the location of his apartments, it made sense for us to meet there.

One of his men was stationed outside his door, ramrod straight and alert. Darius addressed him before walking in. "Arta, could you saddle Kidaris please? Take a good lamp and wait for me in the stables."

"Right away, my lord."

I wondered where Darius planned to ride as I followed him into his rooms. I had not been there since the first day Pari had coaxed me out of my dark cave of despair. I stood stiffly to one side, not going in very far. Entering into his personal domain made me uncomfortable. I felt that I was intruding into his private world. That I didn't belong there.

With a careless motion, Darius dropped his packages upon a green sofa with silver lion's feet. "Pari, let me see the riding gear."

Pari handed Darius her bundle. Unfolding it, Darius pushed aside a sachet of mint, rosemary, and eucalyptus before unearthing a pair of clay-colored linen trousers, quilted at the seat and gathered on the side seams for easier movement. The top was made of two layers of sheer white linen, split on the sides. It was a feminine outfit, judging by its size and cut, and the

225

embroidery at the edges of the sleeves and the hem. "This was my mother's. It might serve. You may try it through there." He pointed to his bedchamber, which connected to his sitting room through an open archway.

I had never donned trousers in my life. I took the garments with uncertain fingers and signaled Pari to follow me. The trousers, which wrapped around my waist with a drawstring, fit well enough. But the tunic was tight around the chest, and too sheer.

"Let's see you," Darius called from the other room.

I made a few attempts at speech, none of which ended in discernible words.

"Well?" he prodded again.

"My lord, it's not decent! I can't come out."

"Nonsense," he called. "My mother used to wear those all the time." To my horror he appeared at the door. I crossed my arms in a feeble attempt at modesty, and bit my lip to keep myself from yelling at him to get out.

"I see." He pulled on an earlobe. "Perhaps there was more to it than I remember." I threw him a dirty look.

He held up his hands as if in surrender. "I'm leaving. Pari, can you sort that tunic out for your mistress? There must be an under tunic somewhere back in the storehouse that I overlooked." On his way out he said, "Sarah, would you please join me when you change?"

I had no desire to be within the same four walls as him after the embarrassment of being seen in diaphanous clothing, but what choice had I? Dressed in my own modest, full-skirted dress, I returned to him, my face flaming. To give him credit, he made no comment.

"I was thinking you could wear this for the opening feast of the equinox celebrations." In his hands he was holding a turquoise silk garment with golden embroidery at the edge of the sleeves and throughout the skirt.

I gasped. "It's beautiful."

"My mother set it aside for my bride. There's a chest full of things in the storehouse."

He said *bride*, singular, which confused me. I came to the conclusion that his mother must have set things apart for his *Jewish* wife. I didn't feel worthy of the gift given that I was a poor sort of wife—one in name only.

"I'll wear it if you wish, of course. But you can have it back afterward."

"Don't you like it?"

"It's exquisite. I . . . it isn't right that you give it to me. You should save it for another."

He sat on the couch and dangled his feet off the end. "You surprise me. In fact, it's a habit with you. You rarely do or say what I expect."

I flattened my back against the wall. "At least you're not bored."

"Irritated, frustrated, discombobulated, infuriated. But not bored. I'll grant you that."

Pari showed her good sense by arriving, which spared me from having to answer Darius's extraordinary comment. She had a clay-colored undergarment folded over her arms. "I believe I have found the right garment, my lord."

"Good. Would you please put the garments on again? And try these," he added, throwing me a pair of soft leather shoes.

"But I just had them on!"

"Humor me."

With ill grace I retired to his inner chamber and changed once again. The tunic was still tight, but I was now covered with a modicum of decency thanks to Pari's fruitful search. "I can loosen it before you leave tomorrow," she assured me.

I pulled the shoes on as I walked back for Darius's scrutiny and was happy to find they fit.

He nodded when he saw me. "Here, catch." He threw a thin summer shawl my way. I draped it loosely over my head and shoulders, glad for the added coverage.

"Off to the stables we go."

"The *stables*?"

"Yes. Surely you've heard of them? It's a place in which they keep horses—those things you don't ride."

I had barely slept in two days. A dear animal I had come to love as my own was gone. I faced a journey I dreaded. I had no patience for cryptic remarks. My voice was syrupy with sarcasm as I answered. "Such a fount of information you are. How *do* you bear being so clever all the time?" There was no hint of offense in his soft answering laughter, however.

At the stables we found his man, Arta, waiting next to a saddled chestnut mare. It seemed huge to me.

"Sarah, meet Kidaris. She's one of my gentlest horses. But she also has the stamina to keep up with the rest of the horses. You'll become very good friends over the next few days. Come close and greet her properly."

No wonder he had insisted on my wearing riding clothes. He wanted me to meet my horse and grow comfortable with her before our early morning departure. And I thought he was baiting me to be annoying. I regretted my acerbic comment and tried to make up for it by being as biddable as I was able.

The horse gave a friendly neigh as I took a faltering step forward. Her pure chestnut coat was marked by a white spot high on her forehead. It looked like a royal tiara. Hence the name *Kidaris*, I realized, which meant *crown* in Persian. "Hello, Kidaris."

228

"She likes being petted like this."

I tried to mimic Darius. Unlike his sure, familiar movements, my touch was hesitant.

"No, don't show her fear. She needs to know you're in charge from the start. Be confident. Step closer. Let her grow accustomed to you."

"She's a lot bigger than I am."

"Yes, and you're still in charge."

I'm in charge I'm in charge I'm in charge. I kept repeating the words in my head, hoping to believe them. Darius handed me a brush and had me gently groom Kidaris. After some time I felt comfortable enough to enjoy being near the horse.

"Good," Darius pronounced. "Now you must learn to sit properly. This is the most important part of riding. You must sit straight so that your weight is divided equally between the two sides of the horse. If your balance is wrong, you will throw her balance off as well, and she won't like it."

He helped me into the saddle and adjusted the stirrups. I could see why I needed the trousers and the split tunic. Darius coached me on my posture. "You're slouching. And your legs are too far forward. You'll lose control that way. Keep your seat using your thighs."

For half the length of an hour he made me sit on Kidaris without moving, critiquing my every fidget. Then he spent another hour showing me the rudimentary lessons of riding. My back was burning by the end of our training. I wondered how I would manage to canter hour after hour, day after day. I felt small and physically unequal to the task.

Pari and I were up late into the night, adjusting the tunic and the turquoise dress Darius had given me. Pari was scheduled to follow in a cart with most of Darius's and my luggage the following morning, accompanied by two of Darius's men.

I hadn't thought it wise to bring Pari with me; she was even more unfamiliar with horses than I was, and had told me she harbored a mortal fear of them. So I had arranged for her to travel with the luggage train; they would travel across the main royal highway, which was a longer but supremely more comfortable ride.

She helped me pack a small bundle of my most basic necessities for the days I would be in Ecbatana without her or my baggage.

"What shall I do without you for ten whole days?" I said as we retired to bed. "What if I make another wreck of things at the feast?"

"You will not. You have learned much in the past few months. Besides, I'm certain the queen will send you assistance. Only this time, don't turn her away."

I groaned and pulled the covers closer about me. It would be the last time I would have the luxury of a bed for some days. But I couldn't enjoy it. I missed the weight of Caspian's solid body resting at my feet.

I lay wakeful through the watches of the night, dreading the morning, certain I would become a nuisance to my husband, and that he would come to like me even less because of it. In my misery, I longed for the comfort of Caspian's presence more than ever.

Finally I remembered to cling to the Lord and His mercy. Every time a fearful thought rushed against my mind, I turned my attention back on the Lord instead of chasing the trails of my disturbing imaginings. Rather than focusing on my fears, I focused on God. And in the end, I slipped into a peaceful sleep.

Darius was accompanied by seven of his men, the rest having been dispatched on various assignments, or directed to remain in his palace. I was the only woman in the train, and the only one who could not ride. He stayed close by my horse, his black stallion towering over my mare. To my surprise, Kidaris tried to bite the stallion.

Darius leaned close and pulled on my reins with a firm hand until Kidaris turned her head with docile obedience. "Keep your horse under control or mine will hurt you both," he snapped. "Hold the reins as I showed you."

"What's his name?" I asked.

"Samson."

Taken aback by the Jewish name I repeated, "Samson?"

"My mother named him. He was huge and strong even as a foal. I've never trimmed his mane in honor of his namesake."

So his mother had taught him something of our history and faith. I had no time to process this brief revelation as he signaled us to start our journey. My whole concentration was spent on trying to cling to my horse.

We started our journey at a trot. I could sense that the men were impatient to canter as soon as the road stretched straight before us, but Darius kept the pace gentle for another hour. I realized that he was giving me time to grow accustomed to the movement of the horse. I was at once relieved and distressed by his thoughtfulness. I knew I was a bother to him and his men. That realization more than anything drove me to try to keep up, to push myself beyond my ability. I could not bear the thought that I caused others inconvenience, for I was convinced that they would turn from me. Had this not been a lesson I had learned well in childhood? Had I not proven a nuisance to my own father, who rejected me because of it?

231

I knew that if I proved useful in some way, I might be tolerated. Perhaps even valued. But deep down, I also knew that except for my linguistic and administrative talents, I had little to offer. I cost more than I was worth. And I wanted with all my might to hide this secret from others for as long as I could.

So after an hour when Darius instructed me on how to canter, I did my best to keep up. I made no complaint when my back began to burn and my thighs started to tremble from strain. I held my back as straight as I could and recited the Scriptures to keep my mind from the pain.

"Are you all right?" Darius asked more than once.

As if I would admit that I felt like my back was breaking. "Perfect," I responded and ignored his concerned look. I was disconcerted by his solicitous attitude. For a man who showed me the sharp side of his tongue at every opportunity, he was being bewilderingly attentive. In spite of his fastidious upbringing, he had no problem squelching the demands of good manners in order to step all over me on most days. It dawned on me that in spite of his protestations, he had softened toward me as a result of my role in dealing with Teispes.

At the outer edges of the fertile plains of Persepolis, we arrived at a thin stream where Darius called a halt. I could not dismount alone. It wasn't that I didn't know how to swing my leg over and down; it's that my muscles would not obey. I just sat atop Kidaris and hoped someone would fetch me down. Darius did. Without a word, he wrapped his hands about my waist and lifted me off the horse like I weighed no more than a sack of wheat. I found my legs were trembling. Darius must have noticed for he kept his hands about my back and held me up until I gained some strength.

Desperate to free him from having to take care of me I said, "I'm fine now, thank you."

One corner of his mouth tipped slightly and he stepped away. "As you wish."

I wobbled my way to a grassy patch on the side of the road. One of the men was rubbing my horse down with dried grass and watering her. The sun had risen in the sky two hours since and I was almost as sweaty as Kidaris. I stretched on the grass and groaned. I knew it was unseemly to lie down before eight men, but I hadn't enough reserves to care. We would be on the road soon enough and I did not know how to face the many hours that still stretched before me. I closed my eyes and tried not to think of it.

A shadow fell over my face and I forced my eyes open. "Drink this." Darius held out a leather container.

"Thank you for your thoughtfulness; I'm not thirsty." During my previous travels, I had been part of a huge train. There were special screens and tents designed for modesty so that the travelers could take care of their needs with a modicum of privacy. With eight men and eight horses as my sole companions, I'd just as soon not drink anything and hope my body wouldn't need to relieve itself until the cover of night. I certainly wasn't about to put any liquid into it if I didn't have to.

"Don't be foolish. You can't ride in the heat without drinking something. You'll be sick before sundown."

I sighed and forced myself to sit up. With a bit of good fortune, I'd perspire the lot out of my skin. He tipped the leather container into his own mouth after I had finished and drank thirstily.

"How long do we rest?" I asked.

He handed me a piece of barley bread. "Not long. Once we and the horses have had a chance to eat and drink, we'll be on the road again."

By the time we remounted, the heat had become overbearing. I pulled my scarf over my brow, trying to shield my eyes. Flies seemed drawn to the scent of the horses; as we started on a slow trot, they gathered around us in thick hordes. Being unselfish beasts, the horses shared their pests with their human burdens. I was too busy trying to keep my seat to swat them away.

The day stretched long as I rode hour after hour, trying to keep up with men who had sat in the saddle since before they could walk. I became aware that the pace was slow for them; for me, however, it was a torment. I felt dizzy from the heat and constant movement.

To my horror, I could no longer delay the need to relieve myself. It was high afternoon, and bright as the day can be. When we took our break, I looked about me, desperate to find a spot that might offer even a little privacy. I had begun to wonder if Darius could read my mind, for he seemed to know my thoughts with alarming frequency.

"Come with me," he said, as he perceived me canvassing the area. I followed him with relief to a copse nearby, which boasted a few skinny trees. Not exactly the height of privacy. I gave him an anguished look.

"I will warn everyone to stay away. You'll be fine here." If he had so much as cracked one smile I would have forgotten my intentions to be on my best behavior and kicked him. He was too wise to do anything but turn his back and move off.

With a burst of inspiration, I took off my long wrap and draped it over a few bushes like a makeshift low curtain. But when I bent down, my muscles were so weakened from the rigors of riding that instead of squatting, I ended up falling on my knees with a crash.

"Are you all right?" Darius called from somewhere beyond.

"Stay where you are!" I yelled, panicked at the thought

234

that he might take it into his head to come and investigate. "I'm fine." *Humiliated. Degraded. But fine.* Had I once really thought I enjoyed traveling?

After this, which proved to be our last rest before we stopped for the night, Darius pushed us hard. Once we left the pleasant plateau of Persepolis, we entered a desert-like stretch of road, which was merciless in its brutal heat. We cantered until I could not even pretend to sit straight. At one point I must have fallen asleep in the saddle, for I woke up with a start when an arm wrapped around my middle. Before I could ask a question, I was lifted high into the air and deposited unceremoniously before my husband in the saddle.

Darius turned around. "Arta, take care of Kidaris, please. Her ladyship will ride with me the rest of today."

I was wide awake now, trying to sit on my husband's lap in such a way that did not bring me in close contact with his body. The inconvenient thing about horses is that such a desire can simply not be gratified. I sat as rigid as an arrow not knowing what to do with myself.

He shifted my weight against him until I was leaning fully into his chest. "Relax," he said into my ear, his voice low and soothing. "Samson is sensing your lack of ease. Stop tensing up and try to go back to sleep."

For the sake of the horse, I did my best to comply. I melted against Darius, wriggling to find a comfortable spot. I felt the muscles of his chest tense up against my back. "You're not very relaxed yourself," I accused.

"Can't a man have some peace atop his own horse?" he growled.

Surprised at his suddenly foul mood I said, "I'm sorry to cause so much trouble to you."

Instead of answering, he pushed my body forward onto the

235

saddle, as far away from him as the tiny space allowed. I swiveled my head to look at him. "Am I too heavy?"

"No, you're not too heavy. Now stop squirming and be still. We have several hours of riding before we break camp."

Chapter Nineteen

By the time the sun sank into the horizon and we had to stop, sleep wrapped me in its hold again and I barely noticed when Darius deposited me on a dry embankment while he and his men took care of the horses and set up tents for the night. The days had grown long; we had managed to ride a fair distance.

In previous years, when I accompanied the king and queen's train on their frequent journeys, I had been astounded by the luxury of their mobile accommodations; most palaces paled in comparison with their tents. The court engineers had devised a complex structure made of leather and bronze, containing many rooms, which accommodated royal formalities. Rich hangings, decorations in silver and gold, bejeweled couches, and bronze pillars gave the illusion that we were ensconced in yet another of the king's palaces, instead of a mere tent. I had heard that the king and his noble generals traveled in similar style even when riding out to war. But Darius's tents were plain soldier's fare, ambulatory and light, appropriate gear for the back of a fast horse.

I was past caring. If he had left me on my bit of dried grass, I would not have complained. He had other ideas, though. "Come. Your tent is ready," he said, crouching next to me. I ignored him, wishing him away so that I could go back to sleep.

"Sarah, get up. You cannot stay out here."

"Yes, my lord." I stayed where I was.

He lifted me up and carried me to the tent. The opening was quite low and he had to bend to enter in. I saw through half closed eyes that a lamp was already burning, and that he had set up a bedroll. He dropped me on the thin mattress none too gently. To my surprise, he did not leave.

"Good night," I said, wondering why he abided.

"I can't leave you like this," he said, sounding irritated.

"Like what?" I asked, equally irritated.

"Sarah, this was your first day in a saddle and you've ridden for hours. If you think you're in pain today, you have no inkling of how you will feel tomorrow. Your muscles will seize and you will be in agony."

I stopped feeling sleepy. "If this is your rendition of an encouraging speech, may I say that it is something short of inspiring?"

"It is no speech. Just truth. You have been brave today, I know. Not one word of complaint passed your lips during the length of the journey. But not all the courage in the world will get you back in the saddle tomorrow if your muscles will not cooperate."

I broke into a toothy smile. "You thought I was brave?"

"That's not the salient point."

"Well, I don't know what to do about the salient point."

He placed a small earthen jar on the bedroll. "This is a balm prepared by the magi, which helps with muscle pain. You need to massage it deeply in order for it to have effect. You can't apply it at skin level; it needs to be pressed deep into the flesh. Do you understand?"

I opened the lid of the jar and sniffed. It smelled like chamomile and licorice. "I understand. Massage it deep."

"Show me."

"*Pardon?*"

"I won't have you waste my good medicine by ill usage, nor will I delay my arrival at Ecbatana due to simple ignorance. Show me you know what to do and I will leave you to it."

"I believe I grasped your simple instructions."

"Then get on with it. I'd like to rest too, if you have no objection."

I remembered that he had already made this ten-day journey once, to arrive home and face a dire emergency, a dying dog, and little sleep, and had been forced to carry my weight for the past three hours besides. "I am sorry," I said and willed myself to sit up.

The sooner I accomplished what he asked, the sooner he would feel released to see to his own comfort. I bit my lip and pulled the hem of my trousers up to my calf. I buried the tips of my fingers into the jar and grabbed some balm. At first I did my best to massage it deep into my flesh, but I had not counted on the pain I encountered at the simple touch. It felt as if my whole lower body was one giant bruise, and no matter where I touched, it hurt. I ground my teeth and did my best to comply with Darius's instructions.

Obviously I failed. He pushed my hand away and took over the massage himself. I squealed, shocked at his touch, and then forgot my embarrassment as the pain took over. I buried my face in my arms to keep from crying out.

He stopped. "Like that. You need to apply it like that."

I nodded and sat up again. "I will."

"Let's see."

Once again I took the balm and did my best to emulate Darius's movements. He stopped me after a few moments. "It won't do. The salve won't take effect like this. You'll have to let me do it."

"No! What do you mean? I'll ride tomorrow, I promise. I won't be a bother to you or the others. I won't complain."

"Sarah, you don't know what you say. Without this treatment, you will be in no condition to ride by dawn." Forgoing further argument, he grabbed the jar and taking a liberal amount of balm he began to massage it into one calf, then another. My embarrassment paled in comparison to the pain. I ground my teeth and did my best to swallow my groans. When he was finished, I barely had the strength to sigh with relief. I pulled down my trouser legs. "Thank you, my lord."

He sat back and did not move. He was wearing the impassive expression that I had come to recognize as a signal for trouble. Usually for me. With sudden certainty it dawned on me that he was not done. I squeezed my eyes shut and begged. *Lord, have mercy.*

"There's more," I said.

"The worst pain will be in the flesh of your thighs."

If I had been his wife in more than name, this situation would have been nothing but a painful inconvenience. But we had shared no intimacies. He had not held me as a bridegroom holds a bride. Which made the notion of baring myself to his touch utterly disconcerting.

Again I realized that the more time I spent arguing, the more I delayed his rest. It was no fault of his that we were caught in this situation. He was trying to help, and my bash-fulness was an added discomfort to him. After all, he must feel as awkward as I in the circumstances. I decided that the best thing for us both would be for me to comply with his wishes, and to do so without fuss.

"Would you turn around for a moment, please?" I asked. There was a spark of surprise on his face. For the shortest moment I thought I caught a whisper of approval in the soft-ening of his lips. Then he turned around and I focused on removing my trousers. I pulled down the tunic as low as it would go and threw the blanket over me as I turned face-down.

"I'm ready," I said.

He was right; the flesh of my thighs was in worse condi-tion than my lower legs. Though he did his best to spare me, I felt dizzy with the agony of it. When he was, at long last, truly done, he said, "I'm sorry to have caused you pain."

"It's not your fault," I said, my face half buried in the blan-ket. "You've done me a service; I thank you."

"I'll wake you before dawn," he said and from the sound of the tent flap opening, I knew that he had left.

I cannot recall much from the rest of that journey other than it seemed interminable, although we achieved in ten days what it usually took the queen's caravan three weeks to accom-plish. After three days my body grew sufficiently accustomed to riding that the pain in my muscles gradually lessened. By the end of our journey I could sit a horse well enough to satisfy my Persian husband's notions of horsemanship. Even on the high mountain passes, far from the breadth and comfort of the royal highways, I kept my seat with confidence. Toward the end of our journey, I was sufficiently accustomed to the rigors of fast travel that I began to take notice of the changing landscape around us. Sweltering desert gave way to the steppes, which gave way to wooded mountains and breathtaking forests. As we entered the region of Media, its splendor and verdure took my breath. Every hour brought us upon a new stream, a frothing river, a fertile field.

We arrived at Ecbatana on the morning of the feast of equinox. As I rode past the city's walls, I remembered again my time of prayer with God. I thought, *I am not riding in alone. The Lord is with me. He will be my help and my shield.*

I recalled the endless practical difficulties that I faced—getting ready for a royal feast in a handful of hours without Pari, looking presentable so that I might undo some of the damage I had done to Darius on our wedding day, facing the queen's questions—and rather than being overcome by anxiety, I felt an inexplicable peace. I knew my capacity for failure; knew how badly I could mishandle this night. But as I yielded to God, I felt more consoled by His power than fearful of my weaknesses.

Ecbatana was smaller and older than Persepolis. Yet its fabled splendor was the subject of many stories, new and ancient. Though I had been there before, I still found the sight of carved, gilded columns and cedar ceilings with beams plated in either gold or silver awe-inspiring. It was as though the very building accused me of being unworthy to walk its august hallways.

Darius and I had been given lodgings in the palace proper for the duration of our stay. I had expected to be assigned space in the women's quarters. Instead when we arrived, I discovered that an apartment had been designated for the two of us. It was a shocking arrangement and felt like one of

Damaspia's artful plans. I tried not to think what motive lay at the foundation of such an unusual provision. Another bet with the king, probably.

I found our chambers to be a tight squeeze. There would be no room for either Darius's man or my Pari. The main room, exquisitely tiled in deep blues and greens with drawings of peacocks and flowers, boasted one bed. I had spent years sleeping soundly on a simple bedroll on the ground; I'd have no problem spreading one on the floor of the tiny annex to our chamber.

What I wanted more than anything was a hot bath. I smelled of horse sweat. An oily mixture of dust and my own perspiration covered my skin. Darius was busy seeing to his men. I decided to try and arrange a bath for him also, knowing that he was no less eager to feel clean. To my delight, I found my old nemesis, the queen's chief handmaiden, standing outside my door when I pulled it open.

She addressed me as her lady and bowed as if she meant it. I remembered not to allow my mouth to hang open for too long. No wonder Darius thought I had tried to trap him into marriage. It was extraordinary how differently one was treated after becoming the beneficiary of a title.

"Her Majesty sent me to assist you with your preparations. She's been on the lookout for your arrival since yesterday."

Trust Damaspia to be one step ahead of me. "Thank you. After a ten-day ride, I'm in dire need of a bath. And the lord Darius will no doubt need one as well. Is it possible to arrange a private one for him in these rooms rather than send him off to the palace bathhouse? They are bound to be very busy so close to the feast."

I used the women's bath, with which I was familiar from previous stays at Ecbatana. The queen's handmaiden sent a servant to see to my every need while she whisked away my wrinkled clothes. Within the hour, I was blissfully clean; I had started to dread I might never know that feeling again. Wrapped in a crisp robe and matching veil that smelled of orange blossoms I wound my way to our apartments.

My husband bid *enter* when I knocked. I found him immersed in a steaming tub.

"I beg your pardon!"

"Ah. I thought you were the servant with more hot water."

I counted the cracks in the ceiling and examined the design in the tiles. Anything to keep me from looking in his direction. "I will prepare in the women's quarters," I said and grabbing what I needed, slipped out. I thought I heard him laugh as I shut the door firmly behind me.

The chief handmaiden herself saw to my preparations. Damaspia clearly had no intention of leaving matters in my hands this time. After hours of careful ministrations I was as ready as I could be for the evening. I returned to Darius and my rooms, hoping he would be presentable by now. Arta opened the door before I knocked.

Darius was arrayed in a long ceremonial silk tunic. Its design, form-fitting and long with a bank of pleats in the front and tight trousers peeking beneath, emphasized his massive chest and made his legs seem even longer. I realized the colors of our garments were made to match; his tunic was of the same midnight blue as my undergarment, which peeked through my overdress of aqua and gold.

I had been made up carefully, my hair arranged in dainty tucks and braids atop my head and decorated with gold bands, my lips painted a deep red that accentuated their fullness.

Darius held out an embroidered box to me. "I believe these match your garments."

Inside the box, I found two identical gold pins in the shape of rosettes, with flawless turquoise centers, and a dazzling pair of hanging gold earrings decorated with more turquoise.

Darius stepped forward. "May I?" he asked, holding out his hand.

I placed the pins in his outstretched palm. He attached one to the top of each shoulder, causing the neckline of my dress to open wider. His lids lowered so that I could not see the expression in them. "They suit you," he said.

My heart was beating so hard I could scarcely speak and I didn't try. With trembling fingers, I hung the earrings in my ears. For a moment we stared at each other. I could not fathom what he was thinking; I only knew that my own heart was filled with longing. In that moment I recognized that longing for what it was. I recognized that I loved my husband.

Unaware of the enormity of my discovery or the sheer terror that filled my soul in its wake, Darius waved a hand. "Shall we?"

I walked alongside him, balanced on my dainty high-heeled slippers, reeling inside. I could not allow him ever to know my secret, I decided. At best he would pity me.

"The king and queen have invited us to a private audience before the feast," Darius said.

"Oh."

"I forgot to thank you for arranging my bath. That was thoughtful."

"Mmm."

"I don't believe I have ever known you to be so parsimonious with your words. Is anything amiss?"

"No." *Of course there is. I'm in love with you and you barely tolerate me.*

The guards ushered us before the royal couple with flattering haste. The king descended from his throne to stand before me; he lifted my lowered head with his own hand. "So this is what you *really* look like?"

"No, Your Majesty. I fear I only look like this when the queen's chief handmaiden is done applying her craft to me."

Artaxerxes burst out laughing. "An honest woman." He turned to Darius. "So how do you like your bride now, cousin?"

"She has certainly improved her appearance."

"I hear she's done more than that. I hear she's cleansed your household of a piece of reeking garbage."

"How in the world would you know that, Your Majesty? We just arrived into Ecbatana."

The king grinned. "I know everything."

Darius crossed his arms. "And I assumed my men reported solely to me."

"Don't hold it against them. I'm hard to resist. Besides, I received the merest hint of a story and am impatient to hear the details."

To my growing discomfort, I found myself the center of the king and queen's attention. They were more exacting in their questions than a military interrogator. I did my best to keep my account as general as possible. The king, dissatisfied with my brief overview, pressed for specifics. And Damaspia, too shrewd to let any detail go and more familiar with my nature, managed to drag out of me the account of how I stole Teispes's key as well as the details of my conversation with the shopkeeper.

"You told him you were a *what*?" Darius barked when he heard that part.

The king sputtered. "You were wasted as a scribe. I should have used you for a spy." Which was quite a compliment coming from the king of an empire whose network of spies set the spine of great foreign leaders atremble.

Thankfully, Darius picked up the thread of the tale at the end and told our royal audience about the poisoned wine. Artaxerxes forgot his good humor. "The man tried to kill your wife?" He seemed lost for words for a few moments. "Though being the king of a vast empire is fraught with many threats, I fear no other kingdoms or rulers. It is our own people who will determine the future of Persia. If we are birthing and nurturing men like your steward, then their deceit will bury us alive down the coils of time. One Teispes can hold many good folks under the yoke of his lies, as you have seen. A whole nation's character can be twisted by the actions of a few corrupt men."

I understood why the king found it hard to swallow Teispes's rampant corruption. Persians believed themselves the most honest people in the world. Woven through the fabric of their religion was the belief that without truth, the universe itself would be undone, lost to perpetual evil. Honesty was more than a mere ideal. It constituted the very foundation of life.

I sympathized with Artaxerxes' outraged distress. And yet, it seemed to me impossible to keep a whole kingdom sheltered from subterfuge and corruption. Beliefs, no matter how lofty, could not overcome human nature. Evil was not a Persian problem; it was a human problem. This was why the Lord, whose standards for truth and honesty were even more exacting than a Persian's, also provided us with sacrifices to cover our inevitable failures.

"And how does the dog fare?" Damaspia asked.

"The dog died, Your Majesty," Darius said, his voice grave.

"I am sorry to hear it. He sounds like a noble creature."

It was considered ill-mannered to cry before the king or queen. I swallowed the pricking tears as best I could. "He was a delightful animal, *duksis*."

247

"A great loss then. And yet, had he not died, it seems certain that our Sarah would have. I cannot regret the exchange."

I was shaken by Damaspia's gracious words. "You are too kind, Your Majesty."

She gave me the benefit of one of her ravishing smiles. "And now we really must inaugurate that feast, my love," she said to her husband. "They will not begin without us."

As we walked down a wide hallway flanked by members of the King's ever-present elite guard, the Immortals, Damaspia addressed me. "There's so much more I'd like to ask you. I have not seen you this whole summer. Why don't you come hunting with me in the morning? It's an intimate gathering of close friends and we'll have time to speak."

At the mention of hunting I blanched. I had hoped not to come near a horse for many days yet. Of course I could not say so to the Queen. "I'm at your service, Majesty."

"One part of the story I left out," Darius said, "was that Sarah had never been on a horse until our journey to Ecbatana. She made it in ten days, but I doubt she'll be much good at a hunt by tomorrow."

I had not expected him to intercede for me. He could have let Damaspia have her way. He could have saved himself the trouble of intervening with a person of higher rank and possibly earning her ire. Instead he chose to inconvenience himself in order to protect me. I thought of how in the whole of my life I could count on my fingers the number of times anyone had spoken up in order to shield me.

Damaspia whisked her beautiful head in my direction. "You kept up with the men without ever having ridden before? How did you manage that?"

Forcing a lightness I did not feel into my voice, I said, "I was so grateful to have escaped death by poisoning that a little saddle sore hardly seemed worth mentioning."

"You haven't lost your sense of humor, I see. Well, we certainly wouldn't wish to put you back in a saddle so soon. Come and visit me before supper, then."

I bowed my head. "It would be an honor."

There was no time for more conversation. We stood before the carved gates of Ecbatana's great hall. The trumpet was blown to announce the royal couple's entrance and every guest stood. Darius and I followed in the wake of Artaxerxes and Damaspia, keeping a respectful distance. To my horror, I found myself the focus of more stares than even the king and queen.

The last time I had entered a gathering of royals and courtiers, I had been the oddity whose appearance had prompted endless laughter. Tonight, the crowd was thirsty for more entertainment. Their curious stares sought me out, bore into me, examined me with minute interest until I felt my heart pound with panic.

The shame of that evening had never left me. Not all the beauty treatments in Persia, nor the most stunning garments in the world could have made me feel like I was acceptable amongst these people. With sudden force my mind returned to my wedding night. I *was* an oddity. I *was* unacceptable. I was ugly. I came to a halt and could not make my feet take one more step. In the middle of the great hall, I stopped, soaked in shame, helpless with fear.

Chapter Twenty

I was shocked out of my paralyzed state when Darius wrapped his fingers around my shaking hand. He smiled at me, ignoring the fact that I had broken etiquette by freezing in the middle of our public procession. "I should have told you earlier this evening," he said as if we were conversing in the privacy of our own chamber and not in the presence of every important head of state, "how lovely you look tonight." He nodded his head once with a kind of gravity, as if assuring me that he spoke truth. Then he pulled on my hand and I followed him blindly to a couch near the head of the hall.

I hung my head low to avoid the weight of so much curiosity directed my way. Darius put a gentle finger under my chin and lifted my head up. "You have nothing to be ashamed of before these people."

"You of all people know why I can't face them. I feel so stupid. They will always think of me as an object of scorn. And they are right."

He crossed his arms and leaned back. "What happened that night concerns you and me. Your account is with me. To them, you owe nothing."

I bowed my head. He leaned toward me and lifted my chin again. This time, he held me firmly until he had my attention. "You are my wife. You are here with me. That's all they need to know. Now stiffen your resolve and win back the ground you lost. This time, I am with you."

"Thank you," I whispered, my voice wobbly.

"What was the first thing I taught you about Kidaris?"

"The *horse*?"

"Your mare, yes. What did I teach you about her?"

"That I shouldn't be afraid of her even though she's bigger than me?"

"Exactly. There isn't that much difference between the people here and your horse."

I couldn't help cracking a smile at that. I was a bit scandalized by his easy scorn of the cream of Persia.

"That's better," he said. "You have a lovely smile."

This was the second time he had called me lovely tonight. In spite of the fact that I knew that he abhorred lying, I could not swallow such a statement from him. I heard his words, but I couldn't bring my heart to believe them.

"You've been very gracious. I am beholden to you. Thank you also for getting me out of the hunt tomorrow. I can't imagine sitting astride a horse come sunrise. Holding my eyes open at the moment is about all I can manage."

Darius leaned over and picked up the bejeweled knife laid at our table, and with it cut a piece of the stuffed quince we had just been served and offered it to me. "I know you're tired. It's been an exhausting week for you. Unfortunately, though I am certain you wish nothing more than to retire, we will be one of the last to leave this evening. We shall feast the night away and show everyone that we are in accord, and that there is no substance to the empty gossip circulating about us."

As he had foreseen, it was late by the time Darius and I retired to our diminutive apartment. As soon as we entered, I headed for the nook where one of the royal servants had delivered a bedroll upon my request. There was no way that I could go to sleep in my heirloom garments. I sat on the mattress and tried to think of a way to undress with Darius in plain view on the other side of the room.

"What are you doing?" he asked, coming toward me.

"Making ready for bed."

"You're not going to sleep here." He tilted his head toward the large ornate bed in the corner of the room. "Get in there."

I'm sure I must have turned scarlet.

He took a step back. "I didn't mean . . . I meant I shall sleep on the floor and you will have the bed. I am not going to drag a woman halfway through the length of Persia and then make her sleep on the floor."

"I am accustomed to sleeping on the ground."

"I don't care."

I was too tired to argue. Without a word I rose and dragged myself to the bed. I sat down and once again tried to work out how to undress in the same room as my husband.

"Sarah? I forgot to tell you; I had word from the men I sent to find Teispes's brother. They will come tomorrow and bring his accounts as well as Mandana's receipts. We will need to go through them and get them in order. Can you help?"

My face fell. The Sabbath had begun hours before. The daylight hours belonged to the Lord. I had broken the Sabbath more than once, but I hadn't fully surrendered my life to God then. I had promised myself that I would not give in to easy compromises anymore. "My lord, I . . . cannot."

He raised an eyebrow. "Of course. I shouldn't have expected that you'd wish to work as a scribe now that you are in an elevated position."

"It isn't that!" I stood up and took a step toward him. "It isn't that at all!" I thought of the irony that prevented me from helping him when at long last I had an opportunity. I could not understand the timing of God. Why would He close this door when He knew it was my only chance at making my husband value me? "It is the Sabbath you see—the Jewish day of rest. The Lord demands that we keep the Sabbath holy. And I . . . want so much to honor Him better than I have done in the past."

To my relief, the tight line of his mouth softened. "The Sabbath. I know what that is. My mother kept it." He turned around. Over his shoulder he said, "It would harm none if we dealt with the accounts one day later, I suppose."

I let my breath out with relief. "I will enjoy seeing what kind of accounts Teispes's brother keeps. I wonder if they are as outrageous as his brother's."

Darius yawned. "The mere mention of accounts puts me to sleep, I own. I'm off to my bed." He blew out the lamps and drenched the room in darkness, thereby solving my problem of how to prepare for bed in his presence.

In spite of my exhaustion, I found myself wakeful, my thoughts awhirl. Once again Darius had stood up for me. He had championed me before the whole court. I thought of his words, *your account is with me.* To be fair, they weren't entirely accurate. My actions had hurt his father also. They had cast a bad reflection upon the queen, upon Nehemiah, upon my own father. I had harmed more than Darius on the eve of my wedding.

But it was the judgment of strangers that had weighed so

heavily on me this night. In their eyes I was an outcast. I felt their sentence of rejection and believed it just. This was my problem: I agreed with them. On the strength of that agreement, I could not be freed from the condemnation I felt.

O *Lord, help me*! I felt so small and lonely. Darius, for all his help, had rejected me himself.

Your account is with Me. The words echoed in my mind like a whisper, but it wasn't Darius's voice that whispered them.

Your account is with Me. I sensed the words repeated once more in my heart, with more force this time.

"*Lord?*" As soon as I said His name, I began to remember the stories of our people. I thought of other men and women, outcast and hopeless, whom the Lord had accepted, watched over, loved: Jacob, Moses, Rahab, Ruth, David. These were imperfect men and women, each one an outsider in his or her own way, whom He had transformed, wanted, changed. Those who against all reason belonged to Him, not because they were free of faults, but because He had chosen them. This was the truth of God. This was His nature, His heart revealed.

I thought how much greater *this* reality weighed in the balance of my soul than the judgment of courtiers I barely knew. *Your account is with Me.* My sins and failures sat in the palm of God's hand; they lay in the balance of His holiness. To Him, I owed my greatest accounting. Could I make my heart dwell only on the Lord's opinion of me, and thereby, be able to ignore the judgments of others, be they good or bad? Could I exchange God's reality for the one that awaited me in the halls of the king's palace?

If my account was with God, then I had more repenting to do. I recalled how hard my heart had been toward Him on the eve of my wedding. How I had discounted God's will and insisted on mine.

That night, my whole soul had been wrapped around *my* pain and fear. I hadn't given a thought to how Darius felt or how my actions might affect our fathers. I had thought only of myself because I had thought so little of God. If I had trusted Him, I would have found the strength to think of the pain of others as well as my own. I would have avoided choices that caused so much damage.

My account with God was in a worse state than any other. But surely the One who had accepted David even after he had committed murder and adultery could find acceptance enough for me? In King David's words I cried out to God:

Do not remember the rebellious sins of my youth.
Remember me in the light of Your unfailing love,
For You are merciful, O Lord.

I spent the rest of my wakeful hours asking the Lord's forgiveness. The more I prayed, the greater the measure of His unfailing love seemed to grow, and the smaller the measure of my rebellion. It was as though bit by bit, His goodness swallowed up my sin. When I finally fell into sleep that night, my dreams were sweet.

The next evening Damaspia dismissed her attendants in order to meet with me alone. She bid me to sit on a golden stool near her and offered me fruit from a bowl overflowing with apples and pears and figs and mulberries and a few fruits I could not name. My new rank had earned me this honor; in the old days, I would have stood at attention in her presence. Without preamble she said, "You've had a hard summer."

I thought she spoke of Teispes. "Yes, Your Majesty," I said. "Though it feels good to be rid of him."

"Him, you got rid of. What about your heart?"

"My heart?" I asked faintly.

"I don't suppose you enjoyed losing your post only to find yourself far from court and abandoned by your husband."

I shifted on the golden stool; it creaked under my weight. In spite of its beauty, it wasn't comfortable. How like Damaspia to set my behind on an incommodious chair while asking her disagreeably insightful questions. "At first, it was devastating. I felt very sorry for myself," I said.

She smiled. "And then?"

I shrugged. "I made a few friends."

"I'm glad to hear it. You must have been lonely."

Even in my years of working at the court I had been lonely. I had merely been too busy to notice, and too tired and afraid to care. At the court, I had had acquaintances, colleagues, superficial friendships. But I had had no one who knew my heart with any degree of intimacy, nor had I known how to reach deeply into the heart of another.

The early quiet days in my new home had made it impossible not to recognize how alone I felt. Without distractions, without the urgency of scribal expectations, for the first time in many years I had had no choice but to feel.

"Yes, Your Majesty," I said, and left it at that.

She folded her hands like an ivory fan and laid them on her lap. "It was my doing that no one tried to reach you all summer. I had good reason. Your husband walked about these walls like a wounded panther for weeks. I feared that if we tried to write you or visit you, he would misunderstand it for some kind of interfering plot and grow even angrier with you. So I stayed away from you, and told Nehemiah to do the same and to bid your father to keep his distance as well.

"After a few weeks, the king sent Darius on some mission to help him cool down a little. He was more himself when he returned. That's when I asked him to fetch you."

I remembered believing Teispes's venomous declaration that the silence of family and friends meant no one cared for me. Now, it appeared the opposite was true. They had stayed away *because* they had cared. I had accepted Teispes's version of events. At the time, it had rung true. But I had been wrong, and in my despair it had been easy to believe a lie.

I saw the queen expected a response and stirred myself. "His lordship has been most kind since his return."

"Oh? Are you a real bride at last?"

I didn't pretend not to understand. Doing my best to keep my expression neutral, I said, "No, Your Majesty."

"Well, it's early days yet. Tell me, how do you like your apartment here in Ecbatana?"

"Very . . . unusual arrangements."

Damaspia laughed. "It took some maneuvering, I assure you. Even the king was scandalized that I would put husband and wife in one room. But with you looking so pretty and under his foot day and night, it won't be long before that cousin of mine will sit up and take notice."

I tried to squelch my annoyance at her interference. I knew she felt responsible, guilty even, for the outcome of this union. Her motives were good, but I couldn't help wishing that she would take her fingers out of my life. "Hardly pretty, Your Majesty," I said, my voice dripping skepticism.

"Do you still doubt it? With those lips, thick shining hair, and all those curves, you'd turn any man's head. And now that you're dressing like a lady instead of an orphaned peasant, you're showing your beauty to advantage. Where did you get that sumptuous robe you wore to the feast last night? That wasn't one of mine."

"Lord Darius gave it to me. His mother set it aside for his wife."

"He *has* been kind. I noticed how attentive he was at the feast last night."

I jumped when she reached out to hold my hand, not as a queen, but as a friend. "Sarah, you were not born as one of us. You cannot imagine what it means to have privilege and influence from birth. You cannot imagine the way people clamor to be with you, only so they can use you. You cannot imagine what it's like never being sure if someone cares for you, or only wants to avail himself of some benefit through you. Trust is not something we can give with ease, and once broken, it's hard to restore.

"That's one of the reasons I chose you for Darius. I knew you were trustworthy and loyal. I knew he would be safe in your hands. The trouble is that he doesn't know that yet. It will take time to heal this damage. But I think it will heal, because the truth is that you aren't who he thinks you are. When he comes to know the real you, he will forgive what you did."

After my time with Damaspia, I stopped for a brief visit with my old colleagues. As usual, they were at work in an airless cubicle in the women's quarters. For some moments I stood at the door unobserved. This would have been my life scant months ago. I felt strangely detached from it. I had thought that seeing them at work would revive my longing. But I felt like a stranger in that room. I no longer belonged there. The insight came as a shock, for I did not feel like I belonged to Darius's household either. Where was my place now? My reverie was interrupted by one of the eunuchs, who, noticing me, jumped up, spilling his parchments on the floor.

I tried to help pick up the sheets, but they wouldn't allow me. It was clear they felt I didn't belong with them either. To them, I was now a lady of rank. They acted awkward with me, and no amount of verbal assurance could put them at ease. I left soon after, knowing I was an unwelcome interruption.

I had a solitary supper in my apartments that night. Of Darius there was no sign. Shortly after I had eaten, one of Darius's men brought a message from him saying that the king had recommended a scribe to replace Teispes and Darius had left to follow up the lead. So much for my efforts to prove my worth to him by my service. Now that he was about to hire a new scribe, he would have no need of my help. I was back to being the nuisance with whom he was saddled. I slept in his bed and wore his mother's bride clothes and gave nothing in return. The spark of hope Damaspia's words had ignited in me began to dim.

Having slept so little the evening before, it was no hardship to slip into bed early. I don't know where my husband spent the night, but it was not in our room.

Chapter Twenty-One

nehemiah sent Darius and me an invitation to visit him in the morning. He had been present at the feast of the equinox, but had not come to greet us. I suspected the rift between him and Darius remained unrepaired. This invitation was his way of extending a peace offering, no doubt.

For my part, I had long since forgiven Nehemiah for his role in arranging my marriage. He had meant me no harm. Indeed, he had paid me a profound compliment believing that a man like Darius would want me for his wife. The discovery that he had not ignored me for three months, but stayed away out of obedience to Damaspia removed any lingering barriers I might have felt toward him.

In Darius's absence, I decided to accept Nehemiah's invitation by myself, although I broke several social rules by doing so. As the wife of a nobleman, I no longer had the freedom of a commoner. To meet alone with a man, even one who was my cousin, was forbidden. But I doubted that Darius would care.

I was a wife foisted on him. He seemed little concerned with my choices.

Besides, I found myself longing for Nehemiah's company. I wished to share with him the joy of my newfound faith; more than anyone, he would understand what that meant to me. I decided not to wait for Darius, and flaunting etiquette, went in search of my cousin.

I caught Nehemiah in the midst of packing. For once, his offices were not in perfect order. No one announced my entrance and I walked in to find my cousin with his head buried in a leather chest. "Going somewhere?" I asked.

"Sarah!" I gulped when he enveloped me in a fatherly embrace. "I'm delighted to see you."

I had not expected such welcome. Neither had he intended to give it, I think, since he stepped away from me with a stiff step. I found both his impromptu affection and subsequent self-consciousness endearing. "I'm going to Susa ahead of the court to prepare for the king," he said, answering my initial question.

"Ah. I'd forgotten the court would soon be moving to Susa. A few months and I already feel out of step with the routines of the royal household."

"Obviously, since you are here unaccompanied. Aren't you asking for trouble?"

"Seeing you is worth it."

Nehemiah gave me a stern glare. "You'd better leave. Come back later with an appropriate chaperone."

"My husband will not care. "

He arched an eyebrow and invited me to sit on an over-stuffed saffron-colored couch. "You've had quite a summer, I hear."

I imagined by now he knew every detail of what I had shared with the king. "Yes, my lord," I said. Technically, he wasn't *my lord* anymore since my rank was above his. But old habits died hard.

"It sounds like you have found faithful friends in your new home."

"That I have."

He nodded. "Good." He looked away for a brief moment. "You've spent some time with your husband, at long last. How does he treat you?"

There were so many ways he could have asked that question. With simple curiosity. With meddlesome intent. With shades of criticism. Instead he asked it with honest concern, his gaze warm with compassion as well as strength. Nehemiah always managed to make me feel like he could handle my gravest problems.

So instead of the flippancy I had intended, the truth slipped out. "He is kind. Appreciative, even, since the Teispes business. But he'll never love me. He won't even touch me."

"And *you* love *him*." It wasn't a question. I should have known he would unearth my deepest secret without effort. Since I'd been a child, the man had known how to burrow inside my mind and expose what I thought.

I buried my face in my hands for a moment. "How foolish can a woman be?"

"It's not foolish to love your husband."

"It is when he can't bear the sight of you."

"I think you are past that at least, judging by the way he looked at you on the eve of the equinox."

"It was his way of shielding me from court gossip. I told you, he's kind."

Nehemiah drummed his well-groomed fingers on the alabaster-top table next to him. "He no longer despises you if he shows you kindness. You've come far in a handful of months."

My smile was tinged with sadness. "I had hoped that I could win his favor by helping him as a scribe. He left his personal aid at his palace to help in Teispes's absence. Until he hired a new scribe, I was supposed to assist him. I thought he would come to see that I was not a complete disappointment. But that's not to be, it seems. The king has found him a man already."

"Your husband must learn to love *you*, not your abilities. You do him no favors by trying to win him with what has far less value than your true self."

I found myself on the edge of tears. "He won't find much to love about me, I fear."

Nehemiah jumped to his feet. "Are you daft, girl?" He exhaled an audible breath before sitting down again. "Sarah, you've never known your worth. You've never known how wonderful you are."

For once I was speechless. Half of me longed for him to tell me what was so wonderful about me. The other half refused to believe any good thing he might have to say.

He was thoughtful for long moments. "I blame your father."

"I am all for blaming my father," I said with a shaky smile. "But what exactly are we blaming him for?"

"Perhaps if I told you about the past, you would understand. You don't know your father very well. Did he ever tell you that he didn't intend to marry?"

"That would require conversation of a personal nature. So, no. He did not."

"He was a scholar from boyhood. A shy man. He told me once that he thought he would never marry, because he couldn't imagine conversing with a woman. Then he met your mother and everything changed.

"She was beautiful as you know, and gentle. Somehow she

had a way of putting others at ease. Your father fell in love with her at first sight, I think. He thought it was hopeless, of course. He couldn't imagine such a ravishing creature returning his feelings, or settling for the humble life he would provide. She did, though. Your mother returned his love."

I picked up an empty silver goblet that was resting on the table next to me and twirled it in my hand, blind to its ravishing workmanship. "I always knew that, somehow. She used to tease my father and make him laugh out loud. I haven't heard him laugh like that in years."

"I think she was the only woman with whom he had a deep relationship, certainly the only one with whom he communicated on a meaningful level. Somehow, she managed to draw him out of his shell. When she died, his world shattered."

A memory of my father staring into space with red-rimmed eyes flashed in my mind. I saw myself as a child, calling out to him again and again, "Abba! Abba!" my voice full of the terror of a little girl who had already lost one parent and now stood petrified lest the other one disappear too. He had ignored my cries.

It wasn't my Abba who had disappeared. It was me. He had stopped seeing me. I had grown invisible to him.

"I was there, remember?" I said to Nehemiah.

"You were there, yes. But you were too young to understand. In the first months of his loss, he was too devastated to pay any mind to you. Then as he started to emerge from that abyss of grief, there you were. He didn't know what to do with you. He had no idea how to care for a child—a daughter."

"I know. I was a nuisance to him."

"Sarah, this is where you are wrong. He loved you. He didn't know how to talk to you, how to show you what was in his heart. But he loved you."

I crossed my arms, the silver goblet half forgotten in my clutched fingers, and sat up straight, my back rigid against his plush sofa. "My lord Nehemiah, I beg your pardon for disagreeing with you. But the truth is, I was a disappointment to my father. I was not as beautiful as my mother, or as winsome, or as sweet. I said the wrong things. I needed too much attention. I required too much care."

"You think your father avoided you because he thought you weren't good enough? Because he thought you demanded too much? *No!* Your father avoided you because he didn't know how to reach out to you. The shortcoming wasn't in you. It was in him."

I blew out my breath in disbelief, but Nehemiah ignored me.

"When I came back into your lives, the damage had already been done. Somehow, you had come to believe that you had nothing of worth to offer. It had nothing to do with your father anymore; it was inside your own heart and mind. You were the one sitting on the judgment seat and finding yourself deficient."

I crossed my arms tighter about my chest. "It was the truth."

"It was a *lie!*" Nehemiah roared, making me jump.

He cleared his throat, and when he spoke, his voice was calm again. "I could see that learning to read gave you a sense of accomplishment. A new attachment to your Abba.

"I believed the Lord had given you the talent for a reason. I also hoped He would use it to bring you closer to your father. To heal this mistaken notion you harbored in your head that you are not special. Whenever I spent time in your company, I was struck anew by how precious you are. But you could not see it."

My eyes grew round with wonder. He thought I was *special?*

"But you wrapped your whole soul around your work. You established yourself in court and became the queen's favored servant. But did you feel secure and happy? Did your success give you peace?"

I chose not to answer and he pressed on.

"Do you know why not? Because you were out of step with God's design. God's design includes the use of our talents. When God created the first man and woman, He gave them many gifts. And then He gave them work that required the use of those gifts. He assigned them a profound task, much more important than anything you can accomplish in your lifetime. They were to take charge of the earth. They were to rule over the world."

I placed the goblet back on the table with a restless move. I could tell Nehemiah was gearing up for a good long lecture. Perhaps that was what I needed, I thought, and forced myself to listen.

"But do you think the Lord counted them worthy because of their abilities?" he went on, ignoring my restlessness. "They hadn't even begun their work yet when He made His first pronouncement over them. He called them *very good* when they hadn't achieved a single thing. They hadn't proven themselves capable. He pronounced them *good* not because of what they had accomplished, but because of who He had made them to be."

I felt myself freeze as I heard those words. I had never thought of God's response to Adam and Eve in those terms. Nehemiah was right. God counted them as good already, before they had done anything worthwhile.

Nehemiah nodded his head, as though he perceived that I was finally beginning to comprehend his meaning. "This is a life of right order, Sarah. The heart that knows the Lord as the source of its beauty and value knows freedom. You have lost yourself in the gifts God gave you. Those blessings have become your master.

"When your inmost being is in step with the right order of God, you reap His rest. Your soul tastes of His peace.

"Instead, *your* inner world produced turmoil, because you lost sight of who you really were. You lived in fear. Fear that you should prove dissatisfactory. For years I have watched you live a disordered life. You've placed your intellect, your ability to learn faster than most, your quickness of thought and understanding at the core of your life. This was never the Lord's purpose for you."

I made an involuntary gesture with my arm; the silver chalice knocked over. It made a hideous noise as it toppled on the polished ground. I hadn't the strength to pick it up. I felt utterly arrested by Nehemiah's words.

"My child, the Lord's care for you has never depended on what you achieve. You were created for His love, not to be His work mule. Your accomplishments are meant to be a response to that love; instead you have made love a response to your accomplishments.

"I don't know if your husband will ever love you the way you desire. I don't know if he will ever see you as you truly are—a woman of rare qualities and beauty. I do know one thing, however. You can feel beloved and fulfilled even without your husband's affections. The steadfast love of the Lord for you never ceases. Never, Sarah."

I brought the edge of my expensive linen sleeve to my dripping nose. "I'm beginning to understand that. I am beginning to believe that the Lord is a very present help in my troubles. I have opened my heart to loving Him again." I wiped the tears from my drowning eyes and wailed, "I wished you weren't going away, Cousin Nehemiah." I realized what I had called him and bit my lip. "I beg your pardon. I meant *my lord*."

He laughed. "Cousin Nehemiah will do. Haven't you been like my own daughter these many years?"

I gaped at him, awash in wonder. Since my mouth was already open, I decided to put it to use. "How did you grow so wise?"

"I pray often." Nehemiah's gaze dripped kindness. "I am pleased to hear that you have faith. You will need it.

"Sarah, I have probably climbed higher than any son of Israel in my generation. Some of our people respect me for it. Others revile me and call me a traitor for living with the Persians and adopting their ways."

I knew what he meant. Having lived in the palaces of the king as a Jew, I had come across the prejudice of many of our people who thought I had grown too Persian. I nodded. "That must make it difficult for you, my lord. Unlike me, you are still very active in the Jewish community."

He shrugged. "It's not difficult if you don't care for what other people think of you. Some judge me a great success. Others turn their backs when they see me. What's that to me? So long as I have the steadfast love of the Lord.

"If one day all the works of my hand should fall apart at my feet, do you think I will lose the knowledge of who I am in God? Not for a moment! My heart may break. But not because I will think myself any less a man for that failure. I will always have my standing before the Lord as His child. I will always know I can go to Him and be welcomed. That is who I am. My work is a small part of me—an assignment from God. Whether He give it or take it away, it will not change how He perceives me.

"This is what I want you to learn about yourself, Sarah."

Before I could respond, Nehemiah's assistant burst in with

some urgent summons and I took my leave, knowing my cousin had already extended more time to me than he had to give. I was in no mood to return to my apartment and chose to go for a stroll in the gardens.

As I walked under an archway covered with pink roses, I pondered Nehemiah's extraordinary revelations. The first thought that came to me was that he thought me *wonderful*. Nehemiah? My accomplished, sought-after cousin thought I was wonderful? I knew he had shown me favor through the years, but I had always assumed that it rose more out of a sense of duty to my mother than any real affection for me.

It seemed I had so many things backward. I thought my father was disappointed in me and I had come to believe I *was* disappointing. I had spent so much time trying to earn his love and he had loved me already.

Nehemiah's last words burned in my mind: *That is who I am. My work is . . . an assignment from God.* I didn't have his ability to rest in the Lord's opinion of me. I had built my own measures of worth and acceptability. They were false; they destroyed my peace. It dawned on me just how doggedly I served these measures. I served them with more fierce determination than I served God. I wanted the good opinion of others more than I wanted the Lord. I suppose I was trying to undo all the years in my life when my father had ignored me.

But if Nehemiah was right, the Lord cared not if I cost too much, or if I proved useful. It mattered not to Him if others thought well or ill of me. His measures were so different from mine.

Overwhelmed by my discoveries, I collapsed on a marble bench and leaned against its carved back. It was a breezy day and I felt the cold creep through my white linen dress. I pulled my legs up on the bench and wrapped my arms around them.

Nehemiah had accused me of living a disordered life. I, who once had charge of bringing order into the queen of Persia's life, could not bring order into my own. I could manage records; my heart defeated me.

Who could set the heart free but God? "Lord," I cried out, in my mind. "You don't see things the way we mortals see them. We judge by outward things, but You look at the heart. So much of my life, I have chased after outward concerns. I have wanted to excel. But You, O Lord, know my heart. Please forgive me for serving the false masters of my soul. Help me to please only You." I thought for a moment and then emended my prayers. "Help me to *want* to please only You."

I ran out of words. Somehow, in the quiet aftermath of my prayers, I grew still in my soul. It was a healing stillness. I knew that I was at the beginning of this journey—knew that having become aware of my sin and desiring to change was merely the start.

Still, I felt as though another great wall around my heart had begun to crack. As if by acknowledging my upside-down values, I had allowed God to draw nearer to me. I felt His presence as that of a cherished Father rather than a distant deity. Like a child calming in the company of a loving parent, I grew contented, and before long, fell asleep.

It must have been past noon when I awoke, stiff from my nap on the hard marble. A blanket of well-being seemed to cover my soul. I grinned, full of joy.

I was too happy to go back to the confines of the palace and decided to continue my earlier walk. The sweet scent of thousands of perfumed flowers clung to me as I walked, making my head spin with their beauty. It wasn't until I reached the inmost wall of the city, standing tall and white like a barrier of ice, that I finally stopped.

From the corner of my eye I saw a little boy coming toward me, his nursemaid a few steps behind. I recognized him. It was Arash, Damaspia's favorite nephew. At three, he was adorable enough to have won an army of admirers. He approached me with bold steps; I had met him a number of times while working for the queen.

"Do you have any parchment?" he asked. I had once given him a small piece, and he now asked for parchment every time he saw me.

"Good afternoon, Arash. I'm afraid I haven't any parchment for you today."

"Oh." One chubby hand scratched his head.

A butterfly with lilac wings, drawn to the scent of the potions in my hair, began to fly around me. "What's that?" Arash cried.

"A butterfly."

With slow, deliberate attention, he repeated the word after me. We had played the game before. Most of the time he already knew the words, but he pretended to learn them, anyway.

"What's that?"

"A wall. Do you know what color it is?"

"White. What's that?" he said pointing to the structure jutting out of the base of the wall.

"Ah. That's a buttress." I assumed this was a new word to Arash. "It helps hold up the wall." I repeated the word, breaking it into syllables to make sure he knew how to pronounce it. A twinkle in his eye alerted me to the fact that one of us was in trouble, and I was sure it wasn't Arash.

At the top of his lungs, Arash started yelling, "Butt-rest. Butt-rest."

A throaty, masculine laugh just behind me made me swivel about in dismay. Darius leaned against the wall, one leg bent at the knee so that his foot could rest on the bricks.

"You're quite the language teacher," he said.

Before I could respond, I spied Damaspia walking toward us. What was this? The meeting place of the nations? Arash was still shouting *Butt-rest* at the top of his lungs. "I'm dead," I muttered.

Darius's mouth tipped in a sideway grin. In the sun, his green eyes appeared like living jewels. I gulped as I looked at him, and turned away. Distracted, I jumped up when I noticed Damaspia standing next to me. She sat on the bench and waved me to take my seat near her.

"What is that child shouting?"

I groaned. By now, Damaspia had caught on to her nephew's words.

"Arash! Cease that at once! You know better."

At the sound of his royal aunt's reprimand, the child stopped his proclamation. I thought he might burst into tears of dismay. Instead, he climbed on Damaspia's lap and began to give her loud, smacking kisses. "Happy?" he asked between kisses. "Happy?" We were all charmed, of course.

"You rascal. Yes, I am happy and I love you. But you are to cease your misbehavior."

Arash smiled at Damaspia and nodded.

Damaspia turned to me. "Did this wretch Darius teach him that?"

I cleared my throat. "I'm afraid it was I, Your Majesty. I was trying to teach him to say *buttress*."

Damaspia bit her lip, and then laughed. "You have an impressive talent for causing trouble without trying."

"And I receive the blame," Darius said, hand on his heart, as though mortally wounded.

"Oh sit yourself on the . . . butt-rest, and be quiet," Damaspia said.

Darius obeyed. "You know, Arash has a point. I find this thing quite restful."

I put my head in my hand.

Chapter Twenty-Two

Darius walked me back to the palace. We strolled at a leisurely pace, both of us silent. The memory of Arash climbing on Damaspia's lap with such confidence haunted me. Damaspia was the queen of Persia. But to Arash, she was just a loving aunt. Even in the midst of being disciplined for wrongdoing, Arash had confidence in that love. He knew he could climb into Damaspia's arms and be wanted there. Even though he had misbehaved, he knew his kisses brought pleasure to his aunt. Arash knew that he didn't have to be perfect to make his aunt happy.

I couldn't help wonder if the Lord's love was like this, full of acceptance even when I had done wrong. Expecting change of me, but loving me before the change came. Was He, like Damaspia, joyful when I came to Him, even in my weakness? Was His loving-kindness that secure?

Yet He was holy too, and could not wave away my sins as if they were of no consequence. That was the point of the many sacrifices He had demanded of my people. The temple in Jerusalem, where I had never been, once ran red with the blood of lambs and bulls so that our sins might be covered. Jerusalem, which stood as a symbol of God's love for His people, also represented His holiness. My heart contracted with the desire to visit the City of God. To offer Him sacrifices there. To know every wall that stood between us was finally crushed by His mercy. Perhaps then, I could run to Him like Arash to his aunt, and I could feel His tender embrace with no barriers of guilt or shame.

Through the fog of my thoughts I heard Darius's clipped voice, louder than usual, bark, "Careful!"

Before I had time to react, Arash's solid little body crashed into my side as he ran past in some private game. He caught me unawares and I lost my balance, falling against Darius. He wrapped his arms around me in an instinctive gesture to steady me. Instead of letting me go as I regained my equilibrium, his arms tightened about me and pulled me all the way around until I was resting close against his chest. I looked up to find him staring at me with melting intensity. His hand trailed up my back. Slowly, he bent his head.

"What are you doing?" Arash asked, pulling on my skirt.

Darius dropped his arms. His mouth tipped up on one side. "Nothing to do with you, little brat. Go find your nursemaid."

Arash sniffed, but obeyed.

"If that child were my father's son, he would have learned better manners by now," Darius said dryly and resumed walking.

I forced my feet to work again. I half expected my legs to tie into a knot, dropping me in front of my husband in a tangle of stumbling limbs. To my relief, everything seemed in normal working order. Even my brain. I said, "If he were your father's son, he wouldn't even see him for two more years." It was a custom among Persian nobility not to present their sons to their fathers until the age of five. The idea was that should the child sicken or die, the father would be too heartbroken.

"My father does not believe in that particular custom. He insisted on seeing me the day I was born, and every day after, when he was not traveling. Even when I went to the palace for my formal training, he would sneak my mother in to visit me at least once a week."

"Your family sounds wonderful. You must have been very close."

"Yours wasn't?"

"My mother died when I was seven. I think we were happy until then. But after that," I said, shrugging. "My father didn't know what to do with a girl child."

"I'm sorry." He threw me a sidelong glance. "We don't know very much about each other, do we?"

"It's not usually a requirement for marriage."

He turned his head away. "I had hoped for something different."

I wanted to ask him what he had hoped for. I wanted to apologize for ruining his dreams. I wanted to tell him that I too had wished for more. But before I had time to form any words, he changed the subject.

"I met with the man the king recommended. He shall do well as the new steward. I sent him ahead to Persepolis already."

I tried to hide my disappointment and gave a polite nod.

"Before he left, I showed him Mandana's receipts as well as the accounts belonging to Teispes's brother. He confirmed all you said. I have sent the records to the royal judge for his consideration. Teispes's fate bodes ill. If he had only committed one crime, he might find himself exiled or imprisoned. But he is guilty of too many infractions of the law. Theft, corruption, attempted murder. He shall lose his life for his crimes."

"He is guilty of much wrong. Still, I cannot help but pity him."

Darius nodded, then slowed his steps until we came to a halt. "Damaspia tells me that there was a time when you helped her, also. She says you saved her from a dangerous plot to ruin her reputation and bring enmity between her and the queen mother. I understand you went to Amestris herself and convinced her of Damaspia's innocence. That must have been an unforgettable experience."

"Let's just say Teispes is a bunny rabbit compared to Amestris."

"Yes, but you were in his clutches longer, and he had more power over you. This is my fault, Sarah. I ask your pardon."

I swallowed past the knot in my throat. "No pardon needed. I confess, before your return, I thought you negligent of your duties. But after I saw how much you cared for your servants, and how Teispes had deceived you, I stopped holding you responsible. You did not know."

"And that's the point. Whereas you *did* find out, and helped my people where you could." He pulled a hand through his dark hair. "Damaspia tells me that is why she arranged our marriage—to thank you for your service. She assures me that you were not the instigator of our nuptials, and neither was your cousin, the cupbearer, but that she herself was behind it from the start. Why did you never tell me? I would have believed you if I had known the circumstances."

I made a point of studying my shoe. "It was not my affair to discuss. It was Her Majesty's business."

"Damaspia said you were circumspect. Our wedding—

that was your plot to break off the marriage? You thought that seeing you, I would renege on the contract?"

My head jerked up. "You royals must all undergo the same training. That is exactly what Damaspia accused me of at first, and it's not true!"

Darius straightened until his back grew rigid. Through tight lips he said, "Sarah, we have a chance for a new start. Let us begin with honesty. I have failed you; I own it. I accept responsibility for my part in this disaster. Do the same. Confess your wrong, and I shall forgive you as you forgave me. Let us have truth between us since we have so little else."

Here we were again. He believed half my story, at least. But the other half still stuck in his throat, and he could not swallow it. I blew my cheeks. "I do confess my wrong, my lord. That night, in my misery, I thought only of myself."

He nodded his head, encouraging me to go on. I didn't have much more to tell. I couldn't lie merely to please him.

"Because of my selfishness, I gave no thought to you or anyone else as I prepared. It never occurred to me how my actions would harm you. I did not design to demean you on purpose, my lord, in order to be released of our contract. But I was so focused on my own feelings that I forgot about God and about everyone else. And I sought no help when I should have."

Darius clenched his teeth. Softly he said, "Still, you lie? As you did to the queen's maidservants when they came to prepare you for your wedding? You look me in the eye and lie?"

I could feel myself turning scarlet. "I did lie that day. But I'm telling you the truth now."

"I tell you, I understand why you did it. Confess it, and I will forgive you. Can't you see that if you lie about one thing, then I must assume that you will lie about others? I'll never be able to fully trust you."

278

What a web of irony he wove about me. In order to make him believe that I did not lie, I had to lie. I shook my head, dumb with misery. My husband turned his back and began to stride toward the palace. I waited a few moments before following him at a plodding pace. Would this chasm of misunderstanding and lack of trust between us never be bridged?

The king had invited Darius to spend the evening at his table. By the time I arrived at our apartment, he had disappeared into the palace bathhouse and must have left for the king's quarters directly from there, for I saw no sign of him. Having no invitations of my own, I spent another evening alone.

Since I had traveled to Ecbatana on horseback, I had been able to bring no more than three outfits in addition to my riding clothes. The rest of my garments clattered in a cart somewhere on the king's highway between Ecbatana and Persepolis. Our baggage train would not arrive for several days. I decided to count having so few engagements as a blessing. At least there was no one to remark on the limitedness of my wardrobe. Or the coldness of my husband.

I missed Caspian and felt lonely for my friends. It had been twelve days since I saw them. Eight more days, and I would at least have Pari with me.

The next morning I awoke to an invitation from the queen to go riding with her and her retinue. I donned my riding habit, and dispatched a palace servant to have Kidaris saddled. To my relief, I found I had not forgotten Darius's riding instructions. My body, now recovered from the grueling journey, settled in the saddle with ease. I joined Damaspia and her ladies and found she intended to ride into the hilly countryside surrounding Ecbatana. We were to picnic in the lush woods beyond the city gates.

Most of Damaspia's ladies already knew each other and spent the early part of our journey chatting pleasantly as they navigated the dusty roads two abreast. Content to ride in silence, I was taken aback when Damaspia led her horse to join me. She signaled for us to slow down. When we were some distance from the others, she said, "Your husband has requested separate rooms from you for the remainder of his stay at Ecbatana."

"I see."

"I thought you were dealing well together."

"He is convinced, once again, that I'm lying to him and says he cannot trust me."

The queen frowned. "I refused his requisition. And the king won't give him permission to move out of the palace."

"Wouldn't it be better to let him go, Your Majesty? He's only liable to grow more riled if you force him to stay with me."

"Perhaps you're right. I shall give him time to calm himself, and if he does not change his mind, then I will move you to the women's quarters."

We rode through the seven gates of Ecbatana at a sedate pace, the queen's guards following us from a respectful distance. Damaspia's revelation weighed on my mind. With depressed certainty I came to the conclusion that Darius would abandon me in one of his residences and lead his life apart from me. Then I remembered how far I had come from the girl at court whose world fell apart because she had lost her post. I had many resources now, to see me through this heartbreak. I had the Lord. I had my friends. I had the truth. I would survive.

When we crossed the last gate, Damaspia picked up the

pace of the ride, and with good-natured laughter, her ladies began a haphazard race. I followed at a more sedate pace, not in the humor for their laughter or for chasing after the wind. At the edge of the road I caught sight of a boy. I turned to study him and was surprised when he waved at me to stop.

He was nine or ten, a dark-eyed boy with tousled hair and dirty hands. He was clearly a peasant child, out on some errand. I brought Kidaris to a gentle stop near him.

"My lady, there's a man what wishes to see you. He's back there." He pointed with his thumb into the woods.

"Who is it?"

"He didn't say, lady. He just pointed at you and told me to fetch you to him."

I narrowed my eyes against the sun as I looked toward the trees. It occurred to me that perhaps it was Darius. What other man did I know in Ecbatana? Although I could not fathom why my aggrieved husband would want to meet with me in the woods when he had easy access to me in our rooms, I figured he would explain himself when he saw me.

The boy, having delivered his message, moved on down the road, back toward the palace. I realized that by lingering behind, I had put a substantial distance between my companions and me. Loathe to keep Darius waiting, I ignored the nagging feeling in the pit of my stomach, and led Kidaris into the woods.

"My lord?" I called out, as I entered a shaded glade.

With disconcerting speed a man jumped before me. I recognized the dark hair, now wild and dirty, the narrowed eyes, the long jaw. "Teispes!"

He grabbed Kidaris's reins before I could react. I tried to jerk them out of his hold and kicked the horse's side, signaling her to gallop away. Just as Kidaris bolted, a strong hand grasped the back of my tunic and pulled me down. I fell on the ground with a heavy thud. My head hit a stone jutting out of the moss-covered forest bed. Its hard impact made me dizzy and nauseated so that I could not move for some moments. Before I had full command of my senses, Teispes pulled me roughly to my feet.

I lifted a trembling hand to the side of my head. My fingers came away wet with blood. I tried to clear my mind. "What are you doing here?" I croaked, disbelief and pain making my voice tremble. I thought of screaming, but the queen and her guard would be far from hearing distance by now.

His grip tightened viciously on my arm. "Why, I came for you. You ruined my life, so I thought I would return the favor." I gasped and began to fight him. He slammed me against a tree. The rough bark must have scraped off half the skin from my back. I went limp in his arms.

I realized that I was too weak to stand a chance against his rage by means of physical struggle. Dizzy from my fall and loss of blood, I could hardly think straight, let alone overcome a wily criminal. Yet my one chance of surviving this nightmare was to best Teispes with my wits.

Before I could think of anything resembling a plan, Teispes pressed me into the tree so hard, the breath was knocked out of me. My knees began to buckle.

"Please," I croaked. "Stop!"

"What? Does that hurt? How thoughtless of me." He stepped away enough to allow me a moment of recovery. I realized that he had enjoyed my pleading and wondered if I could use that against him.

Gulping, I asked, "How did you get away?"

His smile was self-satisfied. "Not every man in Persia is

282

above a good bribe. When I escaped, I went to Aspasia first. But she had left, thanks to you. You drove her away from me. Then I came to Ecbatana to find my brother, only to discover your dear husband had him confined in chains. All my riches are gone. Everything I had worked so hard for disappeared because of you. So I decided to pay you a visit before I moved on to a more pleasant part of the empire."

"It was clever of you to find me."

"I knew you were in Ecbatana. But I didn't think it wise to enter the city. Your husband will have heard of my escape by now, and will be on his guard. So I decided to camp in the woods, knowing sooner or later you would rouse yourself out of the palace. I am a patient man. And justice was on my side, for no sooner had I spied you in the queen's train, than the peasant boy happened to walk by, and for a piece of bread, agreed to fetch you to me. You were so obliging to loll behind the others, out of earshot and the help of the palace guards."

"You always were a step ahead of me."

"How kind of you to notice. If it weren't for Darius coming home so precipitously, I would have rid myself of you and your meddling."

I thought of Caspian and ground my teeth. Trying to keep all emotion out of my voice, I asked, "Where do you plan to go now?"

He laughed. His teeth were dirty, like the rest of him. "Do you think to win me over with friendly conversation? You should have tried that in Persepolis. It's too late now." He pulled out a knife from its leather sheath at his side and pointed the blade at my face. "My only regret is that in killing you, I will be doing Darius a favor."

"Allow me to disabuse you of that notion."

Darius! Both Teispes and I turned toward him in shock. He

was on foot, which explained why neither of us had heard his approach, and stood facing us from the other side of the glade. In one hand he held a bow, a black-tipped arrow already notched, pointed at the ground. "Let my wife go, Teispes."

With a vicious move, Teispes pulled me in front of him like a shield. He pointed his knife dead against my heart. "Move if you want her dead."

"If you put one scratch on her, I will tear you apart," Darius said. The hair on my arms stood at the menace that dripped from his voice. "Let her go. This is between us."

Teispes pushed the knife harder into my chest. I grit my teeth as its point pierced my flesh. "So you really do care for her." His smile was twisted. "That's good." He looked about him wildly. "I'm going to get on my horse now and I'm taking her with me. If you want her alive, you will give your word not to follow. She'll come with me to ensure you keep your promise. At the first sight of pursuit, I will kill her, and with pleasure."

Darius seemed as immobile as a statue to me. I could see his hand clenched on the notched arrow, held steady at his side. "My wife isn't going anywhere with you, Teispes. Let her go."

"So you can kill me? I don't think so."

The knife at my breast kept pressing harder. I bit my lip to keep from screaming, worried that I might distract Darius. Without warning, Teispes began walking backward, dragging me with him, still held before him like a shield. From the corner of my eye, I saw his horse, tied to a tree.

For a moment, he loosened the knife away from my chest in order to pull us up on the horse, but as soon as he was settled in the saddle with me pressed against him, he shoved the point of his knife into my skin again until the fabric of my riding tunic was stained red with blood. It was a superficial wound, but it stung like a hundred bee stings. I tried to gulp down the panic that bubbled just beneath the surface of my mind. I knew if he managed to ride out of there with me, I would be dead within the hour. He was too filled with hatred to let me live.

"Sarah, hold still," Darius said. His voice was calm. I remembered the day he had killed the lion, how true his aim was, and how by remaining immobile, my life had been spared. I held my body rigid. With a motion so fast I almost missed it, he raised his bow, took aim, and released the arrow.

Teispes screamed, his voice loud in my ear. I tried not to flinch as Darius's arrow flew straight toward me. For once, being short was an advantage, for Teispes towered over me in the saddle. Desperately, he threw himself to the side, with me still clenched hard in his arms, but the arrow was too swift, and it caught him in the neck. His body continued in its sideway motion, pulling me with him. I flailed as I saw the ground coming toward me, trying to grasp hold of the horse's mane. But Teispes's weight pulled me down and for the second time that day I was toppled off a horse.

Time grew unnaturally slow; I became aware of Darius yelling my name and running toward us. I saw the thin blades of grass rushing up toward me. I noticed the black tip of Darius's arrow protruding out of the side of Teispes's neck, his face a frozen mask of horror. And then I hit the ground. I remember Teispes landing on top of me—remember the pressure of his body as he pressed upon me, his weight overwhelming in death. I became aware that his hand had become trapped under me, his knife still grasped in frozen fingers. My face was in the dirt. I could not move, but I could feel the knife, now buried in my flesh.

"Sarah!" I saw Darius's leather-clad legs as he knelt by my

side. The weight lifted off my back as he pushed Teispes's corpse away from me. With gentle fingers he turned me over. I moaned with pain.

"Oh, Sarah." I must have been a frightful sight, my head and face caked with blood and dirt, a knife protruding from my chest, blood covering the front of my tunic. He tore part of my tunic with a quick slash of his knife and began to examine my wounds with care. Even in my shock I could sense the trembling in his fingers as he touched me. I was too shocked to be embarrassed.

Have mercy on me, dear Lord, have mercy! I took a deep breath and forced my lips to move. "Am I going to die?"

Chapter Twenty-Three

"No. No, sweetheart. You won't die." For a moment I forgot that my head pounded and my chest felt like it was on fire. My mind fastened on the word *sweetheart*. Had he really called *me* that or was I beginning to hallucinate?

"It's not as deep a wound as it appears, in spite of all the blood. The knife went sideways and was deflected by bone."

I swallowed. Relief flooded me at the knowledge that I wasn't dying, but it didn't change the fact that I felt like it. "It may not seem as deep as a well to you, but I assure you, it is impressive from this angle."

A deep breath leaked out of his lips, half sigh, half laugh. With exquisite gentleness, he pulled my tangled hair out of my face. I thought I might be losing my wits as the ground began to shake beneath me and a pounding noise filled my ears. Then I saw the queen and her retinue cantering toward us on their horses.

"Sarah!" Damaspia cried as she jumped from her horse

and threw herself beside us on the ground. "Is it fatal?" she addressed Darius.

"No," he said, forgoing her title or even a polite nod. "She'll recover with good care."

"We ought to get her to the palace. Artaxerxes' personal physicians shall tend to her."

"I must first deal with this knife and bind the wound. She has bled too much. I have to staunch the flow before I haul her atop a horse."

He turned back to me. "Sarah, I have to pull the knife out. It won't be pleasant."

"Can't you do it later? When I've passed out would be a good time."

He lifted my hand to his mouth for a soft kiss. My heart skipped a beat. "No, I can't. I don't want infection to set in, or allow you to lose more blood. Delay is dangerous."

I closed my eyes. "Do as you think best."

He was slow and meticulous in removing the knife, not wanting to tear the flesh further. The pain was so intense that I feared I might lose the contents of my stomach. In the end, I couldn't help screaming. I kept repeating the name of the Lord in my head, clinging to Him for strength. For a moment, the agony subsided when the knife was finally pulled out of me, and I was able to catch my breath. Then Darius pressed hard against the wound with bandages he had produced from somewhere, and even though I clenched my teeth to keep from groaning, I couldn't stop the tears that flowed.

"Shhh." He wiped the moisture from my cheeks. "It's almost over."

I didn't know why he was being so tender, nor did I care, so long as he did not stop. I supposed he felt sorry for me.

I must have finally lost consciousness, for when I next came to myself, I was in his arms as he walked toward his horse, Samson.

"Where were you hiding Samson? I thought you were on foot," I said, groggy, but wanting to keep my mind on something besides the misery of my body.

"He was on the other side of the glade, hidden behind the trees."

Damaspia motioned for one of her guards to come forward, and Darius handed me to him as he mounted. The guard gave me back to my husband, trying not to jostle me in the process. Darius's arms cradled me. He smiled into my eyes. "Just like old times."

The motion of the horse intensified the pain in my head and chest. I began to realize that I hurt everywhere. Two falls and Teispes's rough treatment had left me covered in bruises. To distract myself, I asked, "How did you find me?"

"I found out this morning that Teispes had escaped. Although I increased the watch around his brother, I could not shake my unease. Finally I came in search of you to warn you to be on your guard. I found out you had gone riding with the queen, and decided to follow. When I caught up with her party, we discovered that you were missing. Then Kidaris galloped into our midst, foaming with exertion and riderless, and we knew you were in some manner of trouble. I doubled back and managed to follow Kidaris's tracks to the glade. Why did you go to him willingly? There were no signs of struggle until the glade."

"He sent a boy to tell me that a man wished to meet me in the woods. I thought it was you."

Darius pulled me closer against him. We were silent for a

while. I wished I would lose consciousness again so that I'd stop suffering. Finally I said, "Could you halt for a moment? So I can catch my breath?"

He brought Samson to a stop. To Damaspia he said, "Why don't you and your ladies go ahead, Your Majesty? We will follow at a slower pace."

"I will have the physicians sent to you right away. They will await your arrival in your apartments."

Darius shifted me in his arms when everyone had ridden past. "Ready?"

I tried to sound confident. "Yes."

"Not much longer. We'll be upon the first wall before you know it."

"I beg your pardon, my lord," I said a few moments later. "I'm going to be sick."

He stopped Samson just in time. I was mortified as I retched before him, for in spite of my urging, he refused to leave me alone. He was concerned that I would start bleeding again, but he had done a thorough job dressing the wound earlier and it did not open. My head pounded beyond forbearance as I disgorged everything in my stomach. When I was finally able to stop, Darius gave me a little wine with which to rinse my mouth. I feared it hardly covered my stench.

Now I smelled as bad as I looked. Back on the horse I croaked, "I bet I looked prettier than this on our wedding night." If my brain weren't so addled, I would never have brought up such a sensitive topic.

I could tell I had startled him as his green eyes opened wide. "You are a terror, little scribe. One never knows what will come out of your mouth."

"Given the memento I just left on the side of the road, I can't dispute the accuracy of that statement."

I could feel his chest contracting under my cheek as he laughed. Into the ensuing silence he said, "I don't know what to do with you."

Wisely I kept my thoughts to myself.

True to Damaspia's word, we found two royal physicians in our room, ready to attend me. They told Darius that he had done a proficient job, but the wound in my chest would have to be sewn. I wished they would leave me be so I could drift into sleep. Instead they poked and prodded me with their instruments, sewed me up like a Phoenician cushion, wiped the dirt and blood off me, wrapped my head, put salve on my wounds and bruises before finally leaving me in peace.

To my discomfort, Darius supervised every step of their treatment. By the time they were done, I was barely dressed, sprawled on the bed with nothing save a short under tunic, and even that had been cut on one side, exposing too much skin. No one seemed to have a care for my modesty.

Alone with Darius, I pulled the covers over me haphazardly, using my good arm. "You seem to have made a habit of this," I said. I was dizzy with exhaustion and pain, but sleep would not come.

He straightened the covers over me with a soldier's precision. "Of what?"

"Of saving my life."

"You seem to have made a habit of endangering it."

I smoothed the linen coverlet with a feeble hand. "Thank you for your care. I am indebted to you." I lowered my lids so he couldn't read my expression. "Please don't feel that you must remain here with me."

He shrugged. "I haven't anything better to do at the moment. Go to sleep, Sarah."

I gave a weak smile. "I know everyone jumps to obey your

every command, my lord. But I've been *trying* to sleep for well nigh two hours to no avail. You don't really think I wanted to stay awake while a needle was pushed in and out of my flesh, do you?"

He ran his finger down my nose in a casual caress. "I'll say this for you; you are courageous."

I wanted him to call me *sweetheart* again, not *courageous*. He made me sound like one of the kings Immortals. "Anything to oblige," I said.

"A less obliging woman I have yet to find."

"Is that the best you can do for bedside manner to a sick, weak creature at the door of death?"

He raised a hand to rub the back of his neck. To my surprise I realized that my words had pricked his conscience. "I was jesting. You've been nothing but kind."

Darius sat next to me on the bed. The mattress dipped under his weight. My head was finally beginning to fall under the spell of the medicated wine the physicians had poured down my throat and I found it hard to focus on his words.

"I sent a message to Damaspia early this morning," he said. "I asked her to separate our rooms."

"She told me." I was finding it hard to breathe. "Not that she will mind me, but I requested that she free you to go where you wished."

My vision was growing blurred and I saw his face through a fog. He studied me intensely. "Is that what *you* want? For me to leave?" He caressed my cheek with unexpected tenderness.

I found the combination of his touch and his talk of leaving too confusing and closed my eyes. "I think I'm going to sleep now," I said.

"Not yet. Answer me first."

"*What?*"

He leaned his face close to mine. "Do you want me to leave?"

"No! No, I don't want you to leave!" As I finally slipped into blessed unconsciousness, I dreamed that my husband kissed me softly on the lips.

A whole day and night passed before I awoke. Sleep had not softened the blow of pain. My body felt like it had been through the battle of Thermopylae, on the Greek side. I could smell the scent of myrrh mixed with blood under my linen bandages.

Added to the agony of half healed wounds and bruises was the urgency of the call of nature. Leaning on my good arm and shoulder, I raised myself to sit on the bed.

Suddenly, Darius was perched next to me, pushing me back into the pillows. "What are you doing? You mustn't try to rise yet."

I blinked. "I didn't know you were here."

He looked as fresh as one of the king's new coins in his crisp linen tunic. I felt dirty and unkempt in comparison. I examined his recently bathed form in dismay. He sat next to me guarding my every move when what I needed was privacy. With inexpressible passion I wished for my sweet friend, Pari. She would know how to help me. But she was plodding somewhere on the king's highways, and too far yet from Ecbatana to help me.

One of Damaspia's handmaidens would serve, I decided, considering the urgency of my need. But I would have to trouble Darius to arrange for one. Hadn't I caused him enough problems? Had he not declared that he wanted a different room, and yet here he was, stuck with me, feeling duty-bound to bide with me while I recovered? Could I add one more inconvenience to an already mounting pile? But what choice had I? I bit my nail, trying to find a way to get him out of the room so that I could at least relieve myself discreetly.

He stepped into the turmoil of my mind with alarming accuracy. "Why do you have such a hard time asking for what you want? I can see you are uncomfortable. What do you need?"

"I have bothered you enough. If you could leave the apartment for a little while—"

"Why? So you can get up and fall on your head again?"

"I didn't fall on my head," I said, my voice heavy with indignation. "That man threw me down. In any case, I wish to get up and . . . do what must be done." I had grown up in a country that was profoundly private about bodily functions. Persians didn't even spit in each other's presence. In spite of his refined background, Darius had traveled among the peoples of many lands, most of whom had no such compunctions about their personal needs. He would have no problem staying in the room and insisting on *helping* me. I could think of few things more mortifying.

Something of the mutiny on my face must have communicated itself to the man. Without a word he rose from the bed and sent Arta, waiting in his usual place outside our chamber, to go and fetch a maid.

"Have their majesties not released you to move to new rooms yet?"

"Who said I wanted to move?"

I frowned, trying to recall the thread of our conversation just before unconsciousness had claimed me. "You did. You and Damaspia."

He sat on the bed once more. "I said I wanted to move yesterday morning. I've changed my mind since then."

I tried to cross my arms and narrow my gaze and found both intentions impossible. One hurt my shoulder and the other my head. Expelling a vexed sigh I said, "Thank you for your noble sacrifice, my lord. I don't know if you feel obligated to me because of guilt or some misguided notion of duty. But I think it best you leave."

"No, you don't. You told me you want me to stay."

Like smoke on a windless day, the hazy memory of yesterday's conversation began to penetrate the cobwebs of my mind. "That's because you were pestering me and I would have said the sunrise was green for the chance to sleep."

Grinning, he put his hand on my pillow and leaned forward. I could smell mint and ginger on his breath. "Someone woke up in a foul temper."

A timid knock on the door saved me from having to answer him. Darius left me alone with the maid the queen had sent, which was a relief. By the time the maid had finished wiping me as clean as I could become without a bath and changed me into a fresh under tunic, I was grey with fatigue.

I had no strength to continue sparring with Darius when he returned to the room. He could waste his time at my bedside if that satisfied him. But he was silent as he poured out another cup of herbed wine and held it to my lips. I drank down the physic without objection and fell back into a restless sleep.

There was no sign of Darius when I awoke. The maid who had helped me earlier was dozing on a stool next to my bed.

Too many troubling thoughts tenanted my mind. I spent time in prayer, hoping that it would soothe my agitated state. I asked God to forgive me for my sharpness toward my husband. What I realized as I prayed was that I had no wish for Darius's pity. I did not desire him by my side for the sake of duty or guilt. In the end he would be sick of me; who could keep up a kinship based on pity or guilt? Before long, these emotions would wear out, would give way to resentment. And I would have to bear his abandonment after having experienced something of his tenderness.

I decided that I preferred rejecting him on my terms rather than waiting to be cast out on his. I prayed more, for I knew I lacked both strength and wisdom. I tried to cling to God the way Nehemiah had told me, tried to remember that my true worth lay in Him. I found my heart still ached at the end of my prayers, for God had not miraculously wiped the love I bore for my husband from me. Yet I also felt comforted. He made it possible for me to bear the pain.

With a sudden snort, the maid came awake. Wiping a thin line of spittle from her chin, she begged my pardon and scurried to fetch some soup.

"Where is his lordship, do you know?" I said, as I ate with desultory appetite.

"He was asked to attend the king, my lady. On account of the man who attacked you. His Majesty wished Lord Darius to make a full report on the matter."

"I see." The germ of a plan formed in my mind. I directed the maid to fetch parchment and quill and sat up to write a short missive to the queen. When the maid left with my letter, I then composed another to Darius.

My Lord,

I thank you for your kind attentions as I have been recovering. I wish to free you of all responsibility in the actions of Teispes. It was never your fault to begin with. I am going to the women's quarters, where I will receive the care I need by women, which is more befitting. Please direct Pari to me when she arrives.

Sarah

I read the note over and knew it to be dry—devoid of the feelings I wished to keep hidden from my husband. Before I lost courage, I left the parchment on my pillow and with painful movements made my way out of bed. I had not yet finished dressing when the maid returned with a litter from the queen.

Damaspia ensconced me in my own private chamber, the height of luxury in Ecbatana, in spite of the fact that it boasted no windows and was as tiny as a child's shoe. My simple exertions had exhausted me. Running like an underground river through my every thought was the knowledge that I might not see Darius for a long time. I had set him free from his false notions of responsibility toward me. With Teispes dead and his palace in good hands, nothing bound us together anymore. He had made his feelings clear toward me in the garden as he had walked away from me. What goodwill he had tried to extend toward an unwanted wife had shriveled on the bed of his suspicions. The one thing Persians hated worse than the pangs of death were lies. And Darius was convinced I was a liar.

The sole beneficial side effect of being stabbed was that I slept for long hours at a time and did not have to linger over my painful thoughts. One day I awoke to find Pari keeping vigil next to me. I threw myself in her arms, shaking with relief at the sight of her.

"There, there, my lady. What's all this?"

I told her everything. I told her about Darius's offer of friendship if I would own up to what I had not done. I told her about his disgust as he walked away from me, and about Teispes's attack. I told her about my husband's sense of guilt and the reason I had left him. I even told her how much I loved him. There was relief in sharing my heartache with someone other than God. Pari never judged me for my foolish fears or precipitous decisions. She listened with patience, holding my hand as I spoke.

When I finished my tale, she shook her head. "First, let's get you well. Then we shall deal with everything else." She was ever practical, my Pari.

When dark humors and despair threatened me, she would distract me if possible, and let me mourn when my heart was too full to bear with distractions. Pari's care coupled with her cheerful outlook proved the best remedy for my battered body. Within ten days, I was striding about the women's quarters with little pain.

To my amazement, my adventures with Teispes made me a favorite among the noble ladies and concubines housed in the women's quarters. I was invited on an endless procession of luncheons and dinners. I began to hide in my room for fear of another invitation.

Damaspia, who was a greater political genius than the king's brightest advisor, encouraged these visitations by keeping my story alive with her own version of the tale. To hear her tell it, I was the most courageous woman in the empire, and my lord Darius the most dashing hero fashioned by the Creator's hand. Without my volition, I became more popular than any lady in Ecbatana other than the queen. I knew that my popularity would only last until the next interesting rumor spread. But I also recognized that Damaspia had launched me into Persian society with a vengeance. I may soon be forgotten, but I was now welcome amongst women of rank.

I remembered how badly I had once wanted this, and was surprised to find it of such little consequence. The friendship I shared with someone as humble as Pari was worth more to me than the opinion of a dozen aristocratic ladies.

When Damaspia sent for me after ten days, I thought she wished for me to regale another woman with my gruesome tale of kidnapping, violence, betrayal, and daring rescue. Instead, I found her alone.

She said in her usual direct manner, "Your husband demands that you be returned to him. Without delay."

Chapter Twenty-Four

I forgot about palace protocol. "What?"

"He says that you've had ample time to recover from your injuries, and demands that I send you back to him forthwith."

"But why?"

Damaspia stretched her foot on an elaborate footrest. "How hard were you hit on the head, girl? You *are* his wife."

"What will you do, Your Majesty?"

"Send you to him. Forthwith. I'm not coming between the affairs of husband and wife. Every nobleman from here to Bactria will rise up in worse fury than in the days of Queen Vashti's disobedience if I do such a thing." She waved her long bejeweled hands like she was sweeping the air. "Off you go to your husband, like an obedient little wife."

I stared at her openmouthed for a moment. She had come *between the affairs of husband and wife* as long as I had been married. My shoulders drooped as I realized the futility of pointing out the queen's inconsistencies to her. "Yes, Your Majesty."

Pari came with me as I returned to Darius's apartment. She couldn't stay there; the residence was too small to accommodate her. But I wanted her with me during that initial interview. I thought her presence would mitigate the awkward opening. A greater coward did not breathe this side of the Nile. The thought of meeting with Darius face-to-face petrified me. What had possessed him to send for me? He should have been relieved to be rid of me without fuss. That's what he had wanted before Teispes complicated his life.

Instead of Arta, another of Darius's men guarded our door. I recognized him from the long ride to Ecbatana, and nodded in salutation.

"Meres. Is his lordship in?"

"Yes, my lady. And awaiting your arrival."

He opened the door after a perfunctory knock, and closed it behind us as soon as we had walked in. Darius spun around to face Pari and me. He was dressed for the hunt in leather trousers and a short tunic whose sleeves gave the appearance of iron scales. It was depressing how the very sight of him seemed to fuel my feelings with fresh power.

"Ha! My truant wife returns at long last."

"I can see we have interrupted you on your way to riding, my lord. Please don't let us detain you." I pointed to his hunting gear.

His smile was dry. "Not at all. I have just returned from the hunt."

"Oh."

He ignored me and came to stand before Pari. "And how was your journey to Ecbatana, Parisatis?"

I gaped at my husband. Where had he learned my handmaiden's full name? And why had he set himself out to charm her, for his manner toward her could have melted an icicle. His warm regard, the way he settled his undivided attention on her, his respectful, courtly manner reduced Pari to another one of his devotees in moments.

"It was very pleasant, my lord. Thank you for the extra care you took in arranging our travels."

"I'm glad to hear you had a commodious trip. Your mistress sings your praises. And I am told you've taken good care of her in her illness."

Pari turned the color of the roses in the king's arbor. "It's no hardship caring for my lady."

"Nonetheless, I wish to thank you." He handed her a slip of parchment, which he must have prepared ahead of time. "Here is an extra ration of wheat for you this month. And a lamb. You can have them sent to your family if you wish, with my compliments."

Pari's eyebrows went up so high they almost fell off her head. "I'm obliged to you, my lord. I've never had such a generous gift."

"You deserve it, Pari. You may take the rest of the day off. When your lady requires you, she will send for you."

Before I had a chance to say one word, or to express my wishes on the matter, Pari disappeared from my presence. So much for my human shield.

Darius settled himself on the couch. "You look better than the last time I saw you. I trust you are recovered?"

"I am. Thank you." It dawned on me that he had kept himself informed of my progress while I was in the women's quarters. I wouldn't have been surprised to find Damaspia herself the source of his information.

He extended a hand toward the couch. "Please, do sit." He was lounging so freely that I would have to practically squeeze myself onto his lap.

"I am comfortable standing."

"But I insist."

I perched on a narrow stool across from him, the only other seat available in the tight chamber.

"Your departure seemed . . . precipitous, shall we say? Would you care to explain?"

"I left a note."

He shifted a long leg down the length of the couch and let it hang from the end. "And such a touching letter it was too. I had hoped you'd feel inclined to consult me regarding such a decision."

He studied me with a calculating stare. Pulsing beneath his pleasant countenance was a storm of anger he kept leashed. My leaving had stung his pride, I realized. "I didn't think you would let me leave if I asked in person."

"You are honest, at least. Now tell me *why* you left."

"I told you—"

"That you wanted women to care for you, I know. Which is why I let you go. I was willing to spare your modesty. But there was more to your actions than the demands of modesty."

I made a careful study of my shoes. They were beaded and sparkled in the light pouring through the latticed window. "First, I have a question for *you*. Why didn't *you* leave? It's what you wanted. Until I was injured, you were set on it. Then you changed your mind. You needn't answer. I know your motive. You felt responsible in some way; but you had no cause. I left, because you stayed for the wrong reasons."

Darius sprang from the couch so fast I almost toppled backward from my stool. He bent toward me until his face was level with mine. "You are mistaken."

There was no room in our constrained chamber for someone as long-legged as Darius to pace. He gave it a good try

303

nonetheless, striding about in curtailed steps. He stopped in front of me and said again, "You are mistaken."

I shrugged and turned away, finding his explosive scrutiny too disturbing.

"I tried to talk to you on the day of Teispes's attack, after the physicians had left. But you fell asleep midway through my explanations. I thought I would speak with you on the following day, but by the time the maid had finished helping you, you were so fatigued that I let you be. And on the third day, when I returned to our chamber, you had taken yourself off without so much as a by-your-leave."

He flung himself upon the couch again. "When I left you in the garden, I was furious with you for your refusal to tell me the truth."

"I did tell you the truth."

"Perhaps. But then we both know you lie convincingly. Nonetheless, I managed to calm myself after an hour or two, and persuaded myself that you just might be as honest and innocent as you sounded. Then Arta delivered an interesting report; he said that you were seen emerging from Nehemiah's chambers without an escort."

I lifted a hand to my temple. "Yes, I did. He had asked us both, but you were gone, and I did not wish to wait. I am sorry, I did not realize how serious an infraction I was committing."

"You visited a single man alone? Without permission? Without even a maid for the sake of modesty? Many noblemen in Persia would set aside a wife for less provocation than this. You seem to have a great fondness for the cupbearer."

"He's like a father to me!"

"So you claim, but how should I know? At every turn you give me reason to distrust you. Which is why I determined to leave you. That morning I sent both the king and queen a request for separate rooms. Or permission to leave the palace altogether."

"I know." But I had not known my visit to Nehemiah had instigated his desire to leave. My transformation from commoner to nobility had been too abrupt. I had yet to internalize the fact that the rules that applied to my life had now changed drastically.

"You only know thus far, and have conjectured the rest. Erroneously, I might add. The truth is that I felt as hard a knock upon my head on that day as you suffered at Teispes's hands. When I walked into that glade and saw his knife at your breast, my blood ran cold. In those protracted moments of deadly danger, I came upon a few startling discoveries. I realized that I might be furious with you. I might resent some of your actions. But I also was not prepared to lose you.

"I told you as I carried you home that I do not know what to do with you. The evidence of reason will not permit me to trust you without reserve. Yet my heart refuses to believe the worst of you. I am at a quandary, as you can see—divided within myself. I know this much. I will not let you go. You are remaining with me, and I with you, and it has nothing to do with guilt or duty."

"You wish to remain with me?" I exclaimed with astonishment. I sifted through his words, trying to understand him. I could not keep the sardonic edge from my voice as I said, "You want me against your better judgment?"

His narrow smile matched the edge in my voice. "I want you enough to take a chance. I know you want *me*. You told me as much."

I did not bother to refute him. He would no doubt laugh in my face. Thus far, his strange courtship was more like a collection of sarcastic accusations than a declaration of sentiment.

He had said nothing of love, nor was he offering trust. And yet, somewhere inside, my beaten-down heart began jumping in jubilation. He wanted me! He wanted *me*!

With as much caution as my imprudent soul was capable of practicing in that moment, I said, "Without trust, we shall unravel at the first test that comes our way."

Darius turned his perfect profile to me. His nose, straight as an arrow, flared with checked emotion. "It is the best I can offer you, Sarah."

Not long ago, I expected him to desert me. Whatever his terms, they exceeded my expectations. I jerked my head into an awkward nod, signifying my agreement.

He gave the ghost of a sigh. "One condition. I want your promise that you will speak to me when trouble springs up between us. No more running away. No more unescorted visits to men. No more secrets. We will discuss our differences. You must tell me what goes on in that head of yours; I cannot forever try to guess."

I shifted on my seat. "I will promise if you make *me* a promise. Promise me you will be reasonable when I make a request of you."

"I make no such promise, for I know your concept of *reasonable*, and it is most unreasonable."

I swallowed a smile. "I shall make a bargain with you, my lord. I will play you a game of backgammon, and the winner shall have his promise. What say you?"

Darius leaned forward. "Done."

I was more than proficient at the game. Being familiar with the board, I no longer had need of counting the points. I could see in my mind's eye where each roll of the dice would land me. I won thrice in a row before Darius began to crush me. He had prodigious luck as well as sound strategy and rolled more doubles in one game than I had rolled in three.

"I believe I get my way," he said when he had thrashed me for the last time.

"How unusual."

"Don't prevaricate. Give me your word."

"I give you my promise, my lord. No more secrets."

We had supper alone in the apartment that night. The truce that he had wrought settled around us like a warm blanket. For the first time I was able to believe that he enjoyed my company. He liked being with me. He laughed with ease in my presence and asked my opinion on matters of importance without condescension.

We were trying a pistachio cake sweetened with honey, a new recipe concocted by the royal chefs, when our supper was interrupted by the arrival of a dust-covered messenger.

"It's from my father," Darius said as he studied the missive.

"Is all well?"

"Yes. But I need to attend to a few urgent matters. It will take several hours. Don't wait for me."

I was relieved as well as disappointed at his departure. So much had happened in the span of short hours. I could scarcely enter into the reality of my husband's changed feelings toward me. It occurred to me that I owed Teispes a debt of gratitude. It was the sight of his knife pressed against my chest that had caused Darius to change his mind about me. Darkness had its role on this earth.

My prayers overflowed with thanksgiving that evening. I thought of God's orchestration of events and the unlikely outcome at the end of so many strange turns and twists in recent months. I did not understand His ways. But with each passing day I grew to trust them. I thought of the words I had once spoken to Nehemiah—that I trusted his ability to make mistakes more than God's ability to make His plans succeed. How little I knew of God's power, and even less of His love if I thought human sin and error could override His ultimate plans.

When it came time to retire, I decided to give Darius the one gift I could: his bed. I snuggled under the covers of the mattress in the diminutive alcove, which he occupied when I was in the room, wanting him to have the comfort of a bed for the night. I wished fervently to be a good wife to my husband. If I could not admit to loving him, I could at least show my tenderness in caring for his small needs.

I was almost asleep when he returned. To my amazement, he lifted the covers and slipped next to me. I sat bolt upright. "What are you doing?" I squeaked.

"I'm joining you in bed."

It dawned on me that he perceived my presence in his bed as an overt invitation. I must have appeared as brazen as the courtesan I had once claimed to be. "You think I came here to . . . you think I was trying to . . . Great heavens above! I was just trying to get you to sleep in your own bed."

"I am sleeping in my own bed."

"Fine." I rolled out of the other side of the mattress and stomped off to the ornate bed. Pulling the blanket down with jerky motions, I stepped back and bumped into a solid mass. Whipping around with a gasp, I found myself facing a wall of muscle.

"My lord?"

"My name is Darius. You could try using it."

I crossed my arms. The memory of the last time I had used his name snuck up the coils of memory, leaving a bitter taste on my tongue. "No I could not. You told me yourself not to be familiar."

Darius wrapped his hands around my arms, uncrossing

them and pulling me forward in one smooth motion. "Lesson number one: you're talking too much."

He pulled harder, propelling me into his embrace. Without warning, his lips descended over mine. My eyes widened.

"Lesson number two," he murmured when he lifted his head. "Close your eyes when I kiss you." He wrapped one hand about my waist and fitted me to his length. With featherlight kisses, he closed my eyes before kissing me on the lips again.

"Lesson number three," he said when he raised his head, his voice husky. "Kiss me back. Like this. And this."

I barely remembered how to breathe when he stopped. "How many lessons are there?" I asked, my voice a thread.

He laughed, deep in his throat. "I'll show you if you say my name."

"Darius," I whispered obediently. It wasn't the last time I uttered it that night.

I woke up to the warbling of sparrows at sunrise. Darius slept next to me, his sprawled body taking up most of the bed. The pale rays of the morning light illuminated his face. In sleep, he lacked the predatory edge that normally stamped his features. His lips, carved and long, held no hardness. I thought of their touch the night before and turned to slip out of bed, embarrassed by my own ruminations.

A hand wrapped around my arm and pulled me back. "Where do you think you're going? You must ask my permission to leave, did you not know?"

I snorted with astonishment. "No."

He nodded. "It's the truth. In the normal course of things, when Damaspia hasn't had her interfering fingers in one's living arrangements, you would be called to my apartments. And you would stay there until I dismissed you."

I pulled the sheets higher around me. "You plan to be a tyrannical husband, I see."

Darius fluffed two pillows behind him and sat up. "I'm merely informing you of aristocratic propriety."

My mouth grew dry as the joy of the enchanted hours we had shared dimmed. It was easy in the privacy of this tiny chamber to think of him as *my* husband. But a day would come, and perhaps soon, when I would have to learn to share him with others. I would come and go to him at his whim, in a long line of other women.

"What is it? You look sad, of a sudden."

I shook my head.

"You promised not to keep secrets from me."

"This is no secret. It's a private thought. You can't expect me to share every thought that enters my head."

"I do expect it. And I won the right if you recall. Now tell me why my bride is sorrowful. You can leave my bed without my permission if it irks you so. Go as you please. I care not."

I attempted a smile. "That is generous of you."

"But?"

How he pressed to have more of me. For years, I had been guilty, with alarming frequency, of opening my mouth and spilling my thoughts without proper consideration. Feelings were another matter. Those I guarded. Now here was the person whose opinion meant more to me than any other, and he was not satisfied with a pleasing shell. He wanted the revelation of my whole soul, be it clean and good, or weak and mired in imperfection. I could not bear to show him my insecure heart and have it rebuffed, have it ridiculed.

Yet I knew what the Lord would want from me. He who

310

wished for truth in my inmost being would want me to show myself as I was to my husband. I was to rest in His forgiveness and acceptance no matter what Darius thought of me.

I opened my mouth, and closed it when no words came out. Clearing my throat, I forced my voice into obedience. "I was thinking of how life will change in time. You will marry again. I will have to learn to share you."

Chapter Twenty-Five

Darius shrugged. "I am not set on marrying again. I was traumatized the first time."

I shoved him in the shoulder. He grasped my wrists and pulled me against him. "I am in earnest. I don't intend to marry another."

I frowned. "Like Artaxerxes, you mean? Marry one woman, and have the rest as concubines?"

He sighed and released me. His forehead grew knotted in thought.

"I intended no complaint, my lord," I said, anxious that I had displeased him. "These are just the ravings of my mind. You see how bothersome they are, and useless? Now perhaps you won't insist on having a share of them."

He remained silent. I licked my lips. "I grew up with a father who could afford but one wife. There were no concubines in our home. I am not accustomed to such luxury. As it is, I am blessed—"

Darius stopped the deluge of my words with a kiss so passionate I forgot what I was talking about. He kissed me until I forgot the whole world. He wove a net of desire about me so thick that I doubt I would have remembered my own name, except that he kept repeating it. There was a desperation in the way he made love to me that morning. He clung to me as one trying to stamp out the shadow of old monsters. I clung back; I had my own monsters to forget.

We ate our morning meal in silence. Darius seemed preoccupied and I still smarted from having misspoken earlier.

"Do you wish to go for a ride?" he asked after breakfast.

"With you?"

"I could arrange Meres to go with you, if you prefer."

"He *is* rather handsome. Can I think on it?"

"No you little wretch, you can't. It's either me or no one."

"Then I suppose it had better be you."

We plodded past the walls of Ecbatana. The world grew quiet and fresh once we left the bustle of the city. It felt as though we were the only two occupants of Persia as we rode side by side.

"My mother grew up in a home like yours," Darius said. He had a disconcerting habit of bringing up topics connected to nothing.

"A home like mine?"

"One husband. One wife. That kind of home. Her father was a simple steward."

"I had heard."

This was no casual conversation, I could see from the determined set of his jaw. He meant to expound on something. I tried to tune my ears to his mood so that I wouldn't miss the point he wished to make.

"My parents' marriage was a love match. They chose each other," he said.

I considered the luxury of loving someone and knowing yourself loved in return. My chest tightened with unmet longing. "They must have been very happy."

"In many ways they were. Still, my mother found it hard adjusting to life with a man who was bound to so many other women. Many a night I watched her hide tears in her eyes when my father sent for another instead of her. She understood when she consented to marry my father that a Persian aristocrat's way of life meant sharing her husband with other women. She could have a part of him or none of him. She chose to have a part. Though she made her decision knowingly, she still paid a price. She suffered from his divided attention."

He wanted me to know that he understood my pain, I thought. That he did not judge me deficient in some way because of it. He wanted me to learn to bear with his way of life as his mother had learned to bear with his father's. "I will try to be gracious like your mother," I said.

He grimaced. "When I was a child, I remember vowing never to do that to my wife. Never to cause her to suffer such pangs of loneliness." He shifted on Samson. "Do you know whose life I wanted?"

"Whose?"

"The son of Bardia, Gobry's father. He had one wife. His children were born to him of the same woman, and they all lived together piled up in one small cottage on our estate. But they were happy. United. I have three half brothers and two half sisters, and I hardly know them. My brothers resent me for being my father's primary heir. My sisters seem to want favors, not affection."

I shook my head. "There are no perfect families, are there? I thought yours came close. I would have given the full length of my hair to experience the love you shared with your parents."

He leaned over and pulled on a fat, silky coil playfully. "Don't go giving away your tresses with such generosity. I like them too well."

I swatted his hand away. "I bet Gobry would have swapped lives with you in a heartbeat."

"I know how privileged I am. I know I am more fortunate than most. But I had always hoped to give my children a better life still.

"I had hoped to marry for love as my parents did. I knew it to be an unlikely dream for a man in my position. Still, I nursed those hopes. I struggled to think of ways that would spare my wife the pain my mother had suffered. When my father arranged my marriage to a woman I had never heard of, I thought that on this point, at least, I could have an easy conscience. Ours was no love match. You did not want me, nor I you. I imagined that would spare you, though I did what I could to welcome you into my home."

"What do you mean?" I recollected little of welcome when I came to him.

"Before I married you, I had three concubines. All came to me of their own will; I would accept no war prize in the form of frightened women. When my father told me about our marriage, I settled each of my concubines into her own home with servants and enough income to live a comfortable life. They can marry if they choose, or remain independent. I made those arrangements so that my wife could enter my home as the only woman in it. It seemed a gracious way to start our life."

My fingers grasped Kidaris's reins with convulsive strength. "You did this even though being wed to me meant an end to your dream for love?" I stared at the ground, blind now to the rich beauty of our surroundings. "You thought of my well-being while I thought only of myself and how to have my own way. I am shamed, my lord, more than ever, of doing you wrong."

He slashed the air with a gloved hand. "I did not say this to shame you. I said it because this morning I saw in your eyes a reflection of what I used to see in my mother's. I suppose even a woman who doesn't love her husband has no wish to share him. I want you to know that for now at least, you do not need to worry over such concerns. Nor will I marry another as long as you keep faith with me and tell me no lies."

My heart brimmed over with pain. What I had promised never to tell him bubbled over onto my tongue. "But I do love you," I cried. Horrified that I had spoken the words aloud, I kicked Kidaris in the side and took off at a gallop.

Outriding a Persian cavalry officer is like trying to outshine the light of the sun. Within moments my reins were in Darius's hands and we had both come to a dead stop.

With one fluid motion, he leapt off his horse's back while pulling me down with him. He drew us a distance away before stopping. "What did you say?"

"Nothing!"

"Did you mean it?"

"Forget I said it. It matters not."

"It matters to me," he said, his eyes soft. "I would like to hear you say it."

I bowed my head. "I said I love you."

The problem with love, I reflected, was that nothing but equal or surpassing love could satisfy its longings. In two short days, I had made enough discoveries to turn my life on its head. I had found that my husband was not indifferent to me. He wanted my company and was unwilling to lose me. In his kindness, he had made a promise to marry no other. I received more honor from him than Damaspia from her king, for I shared my husband with no concubines.

And yet strangely, I was not satisfied. I hungered for more. My husband wanted me, but he did not love me. Kindness, desire, thoughtfulness could not replace the absence of his love. Could not make up for the fact that when I confessed my love to him, he kissed me with passion, with possessive delight, but he made no declaration of his own.

Nor could I put out of my mind the fact that when he had spoken of having no woman save me in his home, he had said *for now at least,* words that rang with ominous possibilities for the future. I knew that his father's expectations as well as the weight of a culture's vast heritage required that he fill his home with women and children. How long would his tender memories of a beloved mother resist the mountainous weight of such a demand? Without the shield of love, of faith, how could he stand fast against what every other aristocrat would deem his proper duty to family and nation?

His promise to marry no other, though reassuring, came with conditions. As long as I kept faith and told him no lies, he had said. If I misstepped, if in his eyes I broke faith, then how fast would he hold to his intention of keeping me as his only wife?

Though he had learned to like me, he had yet to learn to trust me. Every day he seemed to draw nearer to giving up his doubts about me, however. I wondered if a time would come when he would believe me without hesitation or question.

I spent many hours during the dawning days of autumn in supplication before the Lord. I had many hours to spare, for Darius, as a courtier, had his responsibilities. His duties occupied his time. I had no like occupation. Hunting and sport, which were the delights of Damaspia's ladies, interested me little. Nor could I while my hours away at skin and hair treatments, enhancing my charms. I did what I must with grudging impatience. But I could not build a life around such employments. My mind was accustomed to useful activity and what little activity it received in Ecbatana consisted of conversation with my husband and Pari, an occasional audience with the queen, and extended hours of torturous thought about loving a man who did not return the favor.

The Lord used those painful days to weave my soul more tightly to Him. If I had been a beloved bride, I would have been tempted to make an idol of my husband. Loving Darius as I did, it would have been easy to fall into my old habit of seeking all my well-being from him. Instead, I turned more to my God and sought to find rest in His loving-kindness. He seemed the only sure ground in my life.

One afternoon when I expected Darius to remain gone until late into the night, the door burst open and he strode in. I had not seen him since dawn, and looked up in surprise. His shuttered expression revealed nothing. I gave up my prayers and stood to face him, feeling unsure.

"Is anything amiss?"

He shook his head. "I interrupted your prayers."

318

"The Lord is likely relieved by the interruption. I pester Him often."

He was in full court regalia, having attended an official state affair. With impatient fingers he divested himself of his jewel-studded belt and leather sandals, and fell on the couch. His intense green eyes watched me with narrow concentration.

I wriggled with discomfort under the sharp examination. "Why are you here? I thought the feast would go on till past midnight."

His smile was sideways and hard. "Yes, why am I here? I asked myself the same question with every step that took me away from my duty. I could say that I grew bored to death with the pontifications of various heads of state."

I sat next to him on the couch, unsure of his strange mood. "Did you?"

"Oh yes. But that's nothing unusual. I have participated in such events since before I had a beard."

"Then why did you leave?"

"I left, little wife, because I missed you."

Any joy I might have felt at such a declaration dimmed by the edge of angry accusation in his voice. "You don't sound happy about it."

He pulled a hand through his hair and leaned away from me. "Why should I be unhappy? It's no surprise that you are more entertaining than a bunch of whiny old lords set on asking new favors. Anyone would be."

I leaned just as far back from him. "What extraordinary talent you display," I said with cold humor. "In the course of a few words you manage to insult the Persian aristocracy and its foreign heads of state, as well as me. You really ought to teach me how you do that."

The corners of his eyes crinkled. "In the interest of self-preservation, I must refuse you, my lady. You have enough weapons at your disposal. It would be suicide to add to your arsenal."

As his temper cooled, my own temperature rose. "I know not of what weapons you speak, my lord."

I found myself in his arms. "Here is one," he murmured against my mouth. "And here is another," he said as he continued to kiss me.

With the last of my strength I resisted him. "It's not fair that you resent me because you miss me."

"I know."

I woke up to find Darius staring out through the lattice window. He had bunched the blue linen curtains to one side and the light of the moon poured into our chamber. Wrapping myself in a robe, I tiptoed to his side.

Without turning to me he said, "The court moves to Susa soon, but I want to return to my estate in Persepolis, Sarah. I want to ensure that everything is in right order."

"Oh, that's wonderful! I'll see Bardia and Shushan again." I thought about Caspian whom I would *not* see and my chest contracted with pain.

He turned to me. "You do not mind going back? You shall miss the feasts and pageantry of the court for most of the season."

"Of course I don't mind. I would rather be with my friends than stuck with lords and ladies I don't know."

He frowned. "You've grown quite popular, from what I hear. Many ladies seek your company now. You'll not long for that?"

"Not so much popular as entertaining. I have no real friends in court, save perhaps the queen. I am grateful for the acceptance I have found amongst the ladies of rank for your sake if nothing else. As to their company, I can do very well without it."

He was silent for a time as he resumed his vigil of the garden through the window. When he spoke finally, his words were measured. "Since Teispes, I have become mindful of how vulnerable my estates are to harm. I am often away and haven't the time, nor the nature, to examine every detail of the management of my lands. I used to think that I could leave such matters to my stewards and servants. Now I see that is not enough."

His breath trickled out like a deflated sigh. "I see how much damage one dishonest individual can cause. So I have a proposition for you, Sarah. I want you to oversee the management of all my properties. That is what you did for the queen, is it not? You would have less to do in my household, as your job would be to manage my managers, so to speak. I know ladies of your station are not expected to work. I realize I am asking an unusual favor, and I want you to know yourself free to refuse me." He kept his gaze trained away through this speech, as though wishing to give me complete freedom in the making of my decision.

My stomach performed a neat summersault. Was he truly throwing what I had yearned for into my lap as if it were a favor to *him*?

I took time to examine my heart before jumping to give an answer. How did I feel about returning to the work I knew and loved so well? If he had made me this offer when I first had wed him, how different my life would have been. Would I have learned to make friends? To place people and their needs above my achievements? If he had offered me this position when I began to recognize my feelings for him, would I have grasped on to it as a means of proving my worth? As the only way I knew to make him care for me, just a little? Would I not have become once again a slave to my own accomplishments?

How great a temptation would his offer prove even now? God had given me a glimpse of His freedom, it was true. But was I ready to face my old obsession, my darling passion, my idol? Could I work without twisting my achievements into a means of winning acceptance and security?

I pressed my eyes shut and asked for guidance. What was the will of the Lord, not my will, nor Darius's, but the Lord's will, in this? I would obey. Though it slay me, I would obey. As I made that absolute determination, a sudden and inexplicable relief flooded me. I had no angelic visitation. No one spoke to me with a voice like thunder. But I *knew* that the Lord was bidding me to grant my husband's wish. He who had knit me together in my mother's womb would guide me daily and shield me from idolatry. And when I failed, He would lift me up, lead me to repentance, wash me clean with the blood of His sacrifices, and set me on the right path again.

Opening my eyes, I gazed upon my husband. Darius's mouth, pressed tight, had grown white with tension as he waited on my response. I realized with dawning clarity that he had more invested in my answer than the convenience of gaining a free scribe. This was a test to him—a test of my nature, my loyalty, my honesty.

I smiled as I gazed on his tense profile. "I would be honored, my lord. To tell the truth, I have been bored half out of my mind. There were days when your whiny heads of state would have seemed the height of entertainment compared to another treatment by one of Damaspia's makeup artists. I would love to serve you as I served the queen."

"Are you certain? I would not punish you for refusing."

"I have no wish to refuse."

A strong tapered hand wrapped itself around mine as he continued to stare through the window. I pressed his fingers and joined him in his study of the moon-drenched garden. He might not love me, but he missed me through the course of one day's absence. He might not trust me with his heart, but he entrusted me with the breadth of his wealth and the care of his vassals. He might resent and fight it, but each day, he surrendered another part of himself to me. My smile glowed with satisfaction.

I thought of how the Lord had parted the River Jordan for Israel in order to lead them into the Promised Land. *Part his heart for me, Lord. Part his soul for Yourself.*

Chapter Twenty-Six

For our journey back, Darius consented to ride along the royal highway with our whole party. The fact that we spent the nights in the king's stage houses instead of tents, and set our pace at the relative ease that accommodated the covered carts containing Pari and our furnishings, made the trip a tranquil experience compared to our mad dash to Ecbatana. Twenty days flew by in a pleasant haze.

Darius had sent word of our coming to the palace in advance. We arrived after sunset to find the whole place ablaze with lamps in anticipation of our arrival. The sumptuous smell of Shushan's cooking greeted us before we had stepped out of the stables.

It seemed to me that most of the indoor staff must have assembled to greet us, for lined up before us stood over fifty men and women, many of them strangers to me. Shushan came forward bearing a bunch of late-blooming roses. "Welcome home, my lord. My lady." She bowed and gave me the flowers.

I threw my arms about her angular shoulders and gave her a proper hug. "I missed you."

She tried to look disapproving, but even in the lamplight I could see her mouth twitching.

"Where is Bardia?" I cried.

"Here my lady." Darius was first in line to offer the old gardener a greeting by kissing him on both cheeks. At the court, he would have outraged more than one aristocrat by his behavior, for a commoner was expected to bow to an aristocrat. Kisses were bestowed on the cheeks of men of rank, only. But my husband gave more due to a man's character than to his rank. My heart melted with approval.

I was home. I had my friends about me. For the first time in long years, I felt that I truly belonged somewhere.

Though part of me celebrated this comforting sense of homecoming, another part of me anguished. This marked the first night I would sleep in a room apart from my husband since my return from the queen's residence in Ecbatana. The separation stung. Swallowing self-pity, I bestowed a small smile upon Darius before retiring to my apartments.

I knew Pari was as tired and grimy as I from the journey, so I sent her to find a maid who could help with my bath and told her to take the evening off. All the dust of Persia seemed to have worked its way into my hair and clothing. Luxuriating in a long bath, I finally emerged to change into a nightgown and woolen robe before dismissing the new maid.

I crawled into bed alone. Henceforth, I would have to wait on Darius's pleasure to see him. I could not run to him at will, or seek him out without serious cause.

The silence gathered about me with oppressive weight. If I had not lost Caspian, no doubt he would be with me now, smothering me with his wet kisses.

In the light of the lamps I took in the rich tapestries, the opulent furnishings given me from the hand of a queen, the embroidered linens. How different my life had turned out from even my wildest imaginings!

So many of my dreams had come true. So many had been lost.

This was the nature of life. Loss, grief, sorrow, regret were woven through the fabric of human destiny as uncompromisingly as joy, hope, and fulfillment. If one's happiness rested only in the capture of one's dreams, then happiness would prove fickle indeed. There were many things I wanted with desperation that I might never have: Darius's love, my father's approval, a child of my own flesh, the ability to go to my husband at will. And what I did have, I might someday lose.

No. If my joy hung in the balance of having everything I wanted, I would always wrestle with unhappiness.

There had to be another way to joy, another highway to happiness apart from gaining all the desires of my heart.

I thought of how King David often spoke like a man who walked on two roads at once. He had one foot placed firmly on the road of suffering, and the other on the road of hope and joy. It wasn't a case of *either, or* with David. He had learned to do both at once, when needed. He could grieve while rejoicing.

I remembered one of his psalms, where he began by praising God for His goodness:

You have not handed me over to the enemy
But have set my feet in a spacious place.

While in the next breath he cried out with anguish:

Be merciful to me, O Lord, for I am in distress;
My eyes grow weak with sorrow,
My soul and my body with grief.

David knew how to walk the path of affliction while being settled firmly in the joy of God's presence. I wanted to learn to be like David, to have eyes that saw the loving hand of the Lord even in the midst of unfulfilled dreams.

A soft knock on the door dragged me out of my reverie. Pari slipped inside, her hair still wet from its recent washing.

"What are you doing here? I gave you the night off."

"I remember. I am visiting, not working."

I grinned and patted the pillow next to me. She scrambled on the bed and sprawled out comfortably. "I noticed a long line of men waiting at Lord Darius's door. He'll no doubt be busy late into the night. I thought you might be lonely on your first night home."

The best—and worst—quality about my friends was that they knew my insides without my having to explain it to them.

"I'm glad of your company." I also rejoiced to find out that the reason Darius had not sent for me was not because he had no wish for my presence, but due to his responsibilities.

"Have you had dinner?" she asked.

"Not yet." I had secretly been hoping that Darius would invite me to eat with him. But if he was as busy as Pari said, he would have no time.

"I'll fetch some," Pari said.

She came back with no tray.

"Oh good. Invisible food. Does this mean I will gain no weight when I swallow it? I hope you brought a lot if that's the case."

Pari chastised me with a stern look. "His lordship requests your assistance."

"Ah." *Assistance.* It was the scribe he wanted, then, not the wife. I donned suitable clothes and made my way to Darius's apartments, Pari in tow. We certainly were about to forge some new precedents here. It was one thing being a scribe to the queen. I worked with eunuchs and women most of the time, and being a commoner, my rare interactions with men hardly raised an eyebrow. But I was part of the nobility now and was held to stricter rules of conduct. Darius had stretched many a protocol by this scheme.

I found him in the company of his scribe. His face seemed rigid, his eyes strained. He lit up when he saw me.

"Sarah! Are you too tired to look at these figures?"

"No, my lord."

"Excellent. Vidarna, my wife shall see to these details. She has ridden far today, so don't drown her with all your reports at once. Show her what seems urgent, and save the rest for the coming week."

Vidarna's mouth went down on both sides as his eyebrows went up. He could not hide his dismay as I sat near him and invited him to begin. Within five minutes, I had him sitting straight, his forehead covered in sweat. Other than his initial skepticism toward me, I found no fault with his work, and gave him the guidance he needed for several minor decisions.

Darius stifled another yawn. "Can the rest wait, Vidarna?"

"Yes, lord."

Darius nodded dismissal. Vidarna gathered the tools of his trade and walked out, followed by Pari and Darius's man. I rose to follow them. Darius grabbed my arm and pulled me onto his lap where he lounged on a wide couch. "Not you. I didn't say you could go."

"I thought you were finished with the scribes."

"The scribes can go to the moon. My wife, I want."

I never made it to my room that night. When I awoke, still in his bed, it was late morning and there was no sign of Darius. I decided to go in search of Bardia as soon as I dressed.

An idyllic fall day greeted me with the merest hint of a chill in the air. I had fetched Pari to go with me and we ambled in lazy enjoyment. One of Bardia's many new assistants told us we could find him in the vineyard.

The sun shone high and bright, sharing the sky with a few fat, white clouds. I found myself laughing for no reason, distracted by the beauty of the day. I was utterly unprepared for the sight that met me when we arrived at the entrance of the vineyard. Row after row of vine, so heavy with grapes that it required a sturdy pole tied to each plant to keep it upright, greeted my astonished gaze.

I gasped with delight. The last time I had stood here, Bardia had pruned the vine with such drastic energy that the place looked more like a stick garden than a vineyard. Now those same plants bloomed with health, bearing so much exquisite fruit, it took your breath away.

"Oh Bardia," I marveled, when I saw him. "It's glorious."

"Try one, my lady. Go ahead." I gave a small bunch to Pari and popped a few grapes into my own mouth. The juice exploded on my tongue with a mixture of sweet and tangy flavors so complex, I grinned from sheer gustatory joy. The aroma of grapes wrapped around my insides like perfume from Damascus.

"Delicious," I mumbled. Before I had swallowed, I popped another handful in my mouth.

Bardia laughed. "Take it slow, my lady. Leave some for the king's table."

"Let the king come and fetch his own. This is my share."

"Wait until you taste the wine. This has been a good year, I reckon."

The sun burst from behind a white cloud at that moment and shone its dazzling light on the fruit before me. The grapes, red and plump, took on a translucent quality.

"Rubies!" I cried. "They look like rubies on the vine. You've grown a harvest of rubies, Bardia."

He gave me a modest smile. "It wouldn't have been much of a harvest if I had listened to you and stopped pruning."

His teasing words stopped me short. With new intensity I examined the fruitful vine before me. I recalled standing near this very spot, clutching a severed branch.

How like the vine I had felt that day, stripped almost to the point of death, everything I held precious taken from me. How I had longed for my old life back. And yet, like Bardia, God had intended to do me good by dismantling my world.

I had thought that my work was the measure of my worth. I had made my accomplishments more important than friendships, more important than my heart, more important even than God.

The more I clutched at my achievements, the sicker my soul had grown. And God, in His mercy, in His uncompromising love, had torn the sickness out of my chest.

I remembered suddenly the words of the Lord as spoken through the prophet Hosea:

Therefore I am now going to allure her;
I will lead her into the desert
And speak tenderly to her.
There I will give her back her vineyards,
And will make the Valley of Achor a door of hope.

The Lord spoke these words to the kingdom of Israel during her season of intense faithlessness. But He might just as well have spoken them to me.

At a time when I had grown empty and faithless, He allured me away from the riches of court life where I had turned my success into the source of my well-being. Instead He brought me into a desert of hopelessness and loss. He did not bring me into this wilderness in order to destroy me; He brought me here to speak tenderly to me. To speak of *His* love, which healed the sorrows of my childhood. To restore to me my true self, which had become buried under the weight of my perverse appetites for human acceptance.

Looking back, I now realized I could never have tasted true happiness while I had remained so soul-sick. The compulsions of a hungry heart can forbear no denial. They can taste no joy unless they have what they want. And even having, they are not satisfied. The only way I had known to find a measure of happiness back then was to succeed, to win approval, to avoid failure. And yet all the success in the world could not truly satisfy me. It merely left me hungry for more.

I now knew that only my appetite for godly things could ever be truly satisfied.

In His mercy, knowing I was headed for more sorrow by having what I wanted, God had stripped me of the things that fed my soul-sickness. And that brought me to—the Valley of Achor—The Valley of *Trouble*. I saw with clarity, that my suffering had paved the way to my healing. My heart no longer grasped hungrily for my old idols. It still wanted them. I could not deny it. But it wanted God more.

Like Bardia's vine, the soil of my early life had been poor. This world was a fallen place. I had battled loneliness and rejection from an early age. But then, when I turned to Him, I knew that God would not allow these losses to annihilate me. He would use them for good, in the end, though the way to His goodness would sometimes lead straight through the desert and into the Valley of Trouble.

I knew He had directed my path there.

When the season came, the Bardia of my soul had grasped His pruning shears and cut into my already weak frame. He had cut into me to give me more abundant life.

Had I borne a harvest of rubies like Bardia's grapevine as a result? I thought of the changes in my life. I knew how to be a friend now. How to accept help. How to open my heart. I knew how to live without being a mighty success, without being admired and accepted. I knew how to love my husband without being destroyed by the reality that he did not feel the same about me. I knew how to taste joy, even when life was not perfect. In the desert of my life, I had learned David's lesson. I had learned to keep one foot on the road of peace while the other remained trapped in pain.

Most importantly, I knew how to cling to the Lord. I had learned how to be satisfied, learned how to trust Him. Well, most of the time. He still had many lessons to teach me. He still had to cover my gaps.

God had given me back my vineyards. He had taken a broken and sickly garden of sticks and turned them into a rich vineyard, bearing jewels. I had my own harvest of rubies.

"You've been eating Bardia's grapes, I see," a familiar voice whispered against my ear.

I swiveled to find my husband's amused face, studying me. He reached a finger and wiped away the grape juice clinging to the side of my mouth. He held it up for me to see, a small droplet of scarlet on the tip of his finger, standing out like blood. "Evidence of your thievery," he said, before licking it clean.

I never would learn to eat without making a mess, I thought with a sigh. "It wasn't really thievery. Bardia offered it. He was proving how wrong I was."

Darius's brows drew together. "About what?"

"Well, I had lectured him on pruning a few months back."

The long green eyes crinkled in the corners. "You lectured my head gardener on pruning? I am sorry I missed that spectacle. What exactly did you lecture him about?"

"About his drastic measures. He was hacking away at the vine and I advised him to be gentler."

"I take it he gave you a lecture of his own."

I threw Darius a suspicious glance. "Did he give you the same one?"

"When I was about seventeen. You are a little slow."

I laughed. For a moment I deliberated on whether to share with my Persian husband the lessons God had taught me in recent weeks. Could he even begin to understand the world from such a different perspective? I decided that more than anything, I wanted to share this part of my life with him. I wanted him to begin to comprehend my faith. I knew I had to start slow. I did not wish him to think I was pushing my beliefs on him.

"The Lord used Bardia's words to show me a glimpse of His wisdom," I said tentatively.

Chapter Twenty-Seven

"The Lord?" Darius pulled gently on my hand and we began to walk toward a wooden arbor covered by a profusion of late-blooming white roses. "Bardia knows nothing about the Lord."

"I know. It's just that God sometimes refers to Himself as a gardener and to Israel as a vine. As Bardia taught me the mystery of the vine, I felt as though the God of Israel showed me how He could use the suffering in my life for my good."

Darius settled us on the marble bench in the shaded privacy of the arbor. He raised my hand, palm up to his lips for a gentle kiss. "I caused you much pain. I am sorry for it."

My mouth fell open at his unexpected apology. "You had every reason to be angry with me when we first met. I must have been a terrible disappointment to you."

He gave a lopsided smile. "Anger and disappointment I knew what to do with. What confounded me was the change in my feelings."

"What do you mean?"

"When I returned to fetch you to Ecbatana, I was still brimming with dislike for you. Then, to my shock, I found a lovely, composed woman in place of the little monster I had come to expect.

"I found I resented you even more for your beauty; I didn't want to admire any part of you. To my astonishment, the vile image I had built of you in my mind began to crumble with such rapidity that I could not keep up with the evidence before me. You were kind and gentle. My most trusted servants adored you. You had the valor of one of the king's Immortals and the intelligence of one of his advisors. You were funny. I *liked* you.

"But the most disconcerting development was when I realized I *desired* you. That very first night. Tired as I was after my grueling ride from Ecbatana, and facing the appalling betrayal of a trusted servant, I found myself moved as you sat next to me in your midnight blue dress. You leaned over to show me your scroll. I remember I had to stand so quickly, I overturned you."

"You jest!" My voice came out in a squeak. "You never wanted me then."

"I did, I tell you. And it put me out of countenance. I wished to stay as far away from you as I could. Desiring you proved an inconvenience I had not counted on. I wanted nothing to do with you. I had no intention of forgiving you. And then I saw how you loved Caspian, and it broke through my resolve to ignore you.

"Things only grew worse on that interminable journey north. The first few days, I had to bear with sitting in the saddle with you nestled in my arms for hours at a time. Then as you grew strong in the saddle, I had to come to grips with the fact that you *weren't* nestled in my arms. The whole state

335

of affairs made me cantankerous beyond forbearance. You must have noticed?"

I leaned against him. "I assumed it was your normal disposition."

"I'm generally as affable as a lamb."

"Of course you are," I said. He laughed.

"You were very kind to me, that first evening in the palace," I said.

"By then, the thought of you remaining a laughingstock in the court stuck in my throat. I did not want you, but I did not wish you to suffer, either. I had planned upon our arrival in Ecbatana to drop you in Damaspia's keeping and be rid of you. I had committed myself to supporting you in public, but I had no intention of spending personal time with you. Then again, I hadn't contended with the queen's devious mind. Having to share a room with you was utter torture. You were witty and charming. I wanted to spend all my time with you, and yet could not bring myself to trust you. I avoided that room as much as I possibly could."

"Ah. I wondered where you spent the nights."

"As far away from you as I could devise. You almost had to die before I realized I could not walk away from you."

My heart melted as I lifted my eyes to his beloved face. "In that case, I bless the day Teispes took me hostage."

"Well, I don't! That was one of the worst days of my life. I don't know how one small woman can cause so much trouble."

As soon as he mentioned *trouble*, my mind brought me back to the fact that all was not resolved between us. There was a shallow foundation beneath my marriage. I wondered with a sick feeling if all the admiration he felt for me now could bear the weight of his mistrust.

Then he whispered my name, softly, like he liked the sound

of it on his lips, and kissed me, and I forgot my worries.

"Do you know, I don't think you did that quite as well as you normally do," I said when he lifted his head. "Perhaps you should try it again. I think you are out of practice."

He must have taken me seriously at first, for he looked disconcerted for a moment, before giving a shout of laughter. He pulled me into his arms with a rough motion. "My life must have been utterly boring without you." Then he kissed me again and we both forgot about the idea of boredom.

That evening, I found myself supping alone with my husband.

"Your father wishes to see you," he said without preamble.

I choked on a piece of lamb. "My *father?*"

"You are not on good terms?"

"It's complicated. I was angry with him for signing our marriage contracts without trying to protect me. You won't understand. You were in the same position and bore your father no ill will."

"Do you wish me to send him away, then?"

"Away? Is he *here?*"

"Yes. Didn't I say? He showed up this evening to ask my permission for a visit."

I stood up, almost upending a tray of food in my haste. "Where is he?"

"I sent him to your rooms."

My father was standing near the far wall, studying a tapestry. He turned around when he heard me walk in. I expected him to remain on the other side of the room, keeping his distance. Instead he stepped toward me with hesitant steps.

"Sarah?" his voiced brimmed with astonishment.

I had forgotten how much I had changed since he had last seen me. "Yes, Father."

"Why . . . why, you're beautiful!"

I had heard a number of similar compliments recently. But none pierced my heart so deeply. I lowered my lids to hide the glaze of tears.

To my astonishment he covered the gap between us and enfolded my hand in his trembling grasp. "Child, does he treat you well? Are you unhappy? Because I will take you away from here if you want. I care not if your husband is related to twelve kings. I cannot bear that you should be unhappy."

I gave him a blank look, almost beyond comprehension. "You would do that for me?"

"Yes! Let's go now. Come. We will leave at once. I have a cousin in Bactria. We can go to him for a start. And then, we shall find our way."

"What? No! I mean, I am not unhappy, Father."

He took a step away. "This is all my fault. I've been thinking about it since the day you wed—that terrible day with everyone scrutinizing you with such vicious judgment. If I had been a better father, you would have been more prepared. You wouldn't have found yourself in a marriage you deplored.

"I've been a terrible father to you. I've been neglectful. I know it. In my ignorance, I have done you much wrong. My own sweet daughter! I don't know how I shall face your mother." To my horror, he broke down and began to sob bitterly.

"Father!" Without thinking, I took him into my arms, trying

to comfort him. He placed a hesitant arm around my shoulder. For the first time since my childhood years, we clung to each other. The bitterness and sorrow of years were washed in our tears.

"I always thought I was a bad daughter. Not good enough, somehow."

"You?" He gaped at me. "You were perfect. What did you ever do that was wrong?"

"I was a bother to you," I said, and after all my prayers, I still could not say the words without a fresh rush of tears.

"I was a crusty scribe who had no idea how to raise such a precious child. That did not make you a bother. It made me a deficient father. Oh Sarah, forgive me. Forgive me."

"With all my heart. I love you, Father."

When our tears were spent, we stepped away from each other. To my surprise, my father grasped my hand and began to pull me toward the door. "Let us make haste and be away from this place. I have a cart waiting outside. We can travel through the night."

"What? No, Father! I don't wish to leave."

"You're only saying that to spare me from danger."

"I am not! I'm saying that because it's true. I love my husband. He's a good man."

"Truly?"

I gave a watery laugh. "Yes, truly. I shall send for him so that you can meet him."

"I met him once at the wedding. It was not an experience I would like to repeat."

"He improves on further acquaintance. Now sit, while I send for him."

Darius came with gratifying speed in answer to my request. "My father thinks you are going to eat him for supper," I whispered in his ear. "So be kind. He came to kidnap me from your cruel clutches and take me away. I've barely restrained him."

Darius sputtered. "Never know what will come out of that mouth," he said in low tones. Then he set himself out to be charming to my father. Before an hour was done, he had another ardent admirer, as if he needed one more. I was relieved that my husband and my father seemed to grow more at ease in one another's company.

My father left late that evening. Darius, on the other hand, lingered in my apartment for hours. I was half asleep when he sat up with sudden speed, dislodging the blankets.

"I forgot!"

"Forgot what?" My speech was slow with sleep.

"I have something for you."

"For me? What?" I was fully awake now.

"A present, which I meant to give you earlier, but you are very distracting."

He bounced out of bed and left my room, still pulling on the sleeves of his tunic. My door burst open scant minutes later. Darius strode toward me, cradling something I could not see against his chest. I sat up, filled with curiosity. To my shock, the little bundle in Darius's embrace moved. I gasped as he dropped a fawn-colored puppy with liquid brown eyes into my arms. He was the very image of Caspian, only much smaller. Expelling a breath, I held him close to my chest. I turned my face toward him, which he licked even more enthusiastically than Caspian used to do. He stole my heart before I had a chance to draw another breath.

"Oh! What a ravishing creature! What's his name?"

"That's for you to decide. He is from the same parents as

Caspian. I heard there was a fresh litter the day we returned, and sent for him right away."

"You're giving him to me?"

"He's your welcome home present. I know he won't replace Caspian. But I think he will come to occupy his own special place in your heart."

I was speechless. Drawing the puppy closer to me, I gave him a small kiss on his wrinkled forehead. I realized that what I really wanted was to embrace Darius, but I was too shy to go to him. Hiding my face against the dog's soft wriggling body, I said, "Thank you, my lord. I already love him."

Darius sank next to me on the bed, sprawling in the careless way he had that took up most of the space. Plumping the pillows behind him, he sat up straighter. "I think a little more gratefulness is in order. You have no idea the lengths I had to go to in order to secure him. Damaspia's agents were there ahead of me."

I giggled, half horrified. "How much gratefulness would you like?"

"Pour it on thick."

I put the dog on Darius's chest with delicate care. "Puppy, say thank you to your master for fetching you to me." With impressive obedience, the puppy began to lick Darius on the face.

"You stop that!" Darius placed the dog in the center of the bed with a gentle, one-handed tug and leaned back against the pillows again. "Not what I had in mind."

"No?" I threw my arms around him and gave him a crushing hug. "Is this better?"

"Mmm. A definite improvement."

I rained down little kisses on his face and neck. "Thank you, thank you, thank you, master. I love my present."

"What else do you love?"

I drew away when I realized what he wanted. His eyelids were at half-mast, and I could not read his expression. "I love you." I said the words with slow deliberation. "I love you so much."

The long lips slanted. "It's amazing how much I enjoy you saying that." It was his turn to draw me into his arms.

Author's Notes

The period in Persian history in which *Harvest of Rubies* takes place is a particularly enigmatic time. For such an influential and long-lasting world empire, the Achaemenids have bequeathed us a surprisingly sketchy history. What we do know about them comes to us predominantly through the perceptions of their enemies, the Greeks. In recent times, historians have begun to doubt the accuracy of some of these perceptions. Emerging archaeological finds, as well as a closer examination of the Greek material have led to interesting new observations, which I have used in *Harvest of Rubies*.

Whenever possible, I have tried to keep an accurate accounting of facts, or at least to present the story line in such a way that is plausible in the context of history. While there is no evidence of female scribes working in the Persian court, there is substantial documentation supporting the role of women as scribes in ancient Mesopotamia. According to respected historian Will Durant, "some women kept shops, and carried on commerce; some even became scribes, indicating that girls as well as boys might receive an education" (*Our Oriental Heritage: The Story of Civilization*, vol. 1). Hence, I felt that placing a Jewish woman in the role of the queen of Persia's Senior Scribe was not unrealistic.

Modern ideas about life in the "harem" provide an inaccurate picture of how royal Persian women in the Achaemenid Empire lived. Although assigned separate quarters, they were not cloistered, and were free to own and manage property. They traveled and hunted in the company of men. Royal princesses could ride, and some were proficient at the use of the bow and arrow. At least one Greek historian mentions that royal Persian women traveled in enclosed carriages. While this was probably true in general, considering their freedom to hunt with men, it is reasonable to assume that in some cases, at least, they would have been allowed to travel on horseback. Women of royal rank were allowed to attend certain public functions and could entertain men other than their husbands under special circumstances (as in the case of Esther who invited Haman along with her husband, Xerxes, for a private dinner in her apartments). Female commoners enjoyed even greater freedom. The *arassara* are an example of this. Women who worked as heads of factories show up occasionally in royal payroll documents.

Persian men displayed prodigious fashion consciousness. Jewelry, exotic perfumes, and luxurious clothing were all the rage. Shoes with platform heels were quite popular in courtly circles among men (Tom Holland, *Persian Fire*). In the novel—I assume this is true for women as well—I depict Sarah in high heels and sumptuous costumes. While we don't have as much information about women's clothing, I was able to use pictures of royal women as seen in seals and statues to describe their fashion.

Some comments regarding several characters in this novel may prove helpful here. While Alogune is a historical figure, the plot involving her in this story is entirely fictional. However, archaeological records indicate that Alogune's son, Sogdianus, goes on to murder Damaspia's son, Xerxes II, shortly after his ascent to the throne. I felt that the plotline involving Alogune would give Sogdianus a convincing motive (besides good old-fashioned ambition) for the later betrayal of his half brother.

There is no extrabiblical record of the existence of Esther or Vashti. The only wife of Xerxes recorded in history is Amestris. This need not indicate a conflict between the Bible and history; Persians were in the habit of only recording the names of the wives and concubines of the king who bore him children. If Esther and Vashti did not bear Xerxes children, then Persian tradition would have left their names out of public records. Some scholars suggest that Vashti *is* Amestris, but there are problems with that theory. I suggest my own theory in *Harvest of Rubies*, though it too offers certain difficulties, the most pronounced of which is the age of Amestris by the time Xerxes marries her.

Several ancient historians refer to Artaxerxes as a kind and tolerant ruler, a personality trait I try to highlight in the novel. While he was known as "the long-handed" because of a congenital defect, he had no problems with his taste buds that we know of. That was literary license on my part. Along similar lines, I was inspired to give Shushan a fake eye when I read an article on the discovery of a skeleton from around this period, which according to Iranian researchers, sported a stone eye.

Some readers have asked about the appropriate term of address for God amongst the Israelite community at this time. By the Middle Ages, the Jewish community had set themselves a narrow standard; any direct mention of G-d, whether orally or in written form, was seen as breaking the Third Commandment. A number of scholars believe that this practice began as an oral tradition that has much older roots. Other scholars contend that this practice was of later origin. I chose the latter, because the biblical writers address God much more freely in their prayers as well as in their teachings. If the book of Nehemiah refers openly to God, then the most accurate depiction of the time is simply to follow his example.

Although we are not certain of the exact era during which the Psalms were gathered in written form, one stream of thought suggests the Persian Period as the start of this endeavor.

Nehemiah's gift of a collection of some of the Psalms is a reference to this significant moment in time.

I hope you have enjoyed Sarah's and Darius's adventures in *Harvest of Rubies*. I look forward to continuing their story in my next book as I write about Nehemiah's journey to Jerusalem. Once again I will tackle the symbol of walls—this time the importance of building them. You can read a chapter starting on page 357.

Recipes

Unfortunately, no recipes survive from the Achaemenid period. However, lists of foods used for the king's servants and retainers give us a good idea of ingredients. The Persians loved using a great variety of meats, and were extremely fond of sweets.

The following recipes are derived from current Persian cuisine. Some of these recipes have been slightly altered from their traditional form in deference to healthy eating habits. I have tried to choose dishes that use ingredients available in ancient Persia, except for one thing: rice. To the modern Persian, life without properly steamed rice is a fate almost as bad as death. But historically speaking, our earliest evidence of rice in Persia dates to the first century AD. This does not necessarily mean that rice would not have been available at Artaxerxes' table; the king had access to the rarest foods from around the world and his cooks traveled to far-flung corners of the empire, gathering recipes and ingredients. It merely means that the average person would probably not be eating rice during this period.

Pureed Eggplant and Onion
(as served to Darius in chapter 15)

2 large seedless eggplants, washed
2 large onions, chopped
5 cloves of garlic, chopped
1 cup whey (You can purchase this in specialty stores. The Persian name is *kashk*.
Or, you can replace whey with 1 cup Greek yogurt, strained over cheesecloth overnight.)
2 tablespoons dried mint, crushed to powder (you can rub the mint between your palms)
½ teaspoon turmeric
¾ cup vegetable or olive oil
½ teaspoon saffron
Sea salt and pepper to taste

Preheat oven to 350. Poke several holes in the eggplants and place on rack in a pan for one hour, or until eggplants are soft.

Tip: If eggplants give you gastric discomfort, peel them, cut them into ¼ inch layers, salt, and leave for several hours. Eggplants will *sweat* a dark liquid. Wiping that liquid off will make them much easier to digest. Fry your eggplant instead of roasting it.

In a large skillet, fry onions in ½ cup oil over medium heat, reserving the rest of the oil. Stir occasionally. Make sure they are soft all the way through as well as golden. Add garlic and stir frequently until golden. Don't allow to burn. Reserve half the mixture for topping. Add turmeric to the rest of the mix and remove from heat.

When eggplant is ready, remove skin, and using a fork, mash until eggplant is completely pureed. Replace skillet over medium heat and add eggplant to the fried onion mixture. Fry for another five minutes, until completely tender. Add salt and pepper. Serve on a serving dish.

In a skillet, add oil over medium high heat. Add powdered mint. Flash fry and remove from heat. Add saffron and spoon over eggplant mixture. Add the reserved onion and garlic mixture to the top of the eggplant. Serve with whey or yogurt. Delicious with heated pita bread or naan.

White Basmati Rice

Well-made Persian rice has grains that are soft all the way through without being sticky. While more complicated to prepare than the average white rice, it is so profoundly tasty that the extra care and time are worth the effort. Serves six:

4 cups basmati rice (do not replace with other rice varieties)
9 cups water
½ tablespoon sea salt
4 tablespoons vegetable oil
1 tablespoon butter, melted (optional)
1 teaspoon saffron, powdered (optional)

Stage 1: *Boiling*—Place rice in a deep bowl. Gently wash with hot water four or five times. Leave rice to soak in clean hot water for an hour.

Fill a large pot (nonstick ideal, but not necessary) with nine cups of water and bring to boil. Empty excess water from the soaking rice and add to pot. Reduce heat to medium high and stir a few times until water returns to boil.

Try a few grains of rice after 6–8 minutes. If rice feels soft all the way through, drain in a colander and gently rinse with cold water. Don't overcook.

Stage 2: *Steaming*—Add oil, ¼ cup water, and a sprinkle of sea salt to the bottom of pot and reduce heat to medium. When water comes to boil, add rice back into pot. Rice grains are fragile at this point so transfer gently, careful not to break the long grains. Sprinkle salt to taste as you are adding the rice.

Place several paper towels over pot and replace the lid firmly. This allows the rice to finish cooking through steam instead of boiling. After ten minutes, reduce temperature to low. Cook without removing the lid for an additional 30–40 minutes.

Serve rice on a platter with melted butter (optional). Add saffron (optional). See below for preparation tip. The bottom of the pot should yield a golden crispy crust of rice, a favorite in Persian cuisine.

- **Tip**: If you are using saffron, use a few grains of sugar in a pestle and with a mortar crush the saffron filaments into powder. Pour two teaspoons of boiling water over saffron. When rice is ready to serve, pour saffron on top. Its aroma and beautiful color will enhance this dish tremendously. However, avoid stains, as saffron can leave a permanent mark.

Chicken Kebab

1 teaspoon powdered saffron (see tip above for preparation)
½ cup fresh lime juice
1 large onion, chopped
2–3 cloves of garlic, chopped
¼ cup olive oil
1 ½ teaspoons sea salt
pepper to taste
2 pounds chicken, cut into 1 ½ inch pieces. Breast, wing, and drumsticks are especially good with this recipe.
For basting: melted butter, juice of one lime, and a pinch of powdered saffron

In a large bowl mix all ingredients (except for basting mixture). Cover and marinate overnight.

The best way to cook this dish is over a charcoal grill, using skewers. Mix butter, saffron, and lime juice and baste chicken as grilling. Chicken should be ready in 10–15 minutes. Turn frequently.

To cook indoors, preheat oven to broil. Spray bottom of your pan with oil. Cook chicken ten minutes on each side if boned, less if boneless breast. Serve with basmati rice.

Lamb and Quince Sauce

(served at Sarah and Darius's wedding)

White rice is often served with a variety of meat sauces, called *khoresht*. Quince is an ancient fruit, celebrated throughout the ages for its beautiful and unique perfume.

1 pound stewing lamb, cubed, washed, and dried
2 large onions, chopped into small pieces
3 cloves of garlic, chopped
3 medium quince, washed, cored, and cut into medium wedges
¼ cup olive or vegetable oil
¼ cup lime juice
1 ½ tablespoons sugar
¼ teaspoon turmeric
¼ teaspoon ground saffron (see tip under white basmati rice for preparation)
A pinch of cinnamon
A small pinch each of ground cardamom, ground coriander seeds, and ground nutmeg (optional)
Sea salt and pepper to taste

In a large skillet, brown onion in oil over medium heat. Stir occasionally until onions turn a golden color and are caramelized. Add garlic and stir until garlic is also a golden color. Sprinkle turmeric and stir.

Add lamb, and turn heat up to medium high. Stir occasionally. When lamb is brown on all sides, set temperature on low. Sprinkle cinnamon. Add ¾ cup boiling water. Place a lid on skillet and allow lamb to simmer gently for 30 minutes.

In a separate pan, flash fry the quince on both sides quickly. Add to the lamb mixture and cook for an additional 30 minutes. Add sugar, lime juice, salt, pepper, and saffron. Allow to simmer gently another ten minutes.

Serve hot over white basmati rice.

Jewel Rice

(also known as Morrassa Polo)

This dish is not only delicious, but its stunning colors makes it a favorite for weddings.

4 cups basmati rice
I large onion
Two large carrots, peeled and julienned finely
¾ cup fresh orange peel, julienned finely, with the white skin in the back completely removed
¾ cup barberries (specialty store) or you can replace with dried cranberries, with each cranberry cut in half
3 tablespoons slivered skinless almonds
2 tablespoons slivered pistachios
½ cup raisins
¾ cup sugar
1 teaspoon saffron
¼ cup olive oil
¼ cup butter
Sea salt

Prepare white basmati rice, above, through the end of stage one. Let it rest in colander.

Bring ¾ cup water to boil with ½ cup sugar. Add orange peel and carrots. Boil until soft, about ten minutes. Drain and set aside.

If you are using barberries, wash by placing in a bowl of water. Gently agitate and leave in water for one or two minutes. Remove barberries from water and place on paper towel to dry.

In a skillet, add half the oil and butter together over medium heat. Fry onions until golden. Add barberries with ¼ cup remaining sugar or cranberries (no sugar is needed as they are already sweetened). Stir frequently and remove from heat after two minutes.

In a large nonstick pot, add the rest of the oil and butter over medium heat. Add ¼ cup water and a dash of sea salt. Bring to boil. Add a couple of spatulas of rice to the bottom of the pot gently.

Then with a spoon add a layer of the mixture of carrots and orange peel, a layer of the barberry or cranberry and onion mixture, some almonds, and some pistachios and raisins. Alternate with rice layer, until mixture is finished. Cover with several paper towels and place lid tightly. After several minutes, lower temperature to **low** setting.

Rice should be ready in 30–40 minutes. Serve it on a large platter, being careful not to break the rice grains. Try to shape the rice like a little hill. If you are using saffron, add a teaspoon of boiling water to powdered saffron and pour over rice. To ensure you don't waste any of the saffron, put a spoonful of rice back into your saffron dish and swirl so that it absorbs any leftover color.

Serve with *Chicken Kebab*.

Acknowledgments

I will always remain thankful to Paul Santhouse, who was the best introduction to the publishing world a writer could ask for, and to my agent, Wendy Lawton at Books & Such Literary Agency, whose instincts seem infallible.

I am very grateful to my best friend, Rebecca Rhee, who shared tons of her precious time and prodigious training on editing *Harvest of Rubies*, making it a far better book than it would otherwise have been, but not nearly so grateful as I am for her irreplaceable friendship. Lauren Yarger and Tegan Willard, a big thanks to you for your excellent and astute editing. Thank you also to Emi Trowbridge, Cindy McDowell, Janice Johnson, and Karen Connors, each of whom made a valuable difference with her suggestions and heartfelt encouragement.

I'm indebted to Kathi and Taylor Smith for providing me with a peaceful writing haven while feeding me amazing food. Thank you also for helping me with the finer details of the art of horseback riding. I'm grateful to my treasured friends Beth and Rob Bull whose mastiff puppy was the inspiration behind Caspian's breed, and whose constant support puts a smile on my face. I am particularly thankful to you for the idea of Caspian being the one to carry the key back to Teispes.

My constant appreciation for my brother, Ario Afshar, who has always believed in me more than I deserved, and has supported me in every way possible.

I highly recommend my zany online writers loop—the ACFW Northeast bunch. It's a relief to hang out with people who speak your language and get your desires, even if it's just online.

A number of professionals made this writing journey a joy: Bill Chiaravalle, whose magnificent cover designs for both *Harvest of Rubies* and *Pearl in the Sand* have created a beautiful brand for my books; Dr. Torger Vedler, who graciously shared his rare knowledge of the period and answered numerous questions about the mysteries of the Achaemenid Empire, as well as led me to the right resources; three talented editors at Moody—Deb Keiser who added a new depth to *Rubies* by challenging me to let go of Caspian, Betsey Newenhuyse who helped me attend to many important details, and Pam Pugh who was both an encourager and a grammar angel; Janis Backing who fortified me continuously with her sweet emails even though it wasn't her job. Thank you all for your incredible support and help.

I would be remiss if I did not thank the many folks at Moody who are key to the success of each book, but whose names may not be mentioned often: people like Ros, Brittany, and the nameless sales force who put so much time and effort in each project. Simply, thank you!

Excerpt from "Walls of Gold"
(not final title)

Darius snapped into full consciousness, aware that an unfamiliar noise had dragged him out of sleep. Years of military training had honed his instincts for danger so that he was already taking inventory of the surroundings before his eyes had adjusted to the starless night. With relief he noted that Sarah slept undisturbed next to him, her body squeezed tight against his side in an unconscious effort to ward off the night chill.

Without making a sound he shifted his head to look for Arta, who was on guard duty. In the firelight, he could see the man sprawled on the ground, his head slumped forward at an awkward angle. Darius's heart pumped with an unpleasant rush as he noticed the dark liquid clinging to the side of Arta's slack face.

Darius shifted his gaze, careful not to move his head noticeably. Besides Arta, he had three men riding with him. Two were gagged and tied, he saw. He caught the attention of the third man, Meres, who was alert and unbound, faking sleep. Meres pointed behind him with a subtle rising of his brow.

Following his signal, Darius noted that there were four intruders. Five, he amended, taking in the massive shoulders of a leather-bound man skulking toward him, holding a wide, short sword. Darius grasped his knife, the only weapon he had kept strapped against his thigh when he had fallen into his pallet late last night, after an exhausting journey through treacherous slopes.

The wide-shouldered man stood over him now. Filled with the peculiar calm that often came to him in the heat of battle, Darius realized that the man held his sword at a curious angle, more as a club than a stabbing instrument. He wasn't intent on killing him so much as subduing him, then.

With a lightning movement, Darius swept his leg, catching his attacker in the ankles. Surprised, the man lost his balance for a moment. Darius rolled to his feet and taking advantage of his opponent's unsteadiness, kicked him hard in the groin. The man dropped his sword and doubled over, in too much agony to cry out.

Darius grabbed the discarded sword and hit the man on the back of the head with the flat of the blade. With a grunt, he fell over, unconscious.

"Consider it a favor," Darius said, knowing from old experience that his attacker wouldn't want to be awake through that pain.

"Darius?" Sarah, awakened by the commotion, was kneeling on her pallet, her eyes wide with shock. Darius swallowed hard. When he had allowed her to join him on their trip, he had not expected anything more dangerous than their daily rides, which upon occasion brought them to high mountain passes. The thought of what might happen to her in the midst of a melee made his gut twist into a tight knot.

He forced his voice to sound calm. "I want you to run behind that outcropping of rock over there, Sarah. Don't move unless I call you."

She didn't stir. "*Now*," he whispered, a sharp bite underlying the command. To his relief, she obeyed.

The rest of their unknown attackers now became aware

that he was not asleep and could no longer be taken unawares. In the periphery of his vision he saw Meres engaging two men while the other two headed in his direction. Darius frowned, perplexed by the fact that they seemed unarmed, except for a long, skinny stave which one of them held casually in one hand. He used the moments he had before they reached him to try to cut one of his men, Sama, loose. He only had time to cut the ties about Sama's wrists and grab a shield before his two opponents were almost upon him.

Darius turned, using the time to take note of small details that might give him an advantage in the unequal fight. In a corner of his mind he was aware that the grass was cool and damp beneath his bare feet and the air crisp in his chest. To his astonishment, he saw that only one man approached him, his gait slow. He was slim, shorter and thinner than Darius, but even in the pale light of the fire it was clear that his compact body was covered by muscle. The man's companion held back, appearing relaxed, in no hurry to come to his aid. They certainly did not seem to expect much trouble from their prey, Darius thought.

Unsure of how the man intended to use such a thin reed of a staff in a fight, Darius flexed his sharp knife in one hand, considering. He stepped forward into a well-practiced stance, and put his weight behind the knife as he lunged at the man. To his surprise the man did not veer either to left or right, but in the last moment, stretched out an arm, and with what felt like almost a soft touch, pushed against Darius's wrist in an arc. Darius found his knife hand traveling wide off the mark, his own strength being used against him.

He regained his balance and turned to face his opponent again. The white staff suddenly whirled in the air, sounding more like a whip than a stretch of wood. Darius pulled his shield in front of his face just in time to catch its downward strike. Amazingly, the wood did not splinter as it came into contact with Darius's thick wicker and leather shield. Instead, it bent and found its way around the shield, whipping the side of Darius's face with a painful strike. He put a hand to his stinging face; it came away bloody. He had never experienced anything like it in battle before.

Darius gripped his knife harder. The man had taken a strange pose, his knees bent, one arm forward, his palm flat, the other fisted around the staff and pulled back. Darius rushed at him, intending to use the weight of his core body to wrestle the man to the ground. Before he had the opportunity, however, his opponent uncoiled with tremendous speed and brought down the edge of his hand diagonally against the side of Darius's neck. The blow bore down on Darius with the force of metal instead of mere flesh and blood. He knew he would have lost consciousness if his neck muscles were not unusually strong. Darius resisted the dizziness that enveloped him, swallowing hard to overcome the urge to vomit.

With a growl, he threw aside the shield and rushed at his attacker, hoping to surprise him with an unexpected counterattack. The man grasped a hold just above Darius's elbow and pressed. It was as if a string had been pulled from his elbow all the way down into his fingers; Darius lost his grasp on the knife, his fingers nerveless.

He managed to break contact and took up a defensive stance, but he realized that he was losing control of the fight. It was clear that his opponent was proficient in a form of combat hitherto unknown to Darius. With sudden speed, the man rushed toward him and flew high in the air as if he had grown a set of wings, landing a kick that felt like the trunk of a tree straight into Darius's solar plexus. Darius collapsed, unable to breathe.

From the corner of his eye he saw his opponent's companion standing to the side, his arms crossed, a relaxed grin on his face as he watched. No wonder he wasn't exerting any effort. He must have seen his friend pull this trick with success more than once. Without warning, the man's grin wavered and his eyes rolled back before he slid to the ground with a noisy crash. Sama stood behind him, holding a fat rock in his hand.

Darius's opponent was distracted for a moment by the noise of his companion dropping to the ground. It was the opening Darius needed. The thought of what this man could do to his wife gave Darius the strength to get back on his feet, ignoring the fire in his ribs. Taking advantage of his opponent's slack-jawed surprise, he landed his elbow into the man's belly and knocked him in the side of the head with a double-handed punch. The man staggered to one side. Darius swept a kick against his knees in the opposite direction and his opponent toppled. On the ground, he was unable to use the staff. Sama joined the melee, and finally between the two of them, and Sama's flat rock, they were able to subdue the adversary, who lay unconscious, a thin trickle of blood falling sluggishly from his fast swelling lip.

They rushed to help Meres; Darius was relieved to note that although the others in the gang of attackers were good fighters, they were nowhere near as extraordinary as the man whom he had faced. Within minutes, Meres's two challengers were quashed, tied with severe knots that held them helpless against one another. The other three men in the gang who were in various stages of unconsciousness were restrained in similar fashion.

Sarah ran to his side. "Are you all right?" She was unable to hide a small quiver in her voice.

"You were supposed to wait until I called you." He tried to

sound stern, but heard relief drown out every other emotion in his words.

"They can't pose much danger now, unconscious and tied up as they are. You took a few hard hits. Anything broken?"

Barefoot as she was now, the top of her head came to his chest. Her hair, wild from sleep and her haphazard run, tangled about her face, and her full mouth, trembling with fear only moments ago, was now flattened into a stubborn line. He found her utterly beautiful. "I may have a few cracked ribs."

"And your cheek is bleeding. It will probably scar. Too bad. You won't be nearly as good looking as Meres anymore."

Darius swallowed a smile. "Then you'd better attend me, woman. Or will you faint at the sight of a little blood?"

He would have laughed at her offended expression if the moan of one of the captives hadn't forced him back to the present situation.

"Search them," Darius said through gritted teeth as Sarah bound his ribs with bandage. "Strip them naked if you have to. I want to know who they are and why they attacked us."

Arta, who had regained consciousness and was nursing a prodigious headache, growled. "Thieves and rascals—that's who they are. Looking for our silver, no doubt."

Darius made a noncommittal sound in his throat. The five men did not strike him as thieves. They fought like professionals, not bandits. Their high-quality horses were well cared for. He could still picture the unusual moves of the slim man he had fought; if not for Sama's help, he had no doubt he would have lost that clash. Those were not the combat moves of a common thief.

He deliberated for a moment on whether to take the time and solve the puzzle of this mysterious attack, or bundle the culprits on their horses and deliver them to the magistrate in

Susa and let him untangle this enigma. After all, the king, who had summoned him and Sarah for a special audience, expected their speedy presence in Susa. No doubt after months of respite in honor of his new marriage, Artaxerxes had decided that he had shown enough grace; the empire required the services of all its able men if it was to function properly.

Something about these men nagged at him. He felt uneasy at the thought of leaving the investigation to someone else. There was a great puzzle here, and he needed to solve it, even if it meant a delay in meeting with the king.

The sun had risen high by the time his men made a small hill of their attackers' belongings in the middle of the campground. Darius picked up the white staff and examined it. It was made of a kind of wood he had never seen. He flexed it in opposite directions several times. It gave with incredible ease, bending in ways that would have broken any other wooden staff. He wondered what the stave was made of to have at once the solidity of wood and flexibility of leather. He threw the stave aside and began to go through the pile of sacks and parcels in front of him.

At the top of the pile rested a flawless box, carved from ivory. Inside, Darius found a dagger decorated with exquisite jewels. He hefted it in his hand; it was a ceremonial piece, more for show than real battle. Nonetheless, this was no ordinary dagger. The consummate craftsmanship and the rare jewels used in its creation marked it a worthy offering for a nobleman of high rank. Darius examined it a moment longer, looking for identifying marks or clues to its ownership. Finding none, he replaced it in the box and set it aside.

Unlike the dagger, everything else in the pile was ordinary and well used. Extra clothes, coins, a couple of jars of oil for the treatment of leather and metal, camping gear. Wine. Dried date cakes. Nothing incriminating. At the bottom of the pile, a sealed leather pouch caught his eye. He did not recognize the seal; the palm tree and stylized lion motif weren't Persian. He showed it to Sarah. "Do you recognize this?"

She studied it before shaking her head. "It's unfamiliar to me."

"Can you break the seal, but retain the integrity of the design? I need to figure out its source once we arrive in Susa."

"I think so. It depends on the quality of the wax." She pulled out her knife and drew a careful line into the seal. With a delicate snap, she broke it into two undamaged sections.

"What do you think you're doing?" The voice was deep and calm. Darius turned and found the broad-shouldered man who had attacked him first regarding him through intelligent brown eyes.

"Ah. Awake at last. Did you have a pleasant nap?"

"You better leave that missive alone."

Darius's smile was ironic. "You aren't in any position to make demands, are you? Who is it for?"

The man said nothing. Darius unrolled the leather and found a short letter inside. "Not very illuminating," he said after he read it.

"What does it say?" the man asked, shifting against his tight bonds.

"You don't know?"

"I just carry them. I don't read them."

"How noble." He held out the letter to Sarah. "What do you think?"

She studied it in silence for a time. "Interesting."

"Really? I found it disappointing. *Carry out the instructions I am sending you. You will be safe and well rewarded.* How is that of any help? What are the instructions, that's what I need to find out."

"Your problem is that you don't know your grammar. You see the way the author of the letter has used the verb *send*?"

Darius shifted from one leg to another. "Are you trying to put me to sleep?"

Sarah hit him in the shoulder. "Listen, your lordship, and you might learn something of benefit. The way the author has used this verb indicates that the instructions are not coming later. Nor have they been sent ahead. Whoever wrote this letter is saying that the instructions should be delivered at the same time as the missive, which strongly indicates that these gentlemen have them hidden somewhere. Possibly on their persons."

Darius pulled down a lock of Sarah's hair, which was sticking out at an awkward angle, and twirled it around his finger. "That is an excellent grammar lesson." He turned to the intruder. "Impressive, isn't she? Would you like to tell me where these blessed instructions are?" He sighed as the man stared back mutely. "I didn't think so."

He bade his men to search the intruders again while he went through the pile of their possessions once more. There were no other items of interest in the remaining pouches—nothing that pointed to the missing instructions. With sudden insight, Darius began to search through the piles again. This time, he wasn't trying to find something, but to ensure that something crucial was missing.

"Where are your travel visas—your *viyataka*?" he asked.

The man's head snapped up. "What?"

"Your permits. You can't be traveling on the king's roads without the required documents. Yours seem to be missing."

"Must have lost them."

Darius kicked the pile in front of him. "I don't think so. I think that's what you were after when you attacked us. There happen to be five men in our party and five in yours. It was too convenient a coincidence for you to overlook. You are travelling the back roads, so your chances of running into the king's soldiers are diminished. But to enter a large city like Susa, you will certainly be asked for your *viyataka*. Much easier to enter the city with the appropriate documents than to try to sneak in without them, which must have been your original plan."

"You forget—you also have a woman, which we don't. So you see, your travel documents would be of no use to me."

Darius knelt in front of his captive and poked him in the chest with his index finger. "You underestimate yourself. It would be easy enough to pay a woman at the gates of Susa to pretend to be of your party."

The man turned his face away from Darius's penetrating gaze. "So what?"

"So, this proves that you aren't simple thieves looking for money. You are on a mission of some kind—a mission secret enough to prevent you from applying for travel documents. Would you care to share what that mission is?"

The man snorted. "Would you care to share yours?"

Darius sighed. "You insist on making this difficult."

By now, his men had searched the intruders and their horses down to the skin, but found nothing. The whole troop had regained consciousness and sat quietly brooding in their ropes, but made no move to resist the thorough personal examination.

Suddenly Sarah stood and walked over to the owner of the staff. "That's an unusually short haircut," she said.

Darius frowned. It wasn't like his wife to be fashion conscious, or to make public statements about someone's lack of style. He edged closer to her, not liking her proximity to the exceptional fighter in spite of the fact that he was bound.

"You must have cut it recently," Sarah continued, refusing to budge from the subject. "Shaved it even, I would guess, from the way it has grown back."

Darius gave his wife a sidelong glance, before bending to examine the man's scalp. In the bright light of the sun, the skin shone white beneath the covering of hair. Then with bewilderment Darius noticed black marks on parts of the scalp. "Tattoos. You have tattoos on your scalp."

The man turned to Darius and gave him a pleasant smile. "First your woman, now you. Are you people obsessed with scalps?"

Darius restrained the urge to give him a good kick and signaled Meres to shave the man's head.

"Leave my head alone!" the man yelled, but was helpless, trussed up as he was, to prevent Meres from completing his task.

His head was shaved in a matter of moments. Meres wiped the blood that flowed from several shallow cuts, a consequence of the man's useless struggles. A short message written in Aramaic became legible on the white scalp, tattooed in black ink.

Sarah gasped as she read it. "That's about the king!"

"What?" The man twisted his head to address Darius. "What's it say?"

"You don't know?" Darius asked, skepticism dripping from his voice.

"Can't read my own head, can I? What does it say? Tell me."

Darius, who had grown rigid after perusing the strange missive, emptied his voice of all inflection and began to read the tattoo aloud. "Rub the poison you have upon one side of the dagger. On New Year's Day, present it to him along with a roasted pigeon as the gift from our satrapy. He will have you cut the bird in half with the dagger, and consume a piece, as assurance that it is not poisoned. Offer him the flesh of the bird touched by the poisoned side of the dagger."

Darius's men looked at one another, puzzled. Arta scratched his wounded head. "What does that mean, besides the fact that some poor sod is going to get murdered?"

"The message is about the king," Sarah explained. "He receives gifts from ambassadors around the empire on the first day of spring, which is the Persian New Year. Often the gifts are symbolic: water from a river, to indicate that the whole river belongs to Artaxerxes; earth, to signify that the land itself is offered to the king. A bird would be a pretty way of claiming that the sky is also the dominion of the Persian monarch. A cooked bird would be tasted by the king as a sign of his approval, which ostensibly is why they have included the knife. But the king would take the precaution of sharing food with the one who has brought it in order to ensure that it is not poisoned. However, the person behind this plot has concocted a clever ploy to bypass that difficulty."

"The king!" Arta almost exploded as he pronounced the word. "Are you certain? I thought the New Year offerings were made in Persepolis."

Darius nodded. "Usually, they are. This year, the king shifted the usual plans so that he could spend the New Year in Susa. The officials around the empire have been notified; in less than a week, they'll be descending on the city with their gifts, assuring the Persian Empire that they are still faithful servants. One of them has been planning to use this occasion in order to poison the king. Only an official of high rank would have access to the king on New Year's Day, so this plot has its origins in a person of consequence someplace in the empire."

There was a moment of stunned silence in the camp. Then

mayhem broke loose as everyone began to speak together. The loudest voices belonged to the intruders, swearing to their ignorance of the plot. Finally a semblance of silence settled over everyone.

Darius crossed his arms, then thought better of it as the movement strained his bruised side. "How can you have the gall to profess innocence? The only thing you are missing for evidence is the dead body of the king himself."

The man who had forbidden Darius from opening the sealed letter now addressed the party. "My lords, my lady, my name is Nasir, from Babylon. These are my four brothers, Nur, Naram, Nutesh. And that one," he said, pointing with his chin to the man with the tattoo, "is our youngest brother, Niqquu-lamuusu. Everyone calls him Niq."

"What a relief," Darius said.

"First, please accept our humble apologies for the manner of our introduction."

Darius noticed Sarah's mouth twitching at the use of the word *introduction*. This fellow was entertaining for a cur and a murderer. Nasir continued. "We intended you no harm. You must have noticed that we went to great lengths to ensure no one was truly hurt. We don't kill people."

"That tattoo bears witness against your claim."

"This is a terrible misunderstanding, my lord. Allow me to explain."

Darius, who now had the task of interrogating the Babylonian brothers, motioned for him to continue, curious as to the story he would concoct.

"My brothers and I are couriers, in a manner of speaking."

"Couriers work for the empire. I doubt the royal machine hired you and . . ." Darius waved his hand vaguely toward the group of tied up men. "Your siblings."

"That is true, sire. Perhaps *courier* is stretching the word a little. We transport things. As you noted, travel in Persia is guarded by strict regulations. Even mail, if sent without royal approval, is read and destroyed upon discovery. But there are those, who for personal reasons, cannot apply for a travel permit, or entrust their mail to official couriers. Most people have secrets they would rather not share with the king's bureaucrats, who could sell a juicy morsel for extra money on the side. In my experience, these secrets are often harmless to the empire. They concern matters of a personal nature—inheritance, love, family squabbles. Our rule is that we never look inside the packages and letters entrusted to us. People's private sorrows and pain are not our concern."

"How convenient. And you don't think with such rules you attract murderers and villains of every kind?"

"No sir. Folks who have murder in mind wouldn't entrust a stranger with their secrets, generally speaking. We are honest men of business. We have no interest in murder. We merely transport documents and goods from one part of the empire to another for a reasonable fee."

"Honest men, you call it?" Arta gaped. "My head is still aching from your honesty, you scoundrel."

"But that was business, sir. It's not as if we were going to rob you of your gold or silver. As his lordship so wisely deduced, we needed to borrow your travel documents."

Sarah tried to stifle a snort, but was not successful. Darius dug his elbow into her side and decided to redirect the conversation. "Explain the tattoo."

"Ah, that. Believe me, my lord, I had no idea what the content of that vile message was or I would never have placed my brother's scalp at the disposal of such roguery. Here is what happened. A man contacted me and offered a great deal of money for my brothers and me to carry that dagger and a couple of missives into Susa."

"What man?" Now they were getting somewhere, Darius thought.

"There's the rub, my lord. He met me at night, wearing a hooded cloak. I hardly saw his face. His only introduction was a bag of gold. He sounded like an aristocrat. But I never found out his name."

"Where was this?"

"In Babylon. But the man was not Babylonian, I could tell from his accent. He paid extra because he wanted to tattoo his letter on the messenger's scalp. He said it was the only way he could be certain that it would not be discovered by royal spies."

"But for my wife's sharp eyes he might have proven right. How came he to tattoo your head without you ever knowing what the message said?" he asked Niq.

Niq shrugged. "They kept me hidden in a room for a month. Except for the man who shaved and tattooed me, I saw no one, not even my brothers. My room had no window, so I couldn't send or receive any secret messages. I had no idea what they had written on my head. I was locked in until my hair was well grown out and covered the message beneath. When I find the rascal who marred me with dishonor I'll squelch him."

"Was he the same man who spoke to Nasir, do you think?"

Niq shook his head. "No. There was no lordly way about him. He was a simple servant, judging by his manner. His master must've held him in deep confidence, though, if he entrusted him with such a job."

Darius chewed on his lower lip. The origin of the plot was proving a dead end if the brothers were to be believed. Although he had foiled the plan by virtue of discovering it, it

371

was essential that he find the traitor, for no doubt whoever was bent on assassinating Artaxerxes, would try again. "To whom were you supposed to deliver the dagger and the missives in Susa?"

"I have no name," Nasir said.

"Of course not."

"But I have a place and time of meeting."

Darius smiled slowly.

STRIKING BEAUTY
COMES AT A PRICE

978-0-8024-5881-0

Rahab paid it when at the age of fifteen she was sold into prostitution by the one man she loved and trusted—her father. With her keen mind and careful planning she turned heartache into success, achieving independence while still young. And she vowed never again to trust a man. Any man.

God had other plans.

The walls of Jericho are only the beginning. The real battle for Rahab will be one of the heart.

Also available as an ebook

FICTION FROM MOODY PUBLISHERS